The Passionate Elopement

Compton Mackenzie

Printing Statement:

Due to the very old age and scarcity of this book, many of the pages may be hard to read due to the blurring of the original text, possible missing pages, missing text, dark backgrounds and other issues beyond our control.

Because this is such an important and rare work, we believe it is best to reproduce this book regardless of its original condition.

Thank you for your understanding.

DAILY EXPRESS LIBRARY OF FAMOUS BOOKS

THE PASSIONATE ELOPEMENT

COMPTON
MACKENZIE

A DAILY EXPRESS PUBLICATION
LONDON

*Made and Printed in Great Britain by
Key and Whiting Ltd., London*

CONTENTS

CHAPTER		PAGE
I.	THE TOILET	9
II.	THE PUMP ROOM	19
III.	THE BLUE BOAR	30
IV.	CURTAIN MAZE	44
V.	THE PUBLICK BREAKFAST	59
	The Order of the Exquisite Mob	61
	THE PUBLICK BREAKFAST [*resumed*]	63
VI.	BAVERSTOCK BARN	75
VII.	SUNDAY MORNING	91
VIII.	THE GREAT REBELLION	99
IX.	THE ASSEMBLY	103
X.	AFTER THE ASSEMBLY	123
XI.	NOX ALBA	128
XII.	WET DAYS	134
XIII.	MONARCHY IN ACTION	139
XIV.	MONARCHY IN REPOSE	149
XV.	PHŒBUS ADEST	158
XVI.	THE CHINESE MASQUERADE	170
XVII.	THE GRAND MINUET OF CATHAY	182
XVIII.	THE CONFIDANTE	191
XIX.	BLACKHART FARM WITH A COCKFIGHT	198
XX.	IN WHICH EVERYTHING GROWS BUT THE PLOT	208
XXI.	CURTAIN POLLS	213

CONTENTS

CHAPTER		PAGE
XXII.	THE CURTAIN ROD	223
XXIII.	SPACE BETWEEN AN HEROICK COUPLET	229
XXIV.	DAISH'S ROOMS	241
XXV.	QUARTS OF BURGUNDY	249
XXVI.	AND THE DREGS OF THE SAME	266
XXVII.	TIME FOR REFLECTION	272
XXVIII.	THE LOVE CHASE	284
XXIX.	THE BASKET OF ROSES	293
XXX.	SIR GEORGE REPINGTON	304
XXXI.	A TALE WITH AN INTERRUPTED MORAL	313
XXXII.	THE HORRID ADVENTURES OF BEAU RIPPLE AND MRS. COURTEEN	318
XXXIII.	THE HIGHWAYMEN	332
XXXIV.	OLD ACQUAINTANCE	343
XXXV.	THE CUTTING OF A DIAMOND	356
XXXVI.	THE SCARLET DAWN	363
XXXVII.	APRIL FOOLS	380
XXXVIII.	BEAU LOVELY	387

THE PASSIONATE ELOPEMENT

CHAPTER I

THE TOILET

THE meagre sun that for thirteen pallid February days had shone with no more brilliance than a rushlight stuck amid the cobwebs of a garret, poured down at last his profuse glories, and Curtain Wells woke up to a fine morning and the burden of conscious existence, with an effort all the more completely unanimous on account of its reputation as an inland Spa. Residence there implied an almost monastick ideal of regularity. Other shrines of Æsculapius, falling from their primitive purity of worship, might set up for adoration a hooped Venus or bag-wigged Cupid, but Curtain Wells would never admit so naked and misleading a pair of Immortals. Her fountains ministered to bodily ailments—Vapours, Winds, Gouts, Quinsies, Consumptions, Fevers quartan and tertian—without pretending to the power of love-philtres or the sparkle of the Castalian Spring. 'Tis true, romantick dusk or sunset candlelight might consecrate the vows of many a shepherd and shepherdess, but those stretched hours of dalliance were always understood to be the sensuous reward of a strict matutinal discipline.

Consequently Curtain Wells woke up as to a bugle-call. Casement-hangings were flung back, shutters unbarred and, wonderful to relate, an occasional window-sash creaked and subsided. A simultaneous toilet would be followed by a simultaneous visit to the cleansing springs. Drums, routs, auctions, ridottos, and masquerades did not avail to keep their votaries abed.

Perchance a velvet patch would hide the wearer's secret blemish less artfully; beneath young Miss Kitcat's eyes there might be a deeper violet than the state of her health warranted; my lady Bunbutter newly arrived from scurrilous Bath might see her nose sharpen to a richer carmine point; but half-past eight o'clock would behold them all bound for the Pump Room, somewhat reticent perhaps, a little fretful even, yet completely subjugated by their self-imposed renunciation.

St. Simon's clock struck the half-hour of seven, and the birds who live tropick days in the eternal summer of chintz curtains seemed to crow remorsefully at any sluggard who was inclined longer to indulge his laziness. The sun spangled their plumage with innumerable pin-points of light until they began to glow with all the astonishing dyes of printed fabricks. They glowed and ruffled until the sluggard forsook his couch and, creeping over the chilly floor, flung them back into a day-long folded tranquillity. Here, then, is an excellent opportunity to catch a few of our fine characters unaware. Follow the guidance of my Muses and you will see hero and heroine, comedian, villain, and chorus stripped of all outward aids to beauty. You may trust the modesty of Clio and Melpomene who will certainly treat their own sex with discretion and admit you to the keyhole not a moment before it becomes your disposition of mind. Pray do not expect a wanton exhibition because you are holding on to the draperies of two pagan young women.

See that fine house in the middle of the Crescent. Mark the flambeaux guttering and sputtering into an odorous death. Note the flattened Ionick columns which lend it such an air of superiority, and the extra story, and the fat bow-windows on either side of the door. Look well at the door with its cornice of airy Cupids for ever playing Hide and Seek behind solemn urns and festoons of carven flowers.

That is the Great House where Beau Ripple lives. Do you wonder at the early hour of rising when you know that his decree was responsible for the united achievement? I cannot think you do; especially if you have read his *Epigrams* published by Mr. Scratch at the Sign of the *Claw* in Paul's Churchyard—those epigrams with razor-keen edge translated into Latin by Doctor Fumble and into Greek by the Reverend Mr. Tootell. We read how, in ancient days, tyrants beguiled their political victims with Impromptus of their own composition and at Curtain Wells it was esteemed an honour to be reprimanded in such polished prose. Mr. Ripple scorned the easy allurements of metre and, although in himself he summed up the profound artificiality of his age, he was wont to say that Verse as a form of composition possessed all the disadvantages of Prose without any of the advantages.

Let us take a glimpse at the Great Man in the Great House while the little maid is pondering the gaudy Valentine stuck in a crack of the basement-steps by the sweep's apprentice.

That carpet of mellow hue was presented by the Captain of an East Indiaman, much addicted to wind. It muffles the footsteps of the courtiers who throng the stairs, and secures a respectful calm. It even enables us to reach the door of his bedchamber unheralded, but as, invisible and armed with reverence, we cross the threshold, the Great Beau is nowhere to be seen. We observe his bedclothes dignified even in disarray, we see the open patchbox, the bottles of Eau de Luce and Eau de Chypre, the black sattin tie and the wig on the stand, but not until, instinct with awe, we drop our eyes, do we behold two pink feet and the Circumference of the least austere portion of his anatomy wrapped, it is true, in embroidered dressing gown, and with the bedspread hung about it like a pall, yet nevertheless an unmistakeable Circumference protruding from beneath the bed. Diana very wisely killed Actæon for overlooking her toilet, and I doubt we deserve the same penalty, for when, the errant button in his hand, we see the Beau emerge with purple cheeks and oaths innumerable, a certain conviction steals over our shocked sensibility that the Great little Man is only mortal after all, of the same temper and anatomy as ourselves, and, as the gods know very well, this is a mighty dangerous and revolutionary discovery.

There stood Beau Ripple dancing and d——g, while a monologue with appropriate action went somehow like this:

Beau. D—— all buttons for being round.

Then he danced.

Beau. D—— all pins for dropping upon the floor and the chambermaids for not picking them up, and my own feet for treading on them.

Then he danced again.

Beau. D—— all beds for being wide.

Then he danced.

Beau. D—— my eyes, I shall be late for the waters.

Then he danced to his mirrour. And the mirrour showed a man of ripe age with smooth round face and a pair of very blue eyes.

Beau. And d—— you, Ripple, for a clumsy old fool.

Hereupon the Great little Man beamed at himself, for the nature of him was so truly kind that he could not be crossed by himself for long, and as for the world, his severity never upset the balance of a well-turned phrase. He was an urbane man, one who had presumably lived all his life in prim and decorous cities but, since he will preside over this story of mine, we shall learn more about him as we go along.

Further round the Crescent, Mrs. Choke let furnished apartments to valetudinarian bachelors, and in one of the brightest of these, Mr. Francis Vernon sat before his looking glass contemplatively combing his wig. His closely cropped curly hair accentuated the lines of a profile already inclined to sharpness, just as his red lips enhanced the surrounding paleness of his complexion. He combed his wig very much as a man strokes a cat.

The caress half-felt loses itself in speculation, and just now Mr. Vernon was gazing at the wrought-iron balcony of the opposite house where Miss Phyllida Courteen, all swansdown and rosy cheeks, was plucking half a dozen snowdrops from a bough-pot. These were to be enclosed in a note and sent by the hand of the first pleasant-looking passer-by to Miss Sukey Morton in the Western Colonnade. And the aforesaid Miss Morton would, in the estimation of Miss Courteen, simper and blush and confide in her dear Phyllida that, though she had known he admired her and indeed, had proffered her a dropped fan more than once at the Monday Assemblies, yet never, *never* had she for a moment imagined that he would *dare* to send her a Valentine, and if he had, she would have *died* rather than take it, yes, *died*, for *what* she would do when she passed him next Monday evening, she could not *think*, especially as he was *known* to be partial to her, and her Mechlin pinner was quite ruined by the *abominable* wax-candles they would use just because the P—— of W—— was not coming that year after all.

Miss Courteen was so much charmed by this loquacious dream that she began to compose an appropriate verse destined to be wrapped round the green stalks of the flowers.

> *The snowdrop's white*
> *And so are you. . . .*

The smallest foot in the world beat time upon the balcony making the iron bars on which she stood vibrate in twanging chords, but failed to summon from the caves of Poesy an echo worthy of the snowdrop's white.

"The last line is monstrous easy," she thought.

The bluebell's blue! and the accumulation of liquids and labials has enchanted her mouth to such a delicious pout that Mr. Vernon is leaning forward and combing his wig more contemplatively than ever, for, although he cannot see his charmer's lips, he feels sure from the attitude of her whole body that her face is infernally captivating, and the memory of her last whispered good-bye assails him and kindles a leaping flame at the back of his hazel eyes.

Such a merciless regard as ours penetrates to the heart and we know that Mr. Vernon is wondering what on earth will come of his affair with Miss Courteen, and speculating how much she will inherit, and whether matrimony is quite so expensive a joy as his friends make out. The thought of money writes an ugly twisted line across his high smooth forehead, and this line broadens into a hundred little tributary lines as he thinks of his debts. So he brings himself back to the obstacles of life in rather a gloomy frame of mind and faces the necessity of his toilet in such a depression of spirits that he selects a suit to match his mood. And that is the reason why Mr. Francis Vernon wore purple sattin on Valentine morning.

All this while, Miss Courteen is quite unable to invent that odious third line, and though she taps her foot to aerial musick and pulls a chestnut curl right over her nose and twists it round her fingers and wonders whether 'white' is a notably difficult word to rhyme, she never succeeds, and just when she has almost succeeded, her mother's voice sounds from the floor above. This disposes of inspiration altogether, for though her mother's voice is very melodious and sounds prodigiously pleasant as it murmurs 'Spadille' or 'Manille' over the card-tables, it will allow no competition, and drives all invisible musick far away.

"Coming, dear mamma," says Phyllida just as Mr. Vernon decides to wear purple and just as we step out of Mrs. Choke's front door thinking it can no longer be indiscreet to follow our Muses to the scene of Mrs. Courteen's toilet.

As we cross the road glittering in the sunshine with last night's rain, we see a tall young gentleman writing busily in a set of ivory tablets as he strolls quietly along the pavement. Mr. Lovely, the young gentleman, looks up very quickly as a three-cornered note flutters down and lodges in a fold of his ruffles. Miss Courteen who felt the note falling, and thinks that after all she need not make more than a pretty attempt to save it, peers over the railing into the upturned face of the young gentleman who bows very low and sweeps his hat round in a very grand curve, and begs to apologize for the awkwardness of his ruffles in thus intercepting a lady's note. And you and I, my inquisitive companion, stand still for a moment and watch the picture, remembering it is merry Valentine morn. The maid with wide eyes and crimson cheeks nestling in swansdown and the young man of the laughing expectant face, in his peach-coloured velvet suit, seem somehow to have caught the spirit of the day: they make us think of broken stiles, of hedges heavy with may, or blue and white April noons, of lambs, and children with pinafores a-flutter gathering cowslip-posies on a wind-washed down, and of all the old and dear delights of Spring.

Says Phyllida, "Oh! pray pardon my clumsiness."

And "Madam," says he very gallantly, "I'm incredibly obliged, for you've given me a rhyme."

"Oh! pray tell me—was it to 'white'?"

"Nay! 'twas harder than that," he murmurs.

"But I think that is monstrous difficult."

"Bright, sight, light," (cheerfully) "height," (regretfully) "night," (hopefully) and "fight," (fiercely).

"Indeed," adds Phyllida, "I thought of every one of them, but not one would fit the sense."

The young gentleman who is a rhymester himself, grows interested. "Might I," says he, "without impertinence inquire your necessity?"

"Sure, 'tis for a Valentine," and as Mr. Lovely's face darkens, she hurriedly adds, "for a young lady, a friend of mine, you'll see the direction writ on the flap."

His face clears again and he asks,

"You wish it delivered?"

"Oh, sir! how did you guess?"

"By accident, ma'am, or a happy intuition, I stepped

out to take the air this fine morning, and chance has discovered for me an incontrovertible excuse for such idle exercise. To be footman to a sister of the Muses is surely appropriate service for a poet."

"Then you are a poet?"

"My publisher affirms it."

"How romantick truly!" but the tail of the sigh is interrupted by her mother's voice, and she has bare time to murmur her thanks, drop a genteel curtsey and vanish. As for Mr. Lovely he has registered a vow to attend the Monday Assembly next week instead of sitting down to Hazard at the *Blue Boar* Inn.

Abovestairs all is confusion because Mrs. Courteen cannot make up her mind between yellow lutestring and orange silk. Phyllida whose heart is full of the dancing springtide thinks her dear mamma should wear the brightest colours and the richest stuffs in the world.

"For if you would only allow the curtains to be drawn back, you would see what a golden morning it is outside," she complains to her mother who answers:

"Women of fashion, Phyllida, dress by candlelight for candlelight."

Betty the maid, agrees with her young mistress, "Sweet, pretty dear lamb," as she asseverates in Hampshire accents, "Orange silk, say I, and God bless the gaulden sun."

Mrs. Courteen who is sitting nearly half-undressed and quite incapable of forming a decision, bids Betty go and find out Thomas' opinion. Thomas is the family footman and a great critick of men, women, and religions. Presently Betty comes back and says that Tammas would prefar yaller.

"Why, Betty, why?"

"Because," answers the maid, "he says silks are for the vain and abominable and lutestrings have a pleasant twang and savour of the psalmist."

So Mrs. Courteen turns from yellow sack to orange sack and from primrose-quilted petticoat to apricock-quilted petticoat in despair, till at last Betty asks triumphantly:

"How would it be, ma'am, if you was to wear your most elegant and truly genteel green sattin seeing that it do be Saint Valentine with a smell of green leaves in the air?"

This provokes a new decision, and causes a great rummaging in drawers and presses and closets until the gown, fragrant with last year's lavender, is discovered, when the toilet too long neglected starts afresh.

"What patches, ma'am?" says Betty.

"My Cupid's bow and the two tears of widowhood."

"What scents, mamma?" asks Phyllida.

"My Citron Essence, child."

Then shoes are buckled, stockings are gartered, and a black mantua placed gently round her shoulders. One more touch of powder, one more brush from the rouge pot, one more flounce and one more flirt while the watchet ribbands in the cap are hastily changed to ribbands of palest apple-green, and a pair of emerald snaps are quickly fastened.

"Does my hoop sit straight? Oh! Lud! I vow I shall be late."

A breathless moment and, in place of the mantua, a tippet of pheasant's feathers is adjusted. Down the Crescent is heard the opening of many doors. Phyllida runs to the window, draws back the curtains so that the sun streams in upon the sicklied candles.

"Has the Beau appeared yet?" asks Mrs. Courteen.

"Here he comes, and oh! mamma, he is wearing a suit of olive-green."

"What great good fortune! what taste I shall display. Green is certainly the fashionable colour," and Mrs. Courteen began to trill to a tune of her own invention....

"I shall be *à la mode*, I shall be *à la mode* and very *bon ton* and *très bon ton*."

Radiant, she descends the stairs followed by Betty carrying an enormous glass goblet. Outside, rubicund

Thomas with heavily knobbed cane awaits her. The widow glances over her shoulder at the crowds swinging down the street, all equipped with glass goblets of various sizes and shapes. She throws an anxious glance towards the head of the procession. The Beau is certainly in green of a shade slightly darker than her own but, nevertheless, distinctly comparable. She tosses her cap in anticipation of the envied triumph and sails in the general direction.

And you, Achates, who have accompanied me so early in the morning to the toilets of some of our principal characters, pray give yourself the additional trouble of thinking what a Great Man he must be to induce these butterflies and moths of fashion to sally worth Cap à Pie perfect at half-past eight o'clock of a February morning.

"Let Bath be true to her bedgowns," he wrote, "in Curtain Wells we are ignorant that men and women undress."

When we think of that apoplectick Circumference which so lately protruded, we can heartily assent to his opinion.

CHAPTER II

THE PUMP ROOM

AS all roads are commonly reputed to lead to Earl's Court, so here at Curtain Wells all roads led to the Pump Room. It dominated the city from the summit of a moderately steep hill as the Acropolis dominates the almost equally famous city of Athens. In certain aspects it bore a remarkable likeness to a Greek temple with its fluted columns and portico haunted by many white pigeons. It was even more like a gigantick summer-house whose interior was always open to the four winds. Any reasonable explanation of a spring that gushed forth at the very top of a hill always eluded those who toiled laboriously up the slope; but, as a more religious butterfly once remarked, Providence plainly designed it to serve some useful purpose by allowing it to gush forth at such an unexpected elevation. The same lady used to regard volcanoes as an uncomfortable if divine method of destroying large numbers of Papists together, and would pertinently observe that if England had admitted the claims of the Pretender, she was convinced what was now a cool, health-giving fountain would have boiled over to the horrid accompaniment of flames and lava. At precisely a quarter to nine o'clock, Beau Ripple paused at the foot of the hill to survey through a monocle his flurried followers. A wag once said that Ripple liked to gaze at life through the wrong end of a spy-glass, because he himself was of so small a stature. Whether this monocle actually diminished his world to the size of an ant-heap, I do not know, but certainly the whole assemblage stopped to recover their breath as if conscious of their utter lack of importance in the eyes of the Great little Man. The Physician-in-chief was solemnly beckoned into hearing.

"Two minutes," said the Beau.

Mr. Oboe the Physician opened the lid of an enormous watch attached to a red silk fob and regarded the dial with an expression of great intentness. He might, so complete was his abstraction, have been feeling the pulse of the Exquisite Mob behind him.

Slowly the minutes rolled by while the Beau took several possessive sniffs of the young spring air. Not an unseemly whisper disturbed the silence. So still was it that above the cooing of the sacred pigeons on the roof of the Pump Room, far down in the valley could be heard the lowing of cows. At thirteen minutes to nine Mr. Ripple let his monocle drop; Mr. Oboe replaced his watch; the Pump Room bell began to clang very fast; the Exquisite Mob started to climb the hill and innumerable glass goblets glittered in the sun. When the summit was reached the Beau called in a loud voice:

"Oboe!"

"Mr. Ripple?" bowed the Physician.

"I allow two more minutes for panting."

"Certainly, Mr. Ripple. Very just, sir."

So the Exquisite Mob like the Hart panted after the Waters or perhaps more accurately before them.

At the expiration of the breathing-space, a diminutive negro known as Gog advanced towards Mr. Ripple, bearing a fluted goblet upon a tray of Chinese lacker. An equally diminutive negro called Magog presented the goblet to Mr. Ripple who turned slightly in the direction of the company and slowly sipped his portion with consummate meditation. When almost half-way towards the bottom of the glass the Beau looked up as if surprized to see his adherents still thirsty. This was understood to be the signal for approach, and the Exquisite Mob advanced to drink while the children, miniatures of foppery, played Hide and Seek or Touch-last round the pillars.

Mrs. Courteen sailed towards a thin little military man with a very long and very crisp pigtail, whose outstanding feature in front was an extremely conical Adam's Apple that bobbed up and down as if his throat were a bowl of water and, rising with his choler, at boiling-point invariably choked him into incoherence.

The Major would have passed for one of those half-pay officers who frequent watering-places and rely for many of their meals upon an acquaintance with the tacticks and strategy of the late Duke of Marlborough, with the miserable failure of Carthagena and the already forgotten personality of his Highness the Duke of C——d.

As a matter of fact, he had followed Mrs. Courteen to Curtain Wells from Hampshire where he owned a small hunting lodge known as Ramilies House, Oudenarde Grange, and Malplaquet Place according to his humour, but for no discoverable reason besides. He had a painted board for each designation, but nobody ever extracted from him the principle on which, from time to time, they were changed. When asked on one occasion why he omitted the famous victory of Blenheim from his titular commemoration, he replied that the omission saved the expense of continually forwarding letters to Oxfordshire. The Major was inclined to resent the homage paid to Beau Ripple.

"A d——d civilian, ma'am," he muttered to Mrs. Courteen.

"Oh! you soldiers! I protest you have no reverence for anybody."

"Not I, ma'am. I don't bow the knee to a living soul. Not at all. 'Sblood, ma'am, the fellow's no better than a low adventurer. Would he fight? Not he. So he forbids us to wear swords. D——n it, ma'am, a soldier without his hanger is like a monkey without his tail. That's what I say."

"So do I, Major, so do I," echoed a suave voice over

his shoulder and the Major turning round, encountered the bland half-bored, half-tolerant smile of the Great little Man.

"Your similes are uncommon happy, Major."

Tarry's Apple throbbed and bubbled and rose and sank, but the Beau passed on contemptuously, and a large flabby man in a suit of snuff-coloured frieze treading upon the Major's toe at this moment, the latter's wrath flowed into another channel.

"My toe, Mr. Moon!" he said furiously.

"Your toe?" inquired the other with great earnestness. The question of disputed property which seemed imminent was quashed by the widow's interruption:

"'Tis too early for argument. Come, neighbours, let us make our promenade. Where is Phyllida?"

But Phyllida was making her promenade at a careful distance behind her mother. Phyllida was taking the demurest little steps with an arm in her beloved Betty's arm and with a swansdown muff held against her cheek to ward off the shrewd Easterly wind, while almost level with the two maids walked a stately gentleman of a pale complexion. And every time the gentleman stopped to survey the promenaders over the tortoise-shell handle of his ebony walking-stick, Phyllida and Betty stopped to see if it was truly a quarter-past nine o'clock by St. Simon's church tower. And every time the gentleman stopped to flick a speck of dust from his purple sattin sleeve, by a very odd coincidence Miss Courteen always stopped to see if her shoe had really become unbuckled. This tends to show that in spite of all the precautions of Beau Ripple, the innermost fane of Æsculapius had been invaded by a strange god. I doubt Miss Courteen, considered by her mother too young for Chalybeate, was learning to drink of that deep well whose waters will never run dry so long as maids and men frequent its precincts.

The Exquisite Mob continued to circle round the Pump Room because the ritual of the Cure prescribed an hour's steady promenade before breakfast. The scarlet heels of innumerable shoes clicked in unison and the drowsy hum of morning small talk rose and fell upon the February air. All agreed it was a monstrous fine day for the season of the year. All expressed the opinion that by no stretch of imagination could such weather be expected to last. All wished it would indeed, and everybody asked his neighbour whether he intended to grace the next Assembly, and the neighbour invariably replied he had every intention of doing so. Everybody bowed or curtseyed very low to Mr. Ripple and Mr. Ripple had a delightfully well-turned sentence for each of his subjects, as if he would reward their energy in rising so early. Occasionally the Great little Man would condescend to take a pinch of the best Rappee with an elderly gentleman. But as he never took snuff with anybody under the rank of Viscount in the peerage of England and as the peer thus honoured was bound to be above the age of five-and-forty, it happened that the elderly gentleman was always old Lord Vanity, the only individual present who satisfied the double requirement.

"How different this scene is from Hampshire to be sure, though for my part I shall ever protest that those who have eyes to see, let them see, and people who accuse us of wasting our time forget how persistently they look for the arrival of the carrier."

Whether or not Major Tarry and Mr. Moon understood this remark of Mrs. Courteen's, they certainly both agreed with her.

"To-day is Session day," muttered the Justice rather gloomily.

"Well, sir, the magistrates will do their business without you," snapped his rival.

"Not unlikely, sir, not unlikely."

"Well, sir, what the deuce are you grumbling at?"

Mr. Moon replied that he was not grumbling, he was merely commenting; and the two gentlemen bickered on across placid Mrs. Courteen like two children over a hedge.

Meanwhile on the farther side of the Course, as the broad path round the Pump Room was called, Mr. Vernon was still keeping step with Phyllida and Betty, but so delicately did the former tread and so far aloof did he appear that no one suspected him of anything so low as ogling pretty Miss Courteen or her maid. Sometimes he would murmur " When will my charmer be there? " and every time he asked this question, the charmer would send a rippling little laugh into her swansdown muff, and flash a glance over the top towards Betty who would toss her head and imply that such curiosity was worth a long-delayed gratification.

At last Mr. Vernon would take out his laced handkerchief and flick presumably at a ghostly Despair. Phyllida would be prodigiously afraid that her dear Amor (by that name only did she know her lover) was growing unhappy at her hard-hearted treatment and, feeling she had tormented his patience long enough, would gently shake her muff until a piece of paper fluttered slowly to the ground. Mr. Vernon would stoop with indescribable grace and distinction of manner, and while Miss Courteen looked very demure indeed and quite innocent of anything or anybody in the world, he would put the piece of paper in his handkerchief and press the handkerchief to his lips and look round the corner of his eyes at Phyllida, who would just by chance be looking round the corner of her eyes to ascertain if her Mamma were beckoning to her. And this used to happen every fine morning during the promenade, and continued to happen for many days afterwards.

Half-past nine o'clock struck, and the promenaders all turned on their heels to hear Mr. Ripple divulge the gaiety of the day.

It is not to be supposed that Curtain Wells was careless of her pilgrims' pleasure. On the contrary every hour of their visit was wreathed in delightful possibilities of enjoyment. At present it was Winter so that naturally most of the entertainments occurred indoors, but in late Spring and Summer a series of Fêtes Champêtres and Fêtes Aqueuses, of moonlight Concertos, harlequin Ridottos, and lantern Masquerades made Curtain Wells a tolerably attractive stage for the marionettes who postured and declaimed upon its boards.

There was much tiptoe attention for the Beau as he ascended a marble pedestal and slowly turned the pages of a notebook bound in tooled Morocco leather, gilt-edged, and of impeccable finish and design.

"My Lords," Mr. Ripple began, whereupon old Lord Vanity, blinking several times at his daughter Lady Jane Vane, took an extra large pinch of Rappee.

"My Lords, Ladies and Gentlemen, I have the extreme honour to inform you that the Publick Breakfast given to Sir Jeremy Dummer for the purpose of commemorating his twenty-first consecutive winter at Curtain Wells will be held (*Deo volente*) at the Town Hall to-morrow the fifteenth instant."

A murmur of delighted anticipation ran round the Exquisite Mob while Sir Jeremy Dummer who was verging on nonagenarian antiquity drew himself up very erect, quivering and doddering with senile pride. "There will be the usual loyal and personal toasts," continued the Beau, "and at the conclusion of the entertainment the Company will adjourn to the Civick Chamber, where I hope the ladies will be already arrived, in order to partake of a dish of tea. I may add that the tea, duty paid, has been generously presented by Mr. Hopkins of the High Street, well known to many of you as the incomparable provider of the rarer dried delicacies which have traced prodigal patterns over so many of your mahogany tables."

The Exquisite Mob murmured its gratitude for the tea and the compliment with much condescension and affableness, while the publick spirit of the tradesman was generally extolled.

"To-night at precisely half-past six o'clock, Mrs. Dudding's Conversazione. Quadrille tables for ninety-six players, Pope Joan for the young and sprightly and—ahem—a Pharaoh table in order that our gentlemen, Mrs. Dudding informs me, may have no valid excuse for absenting themselves on the score of dullness. Chairs at precisely half-past ten o'clock and I must request you, my lords, ladies and gentlemen, to warn your chairmen that quarterstaff play with the poles will be visited with your acutest displeasure. I am sorry to complain of an abuse on a morning when the prospect of Nature is so vastly pleasant, but last week the whooping and halloa-ing of the partizans caused me to place Basto upon the Ponto of my Vis à Vis."

The Exquisite Mob sighed in sympathetick consternation as, with a perceptible break in his voice, Mr. Ripple made this confession.

"And since I am temporarily launched upon unpleasant topicks, I must beg for earlier and less riotous hours at the *Blue Boar*. It is exceedingly ungenteel to throw quart bottles of Burgundy at the watch. The latter is a fine body of men devoted to the service of an orderly and decent society, and does not deserve a crown of plaisters as the result of publishing the hour of the night and the state of the weather. However, I will mention no names, gentlemen."

Lord Vanity, not feeling himself included in the last vocative, took a pinch of Rappee and gazed very fiercely at my Lady Bunbutter through the rheum and water of his ancient eyes. As her ladyship showed no signs of a guilty conscience, the Earl took a second pinch and muttered "devilish young cubs" under his breath.

"On Sunday," the Beau resumed with his old suavity of enunciation, "the waters will not be drunk until the fulfilment of Divine Service. On Monday the usual Assembly will be held, and a Cotillon will be danced at twelve o'clock precisely. Chairs at half-past twelve o'clock precisely. And now, my lords, ladies and gentlemen, nothing remains for me but to wish you a vastly enjoyable breakfast, a happy issue from your divers infirmities and a very good morning."

This benediction was the recognized sign of dismissal ; the Beau descended from his pedestal and the Exquisite Mob betook itself down hill, although a few individuals waited behind in order to consult with the former on matters of etiquette, fashion and gentility, his advice being considered the most refined in the country.

Mrs. Courteen sailed down upon Mr. Ripple and asked whether she was right in thinking that the moment when green should be worn was arrived.

"I think so, ma'am," the Beau assured her. "I think so : to be sure, a few of our more conservative fops hold that green should never appear before the Queen's birthday. But I differ from them, ma'am, I differ. You will observe, madam, that I differ."

Phyllida had rejoined her mother by this time, and Mr. Ripple saluted her freshness with a courtly bow.

"Many Valentines?" he inquired with a quizzical droop of his left eyelid.

Phyllida blushed, protesting.

"No, indeed, sir."

The Widow hastily assured Mr. Ripple that her daughter was not near old enough to dream of such follies, while Major Tarry and Mr. Moon, whose skirts were stiff with Valentines intended for Mrs. Courteen herself, looked very severely at the sun as if he were in some way responsible for the madness of love in the air.

"Tut-tut! Youth's the time for love, as Mr. Gay sings, and though I do not encourage the interchange of passionate sentiments among those who are seeking to recover their health, I regard St. Valentine's Day as a very proper festival for young men and maidens in whose hearts no degeneration is yet apparent." With these words Mr. Ripple drooped his left eyelid lower than ever.

"Fie! sir, we shall have the child vapoured like any

woman of fashion, if you put such inflammable ideas into her head," complained Mrs. Courteen, who was just beginning to be more than a little jealous of her daughter.

"Not at all, ma'am," said the Beau, "I swear I saw an agreeable spark toast Miss Phyllida in Chalybeate—the irreverent dog—but I forgave him; upon my honour, I was near doing the same thing myself."

Now Phyllida was not at all anxious for her mother to think she had an admirer, and yet with youth's vanity, she could not resist a half-acknowledgment of the Beau's rally. Luckily for her, Major Tarry, who always resented his removal from the centre of attraction, thought it was time to assert his existence by demanding rather pompously if the Beau saw anything unusual in the sky.

"Yes, sir," the latter agreed. "I see the sun, which is very unusual at this season of the year."

Mr. Moon gaped a smile, and Tarry's Apple began to rise. He had anticipated a surprized negative from the Beau, whereupon he intended to look very mysterious and say that after all perhaps he was mistaken. Thus, having impressed the bystanders with the notion that they were talking to a man of superhuman vision, he would offer an arm to Mrs. Courteen.

"Run, Betty," exclaimed the latter, "and tell Mr. Thomas we await his escort."

Thomas was at the footman's Pump Room, a hundred yards down the hill. Here, every morning he mused regretfully upon the decline of beer-drinking. Chalybeate to him was a sort of Jacobite liquor which was slowly supplanting the honest Esau ale. As for streams that spouted inexplicably from solid rocks, these he held to be an infringement of Moses' prerogative. He would unscrew the knob of his footman's cane for a morsel of Parmesan cheese and chew the cud of bitter reflection, while with the butt of his nose he would polish the silver ball till it shone with equal splendour.

Betty found him thus occupied and, as he stalked after

her in obedience to his summoning, she heard him mutter several times in quick succession, " Wells of Sodom! Waters of Gomorrah! Pillars of Salt! "

Mrs. Courteen as she curtseyed her farewells to the Beau sank to the ground like a deflated balloon. This done she gathered her party into hearing and occupied their outward attention as they walked in the direction of the Crescent with a long and disjointed account of her health.

" Why will you shake your muff so vehemently? " complained the Widow.

" 'Tis full of dust," said Phyllida.

If it was, I am afraid Miss Courteen was trying to throw some of it into her mamma's eyes.

CHAPTER III

THE BLUE BOAR

WHILE the Exquisite Mob circled round the central fane of Æsculapius, Mr. Charles Lovely had enough lack of taste and orthodoxy to make a heretick promenade in the low-lying water-meadows at the foot of the town.

He had knocked three times at old General Morton's house in the Western Colonnade and delivered Miss Courteen's Valentine into the hands of Miss Sukey Morton's maid. She, poor soul, wore round her neck a brass button attached to a piece of string still reminiscent in tarred perfume of the Dorsetshire jetty down which she had wandered a year ago. It was streaking her breast with verdigris as if in some way prophetick of a heart that all too soon would be tarnished more irreparably by that faithless lover beyond the seas.

Consequently Miss Morton's maid received the paquet with a sympathetick reverence learnt in long morning dreams when the sunlight splashed the walls of her garret in waves and ripples of faint gold.

"Any name, your honour?" she asked.

"I believe not."

"And no message?" she paused in bright-eyed hope of an assignation which was to be the first step in the softening of her mistress' hard and imperious little heart.

"None at all so far as I know, my dear," and Mr. Lovely passed on down the deserted street towards the meadows.

The little maid stood on the steps regarding him.

"Tes a Valentoine surely," she thought, and held the envelope between her and the discoverer sun. A red heart glowed through the paper, a red heart pierced by a flaming arrow.

"And who'd ha' thought she had a bow and her be so spoitful."

She sighed as she gazed after Mr. Lovely.

"He do look proper and happy surely."

The elegant young gentleman had, in fact, caught some of the harlequin grace of a fine morning in the prime of the year as he avoided the cracks in the paving stones to bring the meadows closer and make the Colonnade less intolerably long.

"Wi' sech a rosy spark, for sure, she've no call to be jealous of me," thought the little maid, as her soul went winging over the great Atlantick whose roar filled the silence of her mind, to meet the soul of her sailor-lover who was at the moment sitting upon an alien beach in the company of two dusky wantons and a bottle of Jamaica rum.

Mr. Lovely turned the corner and the little maid vanished at the sound of a bell summoning her to tie one of her mistress' pink bows to a more modish angle.

Our hero, for since perfect confidence should exist between us, I will no longer attempt to conceal his identity, continued to walk to the tune of a lyrick always provided the measure did not compel him to step upon one of the fatal cracks. Soon he came to a road which ended in green fields sodden with winter rains, but soft and grateful after the arid pavement.

Face to face with the pale blue February sky, he took up more earnestly the intention of the half-fledged songs that occupied his brain. Strange songs they were, fanciful and unrestrained in the eyes of their author and his contemporaries who did not recognize in them an echo of one Mr. Herrick, dead, and now forgotten by the world of literature. His mother had read the poems to him as a child. The *Hesperides* of 1648 was the only book owned by the lodging-house in Westminster where a dingy year of childhood had dragged out its course. In his youth, he had loved their sharp, elusive harmonies, and when he attained years of composition, could never free his own lyricks from extravagance so acquired, however assiduously he attempted to follow Augustan models. To his credit, be it added, he was always sincerely ashamed of his barbarick numbers and, as he grew older, was often successful in expressing the heart of a riotous evening in a clear-cut drinking song. Perhaps this vain pursuit of formalism in words made him neglect his private life, which ran a wild career checked by nothing stronger than the strings of his purse.

As he leaned over a stile and watched the cattle in the meadows, out of the past there came like an arrow of song shot from the gloomy depths of London,

> *Ye have been fresh and green,*
> *Ye have been filled with flowers,*
> *And ye the walks have been*
> *Where maids have spent their hours.*

But Mr. Lovely was dissatisfied. He felt the sentiment would have reached a larger dignity, a more epigrammatick crispness, a more trenchant elusiveness, if it had never strayed beyond the bonds of an heroick couplet. He deplored his ineradicable early impressions and vowed to study the classick models with a still more fierce ardour of imitation.

But having formed this resolution, our hero was just as discontented as before. The sun shining into his heart, found no reflection there.

"These d—d late nights are killing me," he complained, ascribing his discontent to fatiguing sessions of play. He bent down to pluck a starry celandine and wasted a few minutes in trying to find out whether he liked butter. The little golden oracle told him he did, but as he was well aware of this fact already, only the flower benefited by an enhanced reputation for infallibility. Nevertheless it was flicked carelessly over the hedge, where it lay stalk upwards in the shade like many another prophet before it. To confess the truth at once, Mr. Lovely had only used the butter to deceive himself, for round about his red-heeled shoes were eight golden petals which seemed to prove that a more intimate question had been asked, and answered unfavourably if we may judge by the banishment of the flower. To console his wounded susceptibleness, he determined to smoke a pipe and, having made up his mind, found the long clay stem was broken. With a pithy condemnation of things in general, he tried to establish the reason of his depressed spirits. Then he discovered his spirits were not depressed, merely unsettled. Burgundy of course. Hazard without a doubt. Should he try Chalybeate? The d—l! not if he knew it. Should he try Chalybeate? She wore a very engaging swansdown tippet. What a fool he had been to come to these meadows! Should he try Chalybeate? The half-fledged lyrick was strangled: the landskip seemed pretentiously bright in proportion to the wintry air which was still abroad and, to crown all, he felt an extraordinary desire to drink a tankard of ale with Mr. Anthony Clare at the *Blue Boar*. The latter might know who wore swansdown in the Crescent. With a sigh of relief, he wrung this admission out of himself, shivered and turned his face towards Curtain Wells, whose houses clustered like a swarm of bees around the sacred hill.

The *Blue Boar*, whither Mr. Charles Lovely was bound, was a hostelry of the conventionally ample type. The rooms with exterior rows of galleries were built round a large quadrangle to which coaches and stage waggons were admitted through an arch that was only just high enough for the vehicles of a more recent pattern. The fixed population consisted of innumerable plump and shapely chambermaids, innumerable dried-up hostlers and grooms, and a certain number of sedate waiters who were all clothed in the same shade of rusty black, and all of whom wished they had settled earlier in life to become footmen. However this canker of thwarted ambition never prevented them from handling anything from a soup-tureen to a guinea-piece with reverence and precision.

The host, Jeremy Daish, was neither round nor rubicund. On the contrary he was remarkably sallow and, in his suit of cinnamon cloth, bore a vague likeness to a well-seasoned Cremona violin. He was the builder, owner, and inventor of the famous *Daish's Rooms* adjoining the Inn and, as the latter served for a recognized adjunct to the more official *Assembly Rooms*, Mr. Daish became a somewhat mildewed counterpart of the great Beau himself, a mezzotint ill-executed of a famous painting in oils. His back was so often crouched in servility that it had acquired a permanent stoop. Rumour said that years ago Mr. Daish was often seen fiddle in hand at West-country fairs and wakes, and supported the legend by pointing out when a lady of the extremest fashion and quality graced his dancing floor with a pair of very high red heels, the solemn innkeeper would steal to the Dais of the musicians and, taking an instrument, would himself bob and play my lady through a minuet with considerable Gusto and Bravura.

The *Blue Boar* was patronized by a select company of fashionable young gentlemen who lent the old hostelry something of the tone of White's or Almack's. Bagmen were excluded from the wing occupied by these elegant patrons, and though from time to time one of the former, with a merry reputation, would be invited to take wine with the quality in return for the tale of a famous and gross adventure, it was distinctly understood that nothing low or vulgar was allowed to penetrate beyond a certain doorway.

Beau Ripple himself would saunter down towards twilight and exhort his youthful subjects on the folly of vice, the futility of play and the obligation to drink the waters at half-past eight o'clock. Mr. Ripple was esteemed a Puritan, but such a genteel Puritan that the young gentlemen, subdued by the length of his waistcoats and his irreproachable ties and solitaires, listened to him willingly enough, and overpowered by the orthodoxy of his wigs and buckles, the fullness of his shirts and the size of his cuffs, heeded his warnings sometimes.

Mr. Lovely strolled through the archway into the yard all fresh and shining after the morning swill. Along the galleries, the chambermaids were hurrying about their work, and the figure of Mrs. Grindle, the housekeeper, glittering and jingling with keys, warned him no loitering in the galleries would be tolerated at that hour of the day. Two horses were being groomed in the courtyard, but as he had discussed all their points both with their owners and the hostlers at least half a dozen times before, he was not inclined to pursue the outworn theme farther.

" Mr. Clare about? " he inquired.

" Han't see him, y'r honour," answered one of the workers.

" 'Es that Mr. Clare? " asked the other.

" Yes, my good fellow, have you seen him? "

" Rode over to Baverstock Regis to see a maiden aunt," the man replied.

" Ho! ho! ho! " roared the first, " dang me if that bean't the best I ever hard. Ho! ho! ho! " and convulsed with merriment, the man slapped his tight-breeched thighs with frequency and vigour.

" You make the very d—l of a noise, Sirrah," said Mr. Lovely fretfully.

" I axe y'r honour's pardon, but when I hard Jock there talking of maiden aunts—ho—ho—ho! and when I minds that shaapely—ah! well it doan't do to mention no naames, but it come over me sudden to laugh," and with this apology, the humorous hostler picked up his mare's near fore-leg, and continued to chuckle at intervals for the rest of the day.

Mr. Lovely began to think Tony Clare was confoundedly young, and when one young man begins to think another young man confoundedly young, it is usually a convincing proof that the pensive young man is deep in love.

"What's a fellow to do?" he sighed as he turned into the coffee-room. It was empty, so he called for a draught of ale, put his feet on the window seat and surveyed the passers-by. He wondered what had become of his friends, and why the d—l all the world was gone mad because the sun shone with unwonted brilliance for the middle of February. Then he remembered it was Valentine day and amused himself with the manufacture of paper darts which he shot at the prettiest young women in range. Unluckily, in an attempt to pierce the ripe heart of buxom Miss Page who assisted at the cookshop, he wounded the Rector on the nose. This set him moralizing on the fortune of Love. Could anything be more incongruous than Love and the Rector. Yet why not? We are all targets of a dimpled nudity. The phrase caught his fancy. Numberless Cupids in attitudes of attack floated before his mind's eye. "Demme!" thought Mr. Lovely, "my brain is like an Italian ceiling. Targets of a dimpled nudity!" He flung back the lattice to its utmost extent and leaned out to the morning whence the chatter of the world without floated into the sunny room.

"Everybody is monstrous good-humoured," he concluded. But somehow it was no longer amusing to quizz the young woman in Mrs. Tabby's ribband-shop through his ivory rimmed perspective. Somehow since yesterday her forearm had grown coarser.

"All the world's growing old," he grumbled disconsolately. But the world would not be vapoured, and laughed and chattered and bobbed and flirted and chirped with all the selfishness of a world that is always young in defiance of the moods of her individuals.

Suddenly the mob of Cupids faded from his mind and the World at which he was scoffing ceased to exist.

Surely at the very end of the High Street, he could discern something which was slowly assuming the magick shape of a swansdown tippet. His heart began to beat very fast and he felt the rushing crimson flood his cheeks. Life was wrapped in swansdown, as, through clouds of the airy texture, his soul soared to unimaginable heights. Then came the descent and, waking as from a dream, he found himself staring down into a pair of wide blue eyes. In his embarrassment he knocked over a pot of jacynths and, above the noise of the fall, heard himself telling a Swansdown Muff he had delivered the paquet. Could anything be more enchanting than the warning fore-finger, save the lips to which it was lifted? Could anything better console his enforced silence than the knowledge that between him and her existed a secret? The swansdown tippet and swansdown muff had vanished, but fragments of broken Terra Cotta strewed the pavement. The swansdown tippet and swansdown muff had floated away to some fairyland of their own, but a blue jacynth perfumed the air.

Certainly the idlers of Curtain Wells had a fruitful subject for an afternoon's debate in the sight of young Mr. Lovely climbing out of the coffee-room window. Besides, if that were not amazing enough, the idlers were immediately diverted by the aspect of young Mr. Lovely gathering up the remains of a shattered flower-pot and clasping a bruised jacynth to his silk waistcoat. They all agreed the incident had no explanation, and were even stirred out of their perpetual lethargy to muster round the entrance of the *Blue Boar* in order to verify a daring speculation that he was going to carry the fragments within.

" Good G——! " said Mr. Ripple, who was approaching the archway from the other side. " Good G——, sir, are you mad? " To Mr. Ripple the shock was great. He had aspirations for Mr. Lovely. To be sure, he was wild, an extravagant young dog, but then he possessed an inimitable assurance of manner, a pretty talent for polite verse-making, and a consummate taste in brocades. The Beau of late had often pondered the choice of his successor. He had aspirations for Mr. Lovely and now he saw his favourite positively panting (the most ungenteel motion and fatal to the fall of a waistcoat), not merely panting but smeared with mould, hugging potsherds, and apparently quite unmoved by his degradation. Is it wonderful that Mr. Ripple cried,

"Good G——, sir, are you mad?"

"Yes," shouted Mr. Lovely.

"Or drunk?"

"Yes," shouted Mr. Lovely.

As he seemed inclined to answer every question in the affirmative, the Beau remarked he wished to see a representative group of the young gentlemen at the *Blue Boar* upon a matter of the gravest social and civick importance.

Our hero ejaculated, "With you in the twinkling of a bedpost," and raced across the yard, up the first staircase, along the first gallery and into the last room.

A light broke upon Mr. Ripple's bewilderment.

"He has discovered some prehistorick relicks. Probably a Cinerary Urn, a Lunette or possibly a gold coin of Rome."

In pleasant anticipation, the Beau who was an intimate friend of Mr. Sylvanus Urban, beheld the folded copperplate illustrating the discovery and the rounded sentences on the opposite page of the *Gentleman's Magazine* in which the excavations would be carefully recorded by Horace Ripple.

"This must assuage my wrath," he decided by the door of the coffee-room.

To tell the truth, the Beau was on censure bent when he met our hero outside the *Blue Boar*.

Already, that morning, he had alluded to the riotous nocturnal behaviour, the assaults upon the watch, the fusilade of empty bottles, but not being able to descry a single offender, he determined that personal and individual remonstrance would be more efficacious. To the *Blue Boar* therefore, he went having first exchanged his suit of olive green for one of black sattin unrelieved by silver and terminated by ruffles whose cambrick fell in severe folds and condemnatory lines.

As he stepped from the Great House round the Crescent and along the High Street, he passed in sombre eclipse upon the gaiety of subjects shining with the reflection of his genteel rays.

Presently Mr. Lovely came back still bearing the marks of the potted soil.

" Was it an Urn? "

Mr. Lovely looked surprized.

" A Lachrymatory perhaps? Or a Lunette? Or," Mr. Ripple grew breathless with excitement, " not an Image of Æsculapius? "

" Pray, sir, are you trying to humour a madman? Because on my soul, I don't know what you are driving at."

" So, sir, your late phrenzy was nothing more than the unbridled haste and inconsiderate volition of youthful folly? " sternly demanded the Beau.

" I'faith, I knocked over one of old Daish's precious pots, and was making haste to remove it from the region of his laments. That's all, and there's my hand on't."

" You will pardon me," replied the Beau drawing back, " I have no objection to shaking a hand stained by honest toil, but I have never shaken a hand sullied by mere zest for uncleanliness."

" As you will, dear Beau," laughed Mr. Lovely.

The Beau was about to point an example to adorn his statement when he was interrupted by the entrance of severe Mrs. Grindle clasping her nose with one hand, and with the other holding at arm's length the offending jacynth by a shred of its roots.

" Mr. Lovely, sir," she began and as our hero pulled forward a chair and the Beau leaned back to listen, she continued, "I have known a cat kitten in one of the maids' beds."

"How very distressing," murmured the Beau letting the firelight play in the diamonds of his rings.

"But never, never," proclaimed Mrs. Grindle swelling like Mr. Handel's *Largo*, "have I known a young gentleman want to turn his bachelor bed into a ploughed field. Mr. Lovely, sir, I'll trouble you to say if this is your planting or did you wish to insinuate that your bed was not made this morning?"

"Mrs. Grindle, madam," replied the accused, "you have heard of beds and you have heard of garden-beds. Mine is a garden-bed. A Parterre impromptu, a Landskip in miniature, a Bucolick of slumber, a dimity Eclogue. In a word—but pray, Mrs. Grindle, my dear Mrs. Grindle, out of regard for me rehabilitate that jacynth without a word to Mr. Daish, and I, out of regard for you, will certainly pay for the washing of the bedspread."

Mr. Lovely smiled so very engagingly and looked so completely innocent of any desire to insinuate anything except Mrs. Grindle's good-nature that the housekeeper gave way, condescended to smile and, as she retired, threw a quick glance in the direction of a mirrour to notice the angle of her snowy cap.

Having reduced Mrs. Grindle to affableness, Mr. Lovely turned his smile towards the Beau. The latter had watched with much satisfaction the progress of his favourite's negociations, thinking to himself that a man who could circumvent such a dragon as the housekeeper would be very well able to keep in order the most self-assertive of Duchesses. He began to relent his indignation and, as Lovely smiled at him, to see in his late impetuousness no more than the natural activity of a jolly young man. Moreover, for a certain reason, he had a genuine affection for the rogue, and was glad to perceive his high spirits.

"I came here this morning in the hope of a serious

conversation with some of your friends. Are they—are they in the—er—taproom?"

"They're all gone after maids."

"Tut, tut, I wish I could make it plain that Curtain Wells exists for the continence, not the encouragement of appetites."

"You must blame the sun, dear Beau."

"In view of the many pleasant hours I have spent basking in the warmth, I should not presume to do anything so ungrateful. But I will remark that the Sun in his human guises is not to be considered a beneficial example to young men at a stage in the history of mankind when maidens are no longer able to transform themselves into umbrageous laurels, thus rendering impertinent and inconvenient what at first seemed appropriate and inevitable. I allude, sir, to the legend of Apollo and Madam Daphne. However, my dear Charles—" here the Beau laid three tapered jewelled fingers upon the extremity of Mr. Lovely's left shoulder.

"You overwhelm me, sir, with your condescension. The omission of the surname by Beau Ripple, is the bestowal of a title."

"Very well put, Charles," said the older man contentedly. "'Fore Gad! you do me credit. Snuff, sir?"

Charles (we may follow the lead of Mr. Ripple) was now veritably astonished. Never could he recall such an instance of the Beau's condescension towards a man of his years; and he dipped his fingers into the proffered snuff-box with greater bashfulness than he would have displayed towards the powder-box of Titania.

"However, though the rest of our young gentlemen are—after maids," the Beau stumbled over the crudity of the phrase, "I am happy to see that you are engrossed by the seemlier pastime of horticulture." Was it fancy or did Charles really see his mentor blow a tuft of swansdown from his cuff? "I wish," the latter went on, "to remonstrate with you on the indecorous character of your midnight entertainments. Owls, under providence, are allowed to shriek and hoot after sundown, but there seems no reason for extending to men the privilege accorded by a Divine Creator to owls. In short, Mr. Lovely, there has been the—there has been an atrocious hurly-burly in this house every night of late. Pray do not interrupt me," he added as Charles made a protesting movement. "I have the fullest data for my general observations."

"Youth, dear Beau, hot-headed, open-handed Youth."

"Yes, yes, I know something of Youth's anatomy from a personal experience of the happy state, but Youth, Mr. Lovely, is a mighty inadequate justification for a circular scar on the forehead of one of our most respected and silver-tongued watchmen—a scar inflicted by the unconsumed but necessary concomitant of a quart of Burgundy."

"It was an accident, sir, young Tom Chalkley of the Foot——"

"I have observed, Mr. Lovely, that if one of these missiles happens to strike the body against which it is aimed the result is invariably an accident whereas if the missile goes wide of the mark it is a d——d poor shot. But it cannot go on, Mr. Lovely. It shall not go on. The residents acting in conjunction with the visitors reserve the right to expel summarily any person who causes publick offence, and I, as their accredited representative, should be in the highest degree culpable if I allowed it to go on. Consequently, my dear Charles, I appeal to you as to one possessed of some influence over the more violent spirits, to do all in your power of persuasion to prevent it from going on."

Now as the successful quart bottle had been thrown by our hero, and as he was usually the chief agent in promoting a disturbance, it is evident that Mr. Ripple secured his unparalleled authority as much by tact as by severity.

"Dear Beau, you shall be obliged," said Charles, "and now pray tell me who wears a white swansdown tippet and lives hard by the Great House."

"I am not accustomed to observe the minor variations in feminine costume," answered Mr. Ripple with some austerity.

"Nay! But a hermit froze to his psalter must have noticed her," protested the younger man.

"The analogy is incomplete."

"I shall be at the Assembly on Monday night."

"You could not be more worthily employed."

"And I shall effect an introduction under your patronage."

"That very much depends."

"On my good behaviour?" asked Charles.

"On the immunity of my watchmen from further assaults."

"Dear Beau, we are all targets of a—" he hesitated, "of a dimpled nudity or an empty bottle. Love and a bottle, there's the world."

"The flesh, I think, sir."

"I 'faith, Satan must have a fine sieve if he can separate the pair."

"I am no theologian."

"Then you'll present me?" persisted Charles.

"You will protect my watchmen?" demanded the Beau.

"On Monday night?" urged Charles.

"Every night," added the Beau. "Unconditional surrender is my ultimatum. But I hope I know how to display generosity towards a vanquished enemy. You will attend the Publick Breakfast awarded to Sir Jeremy Dummer?"

"Truly I——"

"Tut, tut, I insist. My old friend Lord Cinderton arrives to-day with his invalid son, George Harthe-Brusshe. I should like the young man to see your cherry and trout-pink cuffs."

"Too unseasonable a combination of colours for breakfast."

"Pshaw! your appearance will give a fillip to his impoverished appetite."

"I 'faith, I believe I know how to flavour my conversation with Attick salt, but I swear I never dressed myself for the Role of condiment."

The conversation was soon entirely of sauces.

CHAPTER IV

CURTAIN MAZE

THE Maze at Curtain Wells was always considered one of the principal sights of the place. Holding this reputation, it was naturally the least frequented. Visitors either went there the second day after their arrival or scuttled round it with a competent escort in the twenty-four hours that preceded their departure. But since no one went there twice and since all the visitors and residents of the Wells were perfectly familiar with the various shrines, its invariable emptiness may easily be apprehended. In summer the gardens of which it was a feature were thronged at the fashionable hours. There was also a Rotunda similar to if less grandiose than the famous Rotunda at Ranelagh Garden. This had not long been in existence, and was only used for balls and masquerades through May and June, when the Maze was spangled with lamps for the delight of the dancers. Even so, very few availed themselves of the shelter of its yew-hedges and always spent the rest of the evening in trying to find their way out, being lucky if they succeeded in making a somewhat ruffled appearance during the last Cotillon.

To Curtain Garden went Miss Phyllida Courteen and Madam Betty her maid: to Curtain Garden they were going when they passed Mr. Charles Lovely at the coffee-room window.

Betty belonged to a type of womanhood that grows with age, increased fat and pursiness, into a nurse such as

Mr. Shakespeare drew in *Romeo and Juliet*. If she had been brought up in a disreputable purlieu of the town, she would have become a personally chaste procuress but, nurtured among the buttercups, she merely had a perpetual desire to see her pretty young mistress aflame through the careless progress of some gay spark or other. Whatever there was of passion in her meadow-born soul fed itself on objective embraces. She was never a maid for a kissing-gate at long shadow time, but when she saw Phyllida's heart flutter with quick emotion before the approach of Mr. Vernon, a primitive phrenzy set her cheeks aglow and fired her eyes to a livelier blue. She adored her mistress with a precocious maternity but, paradoxically enough, without any of the mother's jealousy of a lover near to his possession. Vernon with his pale face and slightly sinister demeanour had caught her fancy. 'Let him mate with my pretty one,' she would say to herself, 'blossom of apple looks most rare and sweet under a grey sky of clouds.' It was this anxiety to provide a physical match for Phyllida which had led her to encourage Vernon's addresses, and her mistress to pay heed to his vows. Her greatest delight was to stand, watching against interruption, in the next alley to the lovers. Here she would thrill her imagination with the thought of frail and timid fingers in the clasp of a strong white hand. The sudden interposition of Mr. Lovely vexed her. Certainly he was handsome enough, but too much of a piece with Phyllida; they might have been brother and sister. Moreover, he was always laughing.

"A man who always laughs is as bad as a dog who always wags his tail. Neither is fit for a maid," she grumbled to Phyllida as they stepped briskly along beneath the tall poplars that fringed the road leading to the entrance of Curtain Garden.

"Truly I vow he has a romantick air," protested Phyllida.

"La! what's romantick? 'Tis no more than reading a

book on the shady side of the street." Betty tossed a contemptuous head.

"Indeed, Betty, I think 'tis a great deal more than that. To be romantick, child, is to have a noble heart, and to have a noble heart——"

"Is to lead the Venite on a Sunday morning," interrupted the maid.

"No! 'tis not."

"Well! 'tes to kneel very obstreperous."

"'Tis no such a thing," said Phyllida, stamping on the pavement.

By this time, they had reached the famous wrought-iron gates of the principal entrance, where an old man in an enormous three-cornered hat and long heavily laced surtout walked up and down. Sometimes he would stop and, over gnarled hands twisted round the ivory crook of his cane, stare fiercely at the stamped effigies of Æsculapius and Flora while he addressed the presiding deities in a wheezy monotone.

"Curtain Garden! Curtain Garden! Lads and lasses, ye'll grow old. Fit for maids is Curtain Garden." Thus having droned a warning to Olympus, he would resume his walk.

In two months the broad gravelled path which he guarded would be thronged by the Exquisite Mob, but at present his only audience on fine days was composed of Phyllida and Betty. On wet days, when not even they ventured out, he would sit in a little pagoda whence every few minutes he would pop out his head, and in the same wheezy monotone lament 'Rain! Rain! on the window-pane!' and retire as abruptly as a cuckoo that has told the hour.

With this aged janitor Phyllida used to have a daily conversation which never varied by a single letter.

"Nobody in the garden this morning?"

"Not a soul nor a body, young miss."

"Are you better of your cold?"

"Very much worse."

As Phyllida used to tell Betty when they had left the gateway behind them, 'he must be very ill indeed because he has been very much worse every day.'

This customary conversation interrupted the argument over Mr. Lovely's romantick character of mind, and when they turned down the path which led to the Maze all discussion went to the wind at the prospect of again seeing her dear Amor.

Vernon had met Phyllida in the Maze but a bare two weeks ago. It happened to be his first visit to the Wells, and he was in the act of being solemnly lost when he accosted her for direction. Betty had encouraged the chance acquaintanceship and Mr. Vernon, who was tired of the mechanick Dryads of Vauxhall, embarked upon a new pleasure. The natural secretiveness of his disposition led him to adopt Amor as a fantastick pseudonym, and neither Betty nor Phyllida had troubled themselves to inquire farther into his antecedents. Indeed, it would have puzzled them to do so, for he had but lately appeared at the Pump Room in response to Phyllida's earnest entreaty, and absolutely refused to meet her at the Assembly Rooms. Consequently, had she felt inclined to indulge a suspicion, there was no one to whom she could appeal except perhaps Beau Ripple: and he, of course, was not to be thought of in connection with so trivial a matter.

You will recollect that Vernon's toilet of this morning was considerably perturbed by the image of Phyllida. Over his coffee he had reviewed the situation with great contempt for himself.

To begin with, he had moved into lodgings opposite his charmer's abode. What foolish enthusiasm! worthy of a stripling of sixteen, as he told himself. Then he had seriously contemplated matrimony. To be sure, he had made a few cautious inquiries and heard it stated on good authority that she was an heiress, but odds his life! was that enough to make him commit himself irreparably. He was jaded, and the rustick seclusion (so he characterized the Wells!) had affected his head. A boarding-school miss with gawky tendencies—a boarding-school miss with the smile of a young nymph—a boarding-school miss with little fingers that tugged the manhood—the weariness—out of his heart! It was impossible. His friends would sneer unmercifully, and he would settle in the country as he had often wished, and by heavens! he would seek her mother's consent. Pshaw! the chit would become more insipid than ever, more delightful, more enthralling, more utterly subjugating. Z——ds! what an impetuous fool he would be considered. No! No! country misses were very well in the country, and might bear transplantation for a season, but London bough-pots should be renewed every Spring. Meanwhile the affair was progressing very well, and if he could pluck a pigeon or two—there were always pigeons in the country—why a Summer in town—and after that—why after that— meanwhile his coffee was growing cold.

But when he saw her radiance among the dark hedges of yew, all his cynical plans withered away, and it would have taken mighty little to transform the libertine into as honest a lover as ever galloped across the horizon of a romantick imagination. What grace! What charm! What movement! What colour! It was incredible she would ever grow old. He rose from the stone seat in the heart of the Maze and saluted her with a sculptured bow.

"That's true romantick," whispered Betty. "See him bow, see him stand up tall and white like a great wax candle."

The swansdown tippet rose and fell to the beating of the eager heart beneath.

"My charmer takes the sun like a flower," said Mr. Vernon, bending over her hand.

Betty's eyes were a very quick and fiery blue as she turned away to her post, and, indeed, the scene would have ravished a block.

Never were yews so dark and velvety, so full of whispered secrets, as the gentle wind stirred their crisped leaves continually. In a silence made by cushions of moss set with many green stars that muffled every footstep, the stone image of Cupid, poised upon his damp-stained pedestal caught from the February sunlight the veritable bloom and semblance of divinity.

Vernon, as he led Phyllida to the seat and saw her eyes flash over the swansdown muff, was sure that such beauty must capture something of the permanence expressed by the statue and remain for ever young, for ever provocative of desire.

High over their heads a flight of pigeons circled against the azure, gathered and broke into a scattered multitude of snowy wings whose fluttering echoes travelled along the sunlight to the sombre heart of the Maze.

The simple grace with which Phyllida seated herself held Vernon entranced. He could have sworn that the stone wings of the Cupid trembled faintly as if, animate and inanimate, the whole world stood ready to scale the empyrean. Blinded by an ecstasy of hope, the man forgot himself, discarded the mean ambitions that for so long had guided his actions, and conceived the idea of a fresher existence. Great moments, like great men, have a solitary life, and there was nothing in Phyllida to respond to the fire which he had waked from a pile of ashes. Actually she was wondering whether her dear Amor had remembered Valentine day, whether, indeed, his burning gaze was a prelude to the offer of a trinket.

" 'Tis surely a pleasant Valentine morning," she murmured screwing up her eyes to the sun.

Vernon cursed the want of practice with young misses which had let him forget what every fair esteemed a man's sacred duty. However, he was a resourceful gentleman and, without any perceptible hesitation, produced from his pocket a paste brooch cut to the likeness of a basket of twinkling blue forget-me-nots.

The history of this little ornament possesses enough

irony to warrant a short digression. It used to hang in the window of a Midland toy-shop, and had made a pretty birthday gift from a young man deep in love to his betrothed. She wore it in her kerchief for ten years and sent it at last to her lover in London with some other trinkets not very valuable, but all of the same fresh beauty. At the bottom of the packet was a faded sprig of whitethorn. The young gentleman—not quite so young now—opened it as a London dawn empearled the city smoke. It had lain all day in his room neglected while the dice-box rattled like a skeleton at the feast of Love—a feast of pimps and blowsy carmine furies. The contents of the packet went with the last of his guineas, and at the division of the stake Mr. Vernon contemptuously accepted the brooch. The latter never troubled himself to take the ornament out of his pocket. Now once more it came back to Youth and Beauty.

As she pinned it to her kerchief, Phyllida thanked him for his sweet thoughtfulness, and wondered if he would always remember this morning.

By this time, Vernon had clambered down from his mountain top. Perhaps the brooch made his descent more easy. Yet I think he was sincere when he swore he would never forget.

Anyway Phyllida believed him and so there is nothing more to be said.

" When we are wed," she began, and startled him with such an abrupt disclosure of her dreams. " When we are wed, I think we will live in Hyde Park. Where is Hyde Park? "

" On the confines of Kensington, my dear."

" Yes, but where is Kensington? "

" A mile or so Westward of Temple Bar."

" I think we will live in Kensington."

" Nay, prithee! would you have us die of dullness.'

" Is Kensington dull? "

" 'Tis very rustick. No! my charmer shall lodge in the Haymarket."

Phyllida pouted. There was a Haymarket in the country town to which she made an occasional visit from the little village of Newton Candover, and she remembered it as a dusty spot not fit for a new pair of shoes.

"I vow I should detest the Haymarket."

"Nay, 'tis the gayest place, with hackney coaches passing to and fro all day. You shall sit at your window and all the fine ladies of rank and fashion will envy you."

"And what will my Amor be doing?"

"He will be looking over his angel's shoulder."

"Then they'll envy me more than ever," said Phyllida with a contented laugh. Vernon pressed her hand and looked round quickly as a man will before he attempts the first kiss. But Phyllida drew back.

"What shall we do when we are tired of sitting at the windows—if one could ever tire of anything so pleasant?" she added with a sigh.

"We'll call a hackney-coach and drive to Westminster Steps, to the river."

"To the river? Now that will be most diverting."

"And we'll hail the waterman with the most elegant wherry, and row up through the dusk to Vauxhall."

Phyllida was staring at him with the round eyes of a child who listens to an old fairy-tale.

"Then what should we do?" she asked earnestly.

"We should choose a box for two and sit with our elbows over a very small table and look at each other just as we are looking now."

"Yes! go on," cried Phyllida clapping her hands.

"Then we should call for chicken-wings and eat our supper and listen to the new song and the musick of the orchestra playing the finest tunes high up among a thousand sparkling coloured lamps and watch the masqueraders and row back to Westminster under a great moon."

Mr. Vernon was so much inspired by the interest of his listener that he began to believe in the reality of this proposed idyll, quite forgetting that it was a chastened account of a hundred similar adventures enjoyed with the domino passion of a night.

"Vauxhall must be the properest place in the world," sighed Phyllida, "I doubt everybody wears their jewels."

"Everybody," replied her lover with a quick glance.

"I should wear my pearls."

"Your pearls?"

"My necklace that was left by Grandmother Courteen. Mamma won't let me wear it till I'm one-and-twenty."

"But supposing you ran away?"

"Oh I should never dare. I should be frightened."

Vernon changed the subject, perceiving at present the courtship was nothing more serious than a Springtime diversion.

He told himself if the child surrendered to his blandishments, it would be an easy matter to induce her to run away. He must weave a strong web of personal attraction round her, and if her prudence sustained her to the end, why perhaps he might commit himself to a serious offer of marriage. He must inquire further into her fortune. He wished it were not so difficult to put an arm round her waist. Innocence was very well and the prospect of a siege amusing enough at first, but a long deferred capitulation would be immensely fatiguing; and yet how charming she was. Not for anything would he have her different.

"When we are wed," he began and for the first time echoed her lately expressed hopes. In some way he felt that she would be to blame, if harm came of it. She had given the cue.

"When we are wed, we shall go to routs."

"But we shall be old and wise and able to go then. It won't be near so diverting then as 'twould be now—if you came to the Assemblies."

"My angel forgets the risque of discovery."

"There could be no more danger in that than there is in sitting here in the Maze."

"Come!"

"I'm sure if we were prudent nobody would suspect us of a love-affair."

"But consider my ardour. 'Twould illuminate the whole matter."

"Well! and if the old maids did talk, they would only talk into their teacups and every one knows that to be monstrous ungenteel behaviour. Lud! I've been censured before. Why, when I was but sixteen I was the talk of the ballroom because I stepped four gavottes with Dicky Combleton, Squire Combleton's youngest son. Every one said I was a forward minx, and he's only a year older than me and that's only last year." Phyllida became very indignant, and Mr. Vernon who lacked humour became very indignant too at being compared to a bumpkin.

"Surely my angel sees the circumstances are slightly altered?"

He clasped her hand, and stroked it slowly, but she was not to be pacified and drew it away.

"For my part, I don't know how you dare say you care for my reputation and sit here holding my hand. Walls have ears and hedges have eyes."

"You would not withdraw your hand if you were sure we were not observed?"

She made no reply.

"Possibly," he went on, "you would let me kiss those sweet lips to a smile—if we were not observed?"

"Indeed, I vow you should never do anything so indelicate."

"Z——ds! my pretty Puritan——" he stopped because Phyllida's eyes were very wide open indeed.

"Oh Sir! no one but a father or a very old man has the right to swear so dreadfully before a maid."

He laughed.

"So oaths depend on age for their propriety? I 'faith

that's a new maxim I've learned this morning. After all, my Phyllida, I am fifteen years older than you."

" That may be," she retorted primly, " and I have often wondered whether I should allow a man of middle-age to make love to me."

Vernon wrinkled with annoyance at such a description. He certainly lacked humour.

" But then, you see, I am in love with you, and not marrying you because our estates join like my cousin Clarice who, we all agreed, was old enough to know better."

" Young enough, you mean. Morality rusts with the years."

" I don't know what you are talking about, but it sounds like a text."

" It is a text, my dear, the text of the man of the world."

" I hate texts, but I don't hate goodness and you must promise never, never to swear again, and—never, never to try to kiss me."

" Not even when we are wed? "

" That's another matter."

" Perhaps when you are old and wise and able to kiss you won't like kissing."

" Oh! I protest, I should like it vastly," said Phyllida with great decision.

" But if you have never made the attempt? "

" A young woman knows by instinct."

" But why won't you make sure in advance? "

" Because 'tis imprudent and wicked."

" For my part, I believe you are playing with me."

And then began a long argument which settled nothing at all and, after ten minutes, left matters precisely where they started.

What Vernon said in jest was in essence perfectly true, but unfortunately he was too vain and she was too young to believe it; for if potential Phyllida knew very well she would not expire if her dear Amor vanished for ever, actual Phyllida who was much younger and far more obstinate was equally sure that a gradual decline into an interesting consumption would be the natural result of such a calamity; while potential Vernon who was anxious to prove himself a very fine fellow was very contemptuous of actual Vernon and not at all willing to admit he would find more than sufficient compensation for the loss of his Phyllida in the ample charms of Miss Diana Flashington of the Theatre Royal, Drury Lane.

And this is the way a large number of world-shaking passions begin, since at first we seldom apprehend our potentiality.

The quarrel was interrupted by the sound of approaching voices just as Betty came flying round the corner with the news that "Mr. Thomas and your mamma be coming as fast as legs can carry 'em this way as ever is."

The implication of a rapid advance is to be understood merely as relative to their usual rate of procedure.

In an instant all was confusion. Miss Courteen wrung her hands and behaved quite as wildly as a grand married lady on the verge of discovery in an ambiguous situation below stairs. Mr. Vernon flicked a number of invisible specks of dust from his purple sattin breeches as though he had been kneeling in devout protestation of honourable love for the past hour, while Betty ran in turn to each of the four alleys leading to their present position, and put a hand to an attentive ear. She quickly ascertained by which path the enemy was advancing and without more ado pushed Mr. Vernon hastily in the opposite direction, thrust a tambour frame into her mistress's hands and composed herself to spell aloud the Agricultural Calendar and Farmer's Assistant for the current year. She was in the middle of some astonishing statisticks of the comparative productiveness per acre of turnips and mangel-wurzels when Mrs. Courteen followed by the majestick Thomas appeared upon the scene. On perceiving her daughter, the latter gave a faint scream and declared the meeting would certainly produce palpitations.

At the utterance of this fatal word, Thomas immediately unscrewed the knob of his cane and drew forth a bottle of salts, Phyllida performed the same conjuring trick with her bag, while Betty after some lace-involved rites in which a crimson garter played a prominent part offered a third bottle not more than a moment later. By the tonick influence of several sniffs Mrs. Courteen was sufficiently revived to ask in a stern voice what Phyllida was doing in this ungodly place. Thomas accompanied the query by muttering 'Canaanites' several times in quick succession under his breath. What the commentary was intended to imply no one knew; but there was a general belief that the footman symbolized states of mind, people and actions of which he disapproved, by the various hostile tribes encountered by the Israelites during their wanderings.

Phyllida assured her mother she was working a peacock in blue and scarlet wool for the seat of a chair, and when Mrs. Courteen demanded why she was not sitting on her own balcony, for the privilege of possessing which she paid an additional five-and-sixpence a week in rent, the daughter protested the East wind chapped her ankles.

" Chaps your ankles, miss? What d'ye mean by chaps your ankles? At your age, I didn't know I had ankles. Woollen hose was what I wore, and I should have been whipped if I had ever dared to think my ankles were not as thick as marrowbones."

Phyllida begged her dear mamma's pardon and hoped to be forgiven, but could not help remarking the sun was so warm that she had felt quite positive her dear mamma would be pleased to see her take the air.

" 'Twas very unkind of you," complained the widow, " to presume so far on my acknowledged indulgence of your whims. You know the miserable state of my health compels me to sip several glasses of the waters after breakfast, and seize the lamentable opportunity to deceive your too confiding parent. How am I to know you have not been sitting in this heathen nook for days in succession?"

Again the footman muttered 'Canaanites! Canaanites!' As this was exactly where Phyllida had been sitting for days in succession, she looked immensely shocked by the question.

"Well! well," said Mrs. Courteen as if resigned to her daughter's iniquity, "go home and pray that you may become a more dutiful child."

Thomas murmured a low Amen and earned for his devotion a derisive and ribald gesture from Betty.

"Aren't you coming too, mamma?"

"No, miss, I am not coming; I must rest myself and compose my mind and soothe my feelings. Thomas, will you arrange my cushion?"

Thomas produced it from under the seven capes of his surtout without perceptibly diminishing his girth.

Said Phyllida to Betty as they stepped out of the Maze, "For my part, I believe she only wanted to be rid of us in order to meet puffy old Moon or skimpy little Tarry."

And this supposition was perfectly true.

CHAPTER V

THE PUBLICK BREAKFAST

AT half-past twelve o'clock of the following day, masculine Curtain Wells began to arrive at the Town Hall determined to eat the health of General Sir Jeremy Dummer with all the vigour of an appetite unspoiled by a morsel of food since yesterday's supper. No procession was arranged by those responsible for the entertainment, but the habit of punctuality instilled by the Great little Beau secured an unrehearsed pageant. There was no marshalled order, but since everybody set out from his abode at the same time, the component populations of the place were compelled to affect a military method of progress.

It was quite unpremeditated and, therefore, the more impressive. The Town Hall designed by Sir John Vanbrugh had been erected by publick subscription to serve as a memorial to those gallant natives of Curtain Wells who fought and died under the Duke of Marlborough. That the aforesaid gallant natives were only three in number and in no case killed in action was no cooler to the furnace of civick gratitude kindled by the signing of the Peace of Utrecht. In their delight at the discomfiture of the quarrelsome Whigs, the citizens expressly stipulated there should be no hint of War and War's alarms in the construction of their Hall. There was to be no cannon eternally belching forth stony smoke, no image or superscription of Mars or Bellona. Greaves, bucklers, spears, culverins, swords, scimitars and grenades were forbidden by name. The central medallion of the pediment should enshrine Civick Unity.

So the reigning Mayor was represented in all the pomp of office grasping the hands of two equally befurred and bechained Aldermen. It was an affecting combination of the real and the allegorical. A second medallion contained a voluminously draped and very substantial lady who with absent gaze spilled from a heavy Etruscan vase a large stream of petrified Chalybeate. Her faraway look might be attributed to an effort at ascertaining what a small Æsculapius was doing to a serpent on the summit of a diminutive Pelion. This was Health. Finally a third medallion held a peer in coronation robes thoughtfully regarding the front of St. James' Palace. A curved scroll announced this pensive aristocrat to be the representative of Society.

Civick Unity, Health, and Society—could any other personifications so justly convey the essential quality of Curtain Wells? And not a pike or arquebus to frighten them out of a rigid serenity.

Upon this sermon in stone, three streets converged, which at half-past twelve o'clock were all thronged. Since the breakfast was essentially a male function, the civick band by a happy inspiration of the band-master thundered out *The Girl I left Behind Me*, as in its wake a number of prosperous tradesmen tripped to the measure of the tune. Haberdashers and cheesemongers, drygoodsmen and fishmongers, butchers, tailors, saddlers, cooks and silversmiths all marched along with a pleasant emotion of relief. Fortified by preliminary tankards of ale and unhampered by prosaick wives and daughters, they retreated from nothing save the business of serving customers. Vapours were dispelled by the breeze of trumpets, and the thoughts aroused by the musick of the song only added a pungent spice to their dreams of food and confirmed their faith in the superiority of breeches over petticoats—at any rate when walking away from the latter.

Meanwhile down the central street came another crowd not marching with the precision of movement inspired by the escort of the band, but still urged to a certain unanimity of gait by the common object of their advance. Mr. Mayor, preceded by his mace, set the time, and a line of Aldermen carefully ordered their pace to his. Behind the Aldermen came the Watch. This was a mistake. The latter should have led the dignitaries, but had spent so much time in buttoning and unbuttoning its capes and belts, in brushing its hats and polishing its staves that it was late, thereby belying its name. So the Watch followed behind and vented its contrition on a mob of boys in occasional backhanded cuffs and current imprecations. Behind the boys marched three small girls—Amazons heedless of the embargo laid upon their sex.

However both these processions were overshadowed by the prodigious pageant that emanated from the street facing the medallion of Society. The last deserves a chapter to itself since no appendix could do justice to its importance. Let me therefore, without being held to have violated the decency of orderly narration, insert at this point a supplementary chapter which may serve as a programme to the entertainment I hope worthily to recount.

CHAPTER V

THE ORDER OF THE EXQUISITE MOB

General Sir Jeremy Dummer in a sedan chair borne by two veterans of the Militia. Beau Ripple in damson-coloured velvet coat and breeches, with waistcoat of old rose sattin trimmed with silver and rose silk stockings clocked with the same.

Mr. Ripple with admirable condescension occasionally

arrested the progress of the march in order to address a word of encouragement to Sir Jeremy Dummer who was inclined to be querulous from want of food and the action of the Chalybeate.

The Earl of Cinderton in smoke-grey silk with cuffs of clouded blue.

The Honourable George Harthe-Brusshe, his son, in a lighter shade of the same.

The Earl of Vanity looking liking a fly, in amber.

Five baronets in various degrees of FEUILLE MORTE.

Four Knights of the Shire trying to look like Baronets and horridly bruised by the palings in their attempts.

Seventeen exquisite young gentlemen all exactly alike and only to be distinguished by the various shapes and sizes of their patches.

Major Constantine Tarry who had devoted the sleep of the preceding night to the preservation of his pigtail's rigour and appeared very pale beside his red coat in consequence.

Justice Gregory Moon looking much the same as usual save for a sprig of yew in his buttonhole.

Mr. Charles Lovely and Mr. Anthony Clare arm in arm. The former wearing a cherry-coloured velvet coat with waistcoat and breeches of trout-coloured silk, the latter in uniform cucumber green. Both laughed very loudly and cheerfully from time to time.

Five elegant young gentlemen including a Lieutenant of his Majesty's Navy, a Cornet of the Grey Dragoons and an Ensign of the Foot.

Twenty-three old men suffering from various diseases.

Thirty-eight old men all firmly convinced that they were suffering from gout but all perfectly healthy in truth.

Forty-five old men equally firmly convinced that they were suffering from other and various diseases, and all equally healthy in truth.

Mr. Oboe the Physician watchful of his patients' demeanour and quick to confirm the slightest suspicion of ill-health.

Mr. Francis Vernon in a tawny suit of figured Manchester velvet.

Fifteen or sixteen gentlemen of various ages, sizes, ranks, costumes, complexions, and states of health.

CHAPTER V (*resumed*)

Beau Ripple mounted the steps that, in diminishing semi-circles, reached the entrance of the Civick Hall and, turning his head, froze into silence with a cold stare of surprize the concluding Crescendo of *The Girl I left Behind Me*, as if the half-drawn breaths of the musicians were suddenly changed to icicles.

The good-natured band was not at all put out by Mr. Ripple's lack of appreciation. His objection to panting was universally known, so the band bore him no malice, but continued to pant.

As the musick stopped, Mr. Mayor began to walk up the steps also. No doubt his ascent would have been as active as the Beau's if he had not been hampered by the civick robes on which he trod at every alternate step. Possibly the freezing disdain of Mr. Ripple had made the steps more glacial than their wont. At any rate, the Mayor whenever he avoided the hem of his robes, always slipped and stumbled, but he achieved the summit at last and greeted the Beau with such fervour that he effected a perceptible thaw.

On these occasions of supreme civick importance, it was customary for the latter to relax his rule of never taking snuff with any one below the rank of Viscount in the Peerage of England, so he offered his box to the Mayor. That functionary with a reverence he had acquired over the counter, inserted two fleshy fingers into the dainty receptacle, withdrew them smeared with Rappee, sniffed the powder with avidity, sneezed four times, and said he saw Sir Jeremy alighting from his chair.

The Beau regarded the Mayor's invasion of the delicate touchstone of quality with a smile of amused apprehension. He explained afterwards that he felt as if he were carrying a sirloin of beef into a queen's parlour. When the convulsions set up by the snuff had outworn their first violence, he fixed his monocle upon the guest's chair. Sure enough, Sir Jeremy was alighting. Mr. Ripple and the Mayor simultaneously descended the steps, and while the former started back with an affectation of surprize, the latter charged forward with eager hospitality.

"Gadslife! Sir Jeremy! You are vastly welcome, sir. This is a great occasion. Twenty-one years. Tet-tet." Thus Mr. Ripple.

"How are you, Sir Jermy Dummer, sir? Come along o' me, Sir Jermy, and I hope yaul heat very hearty," said or rather shouted the Mayor.

"*Eheu fugaces!*" murmured Mr. Ripple.

"Heh?" asked the Mayor.

"*Postume, Postume.*"

"Hoh!" said the Mayor. "I beg yaw pardon, Mr. Ripple. Will you take a harm, Sir Jermy?"

The poor old knight clutched at the fur of the Mayor's robe as the two of them stumbled up the steps behind Mr. Ripple.

In passing through the antechamber, the old man dropped his hat and cane.

"I shouldn't leave my hat an' cane here if I was you, Sir Jermy," said the Mayor. "While some's heating, some'll be thieving."

"I have not the slightest intention of doing anything so insane," quavered the ancient soldier, "can't you see that I dropped 'em by accident?"

The good-natured Mayor stooped to recover the accessories. "I beg yaw pardon, Sir Jermy. Follow me. The banquet's in here."

The huge folding doors were flung back, and the sight of so much food kindled a gleam in Sir Jeremy's rheumy eyes and waked a cackle from his lean throat.

"Glad to hear such a jovial laugh. Wittles is wittles when hall's said an' done. Hain't that true, Mr. Ripple," said the Mayor turning to the Beau for confirmation of this statement.

"Victuals are victuals, sir, as you very justly observe."

Upon these three celebrated figures broke the buzz of the excited crowd from the centre of which Lord Cinderton and Lord Vanity withdrew themselves.

"Let me present Sir Jeremy Dummer, the Earl of Cinderton. Sir Jeremy Dummer, the Earl of Vanity." The latter offered his snuff-box to the old votary of Health, who declined it saying,

"No! thankee, my lord, not before I eat. D——e if ever I took snuff before I ate."

His worship the Mayor was then presented to the two noblemen and, discoursing amicably of the outlook on European politicks, the five great men threaded their way towards the principal table.

There was a tremendous shuffling among the innumerable waiters as Mr. Daish urged them to unparalleled exertion. They ran hither and thither like recently fertile hens. One half of them pulled out chairs from the tables and the other half pushed them back again. Some fled bawling for the soup. Others conversed in excited whispers. At last the assembled company to the number of three hundred persons stood each member in the place he had selected.

What caused a further delay? Why did Mr. Daish hurriedly wave back the white-capped cook bearing the first tureen?

Through the doorway pattered little Mr. Archdeacon Conybeare. "I'm late," he muttered, "I know it, I'm aware of it. I'm late. Maria, my love, I'm late, I'm very late."

The Beau was looking at the large clock below the gallery at the far end of the hall.

"Will you ask a grace, Mr. Archdeacon?" he said.

The Mayor smote the table with a silver hammer as the parson slipped into his place.

"For what we are going to receive . . . my dear Mr. Ripple, 'tis no use to tell me the contrary, I know I am very late."

The Publick Breakfast had begun.

I think it was the great Dr. Johnson whose forehead while he ate was dabbled with perspiration and the veins of it red and swollen. At any rate the Mayor had a similar appearance. He devoured his food as if he feared the cherubs sporting in the gilded panels of the ceiling would descend and snatch it from his plate.

Mr. Ripple ate very modishly. One would have said he had watched the honied meals of many butterflies. For all his fork's fastidious action, it managed to pick the best of a Fricassée. Rounds, ribs, and sirloins, he deplored.

Sir Jeremy Dummer evidently felt that his sensibility to the honour awarded to him deserved practical gratitude. He eat voraciously. The old fighting spirit abode in him for a space and he handled his knife like his hanger. He slashed at every course that came along, but, accuracy being impaired by muscular fatigue, he was content to swallow much of his food whole.

Sir Jeremy Dummer ate:
Two plates of turtle soup.
The better part of a codfish.
The wing of a capon.
The wing of a duck.
The breast of a pullet.
A hot buttered apple dumpling and two or three slices of ham which he had not noticed before.

Sir Jeremy Dummer drank:
Two tankards of old ale.
One bottle of Madeira.
Two bottles of Port.

And on the following day, Sir Jeremy Dummer died. He had always been famous for trencher-play until condemned by Oboe to milky sustenance to which through twenty-one winter seasons he never willingly yielded. This commemoration of his abstinence was his opportunity and his revenge. Could he have made a worthier end? For my own part, I should not presume to say so.

Meanwhile, unconscious of this premature obituary, Sir Jeremy Dummer enjoyed the breakfast amazingly. At first he was inclined to peevishness through not being seated upon a sufficiently high chair. Mr. Daish, however, with ready tact secured one of the Civick cushions and so enabled Sir Jeremy, comfortably ensconced in crimson velvet, to eat his last breakfast at ease.

Mr. Lovely having made the acquaintance of the Honourable George Harthe-Brusshe, by whom he had seated himself at the particular request of Mr. Ripple, discussed with animation the food on his plate and the last foppery of the town. Mr. Harthe-Brusshe, a lantern-jawed young gentleman with a sincere devotion to turtle-soup, observing that Mr. Lovely was about to leave his portion, begged him to hand it over. Charles who invariably encouraged every man's idiosyncrasy sent the word down the table to pass up every neglected plateful. This request was readily granted and presently Mr. Harthe-Brusshe found himself surrounded by half-a-dozen portions. Thereupon he declined all other dishes and was faithful to soup for the rest of the meal.

"I suppose you find the difference in temperature sufficient variety?" asked Mr. Lovely in a tone of great interest.

"That's so, sir," replied the other as he refused beef and veal for the sake of a moderately warm fifth plate of soup.

"I doubt you keep a bottle of it always to hand," remarked Lovely.

"It would tire me too much. It tires me to keep things to hand."

Here the Honourable George Harthe-Brusshe sighed with exhaustion and seemed to desire silence.

Charles turned to his other neighbour who happened to be Mr. Francis Vernon.

"Are you making a sojourn here, sir?"

Vernon noticed the richness of Mr. Lovely's attire, made a rough calculation of the value of his buckles, brooches and solitaire, and answered very politely he hoped so indeed.

"I've not yet seen you at the *Blue Boar*, Sir. We make up a pleasant party in the old Coffee-Room every night. There's young Tom Chalkley of the Foot, Tony Clare, Peter Wingfield, Jack Winnington, Harry Golightly of Campbell's Grey Dragoons, Blewforth of the *Lively*, and as many more of us pass the time very pleasantly over some tolerable Port and very excellent Burgundy."

"I doubt the company is delightful."

"I' faith, that's very true for when the wine makes us loquacious, d——e, we sing, and when it makes us mum, why, d——e, the dice-box talks for us. You'll join us, Sir?" he added, turning to Mr. Harthe-Brusshe.

"Proud," murmured that gentleman pensively regarding the rich scum slowly hardening over the plate of soup to be attacked next.

"Let me see," said Charles, "to-night we must positively keep quiet in deference to the Beau. Monday night I've promised to go to the Assembly."

"What's that?" said Mr. Anthony Clare, a florid young gentleman on the opposite side of the table.

"Blewforth!" he called out to a naval officer farther along. "Charles has forsook letters and is going to try life for a change."

"Good G——," said the Lieutenant solemnly. "Charles crowding all canvas after a petticoat?"

Charles looked somewhat disconcerted by this immediate perception of his motives.

"I 'faith, you're in the wrong, Blewforth," he protested, "'tis to please Ripple and that's the whole truth of the matter."

A roar of laughter greeted this excuse, and every young gentleman in hearing vowed to exchange dice for dancing on Monday night.

"I saw Charles leave a note at a house in the Western Colonnade," remarked Ensign Chalkley of the Foot.

"A Valentine for a hundred guineas," said Clare.

"Name the charmer," shouted Blewforth, "name her, and egad, she shall be the toast of the afternoon."

Mr. Vernon felt relieved. Somehow he had half suspected Lovely was in pursuit of Miss Courteen. If he had not decided to wear purple sattin on the day before and buried himself in the closet to extricate the suit, he would have been still more suspicious of Lovely. The latter ignored the friendly jeers.

"Shall we say Wednesday night, sir?"

"I shall be honoured."

"May I beg the favour of your name, Sir? 'Tis customary with us to elect our associates."

"My name is Vernon. Francis Vernon of the Crescent, Curtain Wells—and London."

It was Charles' turn to display apprehension. Here was a man well dressed, of genteel appearance, living in the Crescent.

"Ah! the Crescent! I once had a notion to lodge there myself."

"'Tis a quiet position," said Vernon.

c*

"So much the better for my Muse."

"You are a poet, sir?"

"I have a metrical fancy."

"Try the Colonnade, Charles," bellowed the Lieutenant, "and your Muse'll speedily become the most famous Toast of the time."

"Blewforth owns a spy-glass," said some one.

"I wish he would own a mirrour," said Charles, "his wig is infamous."

"His head is swollen since the w-war," stammered little Peter Wingfield, "or else he was w-wounded in the wig." Blewforth, impervious to smoking, gave a loud guffaw.

Lovely and Vernon agreed to meet on the following Wednesday and the conversation moved on general lines till the silver hammer of the Mayor summoned the company to attend to the toasts. The eyes of the room were on him as away up at the high table, he rose burly and majestick.

"Mr. Alderman Jobbins," he proclaimed, "the King!" Mr. Jobbins, the youngest of the city fathers, blessed his sovereign with unctuous pride, and the toast was drunk amid acclamations whose echo was drowned in broken glass. Curtain Wells knew when to borrow from military manners.

Then the assembly tilted on its chairs after filling new glasses, and composed itself to listen to Beau Ripple who had risen, monocle in hand.

When the murmur of delighted anticipation had sighed itself out on the wings of a loud 'Hush,' the Great little Man with indescribable suavity begged the company's permission to say a few words.

"Mr. Mayor, my lords, and gentlemen, may I say citizens? (a voice, 'You may') for I think I am giving utterance to the sentiments of this salubrious town when I protest that upon an occasion of such unique interest and such immense significance, we no longer recognize any distinction between visitors and residents (loud applause). We are assembled this morning in order to honour a man for whom no honour is sufficient. We are celebrating the twenty-first consecutive winter at Curtain Wells of Sir Jeremy Dummer (loud cheers). He has been faithful to us, gentlemen. Each year towards the close of the equinoctial gales, his coach has clattered over the cobbles of Curtain Wells. Each year he has alighted at the door of Number Seventeen, the Crescent. Each year he has torn himself away from the gaiety of London in order to set us an example of perseverance. Each year his arrival has encouraged other gentlemen of grave address to put their faith in the cleansing springs of Chalybeate. To be sure, his gout is as virulent as ever, but has he despaired? No (cheers). Has he tried other remedies? No (cheers). He has only been the more firmly convinced of the profound malignity of his disorder and the more resolutely determined to annoy it by any and every means in his power (continued applause). Twenty-one years ago Curtain Wells was a different place. We had, it is true, this Civick Hall. We had Crescent and Colonnade, Curtain Garden and Curtain Rotunda, Curtain Wells and Curtain Pump Room, Curtain Hill and Curtain Dale. But we had not your respected Mayor. In those days he was a younger, shall I add, a more foolish man? I myself was still overshadowed by the reputation of my great predecessor Beau Melon whose alabaster bust consecrates the Assembly Rooms.

"In those days, gentlemen, coaches very rarely exceeded the rate of four miles an hour, and, as you have heard, the New Machine proposes to travel at an uniform speed of six. Twenty-one years! This valetudinarian majority should make the youngest of us pause and reflect. Twenty-one years of Chalybeate (a groan from the back of the room).

"Mr. Mayor, my lords and gentlemen, I propose the health of Sir Jeremy Dummer and venture to assert that the time-honoured toast was never before fraught with such significance. The health of Sir Jeremy Dummer! It is in order to commemorate his health that we are assembled. Gout has done many ill deeds, ruined many tempers, spoiled many legs, but for this at least we should be grateful—it has afforded us the spectacle of a gallant gentleman faithful to his earliest prescription, hopeful of an ultimate cure and charitable to the town of his adoption. (Loud and prolonged applause.) One moment, gentlemen: let me add that the guest of this entertainment has expressed a desire to present the town with a new set of mugs for the publick fountains." (Volleys of applause.)

Beau Ripple after leading the toast with three very urbane Huzzas resumed his seat, and Sir Jeremy Dummer doddered up to make his reply. As it consisted chiefly of a long and detailed account of his symptoms and extended over half an hour, and as you, with knowledge of his speedy death, will not bear it with the slumberous equanimity of his contemporaries, I shall not recount it. It is enough to say that when it was concluded, everybody woke with a start and cheered vociferously. Then the Mayor proposed the health of Mr. Ripple, and somebody else proposed the health of the Mayor, and so on until all the dignitaries had had enough wine drunk to their long life to ensure for every one of them an undiseased immortality.

When the toasts were finished, the quality adjourned to the Civick Chamber to meet the ladies over a dish of tea, while the quantity marched off to put the seal on a great occasion by talking it over in the various taprooms round the town.

Vernon was not inclined to brave the extension of the affair when he perceived his new friends cautiously escaping from the Beau. He hated to be conspicuous, and it was a small pleasure to meet his Phyllida among the dowagers. Indeed, he was beginning to wish he had been less hasty in taking lodgings in the Crescent, and the prospect of the *Blue Boar* was already alluring enough to make him inquire the price of a room in that merry house. So he asked if he might take Mr. Lovely's arm.

In the square, the elegant young gentlemen made a bright knot.

" What's to be done? " cried the Lieutenant.

" L-l-let's ride over to B-Baverstock Regis, and s-see T-Tony's m-maiden aunt," stammered little Peter Wingfield.

" Bravo! " shouted Charles.

Clare looked up in surprize. Charles was seldom willing to play the game of light love. Could that chatter of Blewforth's have gone deeper than he thought? There was a strange excitement about him—an excitement that was aroused by something stronger than the civick wine. Was he in love? Mr. Anthony Clare was puzzled.

" You must know, gentlemen," said Mr. Lovely, " that this maiden aunt is of a very singular complexion. 'Tis usual, as we are all aware, to look to maiden aunts for legacies and presents, but this lady, as I know by the state of Tony's purse, gets more than she gives."

" Fie! Charles," protested his friend, " I vow your point of view deteriorates." What could be the matter with him?

" Well, gentlemen," he continued, " since you are so set on meeting my relatives, egad! you shall. We'll ride over to Baverstock to-night; there are dances in Baverstock Barn, and the maids—maiden-aunts will all be there. You'll come, Charles? "

" Not another word. I'll lead the love-chase or, shall we say, the legacy hunt? "

" And you, sir? " Clare continued with a bow to Vernon.

After a moment's hesitation due, no doubt, to bashfulness, the latter assented, and in a trice the whole party went whooping and holloaing in the direction of the *Blue Boar*.

And all this time, Phyllida was counting the kisses in her teacup while she watched Miss Sukey Morton search energetically for strangers.

CHAPTER VI

BAVERSTOCK BARN

VERNON left his companions at the door of his lodgings in order to adapt his dress to the road, having settled with them to meet presently at the *Blue Boar* where a horse was to be saddled in readiness. He wondered while pulling on his riding-boots what was the monetary value of his new friends. They talked of play; but was it high enough to make their fellowship worth joining? They were all apparently expensive in their tastes and habits, but seemed so young and irresponsible. That however was rather an advantage. They belonged to the World, the World that is of St. James' Street; yet if they were callow pigeons, why were they learning to fly so far from the nest which bred them?

Now Mr. Vernon had got hold of a wrong analysis. These young men of Curtain Wells in spite of their outward freshness were not at all fit for the table. They had tough breasts beneath an array of fine feathers. This society of theirs, so remote from the larger society of London, with a toleration of good and bad alike, was in its essence eclectick, like a regiment or a college. An air of genial self-satisfaction clung to it nourished by rules and opinions and traditions which had never been proved to be false or harmful. The members were all clipped to a pattern and displayed a wealth of blooms in a prim setting. Even Lovely straggled too much, and was only allowed to disturb the fellowship on account of his decorative qualities and because he was evidently only a strong sport from the conventional habit of growth.

Vernon in making up his mind to join this elegant association was quite unaware that the condescension was on the side of youth. He was willing to instruct them in the ways of the great world, but found what he had been compelled to learn, they knew by inherited instinct. He was ignorant of their existence: they on the other hand had experienced many Mr. Vernons. Still he was endowed with too much insight not to understand almost immediately that he must imitate their standards, and soon caught the tone of his companions well enough to be voted an acquisition.

However, as he wrestled with his riding-boots, he was distinctly at a loss. This ride to Baverstock was presumably an expedition of gallantry, and yet he had felt it unwise to obtrude a jest appropriate to the occasion. The conversation had possessed a certain elusive ribaldry; women were discussed with frankness, and yet he had not ventured to boast of his own conquests. These young men chattered of love, much as they would have talked of fox-hunting. Love was a theory, a philosophy with a cant terminology of its own. And yet the analogy was incomplete. No man would hesitate to chronicle his leaps, but then no man would confess to having shot a fox. There was the rub. He was a fox shooter; these were hunters. Gadslife! How absurdly young they all were. And this Lovely? He was evidently more prudish than the rest of them —a man of sentiment who objected to either mode of death. He would like to see this paragon of virtue who had stared so coldly at the tale of old Sir John Columbine and his frail exquisite consort, put to the test. From that moment he began to hate Charles, and stamped his wrinkles out of his boots with considerable feeling. He would devote himself to emptying Lovely's purse before he tried the rest of them.

Vernon in a very pleasant frame of mind strolled through the chill of approaching twilight. The humiliation of Lovely was in a way achieved as soon as conceived. This was how Vernon always escaped from awkward situations. He so seldom faced facts.

An outraged husband once threatened him with a riding whip, and Vernon promptly climbed out by the window. In the street he only remembered he had successfully seduced the wife, and forgot the uncomfortable epilogue. He behaved to futurity in the same generous way as he treated the past.

Presently he found the company assembled in the yard of the inn, with a dozen horses pawing the cobbles impatient of the cold. They were soon mounted and the arched entry rang again with the sound of hoofs as they trotted through the High Street.

"Which way?" shouted Vernon who was in front.

"Straight ahead and turn to the right," answered Clare. "We've eight miles to go and a good road to go on."

"Huzza!" shouted Vernon who felt that extreme heartiness was the correct attitude.

In the clap and clack of the horses' hoofs, the affectation passed unnoticed.

How the fat shopkeepers stared to see these young gentlemen cantering away in the late afternoon, 'Some wild frolick,' they thought and turned half-regretfully to attend to their customers who were just as much interested in the jolly troop as themselves. Children scrambled from the gutters on to the pavement with yells of dismay as the horsemen scattered their mud pies. Little girls effected heroick rescues of favourite dolls from the very gate of death and little boys bowled their hoops between the legs of wayfarers with more assiduity than usual, in their struggles to avoid the legs of the horses.

Lieutenant Blewforth like most sailors was an inferior

rider, but on this occasion he surpassed himself, and sat his horse like a Bedouin. He only wished buxom Miss Page would step to the door of the cook-shop and behold his prowess. Unluckily at the very moment when his ambition was in process of achievement, his mount swerved, and the gay Lieutenant found himself at his charmer's feet. The inevitable idler secured the horse, and Blewforth, having no small change, was obliged to reward him with a crown, and what is more look as if he enjoyed the expense. To give him credit, he certainly succeeded.

"Do you always propose yourself in that precipitous manner?" Charles inquired as they cantered past the last house and gained the hedgerows. "You pay very little heed to her corns."

The Lieutenant uttered an enormous guffaw that made his mount swerve again.

"The Royal Navy is always so d-devilish romantick," stammered little Peter Wingfield who looked like a precocious boy beside the burly officer.

"By G—," puffed Blewforth, "that reminds me of a good story I heard of an ensign in Bolt's. He was a d—d bashful man, and couldn't abide the women. One day he was making his compliments to the Colonel's daughter—a gaunt hussy of thirty-five summers or winters. He hung back outside the parlour-door for some time, mustered up courage to enter at last, dashed into the room and, tripping over his hanger, found himself kneeling at her feet. This was a bad beginning truly, but in trying to retrieve the position, he clutched the air and caught hold of her skinny hand. They were married in the spring, and the garrison said he badly wanted her money."

In the outburst of laughter which hailed the climax of the story, Vernon asked with much interest what the young woman's dowry was worth. The subject fascinated him.

"Don't know, sir," replied Blewforth, "but I saw

the jade at Portsmouth last year, and I'm d—d if £50,000 would have made her endurable."

They were riding through a pleasant country of meadows and small streams; so Charles walked his mare to admire the willows empurpled by the fast gathering dusk. Vernon seized the opportunity for conversation.

" A fine landskip," he remarked.

Charles looked up half-angry. He disliked a man who suited his words to his own supposed tastes.

" It might be finer," he said shortly.

" Without a doubt," replied the other. " You'll pardon my ignorance, Mr. Lovely, but of what does the entertainment before us consist? "

Charles' face grew clear again at once—at any rate, the man did not claim omniscience.

" The entertainment, sir, is composed of fiddles and country dances enjoyed by the light of tallow-dips in an old barn. There will be some ploughboys, shepherds and farmers, with a few milkmaids and farm wenches, and the whole will resemble a painted Dutch interior."

" And you propose to join the merrymaking? "

" We do."

" It should be a diverting experience."

" I hope so indeed. My friend Clare vows he has discovered a Venus masquerading in fustian."

" His maiden-aunt in short? "

" The same. Like all small societies, sir, we have our intimate jests which to a stranger must seem excessively threadbare."

" On the contrary," said Vernon, " they possess an engaging spontaneity which flatters me with the suggestion that my own youth has not vanished irreclaimably. And yet," he said, " I am a man whom the world insults by claiming as its own."

" You have travelled? " inquired Charles.

" I have made the Grand Tour."

"That is a pleasure which I still owe to myself and to my country."

"You lack energy?"

"Of the kind expressed in gold."

"An hour's good luck at the tables."

"I've enjoyed some dozens," interrupted Lovely. "Almost enough to pay for twice as many less fortunate periods."

"Then why continue to play?"

"Why fall in love? Why die in a consumption? Why live this life of ours at all? Your question, sir, takes little account of mankind's innate perversity, and no account at all of his tastes and disposition of mind."

"On the contrary," argued Vernon, "I esteem all these at their greatest effect, but regard with equal reverence the doctrine of free will. I myself—but why should I fatigue you with personal anecdotes?"

"Pray continue," said Charles eagerly. He was always alert at a confidence and plumed himself on his ability to read human character. In this case curiosity outran discernment, and he failed to see the improbability of a man like Vernon exposing his temperament without securing a compensatory advantage.

"I myself, Mr. Lovely, was once addicted to the equally expensive habit of intrigue, but I found it led me into so many cursed situations that I forced myself to enjoy less compromising pastimes. I chose cards."

"Ah! cards!" commented Charles.

"But here again," Vernon continued, "I found the introduction of a passionate element ruined at once my pleasure and my skill. I was confounded. To be sure there remained wine, but whoever heard of a man's will exercised by wine? To be frank, Mr. Lovely, I was unwilling to take the risque of defeat."

"So I am to regard you as a disappointed voluptuary, a hedonist philosopher whose premisses induced him to a false conclusion. No, no, sir, keep your logick for speculations upon the soul, not the body."

"Sir," answered Vernon, "I found, indeed, that pleasure tormented by passion was no pleasure at all, but pleasure divorced from any ulterior emotion I soon discovered to be the highest good."

"So you would persuade me that you're an Epicurean who flings withered rose leaves and drinks sour wine. Come, come, sir, I wager your fingers would twitch and your lips quiver if one of us held a dice-box with a deep stake on the main."

"I deny that."

"We shall see."

"I hope we may."

"Ay, sir, and I wager this affectation of indifference will not outlast a week's ill luck, and as for woman, why the very dairymaids to-night will kindle a spark in your eyes."

"My life on't, they will not," cried Vernon.

"Foregad! you wear too stolid a mask to convince me it is your natural countenance."

This duologue, which seems to show that Mr. Lovely was younger and less wise than we might have thought, was interrupted by the shouts of the riders in front who wanted to know whether Charles imagined they were part of a funeral pomp.

"For d——e!" shouted Mr. Golightly, "we are all nodding like plumes and the twilight obscures the undeniable charms of the prospect."

Baverstock Barn, like a great cathedral, loomed upon them at last. As they dismounted, revelry and the drawling chatter of rustick voices, mingled with the tuning of fiddles, came from within, while the flickering light from the open door enchanted a heap of roots to the appearance of huge gems.

Clare approached the entrance while the rest stood by their horses.

"Farmer Hogbin!" he sang out.

"Who be caaling?"

"Mr. Anthony Clare!"

"Come in now, do 'ee come in."

"I've brought over a party with me, farmer?"

"Maids, do 'ee hear that? Maister Clare have brought wi'un a passel o' gallantry."

There was much jingling merriment from the maids.

"Now then Jock, Tommas, William, Jarge, Joe, Sam, Peter, Ern, move your shanks and stable they hosses."

The farmer, a huge Falstaff of a man quite in proportion to his barn, towered in the doorway obscuring the light, while the farm hands clumped with heavy legs towards the horses.

"Gi' they pleanty o' oats, my lads."

"A' right," mumbled the lads in chorus.

"Come in, my gentlemen, come in. Never mind for a speck of mud; the maids'll dust 'ee."

This sally provoked a ripple of laughter from the maids, and a chuckle from the young gentlemen.

The farmer surveyed them solemnly as they stepped into the barn.

"Why, you be all in top-boots?" he shouted. "Ho! ho! my maids, ye'll get thy twinkling toes rarely trod on, or shall I lend 'em my slippers to each in turn?"

This was considered splendid fooling, and laughter again resounded.

"Nay, farmer, you're in the wrong," said Charles producing a pair of pumps from the pockets of his riding coat.

"Why! dang me, if they han't brought a King's wardrobe wi'en. Eh! maids, you must mind your modesties to-night."

The maids, huddled together like a bunch of red apples, were set shaking with laughter at this warning—as if by a boisterous wind.

"Who will help us with our boots?" asked Clare

as he subsided upon a truss of straw and flung his legs wide apart.

There was considerable whispering from the heart of the bunch till one of the maids was pushed by her companions out into the open with ejaculations of " Go on, stoopid."

" Thee needst not let on to be so backward." " Thee wast forthy enough behind the kitchen door yester'een." " Eh! bustle thyself, great gowk," and others of like freedom of opinion.

The maid selected for Mr. Clare was blooming indeed.

" Cream and claret," murmured Charles.

" Gad! a Venus by a Dutch master truly," commented Vernon.

" She's no g-ghost," stammered little Peter Wingfield.

Farewell and adieu to you, gay Spanish ladies,
Farewell and adieu to you, ladies of Spain,

sang or rather bellowed Mr. Blewforth, slapping his thigh with a nautical zest.

Our Blewforth, careening far nearer than Cadiz
Will give to green fields what was meant for the Main.

continued Charles to the same tune.

" Give what? " asked Tom Chalkley.

" The breezy charm of his manner," replied Charles.

Now ensued jests, giggles, laughter, pranks, and struggles, as each gentleman persuaded a fair to wrestle with his riding-boots. Vernon who had forgotten to provide himself with pumps remained aloof from the merriment not sorry for an opportunity to convince Mr. Lovely of his remoteness from anything so vulgar as excitement.

Great was the mirth of everybody when the Lieutenant produced an enormous Valentine that depicted a peculiarly fat Cupid winking at a dairymaid over a brimming bowl of milk. Greater still was the mirth when he presented the token with much earnestness to the bashful lass they called Margery, and it became uproarious indeed when he explained he had wished to offer it on the preceding night, but had been deterred by Mr. Clare's reputed jealousy.

"Whoever heard tell of such a thing in the milk before?"

"'Tis a Cupid, Margery," said Mr. Clare.

"There now and if I didn't go for to think it were a baby," declared Margery.

Farmer Hogbin coming back from attending to the horses in time to hear this remark called out in his great voice:

"Don't 'ee fret thyself, my lass, what thee wants'll come soon enough, I warrant. Now, my gentlemen, take your partners, we was just a-going to begin a round dance. Tune up your squeaking boxes, fiddlers, and tip us *Come lasses and lads.*"

The fiddlers smiled encouragement at the dancers as they struck off with the gallant old tune. Even Mr. Vernon, boots and all, was made to give an arm to buxom Mrs. Crumplehorn, the cowman's wife. The sanded floor of the barn resounded with the perpetual tripping of toes and heels.

Come, lasses and lads,
Take leave of your dads.

The waist of every fair was encircled by a neat arm that tapered to a fine wrist as the dancers swung down to their places. Little Peter Wingfield unable to enfold the ample Polly was given her pinner as if he were indeed the child his appearance and behaviour proclaimed him.

Every one admired the first two couples that took the middle. Mr. Lovely was so graceful and Mr. Clare was so thorough. Round they went and down they went and across and through and over and under while the rest of the dancers clapped and tapped their appreciation. Faster and faster went the fiddles, faster and faster went the shoes. Thicker and thicker rose the sand and saw-dust from the floor until the barn seemed to be the centre of a raging storm, such a wind the petticoats made and so dense became the atmosphere. Thunder was added when the gigantick farmer and the burly Lieutenant, whom merry chance had thrown into the arena together, charged through their Pas Seul, bellowing the while with Gargantuan laughter.

At last the fiddles stopped and, panting mutual congratulations, the exhausted couples subsided upon the various trusses of straw laid along the side of the barn. Even the ivory paleness of Mr. Vernon's cheeks wore a faint tinge of carmine, and some curls of his modish wig were very slightly ruffled.

Jock, Tommas, William, Jarge, Joe, Samuel, Peter, and Ern, who had gathered into a critical knot, feeling themselves eclipsed by these active visitors, were released from their sheepishness by a demand for the bowls of spiced ale.

After this, they played Kiss in the Ring; and it was truly a most exhilarating sight to see Mr. Anthony Clare with flapping coat-tails in pursuit of the blooming Margery who was soon caught not very unwillingly as we may suppose. It was ludicrous in the extreme to see little Peter Wingfield darting hither and thither like a little brown rabbit. His little white wig seemed to twinkle like a tail set too high on his little brown body. But he let himself be caught by Polly beneath a lingering spray of mistletoe, and how all the world laughed when she lifted him up and gave him a resonant kiss on his little red lips. As for the large farmer and the burly Lieutenant they thundered after every maid in the barn quite regardless of any rules and, as I think, kissed the most of them very heartily indeed.

But the chief excitement of all was caused by a great white owl that came flapping down from the rafters and put out half the candles with his great sweeping wings. How all the lasses screamed and how earnestly the lads reassured them, and though the former were repeatedly told that owls while feeding on mice had not yet imbibed their habits, they persistently held their skirts a little higher than usual and nestled very close and comfortable to the exquisite young gentlemen from the *Blue Boar*.

Then, of course, they all danced *Sir Roger de Coverley*, and drank more spiced ale while they rested. Somebody called on Charles for a song and he gave them one of his own which everybody agreed was much too serious for so jolly an occasion. Charles swore he had composed the tune himself, but everybody else vowed they had heard it before, and as for the words, there was not a trace of originality about them. However, his voice was pleasant enough as he sang:

> *When in the dews of early morn*
> *My Chloe trips for may,*
> *Across the fields of springing corn*
> *I watch her pass,*
> *The fairest lass,*
> *That e'er was won with vows of love*
> *Upon a summer's day.*
>
> *Ah! shame that I should leave thee, dear,*
> *And cross the roaring sea,*
> *That I should leave thee lonely here:*
> *Think not, sweetheart,*
> *Because we part*
> *And I to foreign lands do rove,*
> *Thou art less dear to me.*

Blewforth protested he had said good-bye with almost identical rhymes in every port of the two hemispheres, and moreover was not ashamed to confess as much. All the maids, however, grew quite tearful and vowed the evening was spoiled; indeed, they made such ado that Charles sang one of Mr. d'Urfey's ballads to cheer their spirits and succeeded in providing such a burst of laughter that the echo of it never died away during the rest of the evening.

Of course, it was decided they must dance *Sir Roger* once more and, that duty accomplished, it was discovered that Anthony Clare and Margery had vanished. Of course everybody wondered where they could have gone, and when they returned in time to take a last sip at the spiced ale, it was noticed that Margery hung back in the shadows with a melancholy expression of countenance that made her companions nudge each other with wise looks.

Soon word came that the horses were saddled and waiting. Good-byes were murmured, and many a promise to come again was faithfully sworn and many a kiss given and taken. The ousted yokels held each a soil-stained hand for their genteel rivals to mount from. The maids stood huddled in the flickering light of the open barn-door; Farmer Hogbin bellowed a last farewell which was thunderously echoed by the Lieutenant, as with flushed faces and half-regretful memories, the horsemen cantered towards Curtain Wells under a sailing moon.

Clare rode by Charles to hear the judgment of Paris upon his tatterdemalion Venus.

" I'd liefer for her sake that you were overseas next barley-harvest," said Charles shortly.

" Plague on the man, what a cold stream it is! "

" My excellent Tony, your Blowzabella will be happier mating on a straw pallet with Hodge than living under your protection in London."

" She would see the world."

" Pshaw! her world is a garden of gillyflowers. She was never meant to be pushed out of sight for an importunate visitor."

" She would return."

"Like a spent primrose fit only for the bonfire."

"I could secure an annuity for her."

"You'll tire of her in London. Drain the claret from her cheeks, smear the downy bloom, and you'll find rank lees and rotten core. Hodge never would. No, no, the thought of so much comely maidenhood languishing for your velvet-sleeved caresses is merely droll."

Clare loved and admired Charles too much to despise his tirades however self-consciously virtuous they might appear. He felt more than ever convinced that his friend was in love, in love too with some one the very antithesis of the dairymaid. He would try one more test.

"But if I told I was in mind to wed my Venus?"

Charles jerked his reins in astonishment.

"Z——ds, Tony, look round you. There are maids more fit I say. Why wed a mountain, however rich in pasture when you can wed a mountain-nymph?"

Clare decided his suspicion was confirmed. Lovely objected to milkmaids on the score of a taste sharpened to an exquisite point of refinement by an ideal passion. He was postulating mere theories of life on account of the charms of one dear She. Who was the witch? She had not withdrawn him from their late junketing whatever her spells.

"Your morality, Charles, did not prevent you from entering very heartily into the spirit of our pastoral piece."

They had fallen behind the others, and through the silent night Charles' voice caught a melody from the wakening year as he rhapsodized.

"Fore Heaven! I love the country. I love these creamy hussies. I love their swains with the sweet earth all about them. I was happy to-night! I was happy with those dear people. I could lose my tricked-out self in that twinkling barn. I bowed to merriment as a tree bows to the wind. I wanted to hear the singing hopes and joys and desires of humble people. There we were, all of us populating a frieze for some merry artist god. We were as wax moulded to some fantastick dancing shape. On these occasions, I can surmize at immortality and imagine the heart of the universe. I doubt you think I'm babbling nonsense, but I'm trying to tell you I was entirely disinterested in our merry-making of to-night."

Clare stretched out to touch the poet's arm.

"Try to think that I, chattering of Margery, am not more personal than you. 'Tis true, I piped a love-ditty, but though it may trouble the bush and brake of a small wood, it would seem thin fluting——"

"To any but her," Charles interrupted. "The thinnest tune will charm one who is nearer than you to the primitive animal too easily quelled by sweet songs. Pipe to a crowd, Tony, but musick dedicated to a solitary shepherdess at the sight of whom your mouth will be awry in a year's time is ill work for her."

"I doubt you're right," said Clare softly. "You are compassionate to poor nymphs to-night, Charles. Have you met a goddess?"

"Tony, I have."

"May you prosper!"

"Thank 'ee. I'll tell you more of her when I know more myself."

They urged their horses to a trot and were silent for a while. Then Clare asked Charles what he thought of Vernon.

"Oh! a statue positively. I doubt the whole affair was to him vastly low."

"Umph! there was a permanent leer carved on his lips. I dislike the fellow."

"Nay! you're too stern in your judgments. He has promised me an evening for Hazard."

Clare smiled. It was useless to remonstrate with a man whom the thought of two dice transformed into a machine with glassy eyes and curiously sensitive fingers.

So they rode silently.

Charles could see Phyllida in the moon-enchanted clouds, sometimes with the trim waist of a dice-box.

CHAPTER VII

SUNDAY MORNING

SUNDAY morning at Curtain Wells was eminently a day of rest. A stroke of organizing genius on the part of Beau Ripple had abolished the fatigues of early Chalybeate by transferring the corporeal obligations of fashionable humanity to an hour which would not interfere with the respect owed to the spirit.

"A glass of Chalybeate," he had remarked, "will promote the proper digestion of the homily. Moreover, the vanity of post-religious promenades will be considerably mitigated by the discipline of the Pump."

At Curtain Wells, therefore, soon arose the pleasant custom of inviting one's friends and neighbours to partake of a substantial breakfast before setting out to St. Simon's parish church. The neighbours, if gentlemen, were expected to provide a suitable escort for their lady-hosts, and there was not a dame in the town who did not make it a point of honour to be armed in at the great West door on fine mornings or handed out of her chair with cautious ceremony if the weather was unsettled.

The Widow Courteen was not the woman to neglect or despise any prescriptive right conferred upon her sex. It was not surprising, therefore, to see Major Constantine Tarry and Mr. Gregory Moon turning solemnly into the Crescent on the first Sunday morning whose events I am privileged to chronicle. The demeanour of neither gentleman would have allowed us even a momentary hesitation as to the day. The Sabbath wrote itself in the devout wrinkles of Mr. Moon's domed forehead and expressed itself in the stiff curls of the Major's military wig. As they drew near to Mrs. Courteen's house the latter voiced a desire to see eggs and bacon upon the breakfast table, and the former encouraged his ambition by repeating a legend of a fecundity among hens unusual at this season of the year. The meditation carried the two gentlemen to Mrs. Courteen's door in silence.

"Your turn to knock, Tarry," said Mr. Moon, in a rather depressed voice, as he fumbled with the steps from which the Major assaulted the door with military abruptness.

To them after a decent interval appeared Thomas in resplendent waistcoat of Sunday and with nose polished to the limit of a nose's power of brightness.

"Is your mistress within?" inquired the Major.

"Within and awaiting you," said solemn Mr. Thomas.

"Then I think, Mr. Moon," said the Major with half a turn, "we will step inside immediately."

"I think we may venture," replied the latter.

They were ushered into the passage where Thomas received their hats and canes. Thomas had such a sober effect on his fellow-men that the slightest action in which he took part was conducted with a ritual at once austere and grand. One felt that the delivery of a hat, smallsword, cane, or message possessed at least the dignity, the entire absence of all worldly considerations that belong to the Sunday alms.

"Will your mistress receive us in the front parlour or the back parlour this morning?" inquired Tarry whose legs were prepared for either emergency.

"In the front parlour," said Thomas. "Miss Thomasina was ill this morning."

"In the back parlour, I presume?" said Moon.

"Very ill with retching and divers pains," continued Thomas.

"Poor Thomasina," said the Major with an attempt at jocularity.

"A feeble animal," said the footman, "and too fond of grass; and the grass of this city is fit only for Nebuchadnezzar."

A bright fire was crackling in the grate, and on each hob a kettle of burnished copper sang with considerable sentiment.

Thomas withdrew, and the Major and Mr. Moon took up the Englishman's position on the hearthrug with coat-tails wide apart to allow the grateful warmth free access to whatever chillness of morning air still clung about their bodies. So they remained, silent, wrapped in the dignified contemplation of an inferior painting in oils on the opposite wall. No doubt in reality their thoughts were far away, possibly in the chaste seclusion of the widow's own room or possibly in the kitchen whence from time to time ascended the pleasant jingle and chink that heralds food's approach.

No doubt they would both have stood there long enough for us to moralize on England and the greatness of England, had not Mrs. Courteen come into the room just then.

Ponto, Phyllida's black spaniel, sidled in with the breakfast and Phyllida herself followed, and the freshness of her in the morning was strewn about the room like petals of roses.

Conversation at breakfast suited itself to the solemnity of the day. The widow sighed at every remark that was made, and in the gentle pathos of her manner indicated placidly her conviction of fleeting time and sorrow, and all those melancholy reflections which are considered proper to the Sabbath. However, at all times she was accustomed to preserve a cloistral rigour of speech before her daughter. No one loved better to gather the easier blooms on the safe side of the garden-god's perfumed hedge, but they could only be plucked in numerous corners of ballrooms and during secluded promenades. The presence of Phyllida made her mother's blood so much rennet. Conversation became mere verbal curds and whey.

However, the Justice talked into his cup of the swift approach of Spring, of the benefit of sun, the intolerable increase in vagrancy, the need for repressing poachers. If platitudes were esteemed as high as rolling hexameters, Moon would have been among the epical poets. As for Major Tarry, he thrashed each topick as if his tongue were a little rattan cane. One felt that any observation was regarded by that gallant gentleman as an awkward recruit. He had an air of drilling the conversation. After breakfast, the various members dispersed to acquire a seemly attitude towards matters of religion.

Since the search for attitudes occupies a vast deal of human energy, it may not be out of place to inform my reader where the half-dozen required for Morning Prayer at St. Simon's were found.

The Widow Courteen found hers hidden between powder puff and patch-box.

Miss Courteen found hers between the lines of a three-cornered note.

Madam Betty found hers in the coral secrets of Miss Courteen's left ear.

Mr. Thomas found his in a Bible as large and heavy as a Bible should be.

Major Tarry found his in the stem of a churchwarden pipe.

Mr. Moon found his in the best attitude that exists.

Soon Mrs. Courteen's chairmen were knocking at the door and the whole party prepared to set out. The widow seated in her chair, hummed a hymn *tempo di minuetto*. The Major marched upon her left and the Justice upon her right, and Thomas marched in front. Phyllida and Betty kept to the pavement and had scarcely time to wonder if all the world would be at church, when they arrived at the porch and found that all the world certainly was.

As the Major had handed the widow into her chair, Mr. Moon handed her out, and the party of Mrs. Courteen proceeded to Mrs. Courteen's pew, while Mrs. Courteen's chairmen carried the chair to an alley beloved of chairmen and proceeded to doze away the Sabbath morning in its damask recesses and were no doubt as comfortable as their mistress in the musty cushions of St. Simon's pews. In the Western gallery, three fiddles, two hautboys, and a bass viol squeaked and groaned with much fervour. In the pulpit the parson squeaked and groaned with equal fervour and in the desk below the clerk squeaked and groaned with most fervour of all. When the parson threatened damnation, the ladies fanned themselves rapidly and when he spoke of alms and oblations, they consoled themselves with carraway comfits.

The service was rather worldly and seemed remote enough from anything at all spiritual, but nevertheless in so far as it was indigenous to fair King Richard's land, it should exact from us as much respect as we owe to a Chippendale chair and that is or ought to be very great indeed. If so much condemnatory fervour was equivalent to breaking these butterflies of fashion upon a religious wheel, it cannot be denied that the exquisite bloom of their ruined wings was a great deal more pleasant to regard than the spattered blood and bones of earlier and more tangible martyrs to an extreme mode.

The parson continued to prophesy hell-fire. But hell-fire means so many kinds of illumination—certainly it had an invincible attraction for these gay moths and butterflies. Perhaps they thought of it merely as a huge aggregation of wax candles by which most of them had more than once been morally singed. If any permanency of emotion was desirable, it would certainly be more endurable in heat and gaiety than in chill aerial solitudes. And, thanks to chickens, there would always be painted fans. This was the sum of the congregation's united reflection during the sermon;

individually, no doubt, each soul played with more particular premises, but the ultimate conclusion was the same for all.

After so much damnation, the blessing was a rhetorical anti-climax. Clouds had gathered during the homily, due, no doubt, to the violence of the preacher, and, as the worshippers tripped out through the great West door, the clouds burst and the streaming rain inclined them more favourably than ever to the prospect of eternal warmth.

The morning's fair promise had been utterly belied, and many appealing glances were launched at Mr. Ripple as he beckoned to his chairmen. Surely he would not be so barbarous as to force so much accumulated fine raiment through mud and water, to drink the latter element in a less pleasing form. But Mr. Ripple was inexorable: he stepped into his gilded chair, regardless of appeal: the chairmen tightened their muscles for the long pull uphill, and Gog and Magog, the diminutive negroes balanced one on each step, guarded their master from interruption. Now ensued shouts, whistles, cockcrows and screams. Hats were waves, canes flourished, and lily-white hands shaken. All this uproar was due to the fact that there were just half as many coaches and chairs as were required, and when these were filled, and on their way to the Pump Room, there remained in the church too many foolish virgins, too many improvident dowagers, too many thoughtless beaux.

The rain fell in torrents, and the last vehicle had turned the corner.

A desolate remnant surveyed the situation. It was wet enough.

Now arose one of those crises which are inseparable from a despotism. Somebody, for his presumption will always remain anonymous, somebody suggested that the idea of climbing the hill of health in such a downpour was unimaginable.

The stranded exquisites depended for the moment entirely on their rouge for colour.

"Rebellion," they muttered and the ominous word flapped over their heads and darkened the gloom more profoundly.

"The Beau will be furious."

"He will never forgive us."

"We shall be banished."

"Curtain Wells will no longer know us."

Again the daring voice was upraised:

"We are strong enough to defy Ripple. He has no right to make us wade through mud for a whim of his own. If we do so, we'll do so in shifts and shirts." The unknown voice gathered force with each new proposition, and the startled exquisites huddled closer in a very ecstasy of perturbation.

"Shall damask flowers lose their beauty, shall silver lace be tarnished and broideries lack lustre because Ripple has commanded the impossible? Silk is the fashion, ay! and watered silk, but not sodden silk. Well was it named the Pump Room, for such shall we become, mere pumps exuding moisture at the propulsion of a tyrant!"

The apparent carelessness of the unknown tyrannicide had its effect ; a suspicion began to creep in that Mr. Ripple's domination was based on insecurity. The thin end of this destructive wedge was enough to break open the fortress of their duty and, the rain stopping for a moment, the stranded exquisites hurried home to discuss the probable result of their revolt over hot rum and lemon. Up at the Pump Room Mr. Ripple missed many a well-known face that Sunday, and his urbane countenance lost some of its smoothness as the minutes rolled by without the arrival of a single person on foot.

At the expiration of the quarter of an hour, he despatched Gog to see what had happened and when Gog came back with the news that the stranded exquisites had one and all departed to their own lodgings,

Mr. Ripple ascended his marble pedestal with an air of determination.

"My lords, ladies and gentlemen," he began, and just then Magog hurried up with the Beau's glass of Chalybeate. The latter looked at it for a moment. Pity and anger fought visibly for the mastery. Anger won, and the remorseless Beau dashed the glass into a thousand sparkling fragments.

"The Pump Room will be closed until—until this—" he faltered over the description of such ingratitude, "until the extraordinary behaviour of certain visitors has been justified, if it can be justified. There will be no Assembly to-morrow night."

The company shivered unanimously and the Beau, dismissing his chairmen, walked forth into the rain with all the dignity in the world. It is said he ruined three suits of unparagoned cut that fatal day by walking about the principal thoroughfares of Curtain Wells for the remainder of a very wet afternoon.

CHAPTER VIII

THE GREAT REBELLION

NOT unnaturally, the only topick of that memorable Sunday was the rebellion. The excitement it raised far exceeded anything of the sort not excepting the Jacobite rising, and the oldest inhabitant of the Wells positively asserted that the landing of the Duke of Monmouth was altogether inferior in the quality of emotional interest.

Sirloins of beef were allowed to freeze into glaciers of fat, horse radish lost its sting, and the most frothy ale was flat in the presence of such an absorbing topick of conversation. When at last everybody, momentarily exhausted, sought recuperation in the Sunday dinner, everybody ate so fast to be the sooner at the coffee-house or the Town Hall or the Assembly Rooms or some such equally renowned haunt of gossip that everybody had a remarkably bad attack of indigestion.

From every doorway the crowds hurried forth after dinner, scorning the sacred forty winks. But coffee-house, Town Hall, and Assembly Rooms were closed, bolted, barred and shuttered, and for a sign over each was a scroll of parchment on which was inscribed in the finest gold leaf:

Closed till further notice. By order. Horace Ripple.

Disconsolately the ladies trooped home again to discuss developments over a dish of Bohea; eagerly the gentlemen trotted to the *Blue Boar* only to be told that nobody save lodgers could be admitted.

Most of them admired the decision of the Great little Man, but the rebels who, having once started, felt bound to hold out if only against the censure of the faithful, laughed very loudly and boldly and said it was all very well to close the places of publick entertainment on Sunday, that was only a loss of two hours' custom to the proprietors, but on the next day, a very different tale would be told. So they prophesied as they tripped home to their pipes and hot rum, with a twirl of their elegant canes, a shake of their exquisite heads, and a *Whack row-de-dow* from their irreverent lips.

The faithful who had seen the Beau in the first flood of his wrath were not so sanguine. They knew that like the late King of France he could say *L'état c'est moi*, and what shopkeeper, innkeeper, or porter, would be brave enough to defy him?

The sun set on a gloomy town and everybody went to bed at half-past eight o'clock having nothing better to do.

Mr. Ripple had earlier in the afternoon assured himself of Mr. Lovely's fidelity, and in the company of the young gentlemen of the *Blue Boar*, passed a very pleasant evening over some capital Burgundy opened at his expense. He sent down messages to my Lord Cinderton and my Lord Vanity begging the favour of their company, and both my lords hurried back as fast as their dignified legs would carry them. Of course, they quite agreed with Mr. Ripple that the outbreak was scandalous and were determined to support his decrees against the whole of society provided they were not included in the excommunication. The news of Sir Jeremy Dummer's sudden decease was brought in, and Mr. Ripple, deeply moved by the melancholy event, ascribed it to the horror with which the old baronet was overwhelmed at the defiance of himself. It was soon announced in every drawing-room that Sir Jeremy Dummer had died of an apoplexy brought on by the sight of the rebel abstainers from morning Chalybeate.

It was arranged, almost in silence, that everybody faithful to the great Beau, should repair to the Pump Room on the following morning, dressed in funereal black, a quarter of an hour earlier than usual. They might not be admitted, but their devotion would carry its own reward, and would certainly afford the Beau confidence in the loyalty of the most of his subjects. It was farther arranged that a deputation of the leading visitors and residents should wait upon him at his lodgings with an address black-edged, assuring him of their sorrow and fidelity. As for the rebels, they must make what terms they could.

At eleven o'clock of Monday forenoon the deputation waited upon the Beau and was ushered over the Turkey carpet into his urbane presence. Apparently he was quite untouched by the almost servile assurance of loyalty contained in the address. He begged leave to inform the company that, while sensible of their compliment, he could not permit any publick amusement until the ringleaders of the revolt had, hat in hand, implored his forgiveness. He added he had reluctantly despatched mounted messengers to Leamington, Cheltenham, Bristol Well, Brighthelmstone, Harrogate, Scarborough, Tunbridge and the Bath, begging his brethren to refuse admittance to any new arrivals until farther warning. He was confident that his appeal would not be disregarded. The abashed deputation withdrew, having effected nothing. Monday passed gloomily enough. There were no chairmen, there were no chairs, there were no coaches, there was no Assembly. The shops were all closed: the Pump Room was closed: coffee-houses, chocolate-houses and taverns were all closed.

The rebels were now merged almost imperceptibly into loyalists but a few still held out, and two of the more callous —I will not affront the living world with their names—went so far as to send out invitations to a party of Quadrille. Six equally hardened rebels arrived at the time appointed. Two tables were formed, the candles were lighted, the guineas stood piled in glittering dozens, the cards were dealt, when suddenly the door was flung open and Mr. Ripple in black sattin, armed with a spade, marched into the room.

"I think, ladies and gentlemen, that I am Spadille this evening," he proclaimed in a voice of ice.

The eight rebels dropped their cards. It was impossible to play with any calmness in the presence of that menacing figure whose contempt was so sublime. The ladies fluttered from the room in dismay.

"Gentlemen," said the Beau, "you will call at my house to-morrow with the humblest apologies for this evening's outrage."

Then he vanished from the room. It only remains to add that the gentlemen did call at the Great House on the following morning where their humiliation was complete if we may judge by an alabaster tablet set up in the portico of the Assembly Rooms where it remained until the other day, when, alas! the famous old rooms, so long the most frequented shrine of wit and beauty in England, were pulled down to make way for a publick library.

The tablet which was in the likeness of the Ace of Spades bore the following inscription:

Sacred to the Memory of Justice, Decency, and Order,
This Tablet was erected by four Gentlemen
In Token of their sincere Penitence and resolute
Amendment.
Also in the profoundest Admiration and deepest
Respect for Beau Ripple, King of Curtain Wells,
for many years,
Arbiter of Fashion
and
Oracle of Wit.
The Great and Only
Spadille.

CHAPTER IX

THE ASSEMBLY

THE submission of the recalcitrants secured once more to Curtain Wells her publick amusements, and the Monday Assembly was announced for Wednesday evening. Everybody determined that it should make up in brilliance what it lacked in punctuality, and all private conversaziones, routs, and Quadrille parties were, by general consent, postponed.

We have temporarily got out of touch with the lesser intrigues of this history, but truly all such were eclipsed by the great Rebellion whose echoes drowned the whispered vows of lovers and the murmur of scandalous small talk. The prospect of peace set everybody at amusement, with vigour refreshed by the momentary lull in the gay tempest of their lives.

An additional excitement surrounded this Assembly because it was everywhere reported that the young gentlemen of the *Blue Boar* would be present in force. This rumour was, indeed, likely to prove true, for the young gentlemen, already determined to discover Mr. Lovely's charmer, were confirmed in their resolve by a desire to reciprocate the Beau's lately implied confidence in a way more likely to gratify him than any other.

The prospect of dancing with young Tom Chalkley of the Foot, Tony Clare, and Peter Wingfield, or Lieutenant Blewforth of the *Lively* fluttered all the young ladies' hearts and very many of the old ones'. Moreover, there were the Honourable Mr. Harthe-Brusshe and Mr.

Golightly, and above all, there was Mr. Charles Lovely who, if he were a poet, was also a man of the extremest fashion and finest taste, and so at once genteel and romantick. Altogether the postponed Assembly promised to be a great success.

Miss Phyllida Courteen hoped that her dear Amor would make an exception for once, but Mr. Vernon declared he would by no means commit himself to such publick adoration of his fair; so she was forced to content herself with the prospect of teasing Miss Sukey Morton about the anonymous Valentine. She knew that her dear Morton would suspect Mr. Chalkley who, with the politeness for which the British Army has always been famous, had once recovered her dropped fan. This somewhat ordinary event had led Miss Morton to colour the whole world to the hue of a red coat. All the dearest confidences exchanged with her beloved Courteen referred to young Mr. Chalkley who was quite unconscious of the amount of room he occupied in Miss Morton's heart, and was used to regard women as musquets for the presenting of arms, but nothing more.

The whole of Wednesday had been spent by the ladies of the Wells in refreshing their bodies with sleep and rouge alternately, and the sickle moon in the frore February sky looked pale and ghostly beside the sleek tapers that twinkled in every window pane and the ruddy flambeaux of the lackeys as they stamped up and down in waiting to escort their mistresses to the ball.

Phyllida was not long in putting on her white muslin nightgown with flowered sack; and as her curls had neither to be subdued by Powder and Pomatum, nor frizzled to a mock vivacity by restorative Tongs, she sat in the bow-window of her bedchamber and stared at the young moon. The curtains were drawn back, but, even so, she could still see innumerable shepherds arming as many shepherdesses through the pattern and, as the fire-light flickered over them, they seemed, indeed, to be stepping a forgotten dance.

"I should like to live in a curtain," thought Phyllida, "and be always young and always happy and always hand in hand with—but after all nothing could be less like a shepherd than Amor," and just then the little flame that had been urging all the figures into motion turned to a noisy puff of smoke; the picture faded from her mind and the voice of her mother destroyed the last gossamer fancy that floated through her brain.

The widow's room was billowy with rejected petticoats on which, like sea-wrack, floated garters, stockings, and gloves; while a large constellation of paste gleamed fitfully through the mirk of a Paris net. In the midst of the delicate havock sat the widow uncertain as ever what colour and stuff would most become the evening.

"The Major spoils my rose lustring and my orange sack makes the Justice look——"

"Like suet," said Betty.

The widow was about to reprimand her for the simile, but as it perfectly expressed what the Justice would look like, she refrained.

"Sure, madam," said Phyllida, who was impatient to set out, "you had best wear your blue brocade."

"The child is right," said the widow emphatically. "Betty! my blue brocade."

Betty did not protest she had already tried on the blue brocade four times because, if she had, the widow would instantly have thought that green would be better, and the argument would have begun all over again.

At last the widow was dressed; the coach was at the door; and in a very short time made one of a long row of equally cumbersome vehicles that extended far down the High Street. Mrs. Courteen peering from the window announced she had caught a glimpse of Lady Bunbutter stepping out of her coach in blue brocade.

This dreadful anticipation of her own entrance was extremely disconcerting, and if there had been the slightest prospect of turning round in the crush of coaches, chairs, footmen, linkboys and gaping cits, she would have instantly driven home to exchange blue for any other colour in her trunk-mail or closet. However, as she could not change her attire, she did the next best thing possible, by blaming Phyllida for her suggestion. As this was the prologue to every assembly, the latter was not much troubled by her mother's annoyance and soon the coach arrived at the very steps leading up to the Rooms. At the moment it drew up, Major Tarry and Mr. Moon stepped forward and flung open the door and handed the widow out and armed her up the steps and gave her name to Mr. Ripple's confidential Secretary who passed it on to another equally confidential footman who bawled it out at the top of his voice just as Mrs. Courteen sailed into the ballroom where Mr. Ripple, with the rosy bloom of triumph on his cheeks, advanced to offer two fingers vailed in gloves of diaphanous chicken-skin.

Curtseys, bows, and compliments lasted until the arrival of the next guest, when the widow with her faithful Ancients surveyed the room in a grand promenade. Phyllida made off to greet her dear Morton with half a glance in the direction of the young gentlemen from the *Blue Boar*, who were grouped rather stiffly at the other end of the ballroom.

The babble of conversation and the swish of fans, the colour all compact of movement, the innumerable tapers, the glitter of many brooches, pins, and buckles, the mirrours, the preliminary notes of the musicians, the shuffling feet, and the tap of the opened snuff-boxes combined in that glorious whole—a ball at the Assembly Rooms, Curtain Wells.

Soon the Minuets would begin, and after the Minuets, the Gavottes, and so on to the Country Dances and the last great Cotillon. The passionate history of the world is writ in crowquill letters on the programs of dances. What Jealousies and yellow-winged Envies hovered on the cool air of waving fans, what vows would be made and broken in those alcoves, now serene and empty, before the last flambeau expired in the gutter outside. What mean Ambitions coiled around every genteel fine hoop!

Yet Mr. Ripple was so suave, Mrs. Courteen and my Lady Bunbutter so full of compliments, Lieutenant Blewforth so jolly and Mr. Lovely so witty, old Lord Vanity so generous of snuff, my Lord Cinderton so distinguished—and as for Miss Phyllida Courteen, she was enchanted to a magical domain where only very slowly did Mr. Francis Vernon blacken a trinket sun with the menace of real passion.

Suddenly her heart began to beat so fast that she feared all her friends would observe her agitation. Surely that young gentleman in primrose sattin and flesh-coloured brocaded waistcoat, who took the polished floor so easily, was the poet of Valentine Day to whom she had confided her note. Surely too, for all he stared at everybody else from time to time, his eyes were really fixed on hers. Perhaps he was a friend of Amor's with a message to deliver—and yet it would be more interesting, she decided, if he were not. Presently Mr. Lovely was bowing over her chair and asking in the politest manner possible for the honour of the next two dances.

She looked round at Miss Morton as if to say she could not leave her without a partner.

"Madam," said Mr. Lovely bowing very low indeed, "if I might be so presumptuous, does the young lady wish for a Vis à Vis, for in that case I shall certainly present my friend Mr. Chalkley of the Foot."

Miss Morton, amid a deal of simpering, confessed she favoured a minuet on occasions, so Mr. Lovely hurried off to fetch Mr. Chalkley before the musicians began to play the opening bars of the dance.

Phyllida was astonished at the coincidence and not sure whether, after all, Mr. Chalkley had not employed Mr. Lovely's offices on his behalf. However, as she had little enough envy in her and was romantically attached to Mr. Amor, she could scarcely refuse to help her dear Morton into the arms of an expectant lover, and if Mr. Lovely had no real inclination to dance with her, that was no great matter, since he was a vastly agreeable young gentleman and would pass the time very pleasantly in the absence of another.

Mr. Chalkley, when summoned by Charles, was extremely indignant and swore he was not come to dance with any jade in the room.

"Pshaw," replied his friend, "you can't stand there gaping all the evening."

"Why don't you make Blewforth dance with the hussy?"

"Odds my life, Tom, why won't you tread a minuet with a handsome young woman?"

"You're too devilish fond of arranging matters for other people to suit your own whims. I'll be hanged if I dance a step to-night!" But all the other young gentlemen vowed so earnestly that Mr. Chalkley was a surly fellow, that he gave way at last and suffered himself to be dragged to the feet of attractive Miss Sukey Morton, whose black eyes flashed very brightly at the sight of Mr. Chalkley's red coat.

Charles, having disposed her friend, offered his hand to Phyllida and soon they were stepping the minuet with infinite grace, admired by every one who saw them.

For her the room sank into unreality and she lived in a rainbow whose colours moved and changed to the slow dignity of far-heard Pizzicato.

The melody to which these marionettes were dancing possessed a strange quality. It was emotion in quintessence, without passion, without abandon. Whatever it had of definite character lay in the half bashful invitation to dance, as if some ghostly puppet master, pale and stately, were beckoning to his performers. As the opening bars of the minuet were repeated at the close only to die away in a poignant farewell, Phyllida felt for the first time, in the swoon of her last courtesy, that she was a doll whose gestures served to amuse a genteel but unearthly audience of monocled Gods.

Actually it was a mere momentary dizziness, a sudden loss of volition on which Charles hung a score of fancies.

" You are feeling faint? " he inquired.

" No, no."

" The heat is overpowering. Shall we sit for a while in an alcove, or shall we saunter in Curtain Garden? " They passed through the crowded room and down a cool passage into a Baroc cloister where stone Satyrs took the place of Angels, and the Cherubim were not easily to be distinguished from Loves.

The young moon was setting behind Curtain Hill larger and more golden than before.

The cloister was hung with amber lights and held innumerable whispers. Somewhere close at hand was a sound of running water.

" You are fond of dancing, madam? "

" Oh, sir, 'tis a very delicate motion truly."

" I fear you thought I was presumptuous in offering my hand for the minuet."

" No, indeed, sir," Phyllida answered quite naturally.

Lovely was rather surprized. He had expected the customary play of a fan.

" You are making a long stay here? " he asked.

" Oh, sir, I do not know, 'tis for so long as my mamma thinks proper."

" I have not had the honour of an introduction."

" No," said Phyllida doubtfully. She was not at all anxious to present Mr. Lovely, and willing enough to take advantage of the Assembly rule that the offer and acceptance of a dance was not necessarily a passport to intimacy on the next day. She did not wish to be treated like a child before the gallant Mr. Lovely who treated her with such deference.

"Did you hear anything more of the Valentine?" said Phyllida with a ripple of laughter.

"Not a word."

"You remember the young woman by whom I was seated?"

"Perfectly."

"'Twas for her," said Phyllida with more laughter.

"Nonsense."

"Oh, yes! indeed, 'tis true, and the best of it is she thinks the Valentine was sent by Mr. Chalkley."

"Never!"

"Oh! yes, yes, yes."

"But he has never set eyes on her."

"No! But she thinks he has—often, just because he picked up her fan once."

"Truly then I did a very politick action in effecting the introduction."

"Oh, sir, she was ravished, you may be sure."

"Gad! I'll send her a Valentine every day of the week, and put one in her Prayer Book on Sundays."

"Oh, sir! but sure, it might end in a wedding, and that's a very serious matter as all the world knows."

"Not more serious than love," said Charles.

"Well, no, perhaps not more than love; but then neither of 'em is in love with t'other."

"I swear they shall be."

"You can't force people to fall in love."

"Can't you?" said Charles very earnestly, so earnestly that Phyllida thought the air was turning chill and that they ought to go back to the ballroom.

"Not yet," pleaded Mr. Lovely. "I thought we might walk towards the Maze."

"The Maze?" said she quickly.

"Why, yes! the entrance is but a few yards from where we are."

"I had forgot," she answered, and then with a sudden determination, "I think we had better go back."

"You're not frightened of the Maze?"

"Oh, no, truly I'm not," Phyllida affirmed. "But I think I heard my mamma's voice and if she sees me here, I shall not be allowed to come to the next Assembly."

Phyllida was feeling a vague emotion of infidelity to her dear Amor and almost dreaded to see his tall shadow in the amber light.

"As you will," he said in some disappointment, "but we han't had a deal of conversation yet."

"That's true," she replied, "but this is only our second meeting. Oh! Gemini!" she went on, "you'll think me forward and bold, but I vow I never meant it in that way."

"Madam," said Charles with a bow, "I should never presume to put upon it an interpretation so complimentary to myself; but, seriously, you will give me two more dances to-night?"

"It would be indiscreet."

"Nay, I do not think so."

"Your friends would laugh."

"I do not *think* so."

Mr. Lovely looked so fierce that Phyllida hurriedly promised two gavottes, and Charles who was something of a Gascon could not help congratulating himself on his speedy success.

They walked back to the ballroom almost in silence, and above the chatter of folk in the lobby, heard the opening of a plaintive minuet.

Lovely, when he had left his partner, walked over to his friends of the *Blue Boar* and was greeted with a shower of sallies.

"How now, Charles, have you been smuggling rare spirits in the cloister?" cried Blewforth.

"Snuggling would be b-b-better!" stammered little Peter Wingfield.

Charles glared at both the young gentlemen, who laughed very heartily indeed, and were not at all put about by his frowns.

"Oddslife, Charles," said Mr. Chalkley, "where have been your eyes these past six weeks to have so lately discovered the fair Courteen?"

"Charles looks at women through dice-boxes," said Blewforth.

"And what's worse, sees double wherever he looks," added Mr. Chalkley.

"Charles," added Mr. Antony Clare, "be wise. Some knave of Clubs will trump your Queen."

"Mr. Clare," said Charles drawing himself up very straight and looking as grand as possible, "I'll trouble you to croak when I ask for your noise; as for you, gentlemen, you're too free with your words, be d—d to the lot of you."

Thereupon Mr. Charles Lovely swung himself out of the room with such an air that the young gentlemen looked after him in some apprehension.

"Egad!" commented Chalkley, "the man must be madly in love for he's lost his wit."

"And his humour too," said Blewforth.

"Don't rally him too hard, boys," said Tony.

"We can't all turn parsons because Charles is bewitched by two blue eyes," grumbled Chalkley.

This was the opinion of the company, and though in their hearts they excused Mr. Lovely, they were loud in their condemnation of his churlish behaviour.

Clare, afraid he was gone to work off his injured feelings by reckless play, soon followed him out of the ball-room, but could not find him at the tables.

Charles had, in fact, turned into the garden. Cupid had pierced him with a long sharp arrow, and he was not yet able to bear a rough hand on the wound. The night air came over him fresh and cool. In the darkness he was more than ever enthralled by the image and pale fancies of an ideal passion. Yet for all he was a poet, or perhaps just because he was a poet, his love was tinted with the hues of convention. She was like those Madonnas who appear to peasant children, Madonnas in crude cœrulean robes sown with tinsel stars. One feels that much of the apparition is due to preconceived opinion. So with Charles, his love, made one of a list of women dating to the Queens of Babylon. There was too much bob-a-cherry about her and too much cream. She stood, too, on such a high pedestal that if she owned feet of cracked clay not a soul could have seen them.

Charles felt very angry with his bachelor friends, and when Clare joined him at the end of an alley was in no mood to be pleasant company.

"Sure, Charles," the latter remonstrated, "you're the last man to tie yourself to the skirts of a goddess."

"There's a medium, between an angel and a woman of the town," said Charles sententiously.

"But the woman was once an angel to somebody, and 'foregad! I believe you do your charmer an injury to make her such a paragon of air. I swear those eyes can flash with more than saintly ecstasy."

"Z——ds! Tony, you are bent on a quarrel. I tell you the child's name shall not be a toast for my profligate friends."

"You are not better than any of them."

"But at least I can reverence purity."

"Aye, and so can Blewforth."

"D——e!" swore Charles, "'tis a pity he don't exercise his talent more openly."

The argument would doubtless have continued, if the sound of voices approaching had not made the two young men pause involuntarily. Two people were passing down the adjoining alley, and it was impossible not to overhear some of the conversation, which was sufficiently ridiculous. A feminine voice declared that soldiers were romantick, and a voice of opposite sex replied that as an attribute of class, it was an undeniable quality, but not for that reason universally applicable to individual members of that class.

"But a scarlet coat is so dazzling," argued Treble.

"Madam," said Bass, "I cannot claim that my profession is romantick. The Law, Madam, has no time for romance except perhaps in the examination of an unwilling witness, but what my profession lacks, my name possesses. Moon, madam, I venture to affirm, is a singularly romantick name."

"It is," murmured the widow, for, of course, it was she.

"The moon is the method of illumination adopted by every poet of distinction."

"How true that is," she sighed.

"I might add that so far as dazzling goes my name is as capable of extreme refraction as the red coat of a soldier. Moreover, madam, the latter is very antipathetick to the complexion of a woman of quality."

"But the coat need not be worn, Mr. Moon. It could exist in a bottom drawer, I should feel it was there, and I could sometimes brush it even."

"Good heavens! ma'am, has not the Law an equal fascination? Do you know that my house is full of legal cases?"

"How untidy!" said the widow reprovingly.

"Arguments *Pro* and *Contra*, trials!"

"But I dislike arguments, they put my hair out of curl and we have so many trials to bear already."

"They need never be used, but they can exist, madam, they can exist in calf on a bottom shelf, and they could be dusted sometimes," declared the Justice. Then in softer accents he began to plead:

"Think, my dear Mrs. Courteen, of Mrs. Moon. Mrs. Moon! I often murmur that short sentence over to myself."

"Do you, Mr. Moon? When?" said the widow, who seemed touched by his devotion.

"Oh! after dinner—or getting into bed, or—" but the third occasion was never revealed, for Major Tarry charged round the corner and carried off the dear questioner to adorn a gavotte.

Somehow the hedges no longer seemed so mysterious and the night not quite so large.

"Gad! what follies!" laughed Charles.

"D'ye know who the lady was?" inquired the other.

"Venus grown fat by the sound of her voice."

"That was Mrs. Courteen."

"Eh?"

"Your charmer's mother."

"Then she must have had a very delightful father."

"That's neither here nor there," said Clare. "Your angel's wings may moult, and she who now goes tiptoe for very lightness will one day—but, pshaw! if you love her, she will always skim the ground."

"Tony!" said Charles, "I've made a fool of myself."

"In the best way of folly."

It may seem odd that Charles should have been so ready to admit the mortality of his goddess, but after all as yet his love was an apparition. No miracles had been worked at the shrine, and she had a mother.

Also Charles began to smell romance, of which he pretended to an exaggerated horror. Like mother, like daughter. He made up his mind to neglect Miss Phyllida Courteen, and having done so, went back to the ballroom with the temerity of a successful anchorite. Yet when he saw her again she was young and adorable, and he was as madly in love with her as ever; all the more perhaps because he realized that one day she would fade. However, he was no longer so full of heroick rebukes for his friends. Perhaps, like the Greeks, he was beginning to understand that romantick Troy was a menace to the common sense of the world.

Charles found the young men in precisely the same position as that in which he left them.

"Oddslife," cried Blewforth, "there's Charles come back. What, man! have you been languishing under the sky? Your mistress has been dancing merrily with Ripple himself, while you were star-gazing."

"'Tis a pity that none of you have enough impudence to follow his example," retorted Charles, "for on my soul you all stand stiff and awkward as the figures on a Gothick tombstone. Gad! I've a mind to tell the ladies how nimbly you tripped it at Baverstock, Blewforth, and as for you, Tom, I'm hanged if I'd be cut out by a beggarly half-pay militia captain," continued Charles pointing to the disreputable Captain Mann who was handing Miss Morton through the gavotte.

"Well said!" Clare joined in, "we shall find it more difficult than ever to believe Blewforth's tales of conquest in the ports of civilization."

"Unless," added Charles, "like a picture by a great master he possesses an immovable reputation and attracts by beauty in repose."

"Ha—ha—ha," bellowed the Lieutenant, "you should have seen me at Minorca. These finicking hussies aren't worth the shoe leather one uses in dragging them round the room." But just as Mr. Blewforth was about to give a discourse on the beauty, grace, and agility of feminine Spain, Mr. Ripple scaled the rigid group:

"Now, gentlemen, you are not dancing. Come, come, this won't do. I've let you off the Minuets and Gavottes, but I insist on the Country Dances. Let me see, Lieutenant Blewforth, I have the very Vis à Vis you are looking for—Mrs. Georgina Bean, widow of the late Captain Bean, of your own Service. She will like to hear the latest Marine Information."

Blewforth struck his colours with an almost humble salute.

"Mr. Chalkley," the Beau continued, "Miss Margery Mansel, a young lady fresh from boarding-school, will certainly suit your accomplishments. Treat her kindly, sir. Mr. Golightly, I insist on your dancing with Lady Jane Vane—your father and hers were intimate friends. Mr. Harthe-Brusshe, your respected father tells me that he has a particular desire you should dance with Miss Mimsy; she's an heiress, sir, and as good as she is wealthy. Come, come, gentlemen, make no doubt that I shall find a partner for every one of you."

The young gentlemen, a little stiffer, a little more awkward, followed Mr. Ripple very mildly across the room. The rest of the Assembly fluttered quite perceptibly at their approach.

Lovely had no opportunity of asking Phyllida to dance with him as by the time he had crossed the room, she was standing opposite Mr. Moon. So he hurried up to Miss Sukey Morton who flashed her black eyes and took his arm with all the grace in the world and discussed the attraction of the British Army with much fan-play and volubility. He met Phyllida in the course of the dance and begged her hand for the Cotillon, but she shook her head gravely with a glance in the direction of old General Morton, and Charles passed on to less interesting encounters much exasperated by the impertinence of old age.

"Why aren't you a soldier, Mr. Lovely?" asked Miss Morton in a wondering voice.

"I like to pull the sheets over my head when I sleep," said Charles very solemnly, "but soldiers always have to put them on top of a pole."

"Oh! but think of war and fortresses and sieges and bivouacks."

"I dislike war, I object to fortresses. For sieges I lack the patience and I abominate bivouacks."

"But the uniform is so gay," persisted Miss Morton, "and so martial."

"A footman's, ma'am, is twice as gay and three times as martial."

"Nay, I vow you're jealous of the Army."

"Madam, is that surprizing, when Miss Morton inclines so much to scarlet?"

"Nay, now you are laughing at me," she pouted, "and I hate to be laughed at. Are you a friend of Mr. Chalkley?"

"Indeed, I hope I may describe myself as such," said Charles.

"Does he paint landskips as an Amateur?" inquired cunning Miss Sukey Morton.

"Not that I am aware of."

The disappointment visible on her countenance recalled the incident of the Valentine, and he made haste to add:

"Though now I come to think of it, I found him cutting out an ace of hearts one day last week."

"An ace of hearts?" said Miss Morton very innocently, "why what would he do that for?"

"I asked him as much, and he muttered something about a torn velvet-patch. But his behaviour that day was monstrous odd altogether, for I remember I found him later on the bowling green of the *Blue Boar* picking snowdrops, and when I rallied him, he asked me for a rhyme to ' white.' "

Miss Morton danced for the rest of the evening as though her scarlet heels were little flames.

The hands of the clock were nearing the magick hour of the last Cotillon, and everybody was hurrying in search of partners and places; when the appearance of Gog and Magog, with Mr. Ripple's marble pedestal, warned everybody that the Great little Man was about to make an announcement. Everybody waited with extreme deference and not a whisper disturbed the religious peace. The room was quite still save for the tinkle of jewellery and the slow sighing of the fans.

The Beau ascended his pedestal, calm and majestick while the listeners craned their necks to attention.

"My Lords, Ladies and Gentlemen. You are doubtless all aware that we have to lament the sudden death of that respected model of fortitude and perseverance, Sir Jeremy Dummer."

A sympathetick murmur floated along the wind of the fans.

"I am happy to tell you that he died as he lived, fighting. He died, if I may use so vulgar a metaphor, in harness—the harness of an old war-horse who, having fought the foes of England during his prime, continued to fight the greatest foe of England during his decay. That energy which erstwhile displayed itself in the trenches of War enabled him for twenty-one years to persecute by every means in his power that enemy of all of us—the Gout.

"He sought to starve it into capitulation by restricted diet, he tried to storm it by sudden charges of Chalybeate. My Lords, Ladies and Gentlemen, it was in the middle of one of these gallant sallies that he died. In a word, he was half-way through a glass of the cleansing liquid when death overtook him. There it stood, that partially empty glass beside the dead form of the veteran. May we not regard this relick as the tears of Æsculapius? Shall we not enshrine these sparkling drops in a lachrymatory and, having sealed the sacred fluid with the city seal, shall we not set it in a prominent part of our civick museum? My Lords, Ladies and Gentlemen, we shall. I have consulted with my brother the Mayor of this town, and he has agreed.

"Moreover, let me remind you of the last words of the great Socrates, his last injunction to his friend to sacrifice a cock to Æsculapius. Let us also, in memory of our deceased exemplar, present a new tap to our publick fountain and so sacrifice, my lords, ladies and gentlemen, not a cock, but a turncock to Æsculapius."

The Great little Man here paused to wipe away the

tears of sorrow and the heat of the atmosphere. " It seems," he continued, " out of place to make any announcement of a new diversion, but pleasure is as inexorable as death."

Here the audience seemed to murmur a mournful assent. " Next Tuesday at 7 o'clock precisely will be held the Chinese Masquerade. This, as you are aware, limits our costumes to those authorized by gold-lackered cabinets and teacups of blue china. I myself shall act as Gold Mandarin and my young friend Mr. Charles Lovely will be the Blue Mandarin. There will be a grand minuet of Cathay, but I will not detain you now with farther particulars of this entertainment. I hope that we shall hold masquerades of assorted characters until May, when we shall make an attempt to start the Fêtes Champêtres which were so successful last year.

" Finally, my Lords, Ladies and Gentlemen, you are aware that an incident of an unpleasantly obtrusive habit deterred us from Terpsichore on Monday night. I am, indeed, happy to say that the curtain has fallen upon the whole affair without a dissentient voice. I should have been inexpressibly grieved if the gloom consequent upon the defiance of my authority, had been at all lasting. May I add that the rebels—if I may call them so without offence—have acted in the handsomest manner and have offered to set up in the portico of these rooms a tablet commemorating the temporary cloud upon your delight. I should be more than mortal if I were not proud of such a token of confidence in my despotism.

" My Lords, Ladies and Gentlemen, I am your very grateful, humble, and obliged servant to command."

The Beau's descent from his pedestal was the signal for much waving of lace handkerchiefs and fans. There were cries of ' Bravo, Beau,' ' Viva, Ripple ! '

Finally when old Lord Vanity stepped up to the dignified lord of ceremonies and solemnly offered him his noted jade snuffbox full to overflowing of the richest brown Rappee, and when the Beau, having dropped his jewelled fingers into the modish soil, drew them forth and raised them to his aquiline nose, a stillness fell upon the room, and above the silence the sniffs of the great Beau, three in number, were distinctly heard by all. It was as if he wished them Good Health. But this was not enough for the Exquisite Mob. Somebody—it may have been our hero—ran post haste for a bottle of champagne, and somebody else rushed off for goblets. Presently, the prettiest Impromptu in the world was enacted, and very proud indeed were the spectators of a scene memorable for many years in the chronicles of fashion.

Delicately veined hands untwisted the silver wire and tore off the gold cap. Somebody fetched a corkscrew, somebody clenched the sombre green bottle between his brocaded knees. An arm tapering to snowy peaks pulled at the unwilling cork. A fairy explosion was followed by the dewy vapours of long imprisoned sunshine. The amber liquid sparkled and bubbled and flowed over the many faceted goblet in cream and foam.

The Beau mounted once more upon his pedestal and drank to the pleasure, health, and beauty of the company, while Lord Vanity and my Lady Bunbutter quaffed an answering toast in deputy for the lords, ladies and gentlemen present. Salvoes of well-bred applause pattered round the room, and the Beau's triumph was hailed with acclamations.

And you, beautiful women and fine gentlemen, roses and carnations of an older century, nothing remains of you for us. Your very perfume is but a name. You are no more to the world of to-day than those glossy candles that spluttered to death in gilt sockets. And yet, from the ruin of elegance, one relick of that famous evening remains; for the silver wire of the bottle of champagne, flung heedless to the ground, caught in a flounce of some Beauty's petticoat. Long ago the gossamer stuff mouldered, long ago was Beauty herself a skeleton, but the wire cherished by Beauty's family may still be seen in a glass-topped table in the corner of a quiet library somewhere in the broad Midlands. O insignificant wire, you are more durable than the flowers who despised you!

And now another famous ball waned to a close, and all the world of taste and fashion went home to bed.

CHAPTER X

AFTER THE ASSEMBLY

MR. CHARLES LOVELY walked back with Mr. Anthony Clare to the *Blue Boar*, and joined Mr. Francis Vernon in the Coffee Room.

The latter noticed that Clare frowned slightly when he saw him, and explained, almost apologetically, that he had moved thither from his lodgings in the Crescent. Charles was delighted and immediately proposed a game of hazard.

"You'll play, Tony?" he said eagerly.

"Not I," his friend answered. "I'm too sleepy, for 'tis confoundedly fatiguing to be on such polite behaviour for so long."

"That's true indeed," cried Charles, "and therefore we need recreation the more." With this he gave a tug at the bell-pull of flowery chintz, and presently Mr. Daish who had sent the waiters to bed, came yawning to answer the summons.

"Daish, bring two bottles of Burgundy like the fine fellow and good landlord that you are."

"Yes, Mr. Lovely, certainly, your honour, but I hope your honour will be careful with the bottles; it would be a terrible thing for the house if the watch was murdered as they nearly was twice over last week," said Mr. Daish, crumpling into obsequiousness at the impudence of his request, and retreating sidelong from the room.

Mr. Clare, seeing that it was useless to argue Charles out of his determination, took a seat by the fire.

"Egad," said Lovely, "what a jealous dog it is, he won't play, but can't bear to go to bed." Clare gave the fire a meditative poke.

"What shall it be, Mr. Vernon? Ecarté?"

"With pleasure."

"Or picket?"

"As you will."

"Why, then, picket, and if we find we grow too sleepy to count our sequences, we shall, at any rate, not be too sleepy to trickle dice out of a box, eh?"

Charles turned with these words to take some unbroken paquets of playing cards from a small mahogany cabinet hanging against the wall. The picture presented was a friendly one as the two men seated themselves at the card table. The fire was burning brightly and rosy shadows flickered over the ceiling. The curtains were close drawn and the ample flowers of their pattern seemed to retain somehow the warmth and the light. By the side of the grate sat Tony in a high grandfather's chair. He had taken off his wig and was staring meditatively at the crisp curls, as it reposed on his knee. The buckles of his shoes spat tiny glints of flame—red, blue and green. Presently he leaned across to a small bookshelf and took down some dry inn volume, but the print danced in the fire-light and very soon he was dozing peacefully, while his wig slipped to the ground and became a pleasant couch for a large tabby cat to purr away comfortable hours.

At the table sat Vernon and Lovely face to face, and the green baize made a prim battlefield for the debonair antagonists. It was a meadow-fight viewed from towering Olympus. Here was pasture profitable enough to some: to others barren as the unharvested sea. No crescent moon lighted it, no sun parched the fresh greenery whose four tall candles flickered only to chamber tempests, storms of tapestry, keyhole zephyrs. At either end were ranged round guineas in wicked little heaps, and along the borders stood serried packs of cards, shorn of their meaner numbers as becomes the apparelled duel of picket. These had been flung contemptuously on to the floor and the survivors lay face downwards on the table with a new and alluring slimness. Their backs were so innocent—mere festoons of flowers and bouquets of rosebuds; yet their very innocence only served to enhance the red and black determination of their faces. How the royal cards reflected in their appearance the temper of their courts. How sombre-suited went the Queen of Spades, how pensive seemed her consort, while the savage Ace was hung with garlands of mourning and sable flowers of Proserpine. The Queen of Diamonds looked harassed; the Knave had a lean eye and the King himself seemed peaked and careworn. The Club Court was a swarthy and more brutal counterpart of the gay Hearts, and the gay Hearts, with ripe dewy mouths, had yet a certain sly sensuality that bred distrust.

Then the tournament began. The stacked guineas sprawled in golden disarray and dwindled and swelled and tinkled to the tune of the game.

Charles was winning. Five times he had made the grand Repique, five times the gallant Pique, thrice Capote had taken captive twelve hostile cards to be redeemed with rippling guineas. Ace, King, Queen, Knave, Ten came in sequences as month succeeds to month. His hands were palaces for the abode of many courtiers. They were picture galleries of the oldest kings and queens in Europe. If he threw away Spades, he took up the red Hearts for which he longed. If he discarded Diamonds, he gained a lusty host of Clubs to serve his purpose.

At last Vernon, who had lost steadily for a pair of hours—six games at an average price of thirty guineas a game—declared he would fight no longer against his adversary's good fortune. "Moreover," he added, "so much counting has set my brain in a whirl."

"As you will," said Charles, who would have liked to

continue with picket, but could not refuse to give his opponent an opportunity to avenge himself at another game.

So they turned to Ecarté.

And now his fortune deserted him. Each time Vernon dealt he turned up a King, and Charles began to dread their florid appearance, as some ambitious minister dreads the veering of his master's favour. Those kings who had hitherto been numbered in his hands in fours and threes, those puppet kings, had won a new dignity from the only game which accords them their rightful place at the head of the pack; each one had acquired, it seemed, a personality that threatened him. Time after time were his Jeux de Règle defeated by the most astonishing combinations of ill luck.

So many times did those confounded monarchs affront him face upwards on the serene baize that he began to suspect Vernon of being a sort of gamester Warwick, a maker and unmaker of kings. Indeed, he went so far as to watch his deals rather narrowly and, being unable to detect anything amiss, became heartily ashamed of his suspicions.

It was now five o'clock of a chill morning; the fire had sunk into ashes, and dawn would soon shoot her icy arrows into the slow-flying bulk of night.

Clare was still asleep in the armchair, but presently the stealthy cold waked him and he jumped up; the candles were guttering away; the burgundy was drunk; the room smelt stale.

"Come to bed, Charles," he cried out.

Lovely, who had lost at Ecarté considerably more than he had won at Picket, drew back the curtains for answer. The dawn was in the East.

He blew out the candles one after another, and in the unreal morning twilight, the aftermath of smoke curled like an outworn pleasure into extinction save of a foul odour.

"We have still a grey hour for the dice," said Charles.

"As you will," replied Vernon.

The dice boxes were brought out, and the ivory cubes began to dance; strange fancies assailed Clare as he watched the gamesters; morbid imaginations, caught from the chilly atmosphere, froze his reason, and the rattle of the dice acquired a macabre significance. They clicked like the hoofs of horses on an iron-bound road. Then they were the castanets of a sinister dance. Soon they were the shaken ribs of Death, the king of dancers, and at the end no more than a baby's rattle, insistent, importunate, maddening.

Charles was winning again.

The various faces of the cubes took fantastick likenesses. *Two* was a patched beauty, leaden-eyed, pallid, pleasure-doomed. *Five* was a skewbald cat and *four* a plum cake. *Six* was a ladder to some evil house. *Three* was a necklace of jet, *one* a Pierrot's velvet eye.

Charles was still winning.

The irresponsibleness of the dice annoyed Clare. They tumbled and rolled so gaily, and it was mortifying to see a man enslaved by acrobats of ivory. The bodies, too, with their absurd waists were like women whom extravagant stays had driven to vomit sweetmeats.

Charles had won. The casement swung open in the sudden winds of dawn; the room was tinted with the cold colours of sunrise. The three men stumbled upstairs disdainful of the morning's gold. A guinea slipped from Lovely's pocket and tinkled down to the foot of the stairs to reward the little scullery-maid who was even now yawning on her pallet upstairs.

A thrush tuned his melodies against the swift coming of Spring, and the purple leaf-buds welcomed the sun.

CHAPTER XI

NOX ALBA

CHARLES was tempted to deprive himself of sleep for the pleasure of bedabbling his pale silk stockings with dew, but vanity killed romance and the fresh light enchanted a still unruffled couch. So he flung his coat over a chair, and the heavy pockets chinked as they fell back against the taper legs. His prayers were all to rosy Aurora when the fragrant linen sheets flowed like water over his parched brows.

Sleep could not pass the melodious batteries of many birds, and Lovely's brain had captured something of the time's clarity. The clock has many secret hours, but those who would know them must follow their slow pilgrimage wide awake. What castles men build to the pipes of the morning!

The world was waking up. Outside the talk of hostlers grew so loud that the birds fled from the inn yard to the still deserted bowling green.

Soon he heard the jangle of pails, the swish of mops and from time to time the sound of a horse's hoof striking the cobbles with a clap. In the distance a posthorn endowed the air with silver tongues. Charles followed its course along the London road. He pictured the cumbrous vehicle swinging in its straps between the black February hedgerows. He saw the postillions blinking sleepy eyes to the Eastern sun. He saw the great London road like a tape-measure unfolded from the gilded case that was London. Already he was at Knightsbridge watching some townbred maid gathering cresses in the little stream. Now he was spurring the horses to a fine lather, for he could see the grooms in a black knot by the *White Horse* cellars. In a trice he was taking the air in St. James' Street, and then suddenly he was a little boy picking his way through Westminster mud beside his mother who was carrying a bouquet of violets to their narrow house near St. John's Church. And now it was winter, and the sea-coal was burning sullenly: there were no violets, and heavy on the leaden afternoon he heard the bell tolling in Millbank Gaol. "God save the poor soul, the marshes will be icy cold to-night," said his mother, and he knew that some prisoner had escaped.

"How late your father is," she went on as she opened a cupboard, set in the panelled wall, to reach for plates and dishes. Then she told him to get out the candlesticks—beautiful silver candlesticks with swan-like necks and curious mazy lines around their bases. The candlesticks were nowhere to be found.

"Where can they be?" exclaimed his mother, pausing to help in the search. Then he heard a sigh and was told to ask Mrs. Gruffle, the landlady, for the brass bedchamber candlesticks. He rather liked these: there was always a delightful quagmire of grease in the little plate where the socket rested—grease that could be moulded into queer little pliable shapes, with shreds of tobacco stuck around for fur. When he came back to the parlour, he saw his father with his legs on the bars of the grate.

"They had to go, my dear, they had to go," the latter was saying.

"They were my mother's."

"I know, I know, but z——ds! You wouldn't have me fail Dicky Claribut?"

"But sure they were not worth——"

"Oons! I pledged my best buckles to him; the candlesticks were for his gentleman. I'm devilish sorry, my dear, but, 'faith, 'twas not to be avoided, and here's young Charles! Charles, my boy, never play, or, if you do, play deep and win."

"Don't put such ideas into the boy's mind," said his mother anxiously.

"Oddslife, my dear, be very sure the ideas are there already."

"How can you have the heart to persist when you know. . . ."

"The heart, madam?" interrupted his father. "Let me tell you that the hearts of the Lovelys are all of a piece—and 'tis cardboard."

Our hero came to his elegant self with a start and was back in Curtain Wells with hot eyelids, and thoughts continually racing over the flowery wall-paper.

It was not long, however, before he was once more in pursuit of the past.

And now he was seated beside his handsome father in a chariot. They were both in mourning and he thought how well the black frogged riding-coat became his parent. As for himself, his black sattin breeches set his teeth on edge as he tried to scratch his knee.

"Where are we going?" he was asking.

"To your mother's brother, Sir George Repington of Repington Hall."

"That's the man whose letters made her cry?"

"The same, young Charles," said Mr. Lovely, ogling a dairy-maid through his black-rimmed perspective, as the object of his glances shrank into a hedge, powdered with cow-parsley, and closed her eyes against the dust of their chariot.

Then, without any warning, they were driving through a stately park, and as they turned a corner, Mr. Lovely senior exclaimed " Good G . . .! A cemetery indeed!" Charles looked up and saw a field full of small cypresses with rank grass growing between them.

His father, who was looking rather pale, signed to the postboy to stop, and "Charles," said he, "do you go on up to the Hall, knock at the door and ask for your uncle, Sir George Repington. I'll wait for you here."

As he set out in obedience to his father he heard him mutter. "This was the very place. I swear this was the place, and not an apple tree left." And then Charles, diminutive enough in his black suit with miniature small-sword of cut steel, was asking two enormous footmen in canary-coloured velvet for Sir George Repington. They looked at him and laughed.

"My uncle," said Charles solemnly.

And they laughed again, but one of them murmured, 'This way,' and walked up a very wide and very slippery staircase, while Charles stumped up behind him. Half way, his sword belt came undone, and the sword clattered down upon the polished oak stairs with a noise that seemed to resound a dozen times through the quiet house. As he did not dare to keep the canary-coloured gentleman waiting, he picked up the toy weapon, clutched it tight in his left hand and entered a big dark room where a gentleman with iron grey close cropped hair sat reading in a chair with a very tall back, his wig balanced upon his toes.

"What the d——l's this?" asked the grey gentleman jumping up.

"Your honour's nephew," said the yellow gentleman.

"Eh! what! leave us, sirrah," and "What do you want?" he said, turning to Charles.

Charles could only watch the long furrow over his nose and wondered how deep it was, when the grey gentleman caught sight of the small sword.

"Eh! what the d——l! give me that," and snatching the weapon, he broke it over his knee and flung it into the grate.

"Please, sir, my father sent me to see you."

"Who's he?"

"Valentine Lovely, sir."

"Good G——! Good G——!" muttered the old gentleman. "And Mrs. Lovely? Did she send you too?"

"Mrs. Lovely's dead, sir."

The grey gentleman looked across the room at a large painting of a girl in white dress skipping with a rope of roses.

"Please, sir," said young Charles, "I think that is Mrs. Lovely."

"It was, boy; it was."

"I wish I had known her then," said Charles.

"Is your name George, boy?" inquired the grey gentleman in a tone that was half eager.

"No, sir, 'tis Charles—after the Prince of Wales."

"A Papist, eh?" said the grey gentleman bitterly. "George was too honest a name for that scoundrel. Well, boy, you can stay."

"Please, sir, I'd rather go back to my father," said the boy. "He's waiting for me."

"Then go and be d——d," said the grey gentleman, and he walked over to the window.

Poor little Charles was left standing alone in the big room. He waited a moment, but as the grey gentleman did not turn his head, he edged his way towards the great door. When he reached it, he looked round at his uncle. The latter was still staring out of the window. The child gave a puzzled sigh and with both hands succeeded in turning the handle. The clocks seemed to tick very loudly as he breathlessly closed the door and set out to descend the wide staircase. The canary-coloured gentlemen having vanished he could hold on to the balustrade with both hands without shame. As he crossed the green sunlit lawn, a blackbird flew into the shrubbery with a shrill note of alarm.

Then he was in the chariot with his father, and this time he was really fast asleep.

And now he was boy and man at once. The picture of the girl with roses became his mother as he had known her, pale and sad. Then it would change and become Miss Phyllida Courteen, strangely like his mother; and sometimes the Queen of Diamonds would be mopping and mowing in a frame of golden Georges.

At last these many dancing visions forsook his brain, and he slept a dreamless sleep, not waking until high noon of a wet and gusty day. When he reached the coffee-room, he found Mr. Francis Vernon perusing the latest edition of Mr. Hoyle, and as the weather was dirty, agreed to give Mr. Francis Vernon his revenge.

This favour was accorded in the handsomest manner possible, and when, late in the afternoon, the young gentlemen all returned from hunting, Mr. Charles Lovely owed Mr. Francis Vernon rather more than he could very easily pay.

No doubt the latter's success is to be ascribed to his opportune purchase of the latest edition of Mr. Hoyle.

CHAPTER XII

WET DAYS

IF cards are the devil's playthings, wet days are certainly his select playtime; and all the days before the Chinese Masquerade were very wet indeed. The Exquisite Mob returned from the Pump Room remarkably depressed in spirit. The forenoons passed away in the coffee-houses and the shops, but in the afternoons when it was wont to exercise itself and air its modes the stuffy parlours of Curtain Wells became vastly tiresome.

The result was that all the young gentlemen played very hard and very deep and very late, and Mr. Charles Lovely hardest, deepest, and latest of all. The old gentlemen all found their gout teased them more lamentably. Even Beau Ripple grew tired of reading the Epodes of Horace and the Letters of Tully to his grey Angora cat. The ladies played Quadrille and talked scandal, while some of them, I grieve to say, supplied a foundation for much of the gossip.

Candlelight intrigues flourished, and there were not a few tragedies in porcelain, when some Sir John Vulcan, returning too soon from his favourite coffee-house, caught my Lady Venus in too ardent converse with some young Ensign Mars. Very red grew the gallant Ensign—near as red as his coat, while Sir John blustered and swore so loud that he almost cracked the walls with his foxhunting voice, and my Lady Venus fluttered her fan to the pace of her dainty heart, tinkling out exquisite little lies as soulless as unreal, but quite as fascinating as some frail musical box. And the trio acted and declaimed their time-honoured parts to a keyhole audience of lady's maid and gentleman's gentleman.

Very diverting the footmen of Curtain Wells found the story that evening, and very savoury it was voted below stairs—nearly as savoury as the stewed trotters over which it was related.

And so the days went by.

Pitter-pat went the rain on the window-panes, pitter-pat went the cards on the card tables, pitter-pat went the spoons in the coffee-cups, pitter-pat went my lady's shoes across the floor to watch for the third person, pitter-pat went many fans and many hearts.

Mrs. Courteen decked herself in the rosiest sattins, bade Betty close the shutters, draw the curtains and light the candles. Then she composed herself to read the last number of the *Prattler* until a knock at the door announced the arrival of Mr. Gregory Moon and Major Constantine Tarry. Both vowed that their enchantress looked vastly well, and nodded agreement with her assertion that she believed she had a very fresh colour, no doubt due to the tonick air of the Wells.

"It flushes one merely to go upstairs," she declared. "I vow I take as much exercise in going up and down stairs as I do in taking my morning saunter to the Pump Room." The climb was euphemistically known as the Saunter. "Lud, lud," continued the widow, "complexions are droll things."

"Monstrous elusive, ma'am," said the Justice rather gloomily.

"Ha, ha," yapped the Major, "I pickled my skin in the Low Countries."

"That would be injudicious for a delicate surface. Height, Major," sighed Mrs. Courteen, "height! How we pine for it. Mortals! Dear! Dear!"

"I remember I once examined a vagabond who claimed to have been there," remarked Mr. Moon. "We ordered him a whipping."

"What became of him?" asked Mrs. Courteen.

"I believe he died shortly afterwards. Well! well! Kill or cure! Kill or cure!"

The widow flashed her white shoulders in an elaborate shudder.

"Talking of kill or cure," exclaimed the Major, jumping up, "did I ever repeat my tale of the Hessian captain?"

"Probably," said Mr. Moon mildly.

"What do you mean, sir?"

"You are somewhat inclined to repetition, sir."

Mrs. Courteen hurriedly assured Major Tarry that she for one had positively never heard it.

"He did not say 'have you heard my story, ma'am,'" the Justice went on in the calm voice of despair. "He said 'have I repeated it?' I merely remarked that he probably has—dozens of times!"—Mr. Moon burst out in the nearest approach to a passionate enunciation that he ever attained.

"I vow you do him an injustice. Pray tell us the story, Major," and the widow tapped the sword-arm of the infuriated soldier three times. The painted chicken-skin fell with so persuasive a touch that the Apple sank to its normal position and, having turned his back on Mr. Moon, the Major began his tale.

"Well, madam, you must know that in the year . . . but before I tell this story, I should like to give you some idea of the disposition of his Majesty's forces."

Mrs. Courteen sighed. She knew what giving an idea of the disposition of the forces meant. It was useless to protest, however, for the Major was already marching round the room in search of appropriate furniture.

He instantly declared that Mr. Moon's chair was necessary to the illustration.

"Pray excuse me, sir," he rapped out.

The Justice, with a reproachful glance at Mrs. Courteen, moved ponderously to the couch.

"Well, madam, here are Thistleton's Dragoons," and he gave a twist to the chair as he spoke.

"Oh, yes! Very droll!" said Mrs. Courteen.

"Here," the Major continued, seizing another chair and planting it vigorously down by the couch, "here is Buckley's Foot."

"Mine, sir," said the Justice.

"Your what, sir?"

"My foot, sir, not Buckfeast's."

The Major withered his rival with an eloquent silence.

"Here am I," he said, snatching from the mantelpiece a diminutive Worcester shepherdess and placing it between the two chairs.

The widow gazed anxiously at the pastoral soldier. It belonged to the owner of the house.

"Here is Tournai. You'll pardon me, sir, but I should be obliged if you would hand me the couch," said the Major fiercely.

The Justice moved wearily to the window-seat. That, at all events, was a fixture, he reflected gratefully.

After much exertion Tarry succeeded in moving the couch in front of the door, so that if the piece of furniture in question was a poor representation of what it was intended to convey, it certainly made of Mrs. Courteen's front parlour something very like an impregnable fortress.

"I should be glad to give you some idea of the enemy's earthworks," said the Major with a covetous glance in the direction of the chintz window-curtains.

Mrs. Courteen's fleeting expression of dismay warned him to prune the luxuriance of his examples, and as at that moment a tap at the door necessitated the instant surrender of Tournai to admit Mrs. Betty farther operations were stopped. Moreover, the sudden capitulation involved the fracture of the Worcester shepherdess which, as Mr. Moon sardonically supposed, served to illustrate the point of the story.

"You're killed, Tarry; you're dead as mutton. I doubt a cure is inconceivable."

Betty held a note in her hands.

"From Bow Ripple," she whispered excitedly.

CHAPTER XIII

MONARCHY IN ACTION

MRS. COURTEEN scarcely believed Betty spoke the truth. Never could she remember such a gigantick wave of elation as swept over her on receipt of the Beau's letter. Yet, without a doubt, it was true. There was the royal notepaper and, as she reverently examined the outside, there was the river of the house of Ripple meandering in regular curves through meadows of sealing-wax. She marked the colour—lilac—as if faintly to adumbrate the imperial purple of Rome. Moreover, the sprinkled sand, a few particles of which still adhered to the surface, smelt of Courts. There were years of authority between the lines of the graceful superscription; the very "C" of the Crescent bellied in the breezes of Royal favour. Major Tarry and Mr. Moon regarded her with an expression compounded of jealousy and respect. Who was this woman, this correspondent with monarchs?

"Pray excuse me, neighbours," murmured the widow, sinking into a chair. The seal crackled musically as with smooth forefinger and shapely thumb she gently withdrew the diaphanous paper from its waxen prison; so must the golden bough have sounded to the touch of Æneas.

THE GREAT HOUSE, CURTAIN WELLS,
February,
MADAM—*I shall do myself the honour of waiting upon*

you this afternoon at half-past Four o'clock in order to the discussion of an Affair of the gravest moral Importance.
In expectation, Madam, I subscribe myself,
Your obliged Servant,
HORACE RIPPLE.

"Gemini!" cried Betty, "the Bow will be here in fourteen ticks."

"Gentlemen," said Mrs. Courteen with that stateliness which follows from intercourse with Princes, "gentlemen, I must beg to be excused."

The Major and the Justice solemnly advanced and, having kissed the outstretched hand, moved sadly from the room. As they went downstairs the former mused on the unrepeated story of the Hessian Captain, while the latter vowed to insert a supplementary chapter to his great Essay on Peace which should deal with the self-esteem of retired Majors. With similar thoughts no doubt Mr. Oliver Goldsmith went home from that famous dinner when General Oglethorpe, at the instigation of Dr. Samuel Johnson, spilled the Port on the bare mahogany board in order to draw a plan of the Siege of Belgrade. At any rate, old Mr. Hardcastle talks a great deal about that famous beleaguerment in the witty and diverting farce of *She Stoops to Conquer*. Mrs. Courteen tremulously sought her toilet-glass. "An affair of the gravest moral importance." Powder judiciously distributed removed any implied indifference in the freshness of her widowed cheeks. Paleness and morality were certainly akin. As for her lemon sack, Betty vowed she would find nothing more becoming to the unique occasion.

A dignified knock at the front door put an end to any longer hesitation, and Mrs. Courteen, like the Queen of Sheba, presented herself immediately.

The Great little Man was pacing the carpet of the front parlour, but at the widow's entrance he turned on his heels with a low bow.

"We are quite alone?" he inquired.

"Solitary, indeed," replied the lady. Surely, surely he could not be contemplating an offer of marriage! Yet certainly such might well be described as an affair of the gravest moral importance. If weddings were not moral, what would become of our weak humanity?

"Madam," said the Beau. "'Tis only after long thought and exhaustive research among the social archives of Curtain Wells; 'tis only after a complete examination of my glorious predecessor, Beau Melon's notes on the amenities of Polite Cures in which he calls attention with a red cross to the special difficulty of tendering advice to perplexed visitors, that I am resolved to inform you of a fact which may distress your maternal heart, complicate your domestick arrangements, disturb your apprehensive piety and not inconceivably lend to-morrow's goblet a very wry flavour. Madam, your daughter is in love."

The widow raised two anguished hands, but Mr. Ripple continued:

"When I say in love, madam, I say so because I am not so cynical of maiden humanity as to suppose that she would sit in vivacious discourse with a young gentleman for the space of one hour and a half measured by the frequent chimes of the publick clock unless she were in love."

"You cannot mean this," palpitated the unhappy mother. "Say you cannot mean it!"

"Madam, I am not used to devoting so much valuable time to the preparation of circumstantial falsehoods. Your daughter is in love."

"But she is so young," protested the widow. "Not more than fifteen or at the most seventeen."

"To you, madam, deaf to Love's alarms, for evermore protected against his showered darts, such precocious ardour must appear improbable, but I have proof of its existence."

"Malicious tongues! The world is so censorious. It

would destroy the reputation of the mother by insinuations against the virtue of the child."

"Madam, pray allow me to narrate the unhappy but indisputable facts of the affairs. You must know that it is a part of my duties—a pleasant part, if I may say so without undue want of reserve—to inspect Curtain Garden from time to time. You will recollect that this forenoon we enjoyed for two hours a glimpse of the sun. Having been kept indoors during the last two or three days, I determined to seize the balmy occasion and perform my rural duties. I observed that the spring bulbs were remarkably forward. I noticed with pleasant anticipation of summer saunters that the paths were in good order, the gravel free from weeds. From the main Promenade I turned into the Maze."

The widow started.

"The yew hedges were neatly trimmed and I noticed some very good examples of topiary; I may mention in particular the transformation of the old Noah into a peacock whose tail will doubtless gain a more vigorous plumage from the warm weather. I wandered along contemplating the various greens of the mosses that adorn the path and muffle the footsteps in a manner extremely suitable to the decorous quiet of the surroundings. During my saunters I delight to rest my mind with the recitation of the Odes and Epodes of my poetick and pre-Christian namesake. I was embarked upon the apostrophe to Lyce:

> *Nec Coæ referunt jam tibi nec purpuræ*
> *Nec clari lapides tempora, quæ semel*
>   *Notis condita fastis*
>   *Inclusit volucris dies.*

"I had got so far, but egad! I could get no farther for the life of me. I repeated the last four lines, and in my attempts to catch the fugitive—Ah!" cried the Beau, "I have it!"

> *Quo fugit Venus? Heu quove color? decens
> Quo motus?*

or to paraphrase with an extempore couplet,

> *Where now is fled thy beauty? Where thy bloom,
> Those airy steps that charmed th' expectant room?*

"To continue, however—this elusive sentence made me lose my direction and I found myself removed from the centre of the Maze by an impenetrable hedge of yew. I was about to retrace my steps when I heard voices on the other side of the hedge. It was a duet, madam—man and maid, flute and bass viol, fife and drum, describe it how you will."

"Did you recognise the voices?"

"Madam, I did not."

"Then how—since you were not able to see over the tops of the hedges without———"

The Great little Man drew himself up.

"Madam," he said, "I regard the physical exertion of bobbing up and down as ungenteel."

"Then how do you———?"

"Because on retracing my steps I passed your maid in an attitude of vigilance, and exactly one hour and a half later I saw Miss Courteen and the aforesaid maid leave the Garden; and vastly well she looked, madam."

Mrs. Courteen asked why Mr. Ripple did not interrupt them. "'Twould surely have frightened them out of love-making for ever."

"Madam, if I am a king, I hope I am also a gentleman."

"I will call the hussy and you shall reproach her, Mr. Ripple."

"Madam, that is precisely what I am anxious to avoid. On former occasions my interference has proved futile and I cannot allow my counsel to be exposed to contempt. In confidence let me tell you that the last three elopements which I tried to stop were all successfully carried through, and I hear that the parties have lived very happily together ever since. I have vowed not to accept again the responsibleness of a prophet. My glorious predecessor, Beau Melon, mentions several instances of his advice being neglected without any ill effects and notes that it is probably injudicious to interfere unless compelled by the prospect of a duel. Let me read you his comments. '*Elopements. Tell the father. D——n Miss. She's won't listen. Fool for your pains. Fifteen times bitten—shy for evermore. Bodies more important than souls in Curtain Wells.*' An ill-constructed sentence, madam, but nevertheless full of truth."

"Then what do you advise me to do?"

"Madam, I should recommend you to pay less attention to your own heart, and give the most of your care to your daughter's."

The widow rose in a state of extreme agitation and rustled about the room to the hazard of all ware under a certain stability. Such a reproach from Mr. Ripple was more than she could bear politely.

However, presently she caught her placket in the wanton arm of a chair and after a short struggle capitulated to stillness.

She began the catalogue of natural virtues. "I vow the child has been reared on the Church Catechism, she was for ever learning collects, texts, parables, miracles, question and answer, sermons, homilies, and aspirations. If I had been allowed my own way with her education, she would have led a life of Sundays; but the late Mr. Nicholas Courteen, her father and my husband, swore the child's intelligence was become like a Crusader's tomb, scrabbled over with pious nonsense ill-digested and ill-writ. Have I not warned her a hundred times that gentlemen do not love the gawky charms of a hoyden? Have I not repeated to her the history of half a score seductions? Am I to blame? Don't I keep a maid to look after her? What else has that hussy to do? I ask you, Mr. Ripple, what else?"

"Upon my soul, ma'am, I don't very well know," murmured Mr. Ripple.

"Nothing, sir, nothing, save to dress and undress me twice a day, give an eye to my gowns and arrange my toilet table. Apparently they think that I should——" The widow broke off to ring violently for Betty in order to reproach her with a careless supervision of Phyllida.

Mr. Ripple seized the opportunity to make his farewells. He swore to himself that nothing should induce him to remonstrate again with a careless mother. He would say a friendly word to the child herself.

The widow thanked the Beau for his advice and promised to be mighty severe with Phyllida.

"Not if you will be warned by me, madam. No, no, I beg you will not think it was to urge severity that I made you this visit. No, no, it was merely to suggest prudence. Your humble servant, madam."

"Your very devoted, sir."

The widow curtsied the Beau out of the room, and, having heard the front door closed, she watched in prim disgust for the entrance of Betty.

That young woman presently came into the room.

"Well, vixen!" said the widow.

"La! ma'am, what is it?"

"Well, gypsy!"

"Not a drop in my family, ma'am, and that's more than some of the cottage-folk near by can say."

"Well, little Impropriety, what excuse have you to hand?"

Betty asked what Impropriety meant.

"Would it be stealing you mean, ma'am?"

"Well, Madam Indecency!"

Betty suddenly saw the widow's amber petticoat gleaming through the unfastened placket.

"Dear love and barley breaks! However did I come to leave that undone! Never mind, ma'am. 'Tis not as if he'd caught a sight of your smock, though for my part I should not be afraid to show clean linen to any man, Bow or whatsoever."

" 'Tis not to talk of plackets that I called you, hussy, but of packets—love-packets, notes, letters, assignations."

Betty began to understand. She remembered how they had met Mr. Ripple that morning in Curtain Garden, and at once connected the two incidents.

" 'Twould be about this very afternoon that you are talking, ma'am? "

The widow was surprized. She had expected an impregnable barrier of mock stupidity.

" It would," she now answered severely.

" Well, there now! And if I didn't say as 'twas very wrong, but indeed, he was so genteel and made such very grand bows that I didn't think as 'twould be kind to refuse him."

" Refuse him what? "

" Why, direction, ma'am, for the handsome poor soul was lost in the Maze. He was just twirling around from North to South like a weathercock on the old Parish Church at home."

" Does it take an hour and a half to direct a man out of a shrubbery? "

" No, indeed, ma'am, but hearing we was from Hampshire, he fell a-talking and said as when he was last there he was staying with my Lord Senna at Camomile Hall, and was bosom friend of Mr. the Honourable John Squills."

The widow grew interested. The latter had once attended a hunting breakfast at Courteen Grange.

" And what was the loquacious gentleman's name? "

" Ah there! indeed, 'twas wrong of me, but if I didn't go and forget to axe him! "

" Idiot! " said Mrs. Courteen, " and where does he lodge? "

" He intends to post to Bristol Well to-night."

" Is this true? "

"La, dearest ma'am, how does I know. But he spoke as though 'twas."

"You are a pair of simpletons. Lud! you might both have been ravished and no one the wiser. I doubt you both deserve a whipping."

Mrs. Courteen dismissed the subject and turned to survey the ravages of emotion on her own face. Betty retired to warn her young mistress.

The widow was considerably vexed. Vain woman as she was, she was not too dull to perceive that the Beau's complaint of her daughter levelled an indirect reproof at herself. The late Squire Courteen, a man of plethorick habit and a good seat, had broken his neck over a five-barred gate more than seven years ago. Some said his recklessness was too deliberate. Certainly the week before, young Mr. Standish had left the neighbourhood in a great hurry. Moreover, when the Will was read it appeared that a codicil had been added the day before the Squire died by which his lady had forfeited every halfpenny of his money if she married before her daughter, and by an ingenious stroke did the same if she failed to find a husband during the ensuing six months. Farther, a provision was inserted that this husband must be ten years younger than herself. It was all very much complicated and extremely malicious.

Mrs. Courteen fanned herself reflectively. She was perfectly happy in the ridiculous attentions and elderly gallantries of Major Tarry and Justice Moon. At twenty-nine she had still possessed enough florid beauty to excuse her ill-spelled love-letters. Moreover, she had a husband and was safe sport for young gentlemen who lost the hounds somewhat early in the day. When she was widowed, most of her attraction vanished. She grew fat and had to content herself with middle-aged suitors for whom she became a placid ideal on the dull journey of their lives. Mrs. Courteen continued to fan herself.

That absurd codicil drifted across her thoughts. If Phyllida married she was condemned to poverty or a young husband. Yet, after all, Moon or Tarry had enough—not much, but enough; but then both firmly believed in the annuity. The bitterness of her husband's dying jest stung her for the first time. What a fool she would be made to seem! Certainly Phyllida must not be allowed a wedding; that was the solution.

How fatiguing solutions were, to be sure! She felt quite vapoured. At any rate she would look after her for the future. If she had a gallant he should be discovered. If Betty's tale were true, why, prevention was better than cure.

"Alas!" sighed the widow. "I shall play indifferent well and yet—no matter. Perhaps I shall hold Spadille every hand of the game." Wafted by this pleasant hope, the widow sailed upstairs to assume the scarlet and black gown and the spade-patch which she wore to propitiate the cards; also to embellish her fingers with rings; also to trim her nails to a perfect curve and polish to whiteness the peering moon at their base. To such cardboard emotions was this lady come whose husband broke his neck out hunting.

CHAPTER XIV

MONARCHY IN REPOSE

ON the following morning after breakfast Mrs. Courteen produced a strip of faded rose ribband.

"Try to match this, child," she said to Phyllida.

"But, mamma, 'tis not possible. The silk is old," expostulated the daughter who was dressed and ready to take the air.

"Nothing is impossible, child," generalized the widow. "Do your best—all that is required of human beings. You may take Thomas with you."

"But, mamma, I don't want Thomas. I would rather take Betty."

"People can't always take what they desire in this world, and a very good thing too," remarked Mrs. Courteen, "for the world would be a wickeder place if they could. Betty must stay and help me."

The widow was determined to begin the supervision of her daughter recommended by Mr. Ripple. It was the old story of Sisyphus and the Stones, of Tregeagle and the Thimble; as mischievous spirits are kept occupied in Tartarus, and condemned for ever to the performance of the impossible, so was Phyllida to be kept from the temptations of idleness, in order to save, if not her soul, at any rate her reputation.

The widow apprehended that obedience would be more easily secured by guile than the direct imposition of a command.

Miss Phyllida Courteen went out that morning with a sullen little frown above her charming little nose, and walked so fast that Thomas was hard put to keep his proper distance behind her as he continued to mutter, "How long, O Lord?" with many a dolorous wheeze and mortified grunt.

In and out of a dozen haberdashers they went. All the young women behind the counters were very polite and amazingly hopeful, but when they came to pull out the long drawers filled with ribbands of every size and colour, they could only produce the gayest pinks, the most brilliant shades of rose, and though they continued to be very cheerful and persuaded themselves and their rather petulant customer that the match was as near as could be expected, they were quite unsuccessful, and the ribbands were put back in the drawers to await a less exacting purchaser.

Finally Phyllida, turning out of the tenth shop, heard St. Simon's clock strike eleven. It was a moderately fine morning, and she knew her beau was at that moment turning into Curtain Garden. She stamped her foot with vexation and disappointment.

"Oh Thomas, Thomas! was ever such a mad errand before?" complained his mistress.

"Velvet! Vanity! and a-whoring after strange silks," groaned Thomas.

"Thomas," said Miss Courteen in her most engaging voice, "you would do anything for me?"

"With God's help," agreed the footman.

"And you'd do a great deal for a shilling-piece?"

"To spite Beelzebub," said Thomas.

"Then, Thomas, step down to the Western Colonnade, make my compliments to Miss Sukey Morton, say I hope she is better of her cold, and will she give Miss Phyllida Courteen the pleasure of her company to Mrs. Pinkle's Conversazione. But perhaps you'll forget that long message?"

Thomas replied in accents of unctuous solemnity:

"Better of her cold and quite recovered."

"Yes, but there's more."

"Waste not, want not," he answered severely.

"Oh, Lud! I suppose I were wise to write it down," with which Miss Courteen tried the eleventh haberdasher. The pinks were just as light, the carmines as crude and fresh as ever.

But at the opposite counter it was possible to buy the most agreeable paper; so Miss Courteen bought a quire, and also a box of wafers marked with a laurel-wreathed C. Then she borrowed old Mrs. Rambone's crow-quill pen with which the accounts were made up every evening in the little back parlour, and Miss Lettice Rambone politely cleared a corner of the counter and brought out a standish, while Phyllida put her swansdown muff on the chair because, though it was high enough to pull about haberdashery, it wasn't high enough for writing-letters. After much arrangement, she wrote:

"MY DEAREST MISS MORTON,—*I hope you are better o your cold. I am truly anxious that you should come and see me this afternoon at four o'clock on a matter of great importance. I am truly distressed by a most unlucky Event. I doubt my dearest Sukey can guess what disturbs her*

Ever affect. and truly devoted
PHYLLIDA.

P.S. *Pray come.*
P.P.S. *I saw a Red Coat not unknown to a certain young lady now resident at Curtain Wells. The said Red Coat made a most polite bow.*"

Ph. C.

Then Phyllida sealed the note with one of her new wafers, and Thomas unscrewed the knob of his tall stick and put the note inside and the shilling-piece in his waistcoat pocket and marched away down the High Street, while Phyllida rushed off with her muff held up to the East wind which was quite cold when one was walking so fast. For the Western Colonnade, you turned to the right, but if you were going to Curtain Garden, you turned to the left, and Phyllida turned to the left.

She had to pass the end of the Crescent on her way, and hurried past, afraid for her life to see Mrs. Courteen sailing round the corner. She was now outside the Great House, and could not help looking up to the big bow-windows to see if Mr. Ripple was there. There he was, very calm and very dignified, but a little out of focus because his windows all had such very thick glass. She caught his eye, and the Great little Man smiled at her. She smiled back and blushed, thinking of the meeting of yesterday. Suddenly the window shot up, and Phyllida turned her head to see the Beau beckoning. She stopped in dismay, while Mr. Ripple, having first spread his handkerchief on the sill, leaned out to speak to her.

"Pray pardon this ungenteel summons, my dear Miss Courteen, but if you would not consider yourself compromised by such an adventure, I should be vastly honoured by your inspection of some proper new prints which have fallen into my hands."

Miss Courteen was overwhelmed by this invitation. What could she do but murmur assent?

The Beau, with a delightfully suave gesture, hurried to open the front door for Miss Courteen who tripped up the dazzling white steps, all swansdown and blushes.

Mr. Ripple begged her to follow him upstairs to the drawing-room and be seated before the fire.

It was a fine high room of good proportions, with three large sash-windows and a wrought-iron balcony running along the breadth of the house. The walls were pannelled and painted white, and the floor was stained and varnished to a glaze of immense brilliancy. The rugs scattered about it were Aubusson, of rare hues in fawn and puce and faded lavender and old rose interwoven with queer dead greens. There were several prints on the walls, mostly after Watteau and Fragonard. The whole room wore the indescribable air that is only to be found in the house of a bachelor of comfortable means, good taste and a certain age. There was no trace of a woman's hand in its arrangement, and yet one felt that the owner, through long seclusion from the other sex, had softened towards it with the years until, secure at last, he was able to admit a feminine cirrhus into the limpid and rarefied air of his remote celibacy.

Phyllida, as she watched the firelight ripple in orange wavelets across the surface of the blue and white Dutch tiles set on either side of the hob, wondered what the Beau meant by this sudden invitation.

Just then he begged to be excused for a moment while he fetched the portfolio containing his new purchase.

She heard the door gently closed and looked round the room.

How tall and white it was, just like Mr. Ripple's hand, smooth and white and exquisitely shaped. Outside, the grey weather mellowed the ivory of the room. There was a curious stillness as of frost, and she watched the reflection of the fire leaping in opalescent miniature about the high windows. There was a new spinet, set at an angle to the rest of the furniture, in a case of light-coloured wood, painted with cupids, zephyrs and roses, all waxen-pale. The tall, quiet chamber began to depress her spirits, so that she felt compelled to strike the extreme treble note of the spinet which through the stillness rang out like the unwonted pipe of a bird in a hot August woodland.

At last, Phyllida, whose whole body was beginning to tingle with the effort of waiting in such breathless quiet, heard some one coming upstairs. Gog, the Beau's diminutive negro, entered with a silver tray; on which small and shining lake swam coffee cups like swans or fairy shells. The Great little Man followed close upon the dusky heels of his squire and soon Phyllida found herself sipping her coffee in easy conversation with the King of Curtain Wells.

"Do you know the Maze?" he was asking.

"Oh yes," said Phyllida.

"A pleasant spot, cool and green."

"It is indeed."

"I often sit there," said the Beau.

"'Tis a pleasant spot."

"Less fortunate than my poetick namesake, I have no plane-tree there, no long-buried Falernian; but I am unjust to my time, for, after all, I have Curtain Garden and Chalybeate that springs from the depths of earth," continued the Beau, half to himself.

Phyllida was not quite sure what he was talking about, but agreed politely.

"My dear Miss Courteen," said the Beau suddenly, "may I say something very abrupt and perhaps intolerably free, but nevertheless something which I feel ought to be said."

"Oh yes, sir," Phyllida replied, wishing devoutly that she was well out of this tall, white room.

"My dear Miss Courteen," he went on, "I am a man who knows something of life on its merely social side. I have been an observer, if I may say so, a naturalist of humanity. My self-chosen attitude has forbidden me all passion, save that which is the recognized privilege of an audience. Of love I am supposed to know nothing, save in that third person whose company is unwelcome and superfluous. Perhaps my devotion to the *Odes* has led me to see too many Lalages, too many Lyces. Perhaps I regard women too much as roses that bloom, scatter their sweets and die. In a word, perhaps I am unsympathetick."

"I don't think you are at all, sir," cried Phyllida, surprized by her own boldness.

"Thank you," said the Beau, with the merest hint of a tremour in his equable voice.

"But," he went on, "if I regard women as roses, I never seek to pluck them: most men do. Miss Phyllida, pray pardon a man of some age who cares more for Youth than he is willing to admit, who is not quite the phantastick, the fop, the cynick that his subjects make him out. You know what Shakespeare says: 'Each man in his time plays many parts.' I, my dear, have remained for more than thirty years faithful to one. That is why I am considered so eccentrick—well, well, I grow loquacious. My dear Miss Courteen, it is very unwise to make assignations in the pride of youth. Assignations belong to the middle-aged, the disillusioned. If you love a young gentleman, make no secret of it, and let the whole world join in your happiness; but if it be necessary to love this young gentleman in Mazes and such clandestine spots, this young gentleman is not worth so much devotion. Who is he?"

"Mr. Amor, Sir," said Phyllida, feeling half inclined to cry.

"Amor? Amor? I don't know the family. Is it by his wish these meetings are kept secret? Yes! yes! I know 'tis very romantick and very rapturous, but, believe me, my dear Miss Courteen, it is not worth the cost. You must think of your reputation."

"I do, Mr. Ripple, indeed I do—all the time!"

"Come, come then, present me to your Amor at the Chinese Masquerade. I'll talk to the rogue, and egad! we'll have the wedding in June. What do you say?"

"I don't think Mr. Amor would be very willing, and I'm sure my mamma would be monstrous vexed."

"Nonsense," said the Beau, "nonsense! You won't be happy, till you've packed yourself into a post-chaise smelling vilely of stale tobacco and horse-cloths. And when you've found some Fleet Street parson to marry you, you'll wish for a fine wedding and a bride-cake, and your tenants cheering and holloaing at the lodge-gates."

Here the Beau showed himself too unfamiliar with the mind of a young woman. The idea of eloping had never yet entered that dainty head of glistening chestnut curls; but from that moment Phyllida began to play with the notion.

"Come, come," he went on, "let's have no more of

clandestine courtship. Heiresses and dace both attract by reason of their silver: libertines and pike have much in common. Moreover, you must think of your mother."

"I doubt you don't know my mamma very well. She swears I'm but a child, but I'm not a child, am I, sir?"

Mr. Ripple put up his monocle and solemnly stared at his fair impenitent.

"You are not a very old woman."

"Besides, my mamma doesn't understand the meaning of love."

"My dear young lady," protested the Beau, "that is a very common error with the young. Don't you think that shaded lane once lisped to her footsteps? Don't you think April once broke as sweet for her?"

"Well, if it did," argued Phyllida, "she's forgotten all she ever knew."

"Come, come, I dare swear she has a secret drawer fragrant with cedar. Find it, my dear Miss Phyllida, and you'll find many old letters, many withered nosegays."

"Indeed, I've searched."

"Perhaps her escritoire is the heart."

"'Tis very well for you, sir, to talk thus, but my parents were never happy."

The Beau mentally cursed the pertinacious memories of servants.

"Then, if that was the case," he went on, "there is the greater reason for your friends to secure you against such an irreparable misadventure. Now come, you'll present me to this Mr. Amor? I may not understand all women, but trust me, I have a tolerable knowledge of men."

The pale February sun cast a watery beam through the high windows and Mr. Ripple's face caught an added lustre, was in fact so bright and kindly that Phyllida promised, subject to Mr. Amor's consent.

And soon they were both bending over the portfolio of prints—very diverting prints they were too, caricatures of the foibles of fashion.

It was certainly very delightful to see tranquil monarch and fervent maid laughing very heartily together at the most prodigious head-dress the world ever saw.

CHAPTER XV

PHŒBUS ADEST

THE Coffee-room of the *Blue Boar* wore a remarkably cheerful aspect on the evening of the day on which we have seen something of Beau Ripple's methods. There had been a splendid run from Oaktree Common across the downs to Deadman's Coppice, where a short check only lent a spice to that glorious final run across Baverstock Ridge until they killed just outside Farmer Hogbin's famous barn. And after the death what delicious musick acclaimed the deed—the baying of hounds, the chatter of maids, the clatter of horses' hoofs, the guffaws of Lieutenant Blewforth, the still louder guffaws of Farmer Hogbin mounted on his raw-boned hunter of sixteen hands, the blasts of the horns, the chink of glasses and the wind getting up in the South-west, all combined in harmonious delight. What a splendid ride home it was and how the riders went over each renowned minute of that for-ever-to-be-famous day. Lieutenant Blewforth swore he would forsake the sea for the life of a country gentleman, and everybody laughed when H.M.S. *Centaur* (so they had named Blewforth and his steed) shied at a belated calf.

"Egad! B-b-Blewforth," stammered little Peter Wingfield, "'tis lucky your stomach was trained on the roaring d-d-deep, for you pitch and roll like a sloop making Ushant."

"Ah! my boy," shouted Blewforth, "my pretty sloop don't shy like this d———d bum-boat I'm pulling."

How Mr. Golightly of Campbell's Grey Dragoons

swore such a run was better than a frontal charge at the enemy's guns and how young Tom Chalkley of the Foot stiffened all over and muttered something about the Cavalry. Indeed the only person to look glum was Mr. Anthony Clare who, though he rode better than any of them and had shown them his horse's heels all the way, missed Charles Lovely.

As they walked along the road, fading into early dusk, and heard the wind sighing in the trim hedges and saw the lights of Curtain Wells seven miles away, Clare cursed that passion for cards which made a man forsake the bleak Spring fallows for pastures of green baize.

But later when the huge cold sirloin that sailed in so sleek, sailed out like a battered wreck, and when pints of generous Burgundy had coloured life to its own rich hue, and when Mr. Daish himself had coaxed the fire to roar and blaze up the chimney, and set out the walnuts and put half a dozen ample chairs round the fire, Mr. Clare could not resist the universal content, but must laugh and make merry and relate the events of the day for the seventh time, with as much zest as any of the returned heroes.

Charles had surely been winning: he was so flushed and talked so loudly. Actually he did not possess a penny, and what was worse, owed Mr. Vernon a couple of hundred guineas. Not much, but enough when you have only cloaths to sell, and not a prospect in the world.

Presently one by one the hunters dropped off to sleep with legs outstretched and doffed wigs and long churchwarden pipes, that one by one dropped from slowly opening mouths, slid along unbuttoned waistcoats and snapped their slender stems upon the floor, until everybody except Mr. Vernon and our hero was snoring the eighth repetition of the events of that famous day.

The room was hot; the drawing of many breaths thick with fatigue, beef and Burgundy induced a meditative atmosphere; the fire no longer blazed, but sank to an intense crimson glow. Mr. Vernon counted up his gains, while Mr. Lovely pondered his losses in silence.

At last the latter got up suddenly.

"The cards?" inquired Mr. Vernon.

"Not to-night. I think I'll take the air," Charles replied.

"As you will," said the other and betook himself once more to his tablets.

Charles paused for a moment outside the Coffee-Room to take down his full black cloak and three-cornered hat. The night wind had brought in its track a melancholy drizzle of rain that suited his own melancholy mood. He wandered rather vaguely across the wide inn-yard, passed under the arch and sauntered along the deserted High Street.

To tell the truth, Mr. Lovely was very unpleasantly situated at this period. His father had been the ne'er-do-weel survivor of a long line of country squires away down in Devonshire. When he had eloped with Miss Joan Repington, to the eternal chagrin of the young lady's brother, a rich banker knighted for his loyal support of the Protestant Succession, Valentine Lovely ran through his own and his wife's fortune in the first six years of matrimony. Thence onwards they lived a hand-to-mouth existence, dependent on Valentine's luck at the tables and the inviolableness of an aunt's legacy of five thousand guineas.

Mrs. Lovely died, prematurely aged, in the birth of a still-born child, and Mr. Valentine Lovely and his young son continued to live the same haphazard existence for another ten years. Charles spent all his time with his father who in the intervals of drink and play taught his heir to step a minuet, sing a merry song, and indite a witty epigram; also he gave him a case of pistols, heavily chased with the Lovely arms, and lent him the family tree for target. Finally he made him proficient in the polite use of the smallsword and the dice-box.

Once, when an early summer made the Bath intolerably hot, Mr. Lovely and his heir posted down to

Devonshire in a crimson chariot putting up at the *Prior's Head* in Danver Monachorum. He spent a week paying unwelcome visits to the neighbouring gentry who looked askance at the crimson chariot and still more askance at the degenerate heir of the Lovelys. Valentine soon tired of so much pastoral exercise and departed to St. Germain's, leaving young Charles in the care of an old stillroom maid, now a prosperous farmer's wife. The boy spent placid hours in rich meadows, ate a quantity of scalded cream, and grew out of knowledge in the six months of his stay. He used to wander down to the park gates—gloriously wrought-iron gates between massive stone pillars that bore on each summit a quintett of cannon balls, the reputed trophy of some sea-faring Elizabethan Lovely. There was a picture in the great hall, of curiously inferior execution, portraying numbers of Devon sailormen led by a huge-ruffed gentleman with a long peaked beard, swarming up the towering sides of the galleon *Jesu Maria*. Charles was taken to see it when the new family was gone up to London town. He also saw the great stone swan over the vast fireplace, with the motto of his house, *Sum decorus*.

Later in the autumn his father returned and the old life of lodgings, inland Spas and long posting journeys was resumed. He had never again visited that remote Devon village, with its cows and pastures and dairymaids and famous chronicles.

Then, just after Charles reached his majority, Mr. Lovely Senior died quite suddenly, and our hero found himself in undisputed possession of the interest on five thousand guineas and as much more in cash, owing to a lucky run by his father in the week before his death.

Charles now indulged the family vice of throwing money to the dogs, and, having lost the earnings of his father, set about realizing a trifle of ready money on the five thousand guineas left him by his mother's aunt. This step brought him into pen-and-ink contact with old

Sir George Repington who wrote him a stern letter of advice, with a postscript offering him a stool in the Repington bank. Charles was furious and did not reply.

About that time he renewed the friendship with Mr. Anthony Clare begun in that far-off summer away down in Devonshire. The latter persuaded him to leave London and come to Curtain Wells, where for a time he lived happily enough on his small annuity. However, just before our story opened, he had been hard hit at loo and had raised a thousand guineas by making over the interest on his inheritance to the friendly moneylender who advanced the needed sum. On the top of this came his losses to Vernon, and now he was stranded indeed.

Therefore the melancholy drizzle of rain suited his melancholy mood. Of course he could borrow, play again and perhaps win, but if he should lose he would be in debt to a friend, a position which he disliked. His father, less scrupulous in this respect, was always content to lay himself under fresh obligations. To Charles, however, something of the pride which sustains a great financial house had descended through his mother and, prodigal though he was, he would never borrow money from a friend. Of course a moneylender was different, but what security could he offer? It looked as if he would have to appeal to his uncle after all. This alternative was thoroughly odious, and Charles racked his brains to discover a way out of the difficulties into which he was plunged.

In such despondent meditation he wandered on until the dancing glare of two large flambeaux, stuck in iron sockets, caught his attention. He found himself outside the Great House.

The project of consulting with the Beau entered his mind, but St. Simon's struck the hour of ten, and he knew Mr. Ripple would be retiring to rest, since he was accustomed to preserve his energy on those nights when he was not called out to preside over an assembly, rout, or masquerade. At that moment the two flambeaux, as if to proclaim their owner's withdrawal from the claims of society, simultaneously collapsed and strewed Mr. Ripple's fair white steps with ashes.

The sudden darkness betrayed the opalescent windows of the Beau's bed-chamber. He had neglected to draw the curtains, and on the blind his suave shadow disported itself in preparation for the night and the next morning.

Charles watched the shadow dip giant fingers into monstrous pomade pots. Now those fast deepening crowsfeet were being vigorously rubbed. Now that swift creasing neck was being smoothed with slow caressing movements. The wig-block displayed itself in generous shadowy curves. Now, surely, the shadow's sudden inaction betokened a contemplation of creeping age.

"And this," thought Charles, "is the destiny marked out for me by Ripple."

He knew if he waited upon him on the morrow, explained his reverses, and promised amendment, the Beau would one day procure for him the monarchy of the Wells, but Charles was not inclined to manipulate the strings of marionettes, himself suspended from a longer cord and dancing for the amusement of a higher power.

The incongruity of the situation, disclosed by the Beau's window, tickled his sense of humour. There was the monarch of an artificial kingdom caulking his wrinkles like a beldame in search of her youth; there he was, that despotick king who prescribed Chalybeate as the Panacea for all earthly ills, in ludicrous terror at the swift flight of his complexion.

There he was, no better than the chief eunuch of a Persian harem with authority over women and the power of lock and key against intrusive fops.

Yet he was a kindly man and a gentleman. He was

feared and loved, a man whom the world called successful. Charles himself liked fine cloaths, found talking pleasant, enjoyed the organization of splendid entertainments, yet he could not condemn himself to eternal celibacy and the preservation of his figure. The restriction of such an existence would be unendurable.

You will remember perhaps that in our first Chapter we caught Beau Ripple in undignified pursuit of a button. We agreed how rash it was for Gods and Goddesses to discover their anatomy to mortals, and here is the very fact being forced home to Mr. Charles Lovely, an understudy to divinity.

Our hero went on his way, fortified against one ambition.

Presently he passed by the lodgings of Mrs. Courteen as the door was being opened to let out the satellite Moon and the appropriately named Tarry. The pair of them paused on the steps to ascertain the state of the weather and discuss the several games of ombre which they had played for mother-o'-pearl counters.

"Gadslife!" murmured Charles, "Ombre for counters! Then is great Anna really dead?"

The expensive lodgings of the Earl of Vanity towered above him and he heard my Lord, with a flowered dressing-gown wrapped about his skinny shanks, d——g his daughter's eyes for being so late at old Mrs. Frillface's quadrille party. Farther down the Crescent was old Mrs. Frillface's house, and outside stood two handsome chairs with the chairmen fast asleep on the cushions, soon to be wakened from the frowsy damask by Mrs. Frillface's bloated footman.

And so on past all the lodgings of Curtain Wells.

There was young Miss Kitcat who was really twenty-nine and single only because, so they said, no one would marry her since that affair with Sir Hector Macwrath, the young Nova Scotia Baronet, more than ten years ago. To be sure, the matter was never rightly explained, and everybody excused the poor child because her mother never set her the best of examples, and as for her father, everybody knew that he thought of nothing but Mdlle. Dançaboute who had such trim ankles and spent so many guineas and even wore the Kitcat rubies at a Ranelagh supper-party. So Sir Hector married the lean heiress of Lord Glew, the chief of the MacStikkeys, and Miss Kitcat remained young Miss Kitcat for many a long day. There she was, swaying sleepily to the motion of the chair while now and then her hair would catch in a splinter of wood as the first chairman stumbled over a loose cobble.

There was little Pinhorn whose father was a ship's chandler at Rye, but had made money as fast as money could be made over the War commissariat; there he was, strutting home from my Lady Bunbutter's, quite inlaid with diamonds, and with a swinging fob near as big as his own bullet head.

Charles gave him a curt good-night as he passed, and wondered to himself how little Pinhorn ever dared challenge Captain Lagge to walk with him in Curtain Meads. Unluckily the Beau had heard of the meeting and went to remonstrate with the gallant Captain.

" What did you say? " asked the Beau.

" I said I would gladly cut the claws of every harpy on the transport," answered the sailor.

" Well, so you may, sir," said Mr. Ripple, " but by Heaven! you shan't do so here."

Next morning the Captain had his orders and was shot through the heart in the Carthagena business. Poor Captain Lagge, he had a wife and a little maid waiting for him in the prettiest cottage between Pevensey and Brighthelmstone.

Charles passed many others whose small histories, could I recount them, would fill this book to overflowing. For each one he could recall some unsavoury episode, some mean adventure that made its hero contemptible.

"Oddslife," thought Charles, "was ever Society so corrupt, so insincere, so entirely damnable?"

By this time he was back in the High Street after a long circuit, and just as he was thinking of crossing the road to reach the *Blue Boar* and bed, he noticed a candle was burning in his bookseller's little back parlour.

"I'll inquire after the sale of my poems," he decided, and without more ado hammered loudly on the door of the shop. Presently in answer to his continuous rappings, a foxy-faced old young man with a premature stoop and cloath both squalid and ill-cut, shuffled through the shop and asked who was there.

"A mendicant poet," cried Charles.

"Be d——d," muttered the foxy-faced man, preparing to go back.

"Come, Mr. Virgin, you'll open to me, Charles Lovely?"

"Go away, Mr. Lovely, go away. I'm very busy—very busy indeed. I never remember when I was so busy before, so full of business."

"So much the better," cried Charles jumping up to smite the signboard that hung over the door till it swung round on its hinges with a rattle and a squeak.

"Now don't be rough, Mr. Lovely. I've had the lady's face repainted. 'Tis beautifully done, Mr. Lovely. Do look. Can you see? 'Mr. Paul Virgin. Bookseller and Publisher. At the Sign of the *Woman*.'"

"Pshaw!" said Charles. "Will you open to me, or I'll turn the woman into a w——!"

"I suppose you must have your way, but oddscods, indeed I'm monstrous busy. Oh! Mr. Lovely, I am so busy, you wouldn't believe."

With this final protest, the old young man slowly drew the bolts of the door and allowed Mr. Lovely to step inside.

There was a musty smell in the shop and the shelves of calf-bound volumes seemed alive in the uncertain flame of the candle. The counter was heaped high with volumes and on the floor lay gigantick tomes bound in jaundiced vellum covers.

Lovely followed the foxy-faced man into the back parlour which in addition to the general mustiness of the premises had a rank odour of printer's ink and newly struck proofs.

" I am so busy, Mr. Lovely. Mr. Antique Burrowes' great work on the Abbeys of England and Wales must positively appear before the publick next week; the subscription lists are filled up, and we expect a very favourable reception, and so we ought, for the woodcuts are beautiful. Look at this one, Mr. Lovely—this is Glastonbury—the Abbot's Kitchen. What a place just for one man! Ah! those monks: what bellies they had."

Charles scarcely glanced at the proof.

" Very proper," he said, " and what about my poems? "

" Ah! you always have your joke, Mr. Lovely. That's always the way with poets—they will have their jokes just when I'm so busy too," said Mr. Virgin sidling across the room to a shelf full of ledgers bound in hideous marble boards.

" How many sold, these three months? "

" One, Mr. Lovely. One copy. You see it entered."

" Who was the purchaser," said Charles with affectation of great indifference. " Not a lady, I presume? "

" Ha, ha, you poets—so fond of the women. Singers and poets always like the women. There was Signor Amoroso, d'ye know him? The famous Tenore, now singing every night at Vauxhall—he used to buy all my books about the ladies. But, pray excuse my chatter, Mr. Lovely. I'm sure I oughtn't to be talking, just when I'm so busy too. Let me see, who was the purchaser—ah! here it is—it was Miss——"

" Courteen? " Charles let slip in his eagerness.

" Ha-ha! ha-ha! " laughed the foxy-faced bookseller,

"Ha-ha! You must keep your love-secrets better than that. No, it wasn't Miss——" he pursued.

"Oh!" said Charles coldly.

"It was Sir George Repington—I remember now—he wrote from the North."

"Sir George Repington?" exclaimed Charles completely surprized. "Humph! I wish him joy of my effusions."

"Oh, no doubt he'll like them or he wouldn't have sent all that way for them. Well! well! some men are mighty whimsical in their tastes, and there's no denying that people do read verses."

"However," said Charles, "I take it the taste is not an extended one?"

"Well! you mustn't complain. You had two hundred taken by subscription and half a dozen copies sold to casual purchasers. You won't lose a vast deal over the publication."

"No," said Charles, "you wouldn't like that?"

"No, indeed I shouldn't, sir, I take a pride in the success of my clients. So did my father, sir, and he became an alderman of this town, though he was a native of Exeter."

"I take it, then, you are not prepared to offer a sum of money on account of a new volume?"

"Ho-ho!" laughed Mr. Virgin, "what a droll gentleman you are to be sure. You will have your joke, and don't seem to regard how busy I am."

"Very well, sir," said Charles, "I'll wish you a good night."

"*Good* night, Mr. Lovely, good night, sir. When I'm not so busy perhaps, another time, I'll be most happy to talk over your—ahem—literary projects."

Mr. Virgin held up the candle to light Mr. Lovely through the shop. The rays happened to fall on a pile of slim volumes reposing on the counter.

"What are those?" Charles asked.

"Ah, 'tis a great pity you can't write verse like that."

"Poems?" said Mr. Lovely in accents of incredulity.

"To be sure—poems, but such poems,—lampoons, squibs, and pasquinades. 'Tis a Satire on the characters of the Bath—very scandalous, they tell me, but odds-cods, 'tas run through nine editions in as many weeks. Now, if your name was Lively, sir, instead of Lovely."

"Mr. Virgin!"

"No offence. What I mean is, if you could write something similar about the visitors to Curtain Wells."

"You'd publish it?"

"Well, perhaps that's going too far, but I would give it my very best attention."

"Humph! Good night," and Charles went out into the drizzle.

On his way home, he saw the Exquisite Mob and the Exquisite Mob-master grouped before a satirist; and very soon he saw them performing their anticks thinly disguised by initials and asterisks.

That is how Mr. Charles Lovely sat down to indite

CURTAIN POLLS
severely lashed
by a
Curtain Rod.

CHAPTER XVI

THE CHINESE MASQUERADE

THE Chinese Masquerade was the outstanding event of early Spring at Curtain Wells. It was the quintessence of refined affectation, the great fount in which many tributary delights found their source. Moreover, in its character there was a national significance. It was not held merely to emphasize the importance of being seriously amused; it was not one of many entertainments sacred to Epicurus; it did not serve to commemorate the fleetingness of life; it was no Burial Service with a ritual of flung roseleaves and spilt wine. The Chinese Masquerade of Curtain Wells was something far more grand than any of these, being a great national act of homage to the beverage of Tea. Of old, Bacchus was saluted in Samothrace, and the festival of wine was celebrated with all the absence of restraint that might be expected from the past. Nymphs raved, Satyrs danced, and garlanded leopards jigged to one wild inspiration. Phrenzy footed it; troops followed troop, broke and dissolved in flashes of white limbs when Dionysus of the sly smile and rosy cheeks bewitched thousands with his strange madness. In fact, the whole affair was an intolerable concession to Nature. At Curtain Wells you saw the centuries at work. There the Bacchantes were corseted and hooped to primness; the Satyrs had high red heels for hoofs, silken breeches for the fur of goats. Instead of velvety leopards that used to amble over tuffets of fragrant thyme, each with a hussy astride his supple back, went greasy chairmen in lurching escort of dowagers and misses. Dionysus himself was changed. He had kept his sly smile and rosy cheeks, but his vine wreaths were become ruffles and ties, while his body glittered, not with youth and health and immortality, but with paste buckles and brooches and solitaires. The crashing cymbals of Thrace found a thin echo in the delicate tinkle of tea-spoons and frail sounds of porcelain. To be sure, the whole of the difference between the worship of Wine and the worship of Tea was expressed by the fact that to honour the former, society took off its cloaths, whereas in order to celebrate the latter, all the world dressed itself up.

Mr. Ripple wore above his suit of amber a robe resembling a golden dressing-gown. He was the Gold Mandarin, decorated with dragons, tall pagodas, flowers and fireworks. The Blue Mandarin, whose robe concealed the pearl-grey suit of Mr. Charles Lovely, seemed as he moved across the room like a blue garden, so many small landskips wrought in azure silks trembled in the folds of his garment. Only these two officers of the Pageant were privileged to remain unmasked. The rest of the company wore yellow vizards whose painted eyebrows soared at a celestial angle over eye-slits, cut almondwise. The general effect was of animated Ming laughing, jesting, talking, and dancing with the lacker cabinets that were used to contain it.

The ballroom had pagodas in each of the corners where the children of the Exquisite Mob dressed to a more exact replica* of the farthest Orientals, nodded and peeped and chirped the austere maxims of Confucius without the slightest idea of their meaning, but all convinced that it was extremely diverting to partake of a grown-up entertainment, and far better to drink real tea out of real cups in a delightful palace of their own,

* They wore pigtails, which were considered unbecoming by the older Follies. Besides, head-dresses were too elaborate to be ruined for the sake of one entertainment.

than to play with acorns and ditchwater in the mildewed Dorick summer-house at the head of the Park avenue.

Chinese lanterns bobbed on golden wires slung from wall to wall whence the gilt mirrours with the wax candles of the West had all been removed. This Eastern light softened the mingled hues of blue and gold to a gorgeous moving twilight stained by the afterglow of sunset. All along the sides of the ballroom were placed for seats queer twisted animals, winged dragons, squat bronzes, Chinese geese, monkeys and parrots in crude shades of green and vermilion, while at suitable intervals were set little houses to contain two persons. These were intended to encourage the intimate amenities of polite conversation.

Outside in the Rococo cloister unknown flowers expanded and curious fruits ripened by lanternlight; and though the flowers were made of linen dipped in scent, they served very well to pluck and offer to a masked fair and as for the fruits, they were all filled with comfits. Finally, here and there, smoking sandal-wood torches lent a remote perfume to the Mise en Scène, and scurled in scented wreaths, about the motley forms of the masqueraders. To say truth, the Eastern veneer was more than usually superficial, even for a veneer. The result of the attempt to secure reality only accentuated the difference between East and West: still the latter enjoyed making believe so far as it consorted with true gentility, and it may very easily be understood that nothing low was permitted by the British Nation in the eighteenth glorious century of Christian civilization.

This was the first masked ball that had been held since Phyllida grew enamoured of Mr. Francis Vernon, so she made no doubt he would avail himself of the opportunity to be present. As soon as the Exquisite Mob was assembled (at half-past seven o'clock precisely, because it was considered vulgar to be late) there was a solemn drinking of tea, no mere handing round of teacups and saucers, but a far more impressive ritual, invented to mark the occasion with due importance.

The Gold Mandarin seated himself on an ivory stool whose claw legs were fretted with diminutive foliage, temples and flying birds. This was set on a small platform draped with broideries at the foot of which was an azure velvet cushion where, with crossed legs, sat the Blue Mandarin.

Mr. Ripple clapped his hands twice to command the entrance of the Procession of Tea. First walked two musicians slowly tapping gongs shaped like saucers with large spoons. These were followed by six children with nodding porcelain Mandarins whose tongues trembled in and out of their surprized mouths. Then came the bearer of the Caddy—a magnificently decorated specimen of lacker-work. On either side of the Caddy was borne a Nankin jar full of milk. Finally, a lacker table on wheels, overhung by a fringed canopy that protected an enormous bowl of rarest Ming whither odorous vapours ascended from the flowery liquid, was pushed along in slow and reverend state.

The company opened its ranks to allow the procession a way until it stopped before the Gold Mandarin's ivory throne. The Beau at once descended, dipped a diminutive teacup into the bowl, took three sips and sighed rapturously. The six porcelain Mandarins were set nodding with redoubled vigour, gongs boomed from the topmost windows of the pagodas, and the procession re-formed and passed into the upper room, whither the assembled company followed it in order to drink in turn from teacups filled at the sacred fountain.

In the crush, Phyllida, who was wearing a gown faint blue like the March sky, felt her sleeve pulled gently by a tall mask in tawny raiment. She recognized the pointed white fingers and whispered 'Amor.'

The mask shook his head to indicate silence, but presently Phyllida succeeded in conveying her cup of tea to the outskirts of the crowd and hurried through a corridor to a side-door opening into the cloister where she waited for her lover's approach. In a minute he was sitting beside her.

She turned to him delightedly.

"Dear Amor! this will be the first ball that I shall have truly enjoyed."

This statement scarcely did justice to the many pleasant hours she had spent to the sound of fiddles, horns, and clarinets.

"Why was my charmer absent yesterday? The Maze was prodigiously dull without the sweet Nymph who loves to haunt its verdurous ways."

"Oh! Amor, we are discovered."

"Faith, is that so?" remarked Vernon, without any apparent concern.

"Mr. Ripple told my mother I was conversing with a gentleman for one hour and a half by the clock."

"Interfering dancing-master!"

"And yesterday I was sent to match a ribband quite impossible to match; I'm sure 'twas done to keep me employed and when I heard eleven chime, I could bear it no longer, but almost ran towards Curtain Garden, and on my way the Beau beckoned me to come in and, pray don't be angry, dear Amor, he was so vastly kind that I told him your name."

"Here's a pretty state of affairs," muttered Vernon.

"He asked me to present you to him to-night, and vowed we should be wed in June."

"Gadslife! I hope you sent him about his business?"

"Not exactly," said Phyllida, "indeed he was so good-natured that I promised—at least I half promised to do so."

"Confusion take him," swore Vernon, "for a prating, meddlesome, tailor-made gentleman. Harkee! I'll not have myself discussed by Mr. Horace Ripple. I dare swear he patted your hands, eh? called you his pretty dear, made old man's love, eh? A plague on his impudence!"

Phyllida shrank from her lover's wrath.

"Indeed, sir, I vow he did nothing of the kind. He behaved with some of that propriety for which I could wish in my Amor." Phyllida remembered a young woman talking something like this in the first volume of *The Fair Inconstant*. Vernon could not keep back a smile. "I doubt I'm not inclined to hear you farther."

Vernon began to chuckle.

"And let me tell you, sir, your behaviour becomes you very ill, and moreover I told him your name, and the milk's spilt, and 'tis useless to cry over spilt milk as all the world knows."

A tear-drop trembled in each corner of Phyllida's eyes, making them seem more clearly blue, as crystals that surround great sapphires enhance their beauty.

"Sweet indiscretion," began Vernon, who having been politick enough to conceal his true name, could afford to be generous.

A very faint sob was the sole response.

"Nay, prithee, dear one," he continued, catching hold of a tremulous hand, "let's have no quarrels at our first ball; I bear you no malice."

"I should never have told him, had I been ashamed of you," she interrupted.

"Just so, adorable creature, but since we had resolved to keep our affair secret, and since we were agreed that stolen meetings, like stolen fruit, taste the sweetest, I was surprized to hear you had told every one."

"I did not tell any one."

"But, my angel, you did."

"Not until I was forced. 'Tis very well for you. You're a man of fashion and independence, and I'm a young woman."

"Incontestable truth!"

"Now you're being satirical, and I vow I detest sarcasm. Indeed, I think it has all been a mistake, and I'll go back to Hampshire to-morrow, and you may go back to your Haymarket."

"Very well, madam, since you dismiss my suit, I will go back to my Haymarket. It may be vastly diverting for you, madam, to break a man's heart. You, secure in the verdant meads and—er—meadows of the county of Hampshire, you, wandering among fields of daffodillies, at peace, beneath a summer sun."

"Daffodillies don't grow in the summer."

"Alas! madam, I am ignorant of these pastoral delights."

This was perfectly true since Mr. Vernon's mother was a lady who thought a bough-pot in Air Street worth the finest estate in the Kingdom.

"I," he continued, "have lived my life in cities, and though I have often hoped to hear the cuckoo wake me at dawn, 'tis very evident I must for ever bid farewell to such vain dreams."

Here, Mr. Vernon, who had inherited considerable histrionick ability on the female side, contrived to get an effective break into his usually smooth enunciation.

"But I don't want to quarrel for ever," protested Phyllida.

Mr. Vernon turned his head away, probably to hide a tear.

"For my part," she went on, "I should be very willing to live always as we are living now."

"My angel!"

"But since the world is so censorious and seems to concern itself with every unimportant young woman's affairs, I thought—I thought——"

"You thought a wedding would put a stop to scandal. How little you know the world. Why! madam, a hasty wedding would set people's tongues wagging at once. Come, come, pay no attention to old Ripple. He knows my name. If he chuse, he can seek me out. I warrant I shall hear no more about it."

"But we shall be watched."

"Then we'll change our trysting-place. At any rate, prithee, let us enjoy to-night." Here Mr. Vernon put on his mask and taking off his gown resumed it inside out. "Do you see, dear charmer, I am both porcelain and lacker, so that no one will be able to say you prefer the one to the other. Hark! the fiddles have begun—let's go and step our first gavotte together."

Phyllida took his arm and they returned to the ballroom. The vizards made all the faces appear fixed and wooden and Miss Courteen could not help looking very often at Mr. Charles Lovely who was sitting cross-legged on his azure cushion and, in contrast to the rest of the masquerade, was plainly a man. Once she fancied she caught his eye, and when he came up and asked her to honour his arm for the third gavotte, she knew she had not been mistaken. Mr. Vernon silently relinquished his partner.

"Who was your late Vis à Vis?" Charles inquired. "I beg your pardon," he added as he saw Phyllida hesitate, "my manners grow as barbarick as my costume."

He had noticed with devout jealousy that Miss Courteen's fingers reposed a moment longer than was necessary upon that sattin forearm.

"How did you discover me?" she asked with frank interest.

"'Twas not difficult."

"But masked as I am?"

"I did not regard your mask—I saw your eyes."

Phyllida was conscious of a blush and a faint quickening of the pulses, all over her body. There was certainly something very satisfactory in such a compliment. It was genuine moreover, for indeed he had discovered her through the distorted yellow vizard which concealed her roses.

Presently the dance began, and, though Phyllida liked every moment of it, she could not help observing Amor, half buried in the greenery of an alcove and, as it seemed to her, forbidding too keen a pleasure.

Charles found it difficult to extract from his partner

more than the ordinary small talk of ballrooms, and as she became more and more absent-minded during the progress of the dance, he let her go at the end of it without a very valiant attempt to detain her for the next. Presently he saw her join a blue mask and lose herself in the flickering throng. Last time he had remarked particularly that her Vis à Vis wore brown and gold, yet the two figures were alike in movement and gesture and he could swear the hands were identical. It was the same without a doubt. Charles bit his nails with vexation, and fretted confoundedly.

"My dear boy, my dear Charles, pray do not gnaw your fingers. Narcissus admired himself, 'tis true, but without carrying his devotion to cannibality."

Charles turned to the well-known voice of Mr. Ripple.

"A thousand pardons, dear Beau, I was vexed by a trifle. The masquerade comports itself with tolerable success."

"I think so," the Beau replied, adjusting his monocle and gazing critically at his subjects. "I certainly think so, but I am never easy in my mind until the Grand Minuet has concluded the entertainment, yet even so, I do not think you will ever find me preying upon my extremities."

Charles laughed.

"They take their pleasures very easily, sir." Again the Beau examined his puppets.

"The burden of amusement certainly weighs very lightly on them, and yet, Charles, I sometimes fancy I detect a shade too much of self-consciousness in their movements. I could wish for a less anxious grace, a less ordered abandon. My monocle which diminishes their size, diminishes their importance; and I must confess that the motion of dancing, if one regards the Ensemble, appears to me nothing less than idiotical. However, do not let my cynical attitude prove contagious—I have watched so many dances."

"Yet you are willing for me to succeed you," said

Charles. "Foregad, Mr. Ripple, I was never intended for a spectator."

"I have energy to keep me in office long enough to let you grow older. Come, come, Charles, admit the career I offer would tempt many more deserving young men."

"But I have passions, feelings, desires, ambitions."

"All very suitable," commented the Beau, "till you grow tired of versifying life. We write poetry, Charles, in order to improve our prose."

"Some men write poetry to the end."

"Usually a bitter end; but, indeed, I would not goad you into accepting my offer. Have your dramas, lose your money, expose your heart to Cupid, commit the thousand and one foolish actions that will afford you a moral occupation for your middle age."

"What would that be?"

"A leisurely repentance."

"Sir, I think you spin the natural functions into silk like the silkworm."

"Well, Charles, and isn't silk a more durable excrement than most? You are still devouring the tender shoots of the mulberry tree; I am already in the cocoon and shall go down to posterity as a very reputable moth vouched for by a cenotaph in St. Simon's Church, Curtain Wells."

"Sir, I doubt they will never say of me ' Vive le roi! ' "

"We shall see, we shall see. By the way, do you know a Miss Phyllida Courteen? Her mother, a widow whose charms are as ample as her dowry, is lodging in the Crescent."

Charles was taken aback for a moment.

"I believe I have met her once or twice at Assemblies."

"At any rate, you know her by sight?"

"Oh yes!" replied our hero.

"Now, I wonder whether you could pick her out from this multitude of masks?"

Charles at once perceived the subject of the question.

"She is standing over there by the second pillar and talking to a mask in porcel—no, in lacker. That's strange."

"What is strange?" inquired Mr. Ripple mildly.

"Nothing—a lantern effect," Charles explained.

Surely he could not be mistaken in those taper fingers. Moreover, they were familiar to him. Where could he have seen them?

"So that is Miss Courteen," said the Beau, looking at her very intently. "Yes, now that you have pointed her out, I certainly seem to recognize her. Who is her Vis à Vis?"

"That I do not know," said Charles rather gloomily.

"Then, pray, be so good-natured as to make an attempt to ascertain and you'll oblige me monstrously. Or stay—perhaps I had better inquire myself."

Mr. Ripple, observing that Mr. Lovely looked somewhat melancholy, patted him on the shoulder.

"Don't look so full of disapprobation, Charles. Inquisitiveness, with ordinary men and women, is a breach of good manners: with kings, it is a condescension. Dear me! how time runs!" the Beau continued, tripping from an epigram to a truism. "I will leave you to superintend the Country Dances. Let them be as Oriental as possible, I beg."

With this admonition the Great little Man threaded his way through the Exquisite Mob.

Charles d——d the Country Dances very devoutly. He was not enjoying the evening at all, and wished he were sitting in the cosy firelight of the *Blue Boar*, lulled by the whispers of playing cards, shuffled and dealt. Where could he raise that two hundred pounds he owed Vernon? Vernon—by G. . . .! now he recognized those taper fingers. Vernon! they belonged to Vernon, he could swear to them. Too often had he watched their delicate harvesting of his guineas. He began to fret more than ever. Suddenly he noticed that everybody was looking in his direction, and became aware that time was indeed running and the moment for the Country Dances had arrived.

Meanwhile Mr. Ripple searched in vain for Phyllida and a Vis à Vis in brown and gold.

CHAPTER XVII

THE GRAND MINUET OF CATHAY

THE Country Dances of these powderpuff Orientals were so truly inappropriate to the celebration that they almost succeeded in convincing by sheer want of fitness. Picture to yourselves two hundred blue and golden marionettes jigging to *Sir Roger de Coverley* or bobbing to *Come Lasses and Lads*. There was Merry England underneath this hugger mugger of yellow masks, yet the sustained motion was decidedly Eastern. Hands across, back to back, right hand, left hand—each change of attitude was marked by a crashing gong; and he who sounded this barbarick instrument was Mr. Charles Lovely. He stood upon a tripod of ebony quite high enough for a hero of comedy, as I am sure you will admit.

As soon as his proconsulate was over, he jumped from the pedestal, and, once more assuming our poor humanity, sought desperately for Mr. Vernon and Miss Phyllida Courteen.

And now the great ballroom was cleared. The Exquisite Mob refreshed itself not with chopsticks, but with two-pronged forks and stout-handled knives. Nor was the fare ascetick rice, but pies of mutton, rounds of beef, custards, gay jellies and dappled puddings. In the ballroom the attendants busily ran hither and thither in preparation for the Grand Minuet of Cathay. Four pagodas guarded four corners; little bridges spanned little rivers of blue silk. There were miniature groves that shielded queer little Chinese gods and goddesses, while here and there were temples with crooked roofs, hung round with silver bells destined to be jingled at set moments of this incomparable minuet. High up near the ceiling among the swinging lanterns one saw the peaked faces of giant kites gazing benignly down. Finally in the very centre of the room was a small fountain with a pond all about it of real water, starred with white water lilies, on the highest jet of which a little god, inflated by air, jigged to the rise and fall of the water. Mr. Ripple had not been able to find Miss Courteen and was interrupted in his search by a call to inspect the scene of the Minuet. Gog was sent to fetch Mr. Lovely and presently the Gold Mandarin and the Blue Mandarin were stepping over each bridge, peering from each pagoda, gently trying the bells, lending a last touch to the rivers of silk and coming to a standstill in silent admiration of the dancing water-god.

"I think," said Mr. Ripple, "we may venture to proclaim the Minuet of Cathay."

"I think so," said Mr. Lovely as he cast a quick eye in the direction of every entrance in turn.

"I could not find Miss Courteen," said the Beau, "have you had better luck?"

Lovely hesitated a moment.

"No," he said finally.

The Beau looked at him a moment.

"I cannot imagine who this Amor can be. He is not down in my list."

"Amor?" inquired Charles, somewhat too suddenly, "is his name Amor?"

"So the young lady informed me, when we considered the situation together. I perceive you know him."

"Indeed, sir, I am acquainted with no one of that name."

"I never imagined you were," replied the Beau testily. "'Tis too plainly a Nom d'amour; but I'll wager you are able to extract a personality from this pseudonym."

"Nay, indeed, I——"

"Very well," said the Beau, cutting him short, "these is no more to be said," and he turned away to order a burly Oriental who on less decorated occasions was wont to assist Mr. Balhatchett the butcher, to sound the gong of invitation.

While the huge sullen instrument boomed a diapason that threatened more than it cajoled, Charles wondered if he had been wise to conceal his knowledge of Mr. Amor's identity. Ripple had obviously not believed him and was moreover very sensitive to any concealment on the part of his subjects. He, as his own subaltern, was especially bound to indulge this foible. Besides, what good had he done? thought Charles. Not much indeed, for soon Ripple would certainly find out the whole affair. He ought to tell him all he knew. Ripple would act for the best and close the Pump Room against the intruder. It would be kill or cure.

But just as he was upon the point of informing the Great little Man, our hero remembered he owed Vernon two hundred pounds. O resolute hero! Be quick to mount your ebony pedestal or we shall think you no better than a walking gentleman.

The Exquisite Mob of crimped and corseted Orientals began to saunter back from supper, and the debate between honesty and honour was adjourned to a more meditative opportunity. By this hour of the evening most of the Masks were tolerably sure of each other's identity, and though it was an acknowledged custom of the Chinese Masquerade as opposed to other masked balls that all vizards should be worn from door to door, the Grand Minuet of Cathay afforded much scandalous talk for the ensuing days, all the more potent because a convention of anonymity was sedulously maintained. It was not surprizing that intrigue should flourish at a dance where half the company was hidden for many moments at a stretch. The Minuet lasted a whole hour. It reproduced in the various side-figures many emotions. It was a hundred dances in a grand Ensemble. The musick was now courtly, now passionate: sometimes it clanged in barbarick interludes of noise: sometimes but three or four flutes twittered above the plash of the fountain.

Over the bridges pattered the dancers: in and out of the diminutive groves twinkled their scarlet heels. Now a couple swayed in a stationary boat on a motionless river: now at the topmost window of a pagoda, cambrick handkerchief and painted fan kept time to the tune. The Gold Mandarin lived in a golden house beside the fountain and, if he chose, could live a century of sound and perfume in that fragrant hour of dancing. Far away at the other corner of the room lived the Blue Mandarin in a small house at the foot of a small volcano that ceaselessly puffed out clouds of incense. Wherever you went in that strange dance of dances some new delight assailed your senses.

Here, before a temple hung with silver bells, a dozen of these blue and golden dolls moved with grace and precision through many variations of the Minuet. They would carry away with them that night no more than a memory of bells and stately movement by the rosy light of many lanterns. Purged of all feeling save for correct gesture, the vizards seemed no more alive than their mirroured counter parts that moved with equal grace upside down in the polished floor of parquet.

But step over one of these bridges where false white flowers hang in scented clusters: go softly through that Bonbon grove, and there in an alcove fretted to the semblance of wrought ivory, you shall see two masks that are enraptured beneath a white moon-lantern, tracing the melody with long caresses. In one of these fanciful resorts, sat Vernon and Phyllida making love among the shadows, as in pairs and dainty quartetts the dancers darkened the carved portal when they passed. For Phyllida, the Assembly Rooms had been snatched up by some powerful magician and set down in a land of Ombres Chinoises. Many a time had she sat in the theatre and watched these silent black and white tragedies and comedies. Now she had joined that whimsical procession which capers across the draughty sheet. She recalled a particular entertainment of this character last December. First the Columbine had pirouetted across and made a light phantastick entrance into the shadow of the house at the extreme corner. Presently came the Pierrot with a lantern swaying atop of a tall pole. Up and down the sheet he had danced with incredible agility, until a Pulcinello shook his bells from the window of the house, and he floated away gathering giant size as he went. Then came Harlequin, dancing almost more beautifully than Pierrot, and a quiet murder was done in the laurel shadows round the house. Pierrot lay dead and Harlequin, the slim and debonair assassin had donned his vizard: Columbine wept a while until the lights were turned up, when everybody agreed that the whole performance was in the best of taste and vastly well executed.

Phyllida came to herself and found Mr. Vernon gazing steadily at her with his velvet eyes, all the more disconcerting set almondwise in the Chinese mask. She shuddered.

To say truth, this exotick minuet of strange perfumes and processions, was not the sanest amusement for a maid who should have lived always among the roses. The heat was growing intolerable, and still her lover with persistent, regular motion bewitched her hand as it lay in his.

The dancers passed and repassed them as they sat in artificial dusk. Phyllida began to hate them when they fluttered their fans and handkerchiefs. They were sickly things these dancers—crotchets and quavers and semiquavers who had captured the semblance of humanity, who breathed and bowed and capered, merely because musick had conjured them into existence.

Suddenly an amazing clangour of gongs and cymbals waked her completely from the fever into which she had been flung, and, waking, she found herself encircled by her lover's arms, his eyes burning into hers and his lips, all that was left alive by the stolid vizard, eager to meet her own.

" Don't," she gasped. " Don't. I hate you, I hate you when you do that."

" Nay, my angel must not be so prudish. Come, kiss me of your own will and we'll gallop to Gretna Green next week."

Phyllida still repulsed him.

" To Gretna Green," he went on. " Drawn by a pair of cream-coloured horses, in a chaise all citron silk and rosy sattin with my Phyllida plunged into the softest cushions and her Amor to love her so fondly while trees and milestones fly past."

Vernon inherited much talent from his mother, and as he breathed his persuasions in the most refined modulations of intensity, half looked over his shoulder, for an audience.

" My Phyllida, your lips are soft as moths."

" Don't, Amor, don't."

" Soft as little moths that in wet garden paths brush the cheeks with feathery wings."

" Release my hand, detestable Amor. I will sit here no longer to be tortured by your boorishness."

" But why will you repulse me? you love me? We are to be wed almost at once. Why were you willing to sit in this dark corner, unless for the charms of love? "

The Minuet was drawing to a close. Long since the musick had departed into wilder channels. This was now no courtly measure, but a barbarick medley of noise, fit for trumpets of India, cymbals of Ethiopia, and the hollow booming of drums that affright wrecked pirates in the green swamps of Madagascar.

Vernon stood up and drew Phyllida closer.

"By G——, child, you madden me with your prettiness. Come, I swear you shall kiss me before the end of the dance. You shall, by G—— you shall!"

Miss Phyllida Courteen, all swansdown and blushes in our first chapter, is scarcely recognizable now. She is growing old fast. She is kindling the faggots that will warm her chill old age.

But still, though passion tugged at her heart strings, the school-miss, the older Eve before the Fall, made her struggle against knowledge.

"I hate you, I hate you like this. Let me go, sir, let me go!"

With a sudden effort, she escaped from his arms, and he, plunging back at the same moment, struck the frail summer house of ivory so that it toppled over in front of the Blue Mandarin who was crossing a bridge over a silken stream that flowed in the direction of his little house beneath the miniature volcano. The Bonbon grove was strewn with fragments. Like Cinderella fled Miss Courteen and was quickly lost in the gold and azure company. With careless air, Mr. Vernon stooped to buckle his shoe and Charles, seeing the taper fingers, stood for a moment petrified upon the ridiculous bridge over which he had been stepping with such an affectation of importance.

Now was his opportunity to probe Mr. Vernon, or rather to lead him gradually into the urbane presence of Mr. Ripple who would certainly probe him deep enough. There was every reason to admonish him for, as he knelt over his shoe, Charles could plainly see his costume was reversible. Such a device was a breach of etiquette, deserving publick censure. Himself as viceroy of Society, should not be backward in arresting a traitor to Society's rules. Of old, the favourites of monarchs had not scrupled to owe money to those whom they denounced as dangerous to the State.

Charles took a step forward.

"Sir," he said, pointing with a tasselled wand whose

hand was a squat Buddha, " you have broken a law of the Chinese Masquerade."

" Indeed," said Vernon, rising from his knees, not at all perturbed apparently by the accusation.

" Yes," went on the Blue Mandarin. Pray let our hero be impersonal for a while. " You are wearing a double costume."

" What a monstrous breach of privilege," said Vernon chilly, unmoved.

" And it is my duty to report the incident to Beau Ripple. Your name, sir? "

It was now the turn of our villain to hesitate. If he frankly avowed his identity, Lovely was bound to say no more about it, but did the interloping young Jackanapes know the heroine of the affair?—he had danced with her once that night. If he said Amor, Lovely might easily inform Ripple and plead ignorance. D——n the young fool! Why didn't he pass over his absurd stream and take his callow brain, stuffed with ceremonies, to the sugar-plum atmosphere of the Beaux' ante-room?

" Why, Lovely, man, don't you know me? 'Tis I, Vernon, what the plague do you mean by so much impertinence? Were you shocked to see me trying to kiss a saucy school-minx, eh? That was little Miss———"

" Her mask, sir, should conceal her name."

With what fair Incognita Mr. Vernon intended to couple himself, will never be known. No doubt a pseudonym as nice as his own would have been forthcoming, since he was of an inventive disposition and had on occasions a pretty turn of fancy.

The musick had stopped; the Grand Minuet of Cathay was finished. Mr. Charles Lovely was aware of a rival to whom, by cursed ill-fortune, he owed money which he was unable to pay.

" Shall I give you your revenge? " murmured Vernon.

The company, still masked, were hurrying in blue and golden bunches to their coaches and chairs.

"Not to-night," said Charles. "But on my honour, Vernon, you must really be careful not to offend against our rules on another occasion."

So, lightly enough, with no appearance of mutual ill-will the rivals passed on. Phyllida was gone home, her face afire beneath her Chinese mask. To her virginal chamber, I shall presently take you in order to hear what Mistress Betty has to say about the ways of lovers. And while we walk in the direction of the Crescent, somewhat overwrought by a plethora of colour, scent, movement and sound, we may be tolerably certain that young Mr. Charles Lovely—no longer Blue Mandarin, but again our admired hero—is seated furiously inditing the most satirical verses on the residents and visitors of Curtain Wells, in order to make money enough to pay Mr. Vernon his guineas, and be able to run him through in Curtain Mead with a clear conscience and a clean smallsword.

CHAPTER XVIII

THE CONFIDANTE

IF Eve had possessed a Confidante, it is probable that the evil wrought by Woman would have been double as great as it is reputed to be. Miss Courteen had stepped into the mud of reality and, not unnaturally, was eager to tell Mistress Betty of the accident and ascertain by candlelight consultation, whether or not her glass slipper was truly lost.

As they drove home in the rumbling coach, Phyllida experienced an emotion of futility as she half listened, half dozed, to the conversation of the Major, the Justice and her mother. To this came Youth. Bumpety-bump went the coach, bumpety-bump went the conversation, bumpety-bump went Thomas' broad back on the Jimmy, bumpety-bump went Phyllida's head, while her thoughts and memories kept pace in the darkness like swift sparks that are blown along by the wind. At last the coach drew up before their house in the Crescent: Phyllida and her mother alighted: Betty opened the door and the coach drove off to put down Major Tarry and Mr. Moon at their lodgings.

The hall seemed drab and unfamiliar; the bed-chamber candle-sticks set out upon the little gate table had an air of reproof about them; they seemed to say as they sat in a prim row: " Look at us, we are quite content. Last night our candles burnt an inch lower, and the candle suffers diminution, but we remain the same. We are quite content."

"My pretty one looks pale," said Betty, full of solicitude.

"I'm tired," said Phyllida.

"Betty," said Mrs. Courteen, "you must help me to undress. The evening has been most enjoyable, and my lady Bunbutter tore her gown on a monkey's tail. Now, Phyllida, do you run quickly to bed, for to-morrow Mr. Moon and the Major have promised to drive with us to see Melton Abbey. You will enjoy the excursion vastly."

"What a whimsical place to visit."

"Whimsical! How can you be so irreverend, Phyllida?"

"But why, mamma, do you suddenly drive to Melton Abbey?"

"Why, child! because I wish to train your mind to be sure. Nothing tests deportment so severely as wandering round a Gothick ruin. However, they tell me that Gothick will soon be à la Mode, and who am I to dispute the commands of fashion?"

Upon the heels of this humble interrogation, the widow betook herself to bed.

"When you have undressed my mamma, Betty, come to my chamber, I have a thousand things to tell you," Phyllida whispered as they went up the narrow stairs.

She lighted all the candles in her room and looked round in sudden affright. It was as if some one had trespassed upon those virginal solitudes while she was away. Yet her room was the same as usual; the dimity covers were all in their places: the fire was burning merrily in the hearth: the bed-cloaths were turned back, fresh, cool and lavendered. Her slippers knelt devoutly by the fender: the fire-irons looked just as stilted and apologetick as usual. Everything was perfectly familiar, perfectly ordinary and perfectly safe; yet something in the room was strange, or was it herself who was altered? Was she out of harmony with this palace of amber morning dreams, this treasure-box of twilight hopes and imaginations?

Down she sat in the big flowered arm-chair and stared at the crackling logs—a stranger to her own possessions, and, as she untied one by one the ribbands from her glinting chestnut hair, she seemed to smell the jasmine of Courteen Grange and hear her father calling below her casement to come down quickly and count the buds on the York and Lancaster rose, as he was used to call in those sweet dead Junes.

Presently came Betty with a soft knock and Phyllida, starting away from the host of childish memories that assailed her, sprang up as the maid came in on tiptoe.

"Now, sit down, Betty, and listen with all your ears, for I dearly need your advice."

"My sweet one, I'm listening to 'ee," said Betty, pulling forward a fat lop-eared hassock and squeezing herself as close to the fender as possible.

"Betty, Mr. Amor kissed me this evening, and what should I do?"

"What were 'ee best to do? Why think no more about it, for indeed I dare vow you're not the first maid that was kissed."

"But the worst of the matter is that, though I struggled hard to escape, and though I detested him for his persistence, yet, oh? Betty, I don't like to tell you—I did not struggle as hard as I might have done."

As she made this confession, Phyllida went carnation red from forehead to pointed dimpled chin.

"There's no call for blushes," said Betty emphatically, "for you must learnt the love of man soon or late, and Mr. Vernon is a proper enough gentleman for sure."

"And he said we should presently elope."

"Oh! time enough to be wed come three years or more," commented Betty.

"Oh! but you would not have me allow a gentleman to take my hand, and kiss me, and call me his dearest life without being married immediately. It would be most unbecoming."

"If all the world knew, 'twould, but then nobody don't know, and that's the best way for all true lovers."

"Nevertheless, Betty, I feel uneasy."

"'Tis only the stirring of your blood, my dear. Only to think," went on the confidante, "that last sweet Spring time you was building great cowslip balls in the green meadows, and now you are quite grown up with a bow of your own to arm you through the minivets and gawottes, so grand as may be."

"Yes, love makes one grow old, Betty. I've aged very much these weeks."

"Well, and 'twouldn't be right otherwise, for Life bean't all a long sweet April month, my pretty one."

"Then truly, dear Betty, you swear you think there is no harm in what I have done?"

"Oh, my dear, harm? Why, what harm could there be with your great fat Betty to watch and guard 'ee?"

"Still, I'm not sure, Betty. There's something tells me not to be sure."

"Then, do 'ee listen hard to me, my dear, while I tell 'ee what I do think about life. Life! 'Tis a garden and 'tis a wilderness, and between them there's a gaäte and 'tis a kissing gaäte. The wilderness is fine for children—a great open plaäce fit for scampering Jack hares and such like, but bare enough and bleak enough when you do grow old, and then you're too fat to get through that kissing gaäte, and then you do wish wi' all your might and main that when you was young you'd gotten into the garden among the sweet flowers."

Betty stopped, exhausted by the allegory.

"Yes, Betty, that is all very well, but you must go

through the gate with the person whom you love for ever and a day."

"Nay, you can meet him inside and say Good-day and thank you kindly to the arm you went in on."

"I don't believe you give me good advice. If I told you that to-morrow morning I was going to run away with Mr. Amor to Gretna Green, what would you say?"

"Oh, God presarve you from the wicked thought, Gretna Green or any other such unlawful heathenish village green!"

"There you see," complained Phyllida, "you do not take me seriously, and it was foolish of me ever to tell you about this evening. But now that I have told you, you must never breathe a word to a living soul—never—never—promise!"

"I do promise," said Betty.

"With the old rhyme—till Christmas—you remember?"

Betty stood up, while a ritual, sacred to the childhood of Phyllida, was solemnly enacted. In a monotonous whispered chaunt, Betty promised:

> *I will not tell at primrose tide,*
>   *At cherry tide I'll silent be,*
> *At barley harvest I'll be dumb*
>   *Till Christmas come and set me free.*

Phyllida was satisfied that her indiscreet confidence was safely locked up in Betty's bosom, capacious, homely, sweet-savoured as an apple-closet.

You have seen the confidante in action. Is it not well that we have banished her from society? No longer may she enter stark mad in white muslin, as the play directs. We have put her away in an old chest with hoops and tie-wigs and gibbets and pirates and Newgate ordinaries and rotten boroughs and watchet ribbands. No longer does she play asterisk to a heroine, because nowadays the adventures of our heroines are entirely introspective. But, as upon all time-honoured institutions, let us drop a tear for the confidante; she has helped a thousand perplexed authors to unfold their simple dramas, she has helped many a sceneshifter to leisure.

Mr. Sheridan could laugh at Mr. Cumberland through this artful, artless medium, but he too had his Lucy. Mr. Smollett depended upon Miss Williams (a lady of the loosest character) in order to help his Narcissa to reveal herself and you, Mr. Goldsmith whose name, like immortal Madame Blaize, is 'bedizened and brocaded,' you had your dearest Neville.

Yet, after all, however much we may regret them, confidantes were very bad for heroines. They would encourage them in all that was most reprehensible. Here you see, is our own confidante encouraging her mistress to play with Love's torch and for all you or she know, get badly scorched by the purple flame. Such temerity is very well for country wenches to whom a green gown is a proper delight for May morning. Betty, with her memories of many barley breaks, junketings and Hallowe'en festivals, where ripe lips are as common as cherries at midsummer, was not the perfect monitor for swansdown misses brought up under Miss Prudence Prim's long rattan, taught to sit up straight and put into corsets almost as soon as they were out of robecoats. In fact she was a confidante, a match-maker, to whom a wedding-ring was a Post Hoc horse-collar, through which to grin at the censorious world.

After all, where's the ultimate difference between sweet sensibility a hundred and fifty years ago and sweet sensibility to-day? We should consider it *démodé* for the latter to gossip with her maid. Now every schoolboy and schoolgirl knows how to spell psychology, and has been awarded a sub-conscious self to enliven the lonely hours. And this sub-conscious self, what is it, under analysis? Why, nothing more than the old confidante in ghostly guise with as long a tongue and as rich a store of bad advice.

So now, having successfully, as I hope, occupied your attention whilst sweet sensibility gets into bed, let us snuff the candles and leave the room to Phyllida and wavering firelight.

CHAPTER XIX

BLACKHART FARM WITH A COCKFIGHT

ABOUT ten miles from Curtain Wells on the Bristol road stood a ruined cottage. With thatch discoloured, torn by gales and sparrows, and with windows made crooked by internal decay, its expression was grotesque and unpleasant. A tangled bed of rotten nettles filled the space before it, and all the vegetation beside was rank and desolate. This cottage served as fitting lodge to a sinister bye-way covered with weeds and almost overhung in summer by hedges dark with masses of black bryony, but in winter and spring sufficiently open to admit the cold grey sky overhead, and the chill Easterly rain, which on the morning after the Chinese Masquerade fell with dreary persistence.

Pray pardon me that I take you so far from wit, fashion, and beauty, along this unsavoury path, but indeed the journey is inevitable if you are at all anxious to understand something of Mr. Francis Vernon's intentions. The road leads to Blackhart Farm, famous, no doubt, in days gone by for the cherries of that denomination; but since the last dying speech and confession of Mrs. Mawhood the name has acquired a new and sinister significance.

Now you understand my apologies; or is it possible you have forgotten Mrs. Mawhood of Blackhart Farm, who was turned off at Tyburn amid the execrations of the mob in 17—? Yet her long black gloves and white face haunted many pillows on the night when she paid the ultimate penalty; and for what was she hanged? Come, come, this history is not the Newgate Calendar—you must search that bloody register.

At the time, however, of Mr. Vernon's visit, Mrs. Mawhood was alive, and, I am sorry to add, flourishing. He followed the roadway for about a quarter of a mile between tall, damp hedgerows, dismounted at a small wicket-gate and, leading his horse, turned aside through a plantation of close-set, withered larches under which the grass grew pale and thin, with a sweet unhealthy odour of fungus. Blackhart Farm appeared in view—a long, low building with slated roof, trim enough, but repulsive and barren. From a pile of chimney stacks smoke was rising hardly through the heavy atmosphere.

The path by which Vernon arrived led immediately to the front door. Had he continued along the cart track he would have reached, by way of a bleak paved courtyard, the back of the house. Only a very shallow strip of garden separated the front of the farm from the gloomy plantation that served as barrier to the curious world.

Vernon tied his horse to the gate of the garden, walked up the moss-grown path between clipped bushes of box, and, knocking with the handle of his riding-whip on the heavy door, waited. Several moments passed, and in the deep silence that surrounded this ill-wished abode, he could distinctly hear a clock ticking on the other side of the heavy door. This, the drip of trees, and the noise of his horse chewing the rank herbage by the gate, were the only sounds that broke the stillness.

At last footsteps shuffled over the stone-paved floor within. A small panel slid away from a grating and a voice of that peculiar unctuous hoarseness only heard in a prodigiously fat man or woman, inquired his name.

"I want to see you, old Mother Mawhood."

"Love o'maids!" said the fat voice, "'tis Fancy Vernon, or I'm not a fat old sinner."

The bolts were pushed back, the latch clicked, the door swung open, and Mrs. Mawhood, whose bulk, but little reduced by Newgate fare, was soon to test severely the three-legged tenement, occupied the portal.

Take a good look at Mrs. Mawhood, while with pursy greetings she makes Fancy Vernon welcome. She is like an idol in a cavernous East Indian temple, or a giant toadstool, or weight of unbaked dough, or in fact anything that is slow, sleepy, and horrible. Almost buried in folds of flesh is a pair of beady black eyes, as steady and wicked as those of a puff-adder or seaman's parroquet. She is dressed in black, and her nails are bitten to the quick.

Mr. Vernon was probably less narrow-minded than the mob which howled at her infamy during the Tyburn journey. At any rate he chatted with her amicably enough on this grey February forenoon.

"How's business, ma'am?" he asked.

"Very bad," she wheezed. "Only three of 'em upstairs and none of 'em real quality. Still, the flowers in the garden vant fresh food, especially the blood-red toolips. Ah! it was two lips that was the undoin' of the hussies, and, 'tis fair they should profit by the harvest."

This devilish joke was followed by a low rumbling chuckle echoed above by a thin wail.

Mrs. Mawhood waddled to the foot of the stairs.

"Keep that d——d brat quiet, you charity bastard," she wheezed angrily. "She'll hev to get up to-morrow," she continued, seating herself in a wide arm-chair beside the empty grate, "and a sickly puling jade she is. I suppose you've come for the Main?"

"No," answered Vernon, "indeed, I did not know there was to be one. Good birds?"

Mrs. Mawhood nodded. "Thirty-two cocks and a Velch main. 'Tis some of those baby gentlemen from the Vells as finks they's seeing life ven a dozen lousy chairmen sveats thesselves 'oarse over a pair of bleeding chickens. And ven they's 'ad their pockets picked, they goes 'ome 'appy."

"Is Moll here?" asked Vernon.

"No, Moll's keeping a gay house Catherine Street vay."

"Egad, I've a pretty little job for Moll."

"Now don't you go leading Moll astray. She ain't been in Bridewell not these two years, and she don't vant to neither."

"This job won't take her there. I'm in need of a housewife for a month, and Moll's a nice homely woman."

"'Oo's she to look after, eh?"

"A pearl necklace," said Vernon.

"And a pretty neck, eh?"

"Tolerable," said Vernon.

"When do you want her?"

"Let me see—February. Shall we say the last week in March?"

"I'll tell her: I shall be sending a hussy from here presently to a nice honest sitivation." Again the chuckle was heard.

"I want lodgings near the Haymarket. Nice and airy—with a balcony if possible, and—well, Moll knows what attracts sweet seventeen."

"That's young for a pearl necklace."

"'Tis hers by inheritance. The lodgings must be cheerful because Miss is shy."

"Oh, Moll knows what every age likes best. She'll buy a dear little singing goldfinch and put him in a cage and hang him up in the window. Who knows? P'raps it'll breed a nice little nestful of goldfinches for Moll. 'Ow many?"

"I can discuss that with Moll herself," said Vernon.

"Ah, but Moll's so soft 'arted. Not less than fifty goldfinches, mind, and if a little hindrance arrives, 'tis to come down to Blackhart Farm—mind—and be cared for by old Mother Mawhood wot's kind even to the pore little flies on the pane."

"You look too far into the future, old lady," said Vernon.

"And so a body should, my fancy boy," the hag answered. "Now I wager you ain't thought nothin' about postillions?"

"Time enough for that."

"Yes, time enough I dare say, but you ought to engage 'em in advance. That's vat the quality does ven they writes to me. Have you got a pair of good honest postboys?"

"No, but——"

"Vell! and good honest boys ain't so easy found in Curtain Vells! Boys who'll do vat's vanted and no questions axed and none answered."

"But I thought——"

"That's all werry fine," said the monstrous old woman. "But p'raps there'll be another elopement. Maids is thick in Curtain Vells, and p'raps you won't find your boys so easy. There's some that don't like the job—don't like two brace of pops behind 'em and a galloping brother and father."

"We shan't be followed," said Vernon contemptuously.

"No, I dare say you von't, but 'tis as vell to be behind a couple of good honest boys as'll use their pops when they're turning a corner and ready to swear they thought it was two gentlemen on the high toby as vas a followin' of 'em so fast."

"Very well," said Vernon, "whom do you want me to employ?"

"Vy, there's my two nephews, Charlie and Dickie Maggs, vot 'ud drive 'ard and fast all the vay to Lunnon town and no questions axed either end, but vot could easily be ansered wiv golden Georges."

"Let 'em wait on me when I send the word, and

hark'ee, they must be ready any time this month, for Miss may take it into her head to run before I expect."

Further intercourse between Mr. Francis Vernon and old Mother Mawhood was interrupted by loud knocks on the door at the back, supported by catcalls, yells, horn-blowing and whip-cracking.

"That's for the Main," said Mrs. Mawhood. "Vill you stay to see the sport?"

"'Tis a Welch main?"

"Ay—thirty-two birds."

"Well, send a boy to put my horse in the stable."

"This way, my fancy, this way," wheezed the hag, as she waddled towards the courtyard where the noise was growing louder every minute.

It may strike the reader as strange that the young gentlemen of the *Blue Boar* (they were all there save Mr. Lovely) should come ten miles to a disreputable farm for the purpose of seeing thirty-two cocks of the game butchered. The Welch Main was a peculiarly bloody form of cock-fighting, as it was determined by a series of rounds fought by the respective survivors until at the end a pair of already vilely scarred and mutilated birds were placed beak to beak by the Feeder to determine the ultimate victor of the Main.

Ten miles was not too far to travel for such glorious sport in the days of the Georges, but that they were compelled to travel at all was due to the squeamishness of Beau Ripple, who had a singular aversion from the game and would allow no cock-pit to be established within his jurisdiction. He used to say the martyrdom of chickens should never extend beyond the demand for painted fans.

Therefore a suitable cockpit had been set up in one of the outlying barns of Blackhart Farm, whither at discreet intervals went Lieutenant Blewforth of the *Lively*, Mr. Golightly of Campbell's Grey Dragoons, Mr. Tom Chalkley of the Foot, little Peter Wingfield, and many other young gentlemen. They would sit in the first tier and allow their exquisite necks to be blown upon by the stinking breath of the second tier which, in turn, was not unwilling to allow the third tier to spit over its shoulders in the intervals of yelling. 'Three to one on the Blotch-breasted Red!' 'Six to five against the Cheshire Pile!' 'Two to one on the Black-breasted Birchin!' and other such bewildering proclamations of their confidence in particular cocks of the game.

Vernon was not at all displeased that his visit to Blackhart Farm should have ostensible justification. Looking back, as he emerged into the courtyard, he noticed all the windows of the house were blind on that side and wondered why so ill-favoured and disreputable a dwelling-place had never been investigated by the servants of justice. So it was, however, not long after this date, and a gruesome day's work it was beneath the hot August sun: and not the least gruesome sight was old Mother Mawhood, monstrous, flabby and terror-stricken, quivering in her chair by the empty fireside, opposite a Robin Redbreast from Bow Street drinking many quarts of beer and regarding her with unfavourable glances, while he listened to the chink of the spades in the flower garden by the plantation. The runners would never have visited Blackhart Farm had not a certain lady of quality, who travelled in a post-chaise with muffled windows, dallied a month too long, thereby raising the suspicions of her eagle-nosed aunt, the Countess of ——, but what has all this to do with cock-fighting?

In the pit the spectators were arranging themselves. In front sat Lieutenant Blewforth and little Peter Wingfield as Masters of the Match. In the front tier sat the leading amateurs of Curtain Wells. Behind them were the shopkeepers, and behind the shopkeepers was the riff-raff of the Wells and its satellite villages.

Everybody was bawling odds at top voice, and occasionally one of the birds crowed. This was an infringement of etiquette and, being considered a sign of cowardice, immediately lengthened the odds against the offender. The tallowy man in a blue kerseymere coat and breeches is one of the Feeders, and is acting in that capacity for the Services represented by Lieutenant Blewforth, while the civilians are employing the good offices of Jimmy Trickett, who on less exciting occasions is one of the hostlers of the *Blue Boar*.

Vernon, looking for a vacant place in the front tier found himself next to Mr. Anthony Clare, who, for all he sat so unmoved, had provided eight cocks for the civilians and stood to lose a pretty pile of guineas.

"Where's Lovely?" asked Vernon, shaking the sawdust from his boots.

"He never comes to cock-fights," Clare replied rather coldly.

"Too brutal for a poet, eh?"

"I have never heard him say so," said Clare.

As a matter of fact Charles strongly disapproved of the sport and it is a significant fact that at this very moment, he was trotting along the Bristol road, tired of lashing Curtain polls and determined, against the advice of his conscience, to stake fifty guineas on the result of the Main.

The latter progressed with monotonous cruelty until, of the thirty-two cocks who began, but two pairs were left, all bleeding profusely. And now with a refinement of brutality, the steel gaffles, hitherto used to shorten the earlier and less interesting matches, were removed and silver ones fastened on in their place, because, the latter, being less deadly, prolonged the miserable contest.

During this momentary lull, Charles entered the barn and was greeted with cheers in which could be detected a note of surprize. Clare moved along in order to make room for his friend, and squeezed Mr. Vernon somewhat unceremoniously in doing so.

"What birds are being set to?" inquired Lovely.

"My Knowsley and Chalkley's Cheshire Pile, and

a White Pile of Campbell's against Winnington's Cuckoo."

The semi-final dragged out its bloody length, until for the final was left Mr. Clare's famous Knowsley cock, his ebony breast dabbled with blood and his red pinions ragged and broken, but still preserving some of the smartness of their slantwise trimming—trimmed so in order that by a lucky stroke an adversary's eye might be put out. The survivor of the two Services was Mr. Campbell's White Pile, stained with crimson.

" Will your bird win? " whispered Mr. Lovely.

" I think so," said Clare, " he comes of a good breed."

" Two to one in Tens against the Pile," shouted Mr. Lovely.

" Done," said Vernon.

" Two to one in Twenties against the Pile," shouted Mr. Lovely.

" Done," said Mr. Vernon.

" Three to one in Fifties," shouted Mr. Lovely.

And this wager also was taken by Mr. Francis Vernon.

The Feeders were setting the birds beak to beak. The shouting of odds was deafening: the gallant cocks were both exhausted by the four previous fights, but the feathers flew, the wings whirred, the gaffles clicked, and the blood flowed fast enough to please the vile faces that looked down through the murky atmosphere.

At last the White Pile, blinded in one eye, began to retreat before the Knowsley.

" I pound the cock," shouted Charles, flinging his hat into the pit.

The Teller of the Law, a seedy vagabond with a red nose, began to count in raucous accents. Twice he counted twenty slowly, and

" Vill any vun take it? " he asked.

" Yes," said Mr. Vernon, and just as Mr. Vernon said ' Yes,' the brave Knowsley cock, the champion of many famous fights, toppled over on his side, dead.

The Naval and Military Amateurs had won the Welch Main, and Mr. Charles Lovely had lost two hundred and ten guineas, not to mention ten pounds for so rashly pounding the cock.

The young gentlemen went back to Curtain Wells much pleased with the afternoon's entertainment, while the riff-raff walked or drove in queer vehicles back to their squalid homes, all save one unfortunate individual, unable to meet a debt of ten shillings incurred by backing the brave Knowsley, who for all he was dying had pursued his antagonist so confidently. He spent the night in a basket close to the roof and was not set down till the next morning by one of the labourers on Blackhart Farm.

CHAPTER XX

IN WHICH EVERYTHING GROWS BUT THE PLOT

YOU will remember, if you have not put this book upon the table meanwhile, that in the last paragraph of the last chapter, we left an unfortunate individual swinging in a basket hard by the roof of a barn. He was hoisted by a pulley amid the acclamations of the mob because he was unable to fulfil an obligation so small that half a guinea would have covered it. There he swung amid cobwebs and bats, fearful every time the basket creaked he should fall into the blood-stained sawdust of the cock-pit. I cannot tell you his name, but that is no great matter since we must examine him not as a man, but as a symbol.

Possibly with the Beau's perspective, we might diminish him to the size of a textual illustration, for this unfortunate man is a textual illustration, and though not etched with the care of Mr. Stothard, will serve his purpose well enough.

Suspension is a disreputable attitude for the human body, whatever way it is brought about, yet I doubt this maltreated anonymity was in better case than our hero. He paid the penalty for laying unwise wagers and found earth on the next morning much as he had left it on the afternoon of the day before. Moreover, he never paid his half-guinea, which was a real source of consolation. But our hero swung that night in an immaterial basket that creaked thrice as damnably as the other, and found no good-natured labouring man to put him on the ground next morning. The only result of opposing the advice of his conscience, was an additional debt of two hundred and twenty guineas to our villain.

To make matters worse, he had to meet his creditor over the breakfast table, and of the many dooms measured out to sinners, this is surely one of the most difficult to face with equanimity.

In despair, he took to drinking the waters with the rest of the Exquisite Mob, and earned a few golden glances from Beau Ripple, but nothing more tangible. Even the advantage of these was neutralized by the Chalybeate, which acted with disconcerting abruptness upon a healthy body unused to medicinal spurs.

The wry water served a good purpose, however, by souring his point-of-view. The liquid iron entered into his soul and he lashed the Curtain Polls in a variety of metres. He also took long walks into the country, and sought by the contemplation of scenery to acquire an impersonal attitude towards his fellow-creatures. After all, there is no better training for a mob-master than the exercise of a satirical pen, and as time went on Mr. Lovely's book increased in bulk, although it never achieved more than a suggestive slimness even when bound in calf.

February faded into March, and in accordance with the season everything began to grow.

Mr. Lovely's book we have already noticed.

Mr. Vernon's seductive arts grew daily more seductive, and, though for a week or two after Mr. Ripple's warning, Mrs. Courteen arranged for the complete occupation of Phyllida's leisure, the growth of Mrs. Courteen's figure necessitated a stricter attention to diet and exercise, and caused her so much anxiety that her vigilance was soon relaxed. So whenever the forenoons were fine enough, Phyllida sat on the moss-grown seat in the centre of the Maze, and, under the patronage of the little stone Cupid, grew daily more powerfully enchanted by the magical personality of Mr. Francis Vernon.

Thomas, the footman, grew daily more unctuous owing to the visit of a gouty dean who, being invited to occupy St. Simon's pulpit, preached a remarkable sermon in seven divisions and twenty-three subdivisions, conclusively establishing the identity of the English Nation with the tribe of Benjamin. Mr. Moon and Major Tarry grew more entirely devoted to the widow, and Thomasina the cat also grew owing to the advent of kittens. In fact, everybody and everything grew prodigiously in the merry springtime.

The list of visitors grew. Rich Mrs. Bendish arrived and made all the dowagers jealous with her chest of precious stones that she brought back from an island in the Caribbean Sea—buried treasure that was actually discovered. Lord Rocquepool came, and his daughters, the Honourable Georgina and the Honourable Caroline de Winqule. The Honourable Mrs. Winter-Green came, and the Welch baronet, Sir Owen Ap Taffy. The Marquess of Hurricane arrived, and several members of the great Wind family. Also, with all these aristocratick visitors, it is not surprizing that Mr. Ripple's snuff bill grew daily.

March came in like a lamb that year, and the sweet season danced in the bleak furrows over which the lank hares leaped and scampered. White violets scented equinoctial dusks, and in every window of the Wells big daffodils hung down their golden ruffs. March went by to the tune of fiddles and flutes. Mr. Ripple had to attend near half a dozen routs every night, and the weekly Assemblies were more fully thronged than ever before.

Every day the jolly sun grew more powerful and the noise of polite conversation was almost drowned by the twittering of the sparrows as they, like their betters, made a chorus of loves, jealousies, hopes, plans and disappointments in a world of chimney-stacks and slanting roofs. They perched in the most fashionable gutters, just as, down below on the sunny side of the High Street, the Exquisite Mob ruffled before the gayest shops.

" How well that chip hat becomes me! "

" What wonderful silks are being displayed this spring! "

" They say that hoops and head-dresses will both show a monstrous increase in size this year."

As if the daffodils had intoxicated the whole race of dyers, nothing but shades of yellow were to be seen. In these happier days for the followers of the Mode, Blonda and Brunetta, those charming sisters, were not compelled to rely on their natural complexions in order to wear a certain shade. In these happier days, powder, rouge and patches availed to make the gaudy apricock glow even beside the blooming peach without injury to either. Therefore the artfully arranged bow-windows with rolls of citron damasks, canary velvets, golden brocades, lemon sattins and orange silks, dismayed not Blonda any more than the sapphire and turquoise of the autumnal mode fretted the vanity of Brunetta. As for young maidens, their fashion like the eternal mountains was always white.

But suddenly on the twenty-seventh of the month the weather changed. Masses of wet grey clouds swept in from the Atlantick, and March prepared to go out like a lion.

And on this very morning *Curtain Polls severely lashed by a Curtain Rod* appeared on Mr. Paul Virgin's counter.

This small work produced far greater consternation than the sudden change in the weather. Though it rained and blew, and whistled and streamed, nobody paid the slightest attention, nobody said 'What a change in the weather,' for all the world was deeply engrossed in reading about his asterisked self and his asterisked neighbour.

CHAPTER XXI

CURTAIN POLLS

THERE had been nothing to prepare Curtain Wells for its chastizement. No wreathèd pamphlet warned readers in the most choice preliminary puff that a sarcastick comet would presently singe their vices, their follies and their vanities. Nobody had been invited to subscribe in advance to his own ridicule. As it were on the wings of a Westerly gale, these destructive little volumes settled upon the fields of Pleasure like locusts on a Bedouin plantation.

Two speculative chap-book pedlars sold the first twenty to as many drinkers of Chalybeate hastening home to breakfast. For those who stopped to buy there was no breakfast that morning. The kidneys and the bacon and the eggs and the ham and the loin chops and the red herrings and the toasted bread were neglected. The vanguard of purchasers were, in reading about neighbours, too much diverted, and, in reading about themselves, too indignant to eat.

Out went the kidneys and the bacon and the eggs and the ham and the loin chops and the red herrings and the toasted bread, frozen stiff in their own fat; and out went the vanguard to warn the main army of fashion that scurrility, satire and malice were abroad in many metres.

"Listen to this, Moon," ejaculated Major Tarry, as, undeterred by the driving wind, he strode along, quoting extracts that were perfectly inaudible to his companion.

"Listen to this, will you listen to this,"

*Like a lap-dog he's fed with a second-best spoon,
And bays as he should at the sight of the Moon.*

"Yes, but listen to this," said the Justice treading heavily in a puddle as he spoke.

*Do not tarry,
M * * n, but marry,
　While you're still upon the wax,
Though above her,
You can love her,
　And avoid the window tax.*

"Very low, very low indeed," said Tarry.

"So 'tis," quoth the Justice, "but the next verse is lower still."

*For that coat of
Him we wrote of
　Will be in your parlour soon,
And be reigning
When you're waning,
　And we whisper hornèd M * * n.*

"Ha, ha," said Tarry, "low, d——d low! But 'sblood, the fellow has humour."

"Humour," said the Justice, "you call this obscene doggerel, humour?"

"In parts, sir, in parts."

"I call it melancholy and libidinous."

Mrs. Courteen was seated at her window disconsolately regarding the rain.

"Gemini, child!" she exclaimed. "What can be the matter with Mr. Moon and the Major that they gesticulate so wildly."

"They're reading books, ma'am," Betty announced.

"Reading books, but they are standing at the street corner like Methodies!"

"They'm beänt gone sick mad for love of 'ee, do 'ee think, Ma'am?"

"Flatterer," sighed Mrs. Courteen. "No, child, they have probably been converted. I detect Methodism in their madness. Te-hee! I must keep that for Archdeacon Conybeare, who so dislikes extremes of sensibility in anything that pertains to so sacred a thing as religion. Ah, dear! Religion, what is it?"

"There's many ways of it, ma'am, I do think. 'Tis true religious not to laugh when the lads tickle thy ankle wi' straws during the prayer for Good King George!"

"Tut-tut, how disloyal!"

Just then the raucous voice of one of the itinerant booksellers shouted "Curtain Polls severely lashed by a Curtain-Rod."

"Run, Betty, and inquire the price at once," cried Mrs. Courteen perceiving that this was the cause of the gentlemen's delay. "'Tis evidently a rumour on the best authority about the Day of Judgment."

Presently Betty returned.

"'Tis a book, ma'am."

"I know that, simpleton, how much?"

"Four shillings and sixpence, ma'am, for a little mimsy book not so thick as the magick history of Jack the Giant Killer."

"But what was inside, foolish one?"

"Oh, 'twas full of stars, ma'am."

"'Tis certainly a work on fortune-telling. Pray buy it instantly, here is the money."

Back came Betty with the volume, and presently Mrs. Courteen fainted.

Downstairs ran Betty, and upstairs walked Mr. Thomas and Betty.

"'Twas the book as done it," said the latter vehemently.

The offending volume lay face downwards upon the quilted apricock of Mrs. Courteen's lap, so Thomas picked it up and began to read:

At the Wells many elegant widows are seen,
But no one so modish as Mrs. C******n,
Her hoop——

So far he read, but, rubicund though he was, modesty was still able to deepen his colour.

"Yes," said Betty, "pray do 'ee read us some more, Mr. Thomas."

"What Jebusite wrote this book? I will smite him and all his works," replied Thomas, flinging the volume into the fire. Whether the odour of burning leather or the profuse drops of Sal Volatile revived the offended Lady I do not know, but she instantly sat up and, in a voice tremulous with anxiety, bade her footman call a chair.

"For," said she, "I must pay a visit of condolence to my Lady Bunbutter, whose propriety has suffered an almost irreparable injury."

She did not stay to change her dress; she passed her suitors still quoting scurrility, one against the other in the wind and rain, without a smile of recognition or sympathy.

Outside my Lady Bunbutter's stood a row of sedan-chairs, and as Mrs. Courteen walked up my Lady Bunbutter's front door-step, the knot of chairmen packed more closely over a copy of *Curtain Polls* indiscreetly left behind by one of their fares. There was a rustle of pages quickly turned by dirty thumbs, and as Mrs. Courteen was ushered in by my Lady Bunbutter's claret-coloured footman, there followed her upstairs a burst of ribald laughter.

My Lady Bunbutter had, by reason of her superior bulk and wealth, successfully repelled all rival claimants to the throne of dowagership. She reigned supreme; moreover her advice on this gusty forenoon was particularly valuable, inasmuch as she had just shaken off the waters of Bath on account of the publication there of some odious verses, in which her name and her person were treated with intolerably small respect. Therefore it was not surprizing to find her drawing-room the haunt of innumerable widows, old maids and long-established wives. There they sat, supplying asterisks with immense volubleness. As it happened, they had just tittered behind their fans over the odiously vulgar, but undeniably appropriate—yes! the odious fellow was certainly witty—when the subject of their malicious laughter and false blushes entered the room.

With the tact bred of many a Quadrille party, my Lady Bunbutter advanced to meet Mrs. Courteen, murmuring, ' poor dear little Miss Kitcat, so spiteful and yet, my dear Mrs. Courteen, since we are all friends, alas! how true! '

Now young Miss Kitcat was still young Miss Kitcat, and simply would not become old maid or dowager, and would allow herself to be ogled by that notorious rake and disreputable—yes! disreputable, card-sharper, Captain Mann.

While the dowagers discussed the situation and vowed that the rogue of an author sadly needed a lesson, Beau Ripple himself, with many an urbane tut-tut was reading *Curtain Polls* in his tall white drawing-room, where the firelight danced and flickered over the gleaming ivory panels.

" Too bad," said the Beau to himself as he turned the scandalous pages. He did not, however, treat them less carefully because they were scandalous, for to Mr. Ripple a book was always a book, and he paid as much ceremony to the emanations of Grub Street as he would have shown to the copper plates of an elephant folio.

" This is, indeed, too bad," said the Beau, " and yet the rascal has wit. Oh, yes, he certainly has wit, but what an excellent example this volume affords of the superiority of prose over verse. A poetick satirist too often sacrifices his good breeding for the sake of the rhymes. Now I should never have said that. No, no, that is too bad, and this—good G——! this is unpardonable!"

The Great little Man jumped up as red as one of the big chintz roses that bloomed so prodigally all over his winged chair.

The King of Fashion looked very small as he stood in the middle of an Aubusson rug, yet I think he never looked more truly a monarch than at this moment. Unfortunately there was nobody to see him as he stood in his little world of mirrours and engravings.

And what had upset his equanimity? Certainly not the following lines:

> Where R*****, gentlest, kindliest of Beaux,
>   To all the world an urbane presence shows;
> Proclaims the tropick joys of China Tea,
>   And rules e'en Fashion with his polished sway.
> At his approach the graceless ruffle shakes,
>   While every waistcoat in its buttons quakes;
> Each conscious shoe more luminously shines,
>   And puckered breeches haste to smooth their lines.

Whatever the Curtain Rod thought of the subjects, to the Monarch he was always complimental.

"Intolerable! unpardonable!" cried the Beau, tapping his snuff-box so fiercely that some of the powder was spilled over the grey Angora cat which was purring against his gold-clocked stockings in the heart of a faded Aubusson rose. Octavia (the cat) sneezed assent. What had upset his equanimity? You shall take a short journey to find out, for I perceive a break in the weather and sweet April is in the West.

We will walk just so far as Curtain Garden, but, pray, do not turn into the Maze where the paths are atrociously damp. Alas, the rain is beginning again, but at the end of that long alley is a summer house, the above of many Rococo Dryads, although 'tis haunted at present by amorous mortals, for I caught the glint of a buckle and a shimmer of chestnut ringlets.

It does not require King Œdipus to guess that those eyes which stare so into the heavens are the blue eyes of Phyllida, while any one would recognize in that smooth voice the careful enunciation of Mr. Francis Vernon.

He, like every one else that forenoon, was reading *Curtain Polls severely lashed by a Curtain Rod.* Perchance the following lines were they that lately enraged Mr. Horace Ripple:

> *Now is it a hoyden, a hussy or Miss,*
> *Who listens to love but refuses a kiss?*
> *'Tis said every morning she flies to the Maze,*
> *And buries her head from the Publick's low gaze.*
>
> *Of Love in a Maze, pretty charmer, beware,*
> *For under the rose there are thorns ev'rywhere,*
> *And if you should chance the wrong turning to take,*
> *'Tis odds that you'll trip on a tall garden Rake.*
>
> *The Cits, when you pass, point you out to their Belles,*
> *You serve as a moral all over the Wells,*
> *And Dowagers, drinking your health in green tea,*
> *Express a faint hope that man will not betray.*

"Those are pretty stanzas for a lover to read," said Vernon, who, to do him justice, did not seem very greatly perturbed by the insult.

"Oh, Amor," said poor Phyllida, "they can't truly be intended for me!"

"For whom else?"

"But who would write such cruel words of a young woman?"

"That puppy, Lovely."

"Mr. Lovely! Oh! no, he's a gentleman and a man of family and a man of taste and a friend of Beau Ripple."

"He may be all this and more," declared Vernon, "but he wrote this book."

"I don't believe it."

"He did, I say, for he informed me so himself—at least he as good as informed me!"

"Amor! you must have been mistook."

"On my life, not at all. He owes me near five hundred guineas, and when I hinted that the expense of inland Spas tells upon a gentleman's resources, begged my pardon, swore he had a literary project on hand, and promised me a hundred guineas on Lady Day. That was the day before yesterday."

"A gamester!" said Miss Phyllida, who, with the injustice of her age and sex, neglected to see that her lover was as much to blame in this particular as Lovely.

"Ay! a gamester," said Vernon with fervid indignation.

"And for the sake of a hundred guineas he was ready to cheapen the honour of a maid?"

"My angel forgets the Chinese Masquerade. Mr. Lovely was piqued by her obvious weakness for a less fashionable, less conspicuous gentleman."

"Oh, I will never forgive him. He has ruined me."

"Nay, come, come, 'tis not so bad as that. Amor will never desert his Phyllida."

"I'm ruined, I'm ruined," she sobbed. "I shall never dare go to visit my cousin Barbara, who is as prim and proper as——" Nothing was prim enough for the comparison. "And she has the most delicious hot buns you ever tasted, and the dearest spaniel and the most beautiful pug-dog. Oh dear! oh dear! Oh dear! how all the neighbours will laugh, and old Rumble the carrier will be telling tales about me in every kitchen in the county, and 'tis all your fault."

"My fault?"

"Yes, yours, for asking me to come and meet you and making love, while all the while there was somebody peeping over the hedges. I'll never forgive you, never, never!—"

"Dearest life, we can put a stop to scandal by being wed immediately. Listen! I'll have a post-chaise ready at dawn, and post-boys in scarlet, and lodgings with a balcony and a goldfinch singing in a cage. My Phyllida, will you come?"

"Oh! I dare not, I dare not—not yet, oh lud, oh lud! how shall I look the world in the face?"

Vernon thought for a moment.

"Where are your pearls kept?"

"In my mamma's trunkmail, but Betty could give me the key—and sometimes in her jewel case."

"On the thirtieth," said Vernon, "there will be a ball at Daish's Rooms, next to the *Blue Boar* where I lodge. You will surely be there, 'tis my Lady Bunbutter's rout."

"Yes, we shall be there," said Phyllida.

"At two o'clock in the morning, I will have a post-chaise waiting by St. Simon's Church corner, opposite Leonard's toy shop. Would you have the courage to slip out, my dearest heart, my Phyllida?"

"Oh, no, I could not travel by night."

"'Twould be safer," urged Vernon.

"No, no, I could not."

"Then for your sake, I'll take the risque and have the post-chaise in the same place at three o'clock in the afternoon of the next day. Promise you will come."

"No, no, I shall never be brave enough, and I must go for I hear voices, and I must never be seen with you again. Good-bye, good-bye," and before Vernon could stop her, Phyllida was running down the poplar alley to escape from Curtain Garden.

Our villain began to wonder whether she would elope after all. If she were shy, he might secure the necklace at any rate. With slow steps, his mind full of silken pearls, Mr. Vernon went slowly homewards. Half-way down the High Street, he passed a narrow street known as Blood Passage from the vicinity of a large slaughter-house. He hesitated; made up his mind, and, turning down it, came to a crooked house over a low tumble-down doorway. He knocked fastidiously with the amber knob of his cane. A slatternly woman, whose last night's rouge was streaked with the matutinal ashes, opened the door.

"Does Mr. Maggs live here?"

"Come in," said the frowsy light o' love.

CHAPTER XXII

THE CURTAIN ROD

THE satirist stood in his publisher's back parlour, and, through the dusty glass of the partition, observed the Exquisite Mob purchase their castigation.

" 'Tis strange," he pondered, " that mankind should be willing to pay four-and-sixpence to be laughed at. Yet it is! "

Mr. Lovely was awaiting a draught for one hundred guineas, and Mr. Paul Virgin, glad of anything that would delay for a while such an unwelcome disbursement, continued to bow and smirk over the counter as the neat little piles of new volumes speedily diminished. At last the hour for the midday meal arrived with a temporary lull in the storm of purchasers. Mr. Virgin turned with a sigh into his little back parlour and, wading carefully through the heaps of uncatalogued tomes, set out with a wry face to unlock his walnut writing-cabinet.

" We were hurried too much, Mr. Lovely, sir. We han't had leisure to bind the book as it should be bound. Ye would hurry us so, Mr. Lovely."

" You wouldn't pay me till the book was published, and I want the money, so d———n all grumbling and be grateful that you'll make a small fortune."

" A small fortune! What a jester you are, Mr. Lovely. I declare you put me in mind of the old plays, such jests! "

Mr. Paul Virgin seated before his cabinet, was writing the draught with tardy fingers.

"There ye are, Mr. Lovely, and never say I don't treat ye with consideration, with generosity, sir, for I dare swear I shall lose fifty pounds sterling by this adventure."

"Be d——d, you peevish rogue. Why all the world of fashion has thronged your shop since nine o'clock this morning."

"Yes, but it takes a deal to make a hundred guineas. Now let me make it pounds, Mr. Lovely, sir. Do let me make it pounds."

The latter snatched the draught from the old young bookseller and, having read it through with much deliberation, transferred it to the seclusion of his innermost pocket.

After this transaction, which was effected with a singular grace, I am sorry to add that he put his tapered finger to his tapered nose and winked several times at the disconsolate Mr. Virgin.

"The books are so ill-bound, look at this one, Mr. Lovely, your honour. The leaves are falling apart already, just because you would hurry us so terribly."

Mr. Lovely stooped and picked up some loose pages.

"Ay, 'tis autumn already with this copy," he said, glancing casually at the page he held in his hand. "Why who wrote this?"

"You did, Mr. Lovely, you did."

"I wrote this—this d——d vile verse, this—" and Charles read aloud the lines that so dismayed our heroine. "I wrote this damnable doggerel? By G——, Mr. Virgin, I never wrote this."

"Why, who else could have written it?"

"That's what I want to know. Come back, you hound," shouted the irate author, grabbing his publisher by the tails of his coat, just as he was edging his way back to the shop. "Come back," he said, jerking him over Mr. Bayle's Dictionary. "You moth-eaten vagabond, you impostor, you thief." Charles began to belabour Mr. Virgin with a folio copy of the *Anatomy of Melan-*

choly. Round and round the little back parlour he thumped the publisher; the dust rose from innumerable ancient tomes. Surely never were books so rudely disturbed since the niece and the Padre flung the library of the illustrious Don Quixote de la Mancha out of the window, and burned a hundred volumes of chivalry.

" How came these d——d lines into my book, eh, sir, answer me that, sir," and having dissected the *Anatomy of Melancholy*, Charles picked up Sir Roger L'Estrange's translation of Æsop to continue the assault.

" I don't understand, Mr. Lovely, sir. Pray desist, Mr. Lovely, your honour, sir. The printer must have printed them."

" 'Sdeath and fury! you rascal, I know that. Who wrote them, who wrote them? "

In order to supply the correct twirl to this note of interrogation, Charles flung the little bookseller to the farthest corner of his little back parlour, at the same time arming himself with half a dozen fresh volumes.

Mr. Virgin cowered in the dust and cobwebs.

" Who wrote them? " Charles demanded.

" I don't——"

" What! " and the —th volume of the *Gentleman's Magazine*, newly arrived from the binder, winged its way in the direction of the quivering bookseller. This he ducked to avoid, but even as he ducked, the five volumes of Mr. Ozell's revision of Urquhart and Motteux' *Rabelais* burst over him like an exploded hand grenade.

" Who wrote them? "

" Truly I don't——"

This time Mr. Prior's *Poems on Several Occasions* carried his wig into obscurity, and the owner clapped a hand to his head just in time to receive the bevelled morocco edges of the *Beggar's Opera* full on the fingers.

" Mr. Lovely, sir, you are too violent."

" Violent, you dog? By G—— if you don't give the name of the son of a w—— that wrote these damnable lines, I'll flay you alive and bind my next edition of poems with your lousy skin." The foxy-faced old young man commenced to wring his hands.

"Mr. Lovely," he almost screamed. "Mr. Lovely, you're mad—go out of my shop."

"Who wrote those lines? Answer, or I'll break up your shop—ay! break it up with your own sign-board. At the Sign of the Woman—at the Sign of the Strumpet! Answer me, you lickspittle vermin, answer me."

Charles had now seized his wretched publisher by the neck-band, and shook him so roughly that the latter, fearing for his teeth, the most extravagant purchase in his mean little life, began to whine.

"A gentleman—a gentleman——"

"Well, you misbegotten toad, I never supposed 'twas a midwife."

"No, certainly not, Mr. Lovely, a gentleman—a gentleman."

"His name, dog."

"I don't know."

"Yes, you do, answer will you."

"He told me 'twas Amor."

"I knew it, I knew it, you sneaking son of a b——, and he gave you twenty guineas to print the verses."

"No, not twenty, only ten, Mr. Lovely, on my soul."

"On your soul! H——l take your soul! Why you were spawned in a ditch, you viper. So you let my honour go for ten guineas. Give them to me."

"Oh! Mr. Lovely."

"Give them to me."

The miserable little old young man produced the money, unluckily for himself, in paper.

"Now since you love money so dearly, by heaven, you shall eat money." And Mr. Lovely, making a bolus of the bribe, crammed it down the reluctant bookseller's throat with his own ruler. Then our hero walked out of the shop.

I hope you will not deny this scene was in the true vein of heroism. Aye! aye! 'tis full of bombast as you very properly observe, ma'am or sir; but that is the part of a hero. He must follow the Prince of Denmark's directions to the players. Aye! aye! and 'tis full of wind, but so was the great Montgolfier balloon, and surely every aeronaut is a hero, even in his descents at the tail-end of a parachute.

So pray judge Mr. Lovely, not as a man, but as a hero, for I think you'll do me the justice to admit I never tried to conceal his position.

But he owes the villain a considerable sum of money. Of course he does, and this awkward fact is perplexing him very much indeed as he strides down Curtain High Street. To tell the truth, when he emerged from Mr. Virgin's shop, he found that when the Fates dipped him into Styx, they made the same mistake as Madame Thetis, with this difference, that, whereas Achilles was left with a vulnerable heel, our hero preserved a vulnerable conscience.

It would have been mighty heroick to march into the *Blue Boar*, run Mr. Vernon through the lungs, wed the injured heroine and tread after death the golden fields of Elysium; but his silly conscience would not allow him to kill a man to whom he was under a monetary obligation.

So he borrowed four hundred guineas from Mr. Anthony Clare, who could ill afford the loan, and putting this sum with what he had earned from lashing the Curtain Polls in an extra thick paper envelope, he sealed it with his own heroick seal. This fulfilment of earthly debts he sent up to Mr. Francis Vernon by the hand of Mr. Daish himself, and set to work to make his conscience less vulnerable by many consecutive pints of heroick Burgundy.

You thought that he was going to turn out poor humanity after bullying Mr. Virgin so heroically? Egad, ma'am or sir, you thought wrong. You doubt anybody can be a Burgundian hero? So he can; there has been more than one Charles the Bold of Burgundy.

The very word is as fire to the most pusillanimous: the very thought of its crimson depths should set us all tilting.

'Bring me a quart bottle of Burgundy.' The phrase is like a trumpet-call outside the keep of Paradise.

'Bring me another quart of Burgundy.' Down goes the portcullis before the hero's charge.

Port may turn a man into a hero—in his dreams; yet I doubt they are too heavy. As for Sherry, it will serve to sharpen the wits of a dried-up attorney, but is poor stuff to weave into heroes. On Champagne, a man will talk like the crew of the *Argo*, but there's the end of the whole business.

Charles drank Burgundy and I promise you some fine heroicks presently.

CHAPTER XXIII

SPACE BETWEEN AN HEROICK COUPLET

A DISCOURAGING fact for the Persii of yesterday, to-day, and to-morrow, is that, however needle-sharp their thrusted rapiers, however thorough their castigations, Society never shows weal or scar at the end of it all.

Here was profligate, card-playing, snobbish, vapoured Society, quite recovered of its whipping and, by candle-time, setting out to perform just those very actions Persius most bitterly abuses.

My Lady Bunbutter continued to observe every Mata-dor in her opponents' hands, continued to rake in ill-gotten guineas, continued to use a quadrille pack with Manille stained, Spadille nicked, Batso dog-eared, and Ponto scratched. The Most Honble. the Marchioness of Hurricane continued to help herself five times to the richest Fricassées; continued to allow her lap-dog liberty to vomit in alien drawing-rooms, continued to breathe stertorous bawdry into the prominent ears of her Italian son-in-law—il Conte di Scirocco—while her daughter the Contessa snored in a corner.

Young Miss Kitcat continued to encourage the addresses of the disreputable Captain Mann, and even went so far as to tap that military scoundrel three times with her fan in coy avowal of his charming naughtiness.

The Earl of Clnderton drank five bottles of Port that very night in order to emphasize his indifference to satire, and slept under his own mahogany table because his lackeys below stairs were too drunk to carry him to bed.

In fact, nobody save the publisher of *Curtain Polls* displayed sign or sense of injury.

Our heroine indeed was vastly affected, but her misfortunes were due to a gloss upon the original.

As it happened, Mrs. Courteen did not discover the reference to her daughter's indiscretion, until she was asked by an inquisitive dowager to explain the allusion in the twelve lines. She managed to conceal her agitation, thanks to the permanency of the newest rouge, but presently called for her chair and arrived home a full two hours before she was expected.

When she sailed into the parlour Phyllida was languishingly occupied with a blue vase of pot-pourri, and the parlour fire was trying to burn up beneath a weight of blackened notepaper.

The suddenness of the widow's entrance alarmed her daughter so much that she dropped the vase, and the contents were strewn over the carpet. The faint perfume that slowly permeated the stuffy atmosphere of the lodgings, should have reminded Mrs. Courteen of her youth, of long June eves and blossoms plucked awhile ago by fingers now wrinkled and stained with years of snuff.

Mrs. Courteen also neglected to remember that so far as ridicule went, she had brought enough of that upon her own head.

However, she recalled neither memory nor fact, and was properly enraged with her daughter's light behaviour.

"You have ruined my good name, child. I can never again look the world in the face. How we shall be laughed at in Hampshire, for be sure that odious Miss Talker whose sister married the Rector of Slumber, has already despatched a copy to her brother-in-law, and you know what chatterboxes parsons always are: I suppose because they preach, though I should have thought, lud! that with so much breath used on Sunday, they might be as dumb as dumb for the rest of the week, and hurt nobody, least of all their own wives and neighbours. But there! what good is it to educate a young woman in the way she should go? I might better have set an example to the village clock. At all events that does possess a face. Put down your handkerchief, hussey."

"Dear mamma———"

"Don't excuse yourself, pray do not excuse yourself, I doubt 'tis all my fault. I doubt I han't looked after you, taken you to Melton Abbey, and prayed for you, minx, yes, prayed for you. And have you got any good from learning the collects for Sunday and the Benedicite and the Athanasian Creed and the thirty-nine Articles? None! A pretty thing, truly, that after so much honourable religion, I should have my daughter pointed out as a——as what no respectable young woman is. Pointed at! And I, your mother, am to be laughed at, mocked at, jeered at, because you suffer every down-at-heel fop to make gross love to you, sheltered from the eye of men——yes! vastly well——but you forget the eye of one above and the tongue of scandal."

"Madam, I am truly, deeply ashamed. If I promise never, never again to cause you the slightest uneasiness, will you forgive me for once, and take me away from this odious town?"

"Take you away? A pretty request truly; and give every old maid in Curtain Wells the opportunity of saying I was afraid to show my face and your figure. Take you away, miss? No, indeed, I shall take you around. I shall try by exhibiting you beneath your mother's protection, to give the lie to these atrocious reports and, next year, miss, next year, we will pay a visit to Tunbridge Wells in order to provide a husband whom you may kiss in the privacy of your own estate, with no one but a wandering gamekeeper any the wiser."

"I never kissed Mr. Amor," protested Phyllida.

"Amor? Amor? And who is Mr. Amor?"

"He is my true love, ma'am, whom I love with all my might and main."

"There's indecency! there's impropriety! Lud! I vow, vixen, you are as wanton as a goddess. You love him, eh?"

"That is my only excuse, ma'am, for having behaved so ill."

"What business, I should like to know, has a child of fifteen——"

"Seventeen, ma'am."

"Fifteen, girl."

"Then, sure, you are reckoning by leap years, ma'am."

"Do not be impudent. I repeat, Phyllida, I will not have impudence. You know dear Doctor Makewell particularly enjoined me not to allow impudence. 'Your heart won't stand it, ma'am.' Cruel Phyllida, not content with deceiving your mother, you are willing to injure her health by impudence."

"You think only of yourself," said Phyllida bitterly.

"Only of myself! Oh! Phyllida, how dare you accuse me of selfishness? My whole life since the death of your father who was a most exacting man and would ride Pegasus, though I told him a hundred times if I told him once that the brute would murder him. Now I've forgotten what I was saying, and 'tis all your fault, ungrateful child. Go to bed instantly and to-morrow I will have all your dresses starched as stiff as leather, so that nobody, not even that spiteful Lady Jane Vane, can say I don't take care that whatever your mind may be, your dresses leave nothing to be desired. Go to bed, go to bed. I can't listen to you any longer. I feel humiliated by your abominable behaviour. Judge of my feelings when I tell you I did not dare invite either Mr. Moon or Major Tarry to escort me home for fear the world would say I was setting you a bad example. Now, perhaps you'll accuse me of not possessing a conscience. Indeed, my conscience is too tender. 'Tis the tenderest part of me, though I have one of the most delicate skins—a skin that bruises if I ring a bell with unwonted celerity."

" Mamma, I——" Phyllida began.

" Pray do not say another word, you have said enough to-night to last a lifetime. Send Betty with my bed-gown worked in crimson hollyhocks and I will try to forget this wretched experience by attempting to ascertain—please get the playing cards—how Miss Trumper managed to secure codille in the last hand but four of this extremely unpleasant and unprofitable evening. Go to bed, Phyllida, don't dally. Here is Betty. Go to bed, Phyllida."

So Phyllida went to bedew her lavendered pillow. Anything was better than listening to her mother's perpetual reproaches. Anything, anything was better. Even to be betrayed. Ha! ha! now I think for the first time you will admit Miss Phyllida to be a true heroine. Poor Clarie Harlowe! How Phyllida had wept over her adventures and, even in the midst of tears, how quick she had always been to thrust the forbidden volumes out of sight when she heard her mother's step on the stairs.

Poor Clarie Harlowe! She began to sign her name to innumerable nobly penitent epistles.

Your cruelly abandoned
      Phyllida.
Your wretched, but still loving
      Phyllida.
Your heartbroken, hopeless
      Phyllida.
Your betrayed daughter
      Phyllida.
Your forsaken, but affectionate
      Phyllida.
Your seduced (or was it seducted, or abduced
 or abducted?) *Phyllida.*

Oh, dear! Oh, dear! what a muddle fine language was to be sure!

I have not yet apologized for my very ancient story, but faith! you must blame the period and the intolerable system of female education. Amor had either to be a Lovelace or a Joseph at a time when young maidenhood fainted before an ardent glance.

After all we do not now apologize for our strong silent men and hysterical girls. Why should we? And yet for my own part I love better your talkative blackguard; I have known so many strong silent men, and they were all fools or Scotsmen.

During this digression, Phyllida has fallen asleep, her face flushed and dabbled with spent tears, her chestnut hair in golden filigree upon the pillow and, where the sleeve of her bed-gown has retreated, a rosy arm whose little fist is clenched in maiden despair.

Poor foolish child! Why would you fall in love? Untenanted, your dearest gate swings in the wind to-night, but you will not mount again upon its topmost mossy bar. You will never again view with the same excitement the huntsmen over the hill-top; they will mean less to you; their pink coats will be quite dingy when next you say good morning to old Nick Runnalls the Whip. For my part, I do not believe that hot buttered apple-pies will taste so sweet when next you eat them in the long cool kitchen with its pot of marjoram and shaded sunlight.

And as for your bed-chamber with casements abob with peering rosebuds, I doubt the shelves will not soon be disturbed to make a place for new trophies. Once you thought it a day of days when you found the thigh-bone of a horse or the skull of a badger. They hang on the walls now, poor relicks of an outworn delight.

All this shall go for a balcony in the Haymarket and a goldfinch in a gilt cage. Foolish child! Away down in Hampshire the goldfinches build green nests in the orchard. Phyllida! sweet, headlong, heedless Phyllida!

* * *

"I blame you, Betty. I blame you, vixen. Why you cannot model yourself on Thomas passes my comprehension." Thus the widow.

"She meant no harm, poor pretty lamb," protested the maid.

"'Tis not what we mean, but what we do that counts in this world."

"Ah! 'tis fine for thee to talk, ma'am, you take good care to amuse yourself, but, little miss, she must dingle-dangle all day long wi' nought to do but dream of doing nought."

"She has her friend, Miss Morton."

"Ay! that black-eyed hussy what pinches the maiden who dresses her lean skimpy rat's hair. I don't take much account o' she."

They continued in this strain for quite two hours, and would never have stopped if the candles had endured.

They went up to bed just as Charles, having finished his third bottle of Burgundy, knocked with vinous assurance at the door of the Great House.

I am not at all certain whether this adventurous action should have been included in this chapter, for I doubt nothing more heroick was ever done even by Hercules at the zenith of his laborious career. It was considered rash enough to wait upon Mr. Ripple in the middle of his siesta. A royal Duke once succeeded in gaining admittance, if very little else; but to wait upon Mr. Ripple when his flambeaux strewed the steps, when the orange light in his porch was winking on its way to annihilation, when the grey Angora cat had settled herself for repose, when not even a mouse dared scamper in the wainscot, and when Mr. Ripple himself sat amid the ruins of his complexion—this was defying the lightning and inviting Jove's revenge indeed.

Nevertheless, fortified by three bottles of a vintage that held the heart of France in its crimson depths,

Charles recklessly knocked at the front door of the Great House, not once, but twice or thrice, with added vigour in the repetition. The sound sent the Beau's taper fingers a full two inches deep into a pomade compounded of some particularly fine Provençal almonds and the fat of foxes, the whole famous for removing those pectinated wrinkles that cluster at the edge of middle-aged lips. The fragrant grease, wedged beneath his nails, caused him to press thumb to fingers with an exclamation of fastidious displeasure.

The clatter of the second and third assault froze him to his chair with a sense of impending calamity.

Gog and Magog were fast asleep dreaming their gaudy dreams of Africa. Mrs. Binn, Mr. Ripple's intelligent cook, was snoring in the starlight of an upper chamber; Polly and Molly, Mr. Ripple's equally intelligent maids, were dreaming discreet dreams also in an upper chamber. Mr. Mink alone of the royal household was awake, engaged upon the overwhelmingly tricky job of frizzling his master's newest wig, and therefore quite unable, during this capillary crisis, to attend to the affairs of the world or the devil, knocked either never so loudly.

Consequently Mr. Ripple had to open the door himself, for if the knocking were to continue, many heads might peer from the Crescent windows, and the morning's rumour of the occurrence damage his authority.

It is characteristick of the Beau that in this critical juncture of affairs, he preserved his faculties so intact, that he was able without affectation to choose deliberately between a dressing-gown of flowered damask and a more diaphanous wrapper of dove-grey China silk. In deference to the season he selected the latter.

As he passed the door of his third dressing-room, he could see Mr. Mink, apparently unconscious of anything untoward in the air, blowing with steady breaths upon a remarkably hot pair of curling-tongs. The calm demeanour of his gentleman restored whatever was still lacking to Mr. Ripple's perfect equilibrium of mind.

With gentle steps, he descended the quiet stairs and, candlestick in hand, proceeded to draw back the cunningly wrought bolts of the front door.

"Mr. Ripple, I must speak to you," said Charles.

"Charles," said the Beau, "this visit is either vastly important or—it is vastly impertinent. Pray what is your business, sir?"

"Business?" repeated Charles, on whom the effort of concentration was beginning to tell slightly. "Business?"

"Yes, business, sir, business; for I presume you are not situated on my doorstep for pleasure."

"I want to speak to you."

"Come to-morrow."

"Nay, sir, I must speak with you now. I'm in a devilish mess, and need the advice of a man who has seen—who has seen——"

"Well, sir?" said the Beau, shading his candle in such a way that the pallid flickering rays lit up the young man's countenance.

"D——! I don't know, Ripple, but for God's sake don't stand there with that infernal candle dancing all over my face. Let me come in."

Whether it was the note of misery in our hero's voice or his drawn face or merely a whim of a great man's naturally eccentrick mind that made the Beau beckon Charles to follow him upstairs to the tall white drawing-room, where even still the fire glowed dully, will never be known. Any way, beckon to him he did, and, having set down the taper on the high mantelpiece, seated himself beside the fire and began meditatively to toast his embroidered morocco pumps.

There they sat in the great drawing-room, the King and his Heir Presumptive, and very ghostly they looked in the wan light, and very unreal the whole experience seemed to Charles in after life.

"'Tis about this book."

" What book? "

" This satire."

" You wrote it? "

" Aye," with great weariness.

" *You* wrote it? 'Foregad, Charles, I should never have believed that."

" But I never—I never wrote those lines."

" What lines? " Mr. Ripple, having admitted much, would admit no more.

"About Miss Courteen and the Maze, and the whole d——d, d——d, d——d——"

No substantive was strong enough to suit the emphatick epithets thrice repeated.

" And who, may I ask, was the author of those graceful stanzas? "

" I know, but—but, Ripple—I owed the blackguard money—the Chinese Masquerade—I knew his name all the while—if harm comes of this affair, 'tis my fault—but by G——, I'll call him out, yes, I'll call him out, I'll call him out, I'll call him out, and I'll——"

" Go to bed," said Mr. Ripple peremptorily.

" What d'ye mean? "

" You fool, you're drunk. We'll talk of this to-morrow. Good night, Mr. Lovely. By the way, who was the author of those graceful stanzas? "

" Oh! h——! Amor. Vernor—Vernon. Anon! Oh, h——! "

" What proof have you of this? "

" Proof, eh? what d'ye say—proof—ha-ha-ha! proof! Why the proof of the pudding's in the eating. Isn't that so? But I've found, I've found the author, and I'll walk with him in Curtain Mead—in Curtain Mead by moonlight, eh? and by the powers, you shall act for me."

" Sir, this flippancy is intolerable."

" Who's flippant—who's intol—erol—erable, sir? I say I'll pay him with six inches of smallsword."

" You forget my rules, Mr. Lovely."

"Rules! Rules? What's the good of rules? He has insulted me and her."

I think you will agree with me that Charles was drunk enough to be very undignified. Mr. Lovely Senior appeared again, maudlin and quarrelsome. The Beau, who remembered him, winced at the resemblance.

"This interview is very repugnant to my sense of decorum," he protested. "I beg you will take your leave, sir. The whole affair needs the elucidation of the morning; this candle is insufficient. Moreover, the hour is late; the fire is low; I make it a rule to be asleep by midnight whenever possible."

"There you go again!" cried Charles, jumping up and walking with feverish gestures and unsteady legs round about the room. "Rules! Rules! Rules! 'Foregad, sir, I tell you, you cannot make rules for life and death."

"But you can make many excellent rules for living and dying. One of the best of these is moderation in liquor."

Charles went back to the *Blue Boar* not quite sure whether he had told Beau Ripple a very great deal or nothing at all. He remembered so little of what he had said that next morning he came to the conclusion that it was nothing at all. He was glad of this, for somehow when the effects of the Burgundy wore off, he did not feel disposed to attempt the barricade of the Great little Man's modish prejudice. Anything in the nature of an intrigue would be distasteful to such an emotional ascetick.

So Charles stayed late in bed on Tuesday morning and took no advantage of the invitation grimly issued the night before.

In the afternoon, being dejected in spirits, and finding all the world gone a-hunting, or a-fishing, or a-wenching, he betook himself to the *World Turned Upside Down*, a noted house for old red wines. While he sat in the taproom discussing life with an elderly bagman, one of the hostlers of the *Blue Boar* to whom he had confided his destination brought him a note.

" D—— his eyes," said Charles, crumpling the paper to a perfumed ball, and flicking it towards the undulating surface of the elderly bagman's rubied nose.

" D—— his eyes," and, turning to his target, he inquired whether the latter would drink Port or Burgundy.

CHAPTER XXIV

DAISH'S ROOMS*

MR. JEREMY DAISH, as I told you many pages back, was remarkably like a Cremona violin. Conceive then this elderly instrument of the Muses making a final inspection of his polished floor, preparatory to the invasion of my Lady Bunbutter's red-heeled rout.

Everything portended a successful evening's entertainment. The hautboys, the flutes, the fiddles and the harp were drinking hot negus extra strong in order to spur them to unwonted achievements of melody. Prudence and Deborah, Mr. Daish's comely daughters,

* I went into Daish's Rooms the other day, for they still exist as the storehouse of a prosperous ironmonger who is not above unbending at Christmas time so far as to display a variety of choice knick-knacks wrought by the Curtain Wells Amateur Copper-Beaters' Association. The famous frieze carved by an Italian immigrant still exists, and makes a suitable background for the exhibition of patent mouse-traps. Among all the brass gongs and Japanese flower-pots, above the mowing machines and oil-stoves of varied price and power I was pleased to detect the old iron hooks whence long ago hung the gilt mirrors that held the unimpaired reflections of this gay history's characters. For a moment, amid the bleak utility of the stores, I half fancied the swish of a broidered petticoat and the whisper of a painted fan, smelt Eau de Chypre and heard the Minuet in *Ariadne*. I shall not visit Daish's Rooms again; the ghosts have too much power to wring my heart with the tears and laughter of spent joys.

"It's a very inconvenient store-room," said the dapper manager, "I think Mr. Bugloss intends to pull it down next year."

who never appeared in the galleries of the *Blue Boar* so that their attendance on occasions like the present might possess the charm at once of condescension and novelty, were busily puffing their caps and smoothing their pinners, and from time to time glancing in the direction of the gilt mirrours just to see that the wax candles were not forming ominous shrouds liable to mar the gaiety of my Lady Bunbutter's agreeable entertainment.

Waiters came and peeped through a door which probably led to the supper-room and the three footmen in black plush laced with silver braid were engaged in a dignified consultation over the glittering knobs of their tall Malacca canes.

The wheels of the first coach crackle suddenly above the murmurous quiet of preparation. Tremendously hooped and highly wigged, my Lady Bunbutter has arrived and is entirely approving of the arrangements made by Mr. Jeremy Daish for the fitting entertainment of a distinguished and fashionable company.

Here comes the latter very splendid, prodigiously well-bred and thoroughly determined to criticize the musick and the supper and my Lady Bunbutter herself with merciless perseverance. Here comes the Most Honourable the Marquis of Hurricane and his eldest son the Earl of Squall and his second son Lord Augustus Wind and Lady Mary Wind and Lady Winifred Wind, and his son-in-law il Conte di Scirocco and the sleepy Contessa, but lud! my lady, her ladyship was unable to appear and begs to send her apologies. Her dog, my lady, has developed a quinsy, most unaccountable.

Here come the Earl of Cinderton and the Honourable Mr. Harthe-Brusshe, and the Lady Angela Tongs, his married daughter.

Here come Mrs. Courteen and Miss Phyllida Courteen with Major Constantine Tarry and Mr. Gregory Moon close behind.

Here is young Miss Kitcat with Captain Mann who

for all he was so disreputable was nevertheless tantamount to the success of the Cotillon.

Here come old General Morton and Miss Susan Morton.

In fact, here comes everybody of any importance in Curtain Wells; and the fiddlers are tuning up.

Yet for all the fiddlers are inviting the world to dance, for all the world declares the whole entertainment promises to be a grand success (though not so grand as it should be, considering the ample means at the disposal of my Lady Bunbutter whose father was able to leave a large fortune to a milliner in Soho), her ladyship herself casts many an anxious glance towards the entrance. The courtiers have arrived but the King is still absent, and absent he is likely to remain having caught a slight nasal catarrh from his contact with the night weather, brought about by Mr. Lovely. For this story his absence was even more important in its consequences than my Lady Bunbutter dreamed, since if the Beau had been present on this occasion I doubt he would have persuaded our heroine to give up all thoughts of elopements, seductions, stratagems and rope-ladder courtships. As it fell out, there was nobody to encourage the unromantick side of her, that is to say, nobody whose opinion she could honestly respect.

Mr. Francis Vernon had hired the old dancing hall for a midnight party of farewell; and the old dancing hall still possessed an oak door which opened on a long corridor which in its turn opened into the new and improved dancing hall of Daish's Rooms. Half-way along this corridor was a recessed glasshouse now bare of vegetation, bleak and unfriendly in the chilly moonlight but a very convenient place for the renewal of true-lovers' vows when one of the lovers had not been invited to my Lady Bunbutter's rout. So in the press of the opening gavottes, as Phyllida passed down the side of the room to wait beside her mother's empty chair, long white fingers plucked at the black silk mittens that netted her soft little hand. Phyllida started and, looking up, saw the fingers withdraw themselves through the space left by a half-opened door.

She looked round in affright, but the fiddlers were busy over the gentle tune and all the world of scandal was dancing or about to dance. The thrill of his touch gave her strength enough to make up her mind and, without more than a moment's hesitation, she slipped through the doorway whose opening was obscured by greenery.

A solitary candle lit the long corridor with fitful draughty light.

"Come," said Vernon; and, taking his arm, she went down the passage which seemed to stretch far away —to ruin perhaps, but the end was not perceptible owing to the scarce illumination.

Soon they were alone in the chilly glasshouse with the moon and a star or two besides.

"To-morrow, my dearest life," he whispered.

"No, no," said Phyllida.

"To-morrow," he went on, "a post-chaise will be waiting by the toyshop, and on the seat a riding hood of peacock blue that to-day I bought for my love."

"No! No! Amor, dear Amor, I am afraid."

"Afraid, dear heart, afraid?"

Far off sounded the musick and far off the laughter of the world.

"Afraid that misery will come of it."

"Misery, my beloved? I will cherish you for ever."

"Amor! Amor! I'm afraid. Something, I cannot say what, I cannot explain my feelings, but something frightens me, I feel—oh! I feel as if I were walking in a dark wet garden. I feel as if—as if the laurels and the evergreens held a knife."

Vernon clasped her to him.

"My dear and my dear, they hold no more than an arrow; the arrow that has pierced our hearts."

Certainly our villain was play-acting, but he was his own audience and that juxtaposition is as near to sincerity as even your hero attains.

" You won't betray your Phyllida? "

The appeal caught fire from the flaming cheeks of a maid and burned a way direct, poignant, passionate, right through the lustre and tinsel of his emotional costume.

" You won't betray your Phyllida? " The question was such an one as circulating libraries knew very well. It was asked by many a contemporary Musidora or Clarinda of fiction. Yet so tremulous were the lips that asked it, lips frail as rose-leaves and, withal, ardent as wine, that Vernon shuddered. For the first time in his life he had raised a force. He was at home with Ranelagh romps, with patched beauties of Vauxhall, mistresses of intrigue whose fans had become a part of their bodies, or better, whose bodies were no more than the appendage of their fans, light, airy things where Love danced in a mask and could be shut up at will.

Now for the first time he stared into eyes which held immortality. He saw himself Point de Vise but intolerably diminished.

Vernon noticed that the cheek nearer to him flamed more crimson and for a while he was troubled by the mystery of Love's birth. Elation swung him to the skies and, catching Phyllida to his heart, he whispered of constancy, swore that love would endure for ever and hardly knew himself for a liar.

He never spoke again of pearls, and from that moment truly desired her for the youth and the mystery of herself.

With a pang of tenderness he let her go, watched her hurry down the corridor like a crimson Autumn leaf that is blown along by the wind. By the little door she looked back at him, and from the tips of her fingers sped elfin kisses which on the wings of the musick of flutes and fiddles were borne in grace and beauty.

She had promised. With a sigh Mr. Francis Vernon went back to superintend the arrangements for his farewell party. She had promised, and, as she slipped unobserved into the glitter and heat of Daish's famous Rooms, never seemed like one who has stood a long while in moonlight.

What mattered the censorious world? The softness of his black velvet sleeve thrilled her, and, forgetting all else, she began to build her house of dreams. What a house it was, with casements that looked on every month of the marching years. Now it was December when the snowflakes were falling. Down the corridor she and her lover moved in the grey light, but the casements were lines with ferns and stars and jewels of frost, so they sought Spring in the changing fire-gardens of burning logs. February went by with her showers and her celandines, her snowdrops and thrushes that sing on bare branches. That casement in her house of dreams was gilded round and the sill carved with posies and true-lovers' knots, for through it she had seen Love for the first time. March came in by night with a great noise of wind, yet even in the gusty darkness she could put out her hands to touch a velvet sleeve as black as the gloom enclosed by the open lattice. Every casement in her house of dreams was full of delight, even the quaint little window at the very end of the corridor whose ledge was the haunt of drifted leaves. In the far-off autumn he would still be by her side.

Somebody asked her to step a minuet, yet while her body danced, while her feet kept tune to the twinkling rhythm, while her fan fluttered to mortal harmonies, her soul was away with Love—God knows the spot, but 'twas somewhere mighty near the top of this green world. Now she was rocking a wooden cradle while the wind in the wide black chimney crooned an echo to the old nursery song she was singing. Ah! sir or madam, when a young maiden starts to build her house of dreams, I think, if she be a wise maid, she builds the nursery first of all.

This wonderful house had a number of clocks, tall clocks, short clocks, thin clocks, fat clocks, round clocks, square clocks, clocks on the wall, clocks on the mantelpiece, clocks in the corners; and every clock was ticking away to a tune of its own, for in the house of dreams there was never a moment that did not deserve perpetual commemoration.

Somebody asked her to step a gavotte. At the end of the garden of this wonderful house was a green wicket, and when you had walked through a coppice of birches and wild raspberries that ripen with the corn, you found yourself on the London road. It ran straight as a dart over hill and down dale, through villages whose cottages were only built to stare at the gay equipages that rattled past, for nothing alive was visible save a few geese on a blue and white pond beneath a blue and white sky. Phyllida's mind was a book of old wives' tales and her London was the golden London of Dick Whittington.

Fled were all the outraged heroines of dog-eared novels in greasy circulation. The long reproaches, stilted protestations, vows, regrets and declarations had vanished. The nodding spinsters behind country counters who selected the literature of their clients and declared how affecting was this tale, how full of sensibility was that one, had gradually lost all definite shape like the volumes they doled out so assiduously. Fled, too, with the vapours of young maidenhood, were some of the sweets. Nevertheless I doubt there was not a soul to regret the old Phyllida save perhaps Betty and Dick Combleton, the Squire's youngest son away down in Hampshire.

Miss Sukey Morton began to talk to her of young Tom Chalkley. She told how he had passed their house, how he had looked up at the window, and how by the greatest ill luck she happened to be rather pale that morning. She babbled on about the imagined progress of an affair which had never truly existed. To Phyllida who should have been sympathetick, it was rather wearisome chatter. Suddenly Miss Morton shocked her dear Courteen very much by asking if she had discovered who was satirized in those twelve lines beginning . . . Phyllida interrupted with a curt negative, so curt that her darling Morton regarded her with black-eyed curiosity.

"And how should I know, Sukey, how should I know?"

"My dearest Miss Courteen, there is no need to be angry about a simple question."

"These discoveries are all so low," complained Phyllida.

"Oh, vastly low, though for my part I think the hussy deserves censure since she has made every young woman ridiculous."

With this commentary Miss Morton left her friend, and Phyllida, wondering all the while if she knew the whole affair, was more than ever firmly determined to elope to-morrow afternoon with her Amor.

CHAPTER XXV

QUARTS OF BURGUNDY

THE old ballroom of the famous Daish's Rooms looked mighty cheerful on the evening of my Lady Bunbutter's rout and Mr. Francis Vernon's farewell entertainment.

The circular mahogany table with finely carved claw legs shone like the fine old piece of Spanish wood it was, that is to say, wherever it could secure a clear space for shining, being almost entirely clouded over by innumerable dishes of fruit and nuts, plates, silver knives and silver forks, two large horns of snuff and half-dozen pairs of branched candlesticks, while in the very centre surrounded by lesser fruits stood a magnificent pineapple.

Round the table stood a dozen or more solid Windsor wheelback chairs, that were warranted to stand firm though the fattest gentleman that ever sat down to dessert tipped perpetually back on them to the utmost limit of his balance. A magnificent fire blazed and roared in the hearth, and round the walls were hung prints of racehorses, cock-fights, steeplechases, prize bullocks, and fat sheep, with bills of sale beneath them and announcements of forthcoming diversions for the young gentlemen of the *Blue Boar* and the more wealthy agriculturalists of the neighbourhood.

It was ten o'clock of a wet windy night and the chairmen were growing quarrelsome as they stamped up and down in the street below.

Mr. Jeremy Daish had been rather unwilling for Mr. Vernon to give his party on a night when he himself would be unable to superintend the commissariat owing to his services being required for my Lady Bunbutter's rout close at hand. However, he had left the strictest injunctions with John the senior waiter to carry off at once all empty bottles in order to the protection of the Curtain Wells watch, which was wont to suffer considerably in their persons on such an hilarious occasion as a party in the old ballroom of Daish's Rooms.

The host stood with his back to the fire complacently surveying the preparations. Vernon's extraction was somewhat ambiguous, and his father may or may not have been the fine gentleman that his mother swore he was. So, as he stood regarding the well-covered table and the tall armchair at the head of it where he would presently take his seat, a distinct feeling of elation seized him at the prospect of being in a position to pass the decanter round a circle of such undeniable breeding. He went over their names—names famous on many a battlefield and many a hunting field. They belonged to a world of broad acres and park gates and double lodges and Corinthian hunting-boxes. They were revered at home by many peasants and wore the mantle of life with an air of easy proprietorship. They possessed something like the dignified stability of the Church of England. They were a force, an institution, a product of insular civilization. In fact, they were English Gentlemen, and Mr. Vernon contemplated their existence with great self-satisfaction. He, too, was an English Gentleman, he reassured himself. It was the consciousness of being one which gave him that pleasant sense of superiority to the rest of the world when he found himself in the congenial company of his peers.

Yet poor Mr. Vernon (I am rather sorry for poor Mr. Vernon) could not conceal from his shrewd self that he had no business to be at all unduly elated at the prospect of entertaining young Tom Chalkley of the Foot, Lieutenant Blewforth of the *Lively*, Mr. Harry Golightly of Campbell's Grey Dragoons, Mr. Anthony Clare, little Peter Wingfield, Jack Winnington, the Honourable Mr. Harthe-Brusshe, my Lord Squall, Lord Augustus Wind and Mr. Charles Lovely.

It was Mr. Vernon's note of invitation to the last which had caused him to d—— Vernon's hazel eyes, in the taproom of the *World Turned Upside Down*. Presently came a sound of laughter and careless talk as the young gentlemen of the *Blue Boar* came swaggering in. Was it merely a sense of eccentricity that made the host fancy he detected a note of condescension in their loud and jovial greeting to himself? Probably.

The early guests talked, as early guests always will, with half an eye on the clock and the other half on the table.

"Squall is late," said Vernon.

"Squall coming?" inquired Blewforth.

"L-l-ook out for squalls," stammered little Peter Wingfield.

"Squall's an ass," said Mr. Golightly.

"So is his brother," said Chalkley.

"Always was," said Clare.

"Wind is coming too," said Vernon. "Augustus, that is, and Harthe-Brusshe."

The young gentlemen of the *Blue Boar* looked peevish; it was tactless of that fellow Vernon to keep them waiting for three such asses as these.

"They are late," said Blewforth very emphatically.

"I'm expecting Lovely, too," said Vernon almost humbly. Somehow or other he felt the slightest inclination to apologize, exactly what for he did not know.

"Charles is always late. He's a d——d careless

fellow," said Mr. Golightly, and one felt the final judgment upon Charles had been passed.

"Charles is not jigging with old Butterbun, is he?" asked little Peter Wingfield.

"Oh! the d——l! not he," said Blewforth. "He's found a red-cheeked hussy with whom he's carrying on an intrigue."

"Eh, what! Never?" exclaimed a chorus.

"What's his charmer's name?" said Chalkley.

"Burgundy," replied Blewforth with a great guffaw that made all the glasses and goblets and decanters on the big oak dresser ring an echo.

"I never thought Charles cared much for wine or women," said Golightly.

"Nor he don't," Blewforth put in. "Nor he don't. That's what beats me. But I tell you I saw Charles Lovely sitting in the taproom of the *World Turned Upside Down*. Nobody goes there unless he wishes to be drunk by nightfall. Eh, boys? So depend on't when Charles does arrive, he'll arrive drunk. But why? That's the riddle."

"Perhaps the fair Courteen has slighted him," said Chalkley. "Serve him right. He had no business to take himself so seriously. 'Tis very fashionable to be a poet, but egad! 'tis devilish low to behave like one."

"Is that Miss Phyllida Courteen?" said Vernon, trying to speak as though he had read her name in the list of visitors published every week by the proprietors of the *Curtain Wells Chronicle and Pump Room Intelligencer*.

"Aye! d'ye know her? Blooming seventeen with a short upper lip, blue eyes and hair the colour of that chestnut gelding, What's His Name sold 'tother day."

"Very poor animal," said Golightly.

"Not at all. I disagree with you."

"Very poor animal indeed," said Golightly.

"It fetched a very pretty price."

"Oh," said Mr. Golightly and the argument was over.

"Does she carry a white swansdown muff?" asked Vernon.

"Who?"

"Miss Courteen."

"Eh? Oh! I don't know," and since Mr. Chalkley's tone of voice implied a lack of further interest on the subject, the subject was dropped.

"My belief is," said Lieutenant Blewforth loudly, and moving as he spoke in the direction of the fireplace —"Egad, Vernon would you take it unkind if I rang for a tankard of ale? I'm as dry as a gunner in action. My belief is," he went on spreading his coat-tails to the genial warmth, " my belief is——"

"Gadslife! B-B-lewforth," interrupted Peter Wingfield, "pray get on with the recitation of your c-creed."

"Don't get excited, little man," said Blewforth. "My belief is Charles wrote that book."

"What book?" said Chalkley, whose acquaintance with the literature of the day was remarkably small.

"Curtain Polls."

"Never heard of it," said Mr. Chalkley.

"Rubbish!" said Clare, entering suddenly into the conversation. "Rubbish!" and yet Mr. Anthony Clare was one of the two people in the room who knew for certain that Charles was, indeed, the author of that satirical trifle.

"It has caused a terrible amount of talk," Blewforth went on. "My old aunt Seaworthy to whom I paid my annual visit yesterday tells me that all the world is very much hurt at being treated with such freedom."

"I d-don't see why Charles should take to drink because he's wrote a book." This was from Peter Wingfield.

"Ripple may have been annoyed. He's confoundedly touchy about a little matter like that and Charles thinks Ripple is a demigod."

The Earl of Squall, Lord Augustus Wind and the Honourable Mr. Harthe-Brusshe came into the room at that moment, and Mr. Vernon, who had been feeling a little outside the intimacy of the company, made haste to propose that, everybody save Charles being present, the wine should be brought in.

Everybody agreed that nothing fitted in more exactly with their wishes than Mr. Vernon's timely suggestion and everybody selected his chair with that preciseness which stamps the beginning of an entertainment. Everybody sat down and the nuts were circulated.

Presently John entered with twelve quart-bottles of Burgundy on a huge tray. All of them had been gently warmed before a slow fire, and all of them were wiped clean of the cobwebs and dust of the several years spent in the ample cellars of the *Blue Boar*.

Vernon had prepared a short oration for the entrance of the liquor and while John reverently stationed a bottle at everybody's right hand, he made haste to deliver it. Perhaps his utterance was a shade too reminiscent of one of the many prologues spoken by his mother at the theatre in Lincoln's Inn Fields, but that did not matter since nobody in the room was old enough to remember that lady's inimitable delivery of Mr. Dryden's rhymed Alexandrines.

"The life of Burgundy," said Mr. Vernon, "is very like the life of a butterfly. At first the grape or caterpillar-grub, feeding upon the richness of the soil, then the cocoon or bottle stage when it languishes for many years in darkness below the earth until—until it emerges glowing with a thousand varied tints of crimson—and, like a butterfly, wings its airy way into the brain of mankind."

The company, with the exception of my Lord Squall

who was sometimes taken in the old family coach of the Winds to hear his father speak in the House of Lords, were not accustomed to lengthy speeches and looked at each other bashfully.

Lieutenant Blewforth with nautical tact saved the situation by drinking Mr. Vernon's health in a very large and brimming pint bumper which he emptied in two sonorous gulps.

As everybody else proceeded to follow this good example, everybody was soon very cheerful, and the advent of the second dozen of bottles was mightily applauded.

However, the master mind was still absent and the drinking, though steady, had not yet enlivened the company to uproarious spirits.

"Where's Charles?" bellowed Blewforth munching devilled biscuit. "Where's that fellow Charles. Demme! He'll never catch us up at this rate and we shall have him sober as a post-captain when we are beginning to amuse ourselves."

"What, you rogue," cried our hero entering just as the Lieutenant bellowed his inquiry. "I wager five guineas, I am two bottles ahead of any gentleman present." In order to clinch the bet he flung his purse in the direction of the table. The gauntlet snuffed in its course two of the candles and fell with a plump into a piping bowl of punch splashing Tom Chalkley as high as his stock and imparting to His Majesty's uniform an odour of hot squeezed lemons that lasted for quite a couple of weeks.

"Charles! Charles!" bellowed the burly Lieutenant, "Huzza for Charles!"

The latter lurched into the vacant chair next to his friend Tony without a word to the host. However, nobody observed this breach of good manners, because everybody was anxiously leaning over to fill every glass in reach of the newcomer as a preliminary to drinking his very good health a score of times, without a heeltap to any one of them.

"Z—ds! Charles. Where have you been?" said Chalkley.

"Drinking old Burgundy with a rogue of a bagman who looked like Ranelagh Garden en Fête, for his face was illuminated with every hue of crimson lamp and I stake my wig his nose was as large and round as the Rotunda."

With the arrival of Charles, everybody woke up and there were calls for a song. The gallant Lieutenant was the first to respond with my Lord Dorset's *To you fair ladies now at Land*.

Let me remind you of that fine old ballad:

> *To you fair ladies now at Land*
> *We men at Sea indite;*
> *But first would have you understand*
> *How hard it is to write.*

"Not at all," cried Charles.

> *The Muses now, and Neptune too,*
> *We must implore to write to you;*

"and chorus, gentlemen, please,"

> *With a Fa, la, la, la, la, la,*
> *The Muses now, and Neptune too,*
> *We must implore to write to you.*

and so on to the last

> *With a Fa, la, la, la, la*
> *Let us hear of no Inconstancy*
> *We have too much of that at Sea.*

And a proper noise everybody made with the *Fa la-la-*

la-la accentuating every *Fa* with a bottle and every *La* with one of Mr. Jeremy Daish's handsome silver spoons.

The song being a very lengthy one allowed everybody plenty of time to drink another quart of Burgundy before its rousing conclusion, and if the company cheered loudly at the beginning, by heavens, they cheered so loudly at the end that the noise was heard above the fiddlers in the new ballroom of Daish's famous Rooms and put everybody out of step in the last Cotillon notwithstanding the heroick efforts of the disreputable, but nimble-footed Captain Mann.

Then Charles gave a new ballad (new that is in the reign of Queen Anne) sung first at Messieurs Brook and Hellier's Club at the Temple Tavern in Fleet Street, but slightly altered by him to suit present company.

> *Since I'm in the Chair and every one here*
> *   Appears in gay humour and easy;*
> *Say, why should not I, a new Ballad try,*
> *   Bright Brethren o' the Bottle to please ye.*
> *This wine is my theme, this is all on's Esteem,*
> *   For Jeremy Daish cannot wrong us;*
> *Let them get Wealth who keeps us in health,*
> *   By bringing neat liquor among us.*

(with chorus of last two lines repeated).

> *Each Vintner of late, has got an Estate*
> *   By brewing and Sophistication*
> *With cyder and sloes, they've made a d——d dose,*
> *   Has poisoned one half of the nation.*

and so on until

> *Now God bless the King, Peers, Parliament Men,*
> *And keep 'em like us in true concord.*

And grant that all those, who dare be his foes,
At Tyburn may swing in a strong cord;
We'll Loyalists be, and bravely agree
With lives and estates to defend her—him
So then we'll not care come Peace or come War
For Lewis, the Pope, or Pretender.

"Ah!" said Mr. Anthony Clare whose father had been a Jacobite, "you've spoilt more than the rhyme by the last word."

This treasonable remark was the signal for more noise than ever because all the young gentlemen of the *Blue Boar* who held His Majesty King George's commission felt bound to uphold the honour of the Royal Navy and the British Army by flinging a large number of Spanish nuts at the head of the disloyal Clare who retorted by emptying a whole ram's horn of snuff over Mr. Golightly so that for a while nothing was to be heard but vollies of gigantick sneezes. Exhaustion reigned for a moment, but presently the sound of hustling and bustling in the street outside roused everybody to fresh vigour of mischief.

My Lady Bunbutter's rout was over, and those of the Exquisite Mob who had been invited were standing on tip-toe on the steps of Daish's Rooms peering into the darkness and blinking in the glare of waving flambeaux. The chairmen were so busy quarrelling over their positions that they paid no attention to their fares and everything was in a very great state of confusion indeed; nor was the clamour abated by Mr. Lovely cleverly hitting the long red ear of the nearest chairman with a Barcelona nut because the injured chairman instantly floored a linkboy who was standing by his side and the linkboy's torch severely burnt the legs of Lord Cinderton's tall footman in his ash-grey livery and the tall footman with a yell of dismay punched a flat-footed waiter on the nose and the flat-footed waiter butted an inoffensive fop in the middle of his sprigged silk waistcoat and the inoffensive fop struck out with his tasselled cane left and right with such force that presently everybody in the street below was fighting with his next door neighbour to the entire delight of the young gentlemen from the *Blue Boar*. Their next diversion was to empty the dregs of the Burgundy bottles upon the heads of the crowd, whereupon all the ladies of Curtain Wells screamed very loud to see such a number of bloody polls and faces.

Then Charles snatched off little Peter Wingfield's tie-wig and, having set fire to it, began to drop tufts of burning hair out of the window, which tufts made an immense smell and blew round and round in the gusty March air in a very alarming manner.

Little Peter Wingfield, having lost his own wig and being too little to snatch Lovely's wig, mounted one of the stout Windsor wheelback chairs and, taking down the print of a famous cock-fight extracted the hook from the wall and laid an embargo on the black silk ties of three of his friends in order to fish from the window for another wig. He succeeded in catching the Marquis of Hurricane's to the intense delight of his undutiful sons the Earl of Squall and Lord Augustus Wind. Of course after such a successful display of angling, everybody else had to try his hand with the picture hook and two more wigs were captured but proved so frowsy that they were burnt immediately. However, Mr. Chalkley caught the hem of Lady Jane Vane's petticoat just as she was stepping into her chair and would without doubt have injured that virgin's modest reputation for ever, had the garment been made of more durable stuff; as it was, the hook would not hold and nothing was disclosed beyond what is allowed by any wet day.

Then Mr. Daish came hurrying in and begged their honours to desist because the watch was coming, and what Mr. Ripple would say when he heard of the riot he did not dare surmize.

Poor Mr. Daish bowed and scraped and was so full of excuses that all the young gentlemen felt quite sorry for him and put him seat foremost into the biggest bowl of punch in order to drown his troubles, whereupon Mr. Daish grew quite cholerick and vowed he would never let one of 'em enter his inn again and made such ado that the culprits all protested he was more noisy than anybody else, and offered to fetch in the watch and have him arrested in his own bowl of punch.

But presently they lifted him out and subscribed ten guineas by sending round Mr. Golightly's hat; and poor Mr. Daish was more full of excuses than ever and hoped that anything he had said that could by the most spirited gentleman be considered derogatory would be forgiven and ascribed to the dismay caused by the hot punch scalding his hinder parts and goading him beyond the bounds of polite remonstrance.

Everybody vowed that withered little Daish was a prince of good fellows and begged him to buy himself a new pair of cinnamon cloth breeches as soon as possible, while Thomas Chalkley of the Foot created much amusement by shouting that he was holding Dunquerque against the French. In order to hold Dunquerque against the French, it was very necessary that Mr. Chalkley should fling out of the window nineteen quart-bottles of Burgundy in quick succession, whereupon Lieutenant Blewforth of the *Lively* not to be outdone vowed Portobello must be taken and proceeded to take it by climbing with amazing dexterity on to the mantelpiece armed only with a long Churchwarden's pipe. Yet notwithstanding all the efforts of Ensign Chalkley to hold Dunquerque against the French, notwithstanding that he was valiantly assisted by Cornet Golightly of the Grey Dragoons, who led a desperate cavalry charge round the whole room mounted upon one of the stout Windsor chairs, Dunquerque capitulated. In other words the dignified Curtain Wells watch marched upstairs with their lanterns and their staves and, standing in a knot by the doorway, demanded the reason for such a riotous breach of the King's peace, not to mention Mr. Ripple's and the Mayor's. But the young gentlemen were all so merry and the watch was so cold that it consented to taste the punch and presently left Dunquerque in the hands of the Allies and marched off warmer in mind and body to a quieter quarter of the ancient borough of Curtain Wells. I am sorry to add that, in passing the door of the Great House, they so far forgot their standing orders as to cry with enormous fervour the hour and the weather exactly underneath Mr. Ripple's window.

With the departure of the watch, peace fell upon the company for a while; a dice box was produced and some packs of cards, but play lasted a very short time and was voted too confoundedly dull for so joyful an evening. So more songs were sung, and it was exceedingly pleasant to hear these young gentlemen shouting the refrains and hammering Encores upon the polished mahogany table. It was exceedingly pleasant to see the wigs on their knees and the long clay pipes keeping time to the tune; but perhaps the pleasantest sight of all was the two sleepy waiters who leaned against the jambs of the door and, with kindly grins on their tired faces, tapped their flat feet to the more alluring measures.

The night was wearing away when somebody called ' Vernon for a song! '

The latter, to tell the truth, had felt out of his element, except during the brief interval of play, but on being called upon to occupy the centre of the room, he cheered up and announced his very great pleasure in acceding to the gentlemen's request.

I wonder if you are at all sorry for Mr. Vernon.

He was very lonely sitting in his high armchair at the head of the table. I wonder if you will forgive him for singing this song, which you will find in Mr. D'Urfey's *Pills to Purge Melancholy*.

In a merry month of May,
On a morn by break of day,
Forth I walked the wood so wide,
When as May was in her Pride:
Here I spy'd all alone, all alone,
Phyllida and Coridon.

Much ado there was God wot,
He did love, but she could not.
He said his love was to woo,
He said none was false to you;
He said he had lov'd her long,
He said love should take no wrong.

Coridon would have kissed her then,
She said Maids must kiss no men
Till they kiss for good and all;
Then she bade the shepherds call
All the Gods to witness truth,
Ne'er was loved so fair a youth.

Then with many a pretty oath,
As Yea and Nay and Faith and Troth,
Such as silly shepherds use,
When they would not love abuse;
Love which had been long deluded
Was with kisses sweet concluded.

And Phyllida with garlands gay
Was crowned the Lady May.

The words were poor, as you will allow, and the tune a mere tinkle, but it had the effect of rousing our hero from the half-sleep into which he had fallen.

" Sing that song again, will you."

" G—— forbid," whispered little Peter Wingfield.

"Nay, sir," said Mr. Vernon, " 'Tis too long to sing over again, but I'll toast the heroine if that will please your zest."

"No, sir," said Charles, "it will not please me at all."

The rest of the company began to wake up to the fact that something was happening.

"I should have thought," Vernon replied, "that Mr. Lovely would have cordially welcomed such a toast, for we all know his partiality to the name."

"Gentlemen," said our hero. Did I not promise you some pretty heroicks a score of pages back? "Gentlemen, I have a tale to tell you."

Charles looked very stiff and very fierce as, clapping on his wig, he began:

"A short while ago I perpetrated an indiscretion in mistaking Mr. Francis Vernon for a gentleman, for which I beg the pardon of everybody present. Mr. Vernon for some reason best known to himself saw fit to bribe my bookseller to insert in a volume I have just published twelve scurrilous lines reflecting upon the character of a young lady whom I—whom I——"

"Admire," suggested our villain.

"No, sir, respect."

"Sir, your virtue should make us all blush," sneered Vernon, cold and contemptuous.

"D——n you and your blushes; blush deeper, then," shouted Charles, slinging the contents of a wineglass into Mr. Vernon's pallid face.

There was silence for a moment until the honourable Mr. Harthe-Brusshe proclaimed——

"The affair should be settled at once."

And this was the only remark that the Honourable gentleman uttered in the whole of the evening.

"With all my heart," cried Charles. "Tony, you'll act for me?"

Mr. Vernon had delicately wiped his face with a

handkerchief of Mechlin lace. A single drop of the wine lingered above his left cheekbone. There, it was not unbecoming.

"I shall be proud to walk with Mr. Lovely in a month's time," said our villain, "but for the present my honour is pledged to a lady."

"Sure, you borrow on mighty small security, sir," said Charles.

The lingering drop of wine that stained Mr. Vernon's cheek seemed to expand for a brief moment.

"I have named my day," was all he answered.

"Mr. Vernon is within his rights, Charles," said Mr. Golightly, "and moreover the weather will be finer next month and we can make up a jovial party."

"'Tis hardly fair to poor Daish to fight in his rooms," said Blewforth. "Ripple would put his shutters up at once."

"H—— take you all," cried Charles, in an access of fury, as he sprang to strike Vernon.

The latter stepped back and with a well-aimed blow sent Charles flying backwards over two chairs.

"'Slife, Charles," said Mr. Golightly very stiffly. "Your conduct is d——d irregular, sir."

"Most improper," said Mr. Chalkley.

"Devilish unrestrained," said little Peter Wingfield.

"Charles was two bottles ahead of us, gentlemen," said Blewforth who held a broad mind in a broad body.

Our hero was still lying where Vernon had sent him among cards and broken glass.

"D——n you all," cried Clare. "Charles is worth the rest of you puppies in red and blue coats put together, and by G——, Mr. Vernon, he shall kill you for that blow."

Everybody was so surprised to hear Mr. Anthony Clare, cool and placid Tony Clare, break out like this that a wave of embarrassment swept over the room. One by one they hurried from the scene of such an irregular quarrel.

It was very entertaining to see them march out so stiff and straight, with nutshells crackling underneath their feet.

CHAPTER XXVI

AND THE DREGS OF THE SAME

MR. ANTHONY CLARE stayed behind to help our hero home to bed. His effort to achieve sobriety had completely exhausted such faculties as remained after so many quarts of Burgundy, and he babbled to his companion foolish threats and impotent defiance in such an incoherent voice that I doubt his enemy, had he been present, would scarcely have been able to discover common sense in any one of his remarks. Charles woke up in the morning full of bile, dressed himself in a splenetick fury and ate a breakfast, conspicuous for its peppery flavours, with petulance and aversion. Then he crammed his gold-laced Kevenhuller hat on his head and went out to interview Mr. Horace Ripple.

In crossing the courtyard of the inn he passed Mr. Chalkley, and for a moment debated seriously the wisdom of challenging him out of hand. This he was the more inclined to do because he fancied the gallant Ensign was regarding him with some disfavour. However, the latter gave him a 'good morning,' and excused his want of geniality on the score of a liver teased out of endurance by hard and violent exercise.

So Charles forgave him his supposed breach of good manners and decided to hear from Tony a full account of the evening's events.

Clare presently overtook him under the archway, and, on being informed of our hero's destination, tried to dissuade him from the projected visit to the Beau.

"Z——ds! I tell you that blackguard shall be turned out of the Wells with ignominy." So much Charles vowed.

"But 'tis no business of yours, Charles," argued his friend.

"No business of mine? Eh! is that so? Then, by Heaven! I'll make it my business."

"Ripple does not believe in settling disputes of this nature by the personal encounter."

"Then, by Heaven!" said Charles, "that being the case there is the greater necessity for expelling him from the company of gentlemen."

"That is all very well," expostulated Clare, "but you are neither the young woman's brother nor, as I believe, her lover. What right have you to interfere?"

"I tell you, Tony," said Charles, "that Ripple has already pondered the advisableness of interfering with Mr. Francis Amor-Vernon and, indeed, begged me to disclose his pseudonym, but I would not."

"You owed him money, in fact?" said Clare, gently tapping the kerb of the pavement with his cane.

"Yes, I owed the dog money."

"And now he is paid?"

"Thanks to your generosity he is paid."

"Charles," said Mr. Clare, laying his hand affectionately on that indignant gentleman's right shoulder, "oblige me, who was able and glad to oblige you, by not proceeding further in this affair."

"'Tis monstrous ill-bred in you to remind me of an obligation under which I laid myself with the most profound disinclination." Charles was growing angry.

"Nay, you know that is not my meaning, but, consider, Charles, this confounded, pasquinading pamphlet book has placed you in such an ill light that the world will be very loth to believe any good of you."

"Ripple is wiser than the raree-show over which he presides."

"Ay! but depend on't, he has already been informed of last night's affair and will be prejudiced against you on account of your quarrelsome overtures."

"'Sdeath! Tony, pray desist from further argument; you do not convince me and will soon rouse my choler."

"As you will," said Tony, and, leaving the company of his friend, betook himself to the solitude of green fields. In the pleasures of country sights and sounds he found some consolation for the undeserved reproaches of a gentleman whom he had gratified at considerable expense to himself.

Charles continued in the direction of the Great House. Being arrived on the topmost doorstep he rang the bell with complete assurance and knocked thrice with the heavy brass knocker.

He was admitted to an audience and walked upstairs to the tall white drawing-room without trepidation or bashfulness. Mr. Ripple had favoured him with so many compliments lately, had begged his advice on so many trifles of publick importance, had in fact adopted him so completely into intimate conversation, that Charles may be pardoned for supposing that, notwithstanding his unceremonious conduct of the night before last, notwithstanding his notoriety as the author of a book of satirical poems, he would still be received with that inimitable and charming condescension which the Great little Man reserved for few indeed.

He found the Beau seated among the roses of his wide-winged armchair sipping what looked uncommonly like a cordial physick. He did not rise to Mr. Lovely's entrance, did not even turn his head, but merely said in a tone, indifferent, lifeless and chill,

"To what may I ascribe the honour of this visit, sir?"

Conceive the shocked feelings of Madame Semele when he, whom she had hitherto regarded with the familiarity born of many amorous meetings, assumed at her own request the attributes of divinity. She died, if you can recall the sad event.

Charles experienced a particle of that dismay when the Great little Man for whom he had hitherto felt an almost playful affection suddenly appeared to him with the attributes of majesty—remoteness, scorn, and inaccessibleness. The pattern upon the Aubusson rug swarm before his eyes in changes of tint and form as frequent as a child's Kaleidoscope, and he found himself in humble obeisance. The Beau twirled the fluted stem of the green Venetian glass that contained his physick and waited for Mr. Lovely to explain his business.

"Well, sir," he said at last.

The abashed favourite stammered his reasons for the visit.

"Pooh, pooh," said the Beau. "Pooh, pooh! a likely story. Your brain, sir, addled by the ridiculous rhymes it has already born with obvious labour, refuses to hatch further monstrous fancies, and is content to send into the world an abortion. The night before last, Mr. Lovely, you waited upon me at an hour both indiscreet and inconvenient. I was ready to overlook this horrid breach of decorum and was indeed willing to receive your apologies on the following day. You found, however, a more engaging diversion in cracking bottles with a bagman. For this I do not blame you—and, indeed, think you will do well to cultivate a manner of company for which you seem to me singularly adapted. Pray understand, however, that, in finding your level, you have had to make a very considerable descent. The rider who has been thrown into a ditch is unable to cry 'View! Holloa!' to the master of the hunt. In other words, Mr. Lovely, you have put yourself in a position where your estimate of polite intrigue is incredible and impertinent. I am very well able to look after the morals of the Beau Monde without the assistance of the kitchen or the tap-room."

"Mr. Ripple," said our hero, "you insult me."

"Unfortunately, sir, I recognize no responsibleness in that direction. I have always claimed the right to speak my mind. If you find my strictures intolerable, the door affords you an easy remedy."

"Mr. Ripple," Charles replied, "I think you are making a fool of yourself."

The Great little Man clutched the arms of his wide-winged chair and gasped. It was certainly twenty years since any one had dared to address him with such a want of reverence.

"You wrap yourself in paint and sattin," continued Charles. "You strut about as if you were indeed the king of a puppet show. But don't forget, Mr. Ripple, that when the puppets perform, when they make miniature love and die small deaths, the publick regards them, not the wire-puller above. The world, your world, will forget you, Mr. Ripple, when it still remembers the inconsiderable passions of your dolls."

"It does not matter, sir," the Beau interrupted in a voice tremulous with well-bred anger. "It does not matter what the world thinks of me, so long as my puppets comport themselves with taste and discretion."

"You fool," shouted Charles, "the wires are twisted."

It is improbable that any one had ever shouted in this tall white room before, and the lustres shivered at the unwonted sound, while a diminutive Dresden shepherdess, fragile as a sea-shell, lost her head, which rolled into the grate with a tinkle of dismay.

"Leave my house," said the Beau.

"Ay! and you dislike to be told that your show will presently appear ludicrous."

"Leave my house."

"Good G——! Ripple. I know I have been to blame, I know my story seems to you absurd; but, by Heaven! I swear those cursed lines were never writ by me, and since Vernon wrote them, why, z——ds, man! can't you see his intention?"

"Leave my house."

"Very well, sir, your obedient servant."

With a very grand bow, Mr. Lovely took his leave of the Great little Man.

When he was gone, the Beau stooped to pick up the head of the diminutive Dresden shepherdess.

"Tut-tut, I doubt the join will be plainly visible," he murmured to himself.

CHAPTER XXVII

TIME FOR REFLECTION

MR LOVELY left the Great House enraged with the owner, with Society and, to say truth, with his own heroick self.

I do not think he was very wildly in love with Miss Courteen, but I do believe he was sincerely vexed with himself for letting her fall into Vernon's power. For a moment he seriously pondered the wisdom of warning her mother of the lengths to which the affair had gone, but upon reflection shrank from a step which would savour, in the eyes of the world, of ill-bred intrusion. After all, the girl was nothing to him, and her reputation—plague on her reputation! I trust you observe the unheroick aftermath of heroick Burgundy. Such bathos of indifference would have sounded strange in the days preceding this forenoon.

Just then my Lady Bunbutter went by in her capacious chair and Charles prepared to make an elaborate bow, but her ladyship merely stared at him in cold disdain, and he was forced to buckle his shoe to save his countenance.

"So everybody knows," said Charles to himself. "Well! I shall always regard Curtain Wells with affection and remember it with regret."

He walked down the Colonnade where Miss Morton lived and, as he passed the house, thought with half a smile of Valentine Day. It seemed a century ago—

that merry morning. Soon he was in the fields, where the hedges were splashed with the silver of blackthorn in profuse bloom.

He crossed a winding path, begun and ended with a notched and scrabbled kissing-gate, and, passing through a small plantation where the daffodils grew tall, went up a rounded hillside along whose clear-cut horizon great fleecy clouds moved solemnly. He stopped for a moment to glance back at Curtain Wells with the March sun spangling the rain-wet roofs before he dipped with a sigh into one of those serene valleys that are only found in England—valleys whose slopes are often darkened by the long shadows of sheep and cattle, whose hollows are bright with moist grass and in summer fragrant with spearmint and creamy meadowsweet.

He took the devious course of a narrow stream and knew the grave delights of rural meditation; yet somehow the image of Phyllida danced before him all the time and whenever he paused, the wind far away over the hillside had a melancholy and foreboding sound.

He met an Elderly Gentleman—a parson by the colour of his cloth—who was poking some decayed herbage with a long cane. The Elderly Gentleman looked up as Charles went by, gave him a 'very good morning,' and said he believed he had seen an adder enter the herbage.

"Indeed," said Charles, who thought the information given demanded an attitude of respectful surprize.

"But nothing amazes me after that wonderful February. When I tell you that half an hour ago I saw an Orange Tip butterfly, you will understand that nothing amazes me."

Charles left the Elderly Gentleman still investigating the decayed herbage reputed to contain an adder, and found himself envying a mind that could invest a day with such easy fame. He had seen an Orange Tip butterfly. Had he met grey-eyed Athene, or beheld the roses and doves of Cytherea, the day would scarcely have held a more splendid memory.

He envied the Elderly Gentleman. To be sure, with a Stoick complacency, he had announced that nothing strange in the natural order could startle him after that wonderful February, but his tone of triumphant excitement foretold an entry in his diary that very night, perhaps was the prelude to a paragraph in the *Gentleman's Magazine*.

He began to imagine the Elderly Gentleman sipping his Port before the Rectory fire, on his knees an open Concordance whose pages were illuminated by dancing butterflies, precocious heralds of the scented spring. He heard the dignified butler told of his reverend master's lucky discovery, heard him asked to hand down the calf-bound diary of such and such a faded year, heard the Elderly Gentleman's chuckle when he found, as he suspected, that the date in his own experience was unprecedented and finally heard him order a bottle of the Port in bin twelve, the first-fruits of the Assiento Agreement.

Charles fell to comparing himself to the Elderly Gentleman, greatly to his own disadvantage.

Certainly the image of Phyllida danced before him in the water meadows, eluded him at every turn and twist of the little stream, and beckoned him along this secluded valley; but his own heart did not beat with the proper amount of answering fervour.

Six weeks ago when he saw her first, all swansdown and blushes, he had been duly elated. She had occupied much of his meditations ever since, but he had no sensation of triumph, no delight in the great fact of her existence. Perhaps that was because she belonged to the world. The butterfly had belonged, as a phenomenon, to the Elderly Gentleman alone. To the rest of mankind it was a legend. The discovery would be recorded in print, but the discovery itself would flutter in secret pale wings powdered with vivid gold, and this March morning would remain a permanent fact in that Elderly Gentleman's heart. He would suffer no disillusion. If others saw that butterfly, why, then, he would enjoy the discussion of it, whether in the *Gentleman's Magazine* beneath a learned pseudonym or over two or three glasses of Port, with details long drawn out to protract the delicious memory.

The ink is faded on the pages of those calf-bound diaries, the Latin epitaph on the Elderly Gentleman's tombstone is now nearly illegible, but since he went down to Elysium alert and heedful of the changing seasons, I believe that his spirit still listens on summer eves to the blackbirds in his beloved orchard and observes with interest and curiosity each separate harebell that blossoms above his mortal remains.

Charles went on his way with much the same thoughts about the Elderly Gentleman as I have set down for my own, and continued to envy his gift of youth.

Presently he met Margery of Baverstock Farm.

Let me remind you, she was the wench to whom Mr. Anthony Clare had paid light court back in the winter. Charles reproved him for his behaviour and apparently his friend had given up his addresses, for the milkmaid looked happy and blooming and seemed not at all displeased to giggle over a hazel wand at Mr. Charles Lovely.

" Good morning, Margery."

" Oh, good morning, zur," said Margery.

" No longer with Farmer Hogbin? "

" I be with Farmer Hogbin's brother Jahn to High Corner Farm."

" And happy? "

" Oh, 'ess, proud and happy."

" Seen Mr. Clare lately? "

Margery blushed expansively.

" Oh! naw! I an't seen him since Baverstock Barn. I be courting."

"Eh, indeed," said Charles, "and who is the shepherd?"

"Wully Pearce."

"And you'll be married soon?"

"Come barley harvest—'ess."

"I will dance at your wedding, Margery."

"We shaänt have daäncing, because Wully says it leads to what oughtn't to happen."

Charles made a wry face.

"Going to wed a Puritan, eh?"

"Nay," said the buxom maid. "He's carter to Farmer Jahn Hogbin."

"Then, surely, he will let you have a merry junketing at the bride-ale."

"Naw, indeed an' he wawnt, because his sister Molly when they were thrawing the stocking last year fell on her back, and Wully's fam'ly is a proud and proper fam'ly and Wully says we mun be married wi' no such nonsense."

This long proclamation of propriety made Margery quite breathless, so Charles, with a bow and the present of a crown, passed on his way. Margery's case gave him more food for meditation. There was a buxom hale wench with the bloom of a peach, throwing away her ample charms upon a puritanical clod whose only ambition seemed to be the preservation of a mealy-mouthed decorum. Pshaw! such prime beauty deserved a better fate. Such a wedding as hers should have made old wives' fireside gossip for a score of years and the tale of it quickened the hearts of every lover and his lass that listened beneath the golden summer moon. Had he the control of the ceremony, by Heaven! they should have danced the dawn in, and every man and every maid should have gone to sleep with a face as pale as the morning sky. It was ridiculous that young Cupid should be breeched for the bidding of a lubberly half-baked ploughboy.

And yet, to be honest with himself, was not he behaving in much the same way as the despised Wully Pearce? Was not his chief objection to Vernon based on the latter's reputation as a man of intrigue? It was Phyllida's attraction to Vernon that made him indignant. Had she chosen to bestow herself on a middle-aged squire with acres and a gaunt square hall and a pack of hounds, would he have been at all seriously disconcerted by the prospect? And Vernon could have no honest love for her, because if a man means to wed a young woman, he does not stigmatize her behaviour in scurrilous verses, even to secure an advantage over a supposed rival. Or does he—when he is not quite a gentleman?

Then occurred to him the story he had heard many years ago of a thin unhappy-looking woman who had spoken kindly to him at some crowded Al Fresco entertainment where he and his father and mother had gone one fine July afternoon. He had asked about her as they drove home to the lodgings, and he remembered his mother's warning finger, while his father laughed over Lord B—— and Mrs. D——.

At the end of the tale his mother, a gentle Christian soul, had said it served the baggage right, and bad him never talk to people to whom he had not been presented by his parents. No doubt the circumstances of the two cases were totally different, but he connected them vaguely in his mind.

Moreover, without any doubt, Phyllida had caught his fancy. She disturbed his view. Yet there was nothing that singled her out from a dozen handsome young women with whom he had danced, whose existence save as a bevy he no longer recognized. Still, whatever he thought about the affair, his opinion would never again be invited and, disinherited by Beau Ripple, he must consider his own position with an eye to the future.

He was bracing himself preparatory to this great mental effort, when he perceived round the next bend of the stream Mr. Anthony Clare, pensively leaning against the rugged stem of a pollard willow-tree.

"Tony," said Charles, "Ripple has dismissed me."

"I know," said his friend, "your writ of banishment, signed, sealed and delivered, is pasted on the window of every coffee-house and occupies a large and distinguished space in the vestibule of the Assembly Rooms. What do you propose to do?"

"I might hire myself out to the amiable Hogbin as carter."

"Pshaw," said Tony, "be serious."

"Or I might take to the road."

"Nonsense, man."

"Nay! I vow such a career has many advantages for a poor man, since he may live and, what is more, die at the public charge."

"You are not in earnest, Charles?" said Mr. Clare, laying an anxious hand upon his friend's wrist.

"And why not, i' faith?"

"What would you gain by such an impulse of folly?"

"My livelihood and, as I said, very possibly my funeral expenses."

"Such flippancy is ill-timed," said Mr. Clare, who was a serious young man and spent much of his leisure with the theory of estate-management.

"Nay! I am not treating the matter as a jest, but truly considering the benefit of adopting such a novel method of existence in these hard times."

"Novel!" said Clare, with a scoffing laugh. "Novel! why, every ne'er-do-weel blackguard for the past hundred years has tried this novel method of existence and every one of them has come at last to the same windy death."

"Oh, as to the last scene," interrupted Charles, "indeed I vow 'tis the best in the play, for it never fails to please the populace, and sure in this dull world a man should try to give a little amusement; I hold that the author of a diverting comedy and the thief who makes a brave exit are the truest benefactors of humanity."

"All this is very pretty fooling, but leads nowhere," said Clare, who had a proposal to make and was vexed by Charles' levity.

"But ponder, Tony, the Gothick atmosphere of such an escapade. Imagine the moated grange, the haunted lane, the shadowy coppice, the phantastick oaths and gestures, the pursuit by moonlight, the clatter of hoofs, the jingle of spurs—all this appeals to an aspect of my character too long subdued by the bonds of convention and the trammels of polite society."

"But, you fool, you would be taken at once. You have no cant of the road and, as a Dilettante, would certainly be regarded with odious suspicion by every regular highwayman between Berwick and Dover. Oddslife, I'll not argue with you further, for I do not believe you mean a word of what you say, and, harkee, I have a plan that will suit either of us better than your cut-throat Braggadocio."

As a matter of fact, Charles had once or twice thought quite seriously of taking to the road. After all, it was in accordance with every precedent of outlawry. As soon as a man was banished from Society, he should compensate himself for the discomfort he incurred. Tony, however, now came forward with a project which, while it preserved much of the charm of highway robbery, held none of its dangers or difficulties. He suggested that since neither he nor Charles had very many ties to attach them fast to Curtain Wells, they should spend a year in making the Grand Tour of the British Islands.

Charles objected on the score of money.

"I have three hundred guineas," said Clare. "That will equip us with all that we require as travellers, and I am sure the world will entertain us for our pleasant appearance and company."

"In fact we are to become beggars—in velvet gowns," Charles commented.

"Adventurers, knights at arms, what you will," added Clare.

Charles was enraptured with the idea, so deeply enraptured that he saw no absurdity in grave Mr. Anthony Clare setting out upon such a career of folly. In fact, it seemed the most natural thing in the world for his friend to spend three hundred guineas on a whim. He himself would have spent treble that sum (had he possessed it) in order to the exploitation of such a witty, ingenious and romantick method of wasting time.

"We must equip ourselves for the parts we are about to play. There must be no shilly-shally, and above all no one must think us anything but eccentrick men of fashion, itinerant beaux, fops on pilgrimage, wandering wits."

"The last phrase is unfortunate," said Clare. Charles laughed hugely.

By this time Phyllida had faded like a summer joy, Vernon was forgotten, nothing mattered except this new and exceedingly entertaining project.

"What is the first thing to be done?" inquired Clare.

"Egad, what should always precede any undertaking of importance—a visit to the tailor."

The two young men beneath a sky growing rapidly overcast, walked quickly through the lush meadows towards Curtain Wells, discussing as they went the merits of rival tailors with infinite vivacity.

Meanwhile in the Crescent, our heroine was engaged upon much the same problem. Possibly the reason that so many timid young women have been brave enough to plunge into an elopement, is the obfuscation of the real issue, the vital stakes, by the need of deciding what they shall leave behind to console their abandoned virtue.

So it was, at any rate, with Phyllida. She was deterred from soft regrets by the desperate necessity of making up her mind between the charms of a muslin frock overlaid with pink rosebuds and a muslin frock sprigged with the palest blue forget-me-nots.

There were a thousand sentiments that might well have restrained her from the wild step she was taking, but everything was forgotten for a trifle; and when finally she slipped out of the door, the only living creature for whom she indulged herself in the luxury of a protracted farewell, was Thomasina the tabby cat, and that was considerably interrupted by the attenuated miaouws of a large family lately arrived. Even Ponto the spaniel had sidled off to a favourite heap of rubbish. Pray do not suppose I am sneering at Phyllida. Heaven forbid that you or I should sneer at a young woman, however impetuous, however foolish. Still, I cannot help observing that the heroism of most heroick actions is to be sought for in the obscure preliminaries to a grand event. Phyllida had known the agony of making up her mind through many a firelit, sleepless night. When the moment arrived for carrying out her resolve, she spent most of the forenoon reading the advertizement of a fashionable mantua-maker. As to her devices for getting rid of her mother and Betty and the landlady and Thomas and Miss Sukey Morton, who called to inquire whether Mrs. Featherbrain's new novel was called *The Affectionate Aunt* or *The Disconsolate Uncle*,— why, they were as old as the first writer of tales and I will not weary you with their repetition. And why should I delay you with the narrative of the attempt to open her mother's jewel-case with a bodkin and a silver paper-knife? Like most toilet receptacles, it was very easily broken.

She hurried down the Crescent with a small parcel of cloaths wrapped up in brown paper and tied with a green ribbon. If you are anxious to know what was inside, I will refer you to Miss Howe, Mr. Richardson's Miss Howe, to whom Miss Clarissa Harlowe confided a parcel of much the same dimensions and contents.

She did not forget her swansdown muff nor her swansdown tippet, and altogether she looked just the same as she looked a good many pages ago and was flushed to just the same frail hue of carmine.

Ding-dong went St. Simon's husky clock, ding-dong, ding-dong.

Pitter-pat went Phyllida's heart and pitter-pitter-pitter-pitter-pat went Phyllida's heart when, exactly opposite the toy-shop, she saw a post chariot and four bay horses and two postillions staring very intently at the sky.

It struck Phyllida how clever it was of her dear Amor to chuse such a time and such a place; for all the world was engaged in directing the start of the Invincible Stage Coach that ploughed once a week between Curtain Wells and London.

Tootle-a-tootle-a-tootle went the long brass horn of the guard and plump-plump went two large parcels into his basket and crack-crack went the coachman's long whip, and 'Now then, Miss, jump in,' said one of the post-boys, still staring intently at the March sky, and before Phyllida knew where she was, she found herself sitting on a rather damp cushion with a peacock-blue riding hood lined with swansdown on the seat beside her, but no sign of Mr. Francis Amor.

In dismay she put her head out of the window and cried to the nearest postillion.

"Mr. Harmor's followin' on 'orseback," he said, with a thumping thwack on the ribs of his mount and a vicious prod with his rusty spurs.

Phyllida drew back with tears of disappointment starting to her wide blue eyes; but before she could make up her mind to stop the chariot and never elope again, she caught the glance of Thomas in open-mouthed amazement. Instinctively, she pulled the musty curtains close, and, lifting the leather flap at her back, could not help laughing aloud to see dignified Thomas mopping his brow with his right hand and waving his tall cane with the left; and just as the chariot tore round the corner of the street, she saw that Thomas had knocked off Lord Cinderton's grey beaver hat. The Love Chase had begun.

CHAPTER XXVIII

THE LOVE CHASE

JOHN GILPIN never rode so fast through Edmonton as, on that memorable afternoon in March, Major Constantine Tarry pounded over the cobbles of Curtain High Street. His scarlet uniform was very bright against the huge iron-grey steed on whose broad back he nodded with hat pressed down as far as his fierce prickly eyebrows, with pigtail bobbing to the motion and with sword whose martial clangour recalled every famous battle in the history of the world. He was conversing with the widow when Thomas burst upon them with the news of Phyllida's elopement.

"Gone, gone!" wailed the footman. "Oh Tyre! Oh Sidon! Hittites on horseback and two Amorites in a chariot!"

"What the d——l do you mean, sir?" snapped the Major, "who is gone?"

"Miss Phyllida," groaned Thomas.

"Gone," breathed the widow, and the odour of diffused Sanspareil permeated the room.

"Gone where?" shouted the Major.

"To the desert beyond Jordan," answered the footman.

"With what viper in sheep's clothing?" gasped Mrs. Courteen.

"Which way, which way, sirrah?" interrupted practical Major Terry.

"Lunnon," ejaculated Thomas, fainting into the arms of a chair.

This was why the inhabitants of the Wells saw a veteran of the Low Countries shaken up like a cherry in a basket. The sedate glories of the town were never more nicely displayed than on this famous occasion. From each bow-windowed shop came forth a bland shop-keeper and half a dozen inquisitive customers.

The little Miss Pettitoes trilled in bird-like accents: ' What an adventure! ' and returned to a counter spangled with their gay little purchases, for the Miss Pettitoes were twin sisters and to-morrow was their birthday.

" What an adventure! " they trilled to each other over a dish of Hyson and ' What an adventure! ' they trilled as they kissed each other ' good-night ' and went each to their bed chambers, identical save for the ribbons of their fascinating little spinster night-caps.

" Hurrah! hurrah! " shouted the boys, as they pushed the maids into the puddles the better to follow so surprizing a cavalier.

" Rot me! " said Mr. Golightly of the Grey Dragoons, as he lifted his tortoise-shell rimmed monocle to his supercilious left eye, and ' Rot you! ' he ejaculated, as an enthusiastick trio of youth sheltered between his remarkably tight-breeched legs.

" Shall we make such an impressive entrance, d'ye think? " asked Mr. Lovely, as he and Mr. Clare came out of Mr. Canticle's shop, followed by Mr. Canticle himself and Mr. Canticle's apprentice loaded with a huge brown-paper parcel.

" Good day, Canticle," said Charles.

" Good day, Mr. Lovely, good day, sir, and depend on't, grey will be the modish colour for gentlemen of quality; and I beg you not to be uneasy about the light-blue lining. That, sir, I venture to predict, will supply the exact touch of genteel eccentricity that consorts so amiably with the friendly madness of the season. I envy you, gentlemen, I envy you; and I beg to wish you many a pleasant adventure. The cut of that riding-coat, Mr. Lovely, will enthral the most fastidious glance, and as for your breeches, Mr. Clare, I should perhaps be considered boastful if I said that they impart a tone, sir, a very distinguished tone to the landskip.   Good day, gentlemen."

The two young gentlemen laughed over Mr. Canticle's prophecies, and excused his loquacity because he had been a limner till the vogue for foreign painters compelled him to apply his art in another direction.

It was certainly a stroke of irony that the offer of a sartorial uncle should make him, a very tolerable exponent of nudity, take up the occupation of devizing cloaths.

By this time, Major Tarry's coat-tails were flapping to hedge-row winds, and his astonishing course was less universally regarded; although, even in open country, the clamorous transit caused much confusion to itinerant carters, while a pair of blackbirds forsook their hardly built nest and retired in voluble dismay to the densest coppice between Baverstock Regis and Curtain Wells.

Mr. Jeremy Daish met our hero with a very lugubrious expression, as he strolled into the coffee-room.

"What has your honour been doing to enrage Mr. Ripple? Oh, Mr. Lovely, read this."

Charles took the proffered note, and half-smiling, half-sighing, perused his decree of banishment.

THE GREAT HOUSE.
CURTAIN WELLS, PRIDIE KAL. AP.

MR. DAISH,—*The uncomfortable events of Wednesday evening compel me to announce that I cannot contemplate with equanimity the protracted Sojourn of Mr. Lovely at your hitherto peaceful House. I have no desire to inflict upon you the invidious course of summary Ejection, but at the same time I am bound to invite a trifle less cordiality in your Reception of all young gentlemen unperturbed by the Gout. The town of Curtain Wells exists for the supply of*

hygiastick Waters; and, since red wine is a notorious antidote to chalybeate, my civick brother the Mayor begs me to point out that we cannot lend our patronage to a house which studiously encourages the circulation of this antipathetick Beverage. In expectation, Mr. Daish, that you will presently reconstruct at once your list of wines and your list of visitors,
I am Mr. Daish, your obliged
HORACE RIPPLE.

"Console yourself, Daish," said our hero, as he handed back the Beau's exquisitely written epistle, "Mr. Clare and I propose to make a long excursion into the country this very afternoon. Have the goodness to order our horses to be in the yard at six o'clock."

"Certainly, your honour, but I hope that nothing I may have said or done or hinted—or—or—or—" poor Mr. Daish stumbled over the awkwardness of the interview, and was more like a Cremona violin than ever, a violin whose strings were snapping one by one.

"Console yourself, Daish," said our hero with an incredibly magnanimous air, "you are not to blame. You must know, Daish, that for a long time past I have had a curiosity to survey this small green earth, unhampered by anything more serious than the impulse of the moment. To-night, Daish, when you retire to rest, when you gather the curtains of your serene bed, when you hark to the clock in the passage striking the moderate and orderly hour of ten o'clock, when you reflect with a sigh of proprietary contentment that you have offended no one in the course of an innkeeper's promiscuous day, when, in a word, your respectable head sinks into your respectable pillow, dally for a moment in the imagination of Charles Lovely and Anthony Clare mocking society, laughing at convention, seated in the parlour of some remote inn and dozing gratefully before a pile of logs.

"Think of us, Daish, in the cool dusks and azure silences of April, at the top of some gentle hill whence we can regard with exhilaration the prospect of a good dinner, a crimson glass, and genial intercourse with travellers. Behold us in your mind's eye, walking our horses down through the twilight, as one by one in cottage lattices the candles twinkle and, high above, the stars betray the night with silver spears. For my part, already I can hear the evening gossip of housewives, and the babble of children in small gardens, and clear against the green West, I can see the many lovers of a little town moving with slow steps along their customary path.

"Thus, my excellent Daish, each solemn nightfall will discover for us a new world, and, when the sun rises on the merry unknown streets of our pilgrimage, we shall think to ourselves what a vast number of jolly people exist in this remarkably jolly world. Oddslife—" Mr. Lovely broke off—" what a surprizing alliance."

As he looked out of the window, we had better look out of the window too, and I think you will be quite disposed to agree with Charles when I show you that vivid yellow chaise drawn by two fiery chestnut horses, and driven by that extraordinarily diminutive coachman, for inside are seated Beau Ripple and the Widow Courteen, and neither you nor I nor anybody else ever saw both so nearly disconcerted.

"Now what the deuce can be the meaning of that?" continued Mr. Lovely.

"Of what you were saying?" inquired Mr. Daish in a deprecating voice.

"The horses! the horses!" was all that Mr. Lovely saw fit to reply.

Major Tarry's earlier progress might well have been the meteor which heralds a cataclysm, for cataclysm this later apparition certainly was. I vow the noise of conversation it caused far exceeded anything of the sort that was ever known.

The Beau found the publicity of such an exit unendurable to his polite soul. That his sacred chaise, which had once bowled along at a high but decorous speed in order to meet the H—r A———t of Great Britain, should achieve such a vulgar notoriety nearly upset the sit of his waistcoat.

His contemporaries felt the Great little Man's humiliation.

Yet compassion did not prevent them from forming numberless conjectures as to the cause of this strange affair. Some said 'Debt!'; others boldly affirmed an intrigue; but as usual nobody guessed the true reason, which was that beneath a gorgeous exterior lurked the gentlest, kindliest heart.

When the Widow, with a very noisy tale of seduction, poured forth her tears upon his cushions, Mr. Ripple instantly reproached himself and nobody else with the disaster, immediately decided he must atone for his negligence by immediately ringing his flowered bell-pull and commanding Magog, who immediately appeared, to run immediately to the stables and command the immediate harnessing of the royal horses to the royal chaise and the immediate buttoning of his diminutive coachman's slender gaiters.

It was with a shudder, if a much polished shudder, that he handed Mrs. Courteen to a place amid the fawn and ivory of the interior of his chaise. With a barely repressed shudder, too, he observed the dabbled rouge of her cheeks, and the open mouths of the cits, and the bobbing of heads at windows, and a horrid bank of black clouds in the extreme South-west that seemed to betoken a night full of rain, and last but perhaps worst of all, the lean sign-post 'To London,' a prologue to G—— knows what unendurable discomfort.

"We have an adventure to hand," said Charles to Clare, as they strolled across the yard of the *Blue Boar*. "We'll follow Ripple!"

"Ripple?"

"Ay! Which way did Mr. Ripple's chaise go?" demanded Charles of a knot of idlers.

"Lunnon Road," they replied unanimously.

"We must get ready at once," declared Charles.

* * *

"How pleasant 'twould be," thought Phyllida, "if I were not alone."

Even alone, it was very pleasant to bowl along a level road at an equable rate of speed. It was very pleasant to try on the peacock-blue riding hood that so became her. It was very pleasant to see the cheerful faces of the many wayfarers encountered by the chariot. The backs of the postillions glowed with scarlet, and a gay contrast they made to the flaming gorse of a wild open stretch of country. Every cottage that nestled back from the road with clipped yews to guard the gate seemed to Phyllida a desirable place to live and love in for ever. It was pleasant to watch the lambs in the meadows, and exciting indeed to count the still sparse primroses starring the hedgerows. It was pleasant to watch the children stand on the topmost rung of a five-barred gate and cheer as they rattled past. Very pleasant it was, though the sight brought a slight lump in her throat, as she thought how often she had done the same thing with Dick Combleton the Squire's youngest son.

Up-hill with many a groan and grunt, and down-hill with a clatter and a dash, and along the level with a ring and a jingle went the post-chariot in the afternoon sunlight. Past farm-house and farm-yard, past villages and churches, and inns with waving signs, past ponds and geese, past many a tired woman trudging home from market and many a jovial carter; past sign-posts and cross-roads and milestones; past smithies with roaring fires and monstrous bellows, past lowing cows and crowing cocks, past journeymen tinkers and journeymen barbers, past a great dancing bear which, had Phyllida but known it, danced not a whit more foolishly for bumpkins than rose-pink Phyllida herself for the malicious eyes of the world of fashion.

After a long climb up a heavy hill, whence a very fair champagne spread before her, the great black and purple cloud caught the westering sun, and suffused the whole landskip with a queer metallick sheen. It made the rooks that swayed in the bare branches of a windy clump of elms take on a strange green lustre over their plumage, and cast a stillness over the world. That view remained with Phyllida all her life, as a pause wherein she had contemplated existence for the briefest moment. Years afterwards, an old woman, sitting in a dim inglenook, would see that fair champagne in the clouds of smoke that curled ceaselessly up the wide chimney, and, above the scent of burning logs, would be wafted the perfume of the white March violets that blossomed at the foot of those swaying elms where the rooks cawed and the dead leaves raced round and round.

"Stop, you blackguards," cried a rasping voice above the noise of fast-approaching hoofs.

"Crack! crack!" went Dickie Magg's big pistol.

"'Ighwayman, Miss," he added cheerfully, as the sound of something soft falling was heard, followed by horse-hoofs in mad retreat down the long heavy hill.

In a moment, the chariot was rocking in a wild gallop down the opposite decline.

Raindrops began to fall, deliberately at first, but soon fast enough, while the earth was slowly blotted out by storm and rain and twilight.

On the summit of the hill, Major Constantine Tarry lay face downwards, having paid the extreme penalty of interference with other people's business. Poor Tarry, he was a bore and a braggart, and had not the slightest intention of being killed, yet I for one regret the manner of his death, up there on the top of that windswept hill. And for all he told you such very long stories when he asked you to dine with him at Oudenarde Grange and Malplaquet Lodge and Ramilies House, he gave you some capital Port, and Sherry nearly as dry as his own anecdotes. Moreover, he really fought in that bloody fight of Fontenoy, and that was a very great honour and should make us forgive a very great deal.

A flash of lightning illuminated the dead body of the veteran lying face downwards in the mud of an English highroad, and a distant volley of thunder accorded military honours to his somewhat grotesque death.

CHAPTER XXIX

THE BASKET OF ROSES

SOME four-and-twenty miles from Curtain Wells on the Great West Road is a tangle of briers among whose blossoms an old damask rose is sometimes visible. If the curious traveller should pause and examine this fragrant wilderness, he will plainly perceive the remains of an ancient garden, and if he be of an imaginative character of mind will readily recall the legend of the Sleeping Beauty in her mouldering palace; for some enchantment still enthralls the spot, so that he who bravely dares the thorns is well rewarded with pensive dreams and, as he lingers a while gathering the flowers or watching their petals flutter to the green shadows beneath, will haply see elusive Beauty hurry past.

Here at the date of this tale stood the *Basket of Roses* Inn, a mile or so away from a small village. When coaches ceased to run, the house began to lose its custom and, as stone is scarce hereabouts, was presently pulled down in order to provide the Parson with a peculiarly bleak Parochial Hall.

However, this melancholy fate was still distant, and old Simon Tabrum had a fine custom from the coaches and private travellers who delighted to spend a night in so sweet a lodging.

The *Basket of Roses* was the fairest, dearest inn down all that billowy London road. The counter, sheathed in a case of pewter, the glasses all in a row, the sleek barrels and the irregular lines of home-brewed cordials, charmed the casual visitor to a more intimate acquaintance. Behind the tap was the Travellers' Room, and what a room it was—with great open fireplaces and spits and bubbling kettles and blackened ingles. Long-buried ancestors of the village had carved their rude initials over each high-backed bench and battered the bottoms of the great tankards into unexpected dents by many rollicking choruses in the merry dead past. The walls of this room knew the pedigree of every bullock and the legend of every ghost for many miles round. Here was the cleanest floor, the clearest fire in England.

Old Tabrum the landlord was the very man for the house—the very man to bring out all that was most worthy in his guests. He always produced good wine and a piping hot supper, never asked for his money till his guests were satisfied and always wore an apron as white as the foam of his cool deep ale.

He was eighty years old now, with a bloom on his cheeks like an autumn pippin and two limpid blue eyes that looked straight into yours and, if you had any reverence at all, made the tears well involuntarily at the sight of such gentle beauty.

Once he was a famous Basso Profundo, but now his voice was high and thin, and seemed already fraught with faint aerial music. The ancient man was a great gardener as properly became a landlord whose sign was a swinging posy. What a garden there was at the back of this glorious inn. The bowling-green surrounded by four grey walls was the finest ever known, and as for the borders, deep borders twelve feet wide, they were full of every sweet flower. There were Columbines and Canterbury Bells and blue Bells of Coventry and Lilies and Candy Goldilocks with Penny flowers or White Sattin and Fair Maids of France and Fair Maids of Kent and London Pride.

There was Herb of Grace and Rosemary and Lavender to pluck and crush between your fingers, while some one rolled the jack across the level green of the ground. In Spring there were Tulips and Jacynths, Dames' Violets and Primroses, Cowslips of Jerusalem, Daffodils and Pansies, Lupins like spires in the dusk, and Ladies' Smocks in the shadowed corners. As for Summer, why the very heart of high June and hot July dwelt in that fragrant enclosure. Sweet Johns and Sweet Williams with Dragon flowers and crimson Peaseblossom and tumbling Peonies, Blue Moonwort and the Melancholy Gentlemen, Larksheels, Marigolds, Hearts, Hollyhocks and Candy Tufts. There was Venus' Looking Glass and Flower of Bristol and Apple of Love and Blue Helmets and Herb Paris and Campion and Love in a Mist and Ladies' Laces and Sweet Sultans or Turkey Cornflowers, Gillyflower Carnations (Ruffling Rob of Westminster amongst them) with Dittany and Sops in Wine and Floramor, Widow Wail and Bergamot, True Thyme and Gilded Thyme, Good Night at Noon and Flower de Luce, Golden Mouse-ear, Princes' Feathers, Pinks, and deep-red Damask Roses.

It was a very wonderful garden indeed.

And because the old man loved flowers, tending them in the early twilight with water and releasing them from many a small weed which he was fain to destroy, but in the end always replanted in a small clearing on the shady side of his farthest meadow, because he loved flowers, the old man, whose first wife died years and years ago on a long past primrose-tide, married in the hale winter of his life a comfortable wench whom he could trust as he trusted his flowers to be true to their seasons. This second wife, more like a daughter than a wife, he delighted to surprize with fragrant rolls of gaily sprigged cloths; and never a summer morning broke but he was abroad in the dewy grass to gather her such a posy of freshness and beauty as can only be taken in the earliest hours of the morning. Mrs. Tabrum, for all she was so young and rosy, had a great feeling for the importance of her position as mistress of a famous hostelry and ordered about little Polly Patch, newly arrived from Mrs.

Margery Severe's select charity school, with a great air of ladyship. Little Polly Patch was a very important young woman too; for the *Basket of Roses* was not a large galleried inn full of grooms and hostlers and waiters and chambermaids, but a house of quite another character, where you were never bewildered by superfluous service but always received with a quiet dignity. Therefore you paid a great deal of respectful attention to little Polly Patch who had a great deal to do with your night's rest and your morning's breakfast. I think Mr. Vernon was a very wise man to choose a domestick fairyland so apt to soothe the sweet alarms of his Phyllida.

Here they would sup while the horses were being changed, and hence they would set out in the darkness, preserving, as they galloped along, a sense of peace and quiet beauty that should be to her the fortunate prelude of a happy adventure.

Vernon had sent word to the house of their arrival, hinted at the fatigues of a gay bridal, and let it be supposed they desired no intrusion.

To the ancient man such a confidence was enough to set his old brain agog with the gallant scenes of his youth. He chuckled over every tankard of ale he drew, told every one of his daffodils the merry secret and piped away at long forgotten melodies until his wife in despair sat him down in the ingle, put a broken fiddle in his hand and bade him play his fancies to sleep. The storm that rose at sunset shrieked about the inn, and the hollow groaning in the mazes of the huge chimney consorted in fitting harmonies with the old man's eerie tunes.

"March is going out wi' thunder and tempest like a roaring lion," he muttered, as a sudden gust of hail was blown against the lattice which pattered and rattled as if a crowd of elfin drummers were beating a wild tattoo without.

"Aye, 'tis a main ugly night," said Mrs. Dorothy

Tabrum, who was laying the shining silver about the snowy tablecloth. " So 'tis, my peony, so 'tis! A main ugly night for daffodils and young brides. Is her chamber ready? " he went on.

" Aye! Aye! "

" Wi' rosy curtains drawn close? "

Mrs. Tabrum nodded.

" Wi' candlelight and the crackling of logs and green bayleaves in the presses? "

" Why, do'ee think I'm gone daft to forget suchlike? "

" And a vase of daffodils by her mirrour? " the ancient one persisted.

Polly Patch came in at that moment.

" All be ready, mistress," she said in a slow voice, solemnly nodding her enormous mobcap while she spoke.

" Now, Polly," said Mrs. Tabrum, "lend a hand wi' this table and lets put 'un a thought nearer to the fire. Ugh! how it blows! " A vivid flash of lightning illuminated the room, and on the heels of a terrifick roar of thunder there was a cry of ' House! House! '

" Hurry, hurry, my daisies, and make who comes there welcome. Jacob! Jacob! " cried the old landlord as, much excited, he rose from his seat in the ingle and quavered towards the taproom.

" You are sure the candles are lighted, Polly? "

" Sarten, mistress."

" And the logs burning brightly? "

" 'Ess, mistress."

" And the curtains pinned together? "

" 'Ess, mistress."

" Then stand by the door, curtsey when you're spoken to, and don't put your thumb in the soup."

" No, mistress."

" Is Mary Maria watching the fowls? "

" Wi' both her eyes, mistress."

" Hark! "

" I'm harking away, mistress."

And while the mistress and the maid harked vigilantly the ancient landlord ushered Miss Phyllida Courteen into the Travellers' Room of the *Basket of Roses* Inn.

As he entered, old Tabrum looked very much like a sexton leading a shy maid to the altar. She, flustered, expectant, murmured soft thanks into the farthest recesses of her swansdown muff, stumbled frequently to the voluble distress of her guide, and seemed afraid to look round the well-ordered comforatble room after so many miles of wind and driving rain.

"Dear soul! And where's the bridegroom?" exclaimed Mrs. Tabrum, as she led Phyllida to a high-backed chair right before the heart of the blazing fire.

Phyllida blushed as she explained Mr. Amor was travelling on horseback.

"Indeed, I expected to find him here," she stammered, "Oh! I hope nothing has happened to him."

"Now, don't 'ee fret thyself, sweet marjoram," said the ancient one, humming round her like a bee. "A'most anything might have happened to him on such a dreadful night."

"Don't 'ee hark to the ancient dodderer," interrupted the dodderer's wife.

"Killed by a falling tree, withered to a cinder by bloody lightning."

"You alarm me," exclaimed Phyllida, jumping up.

"Hold thy ancient foolish tongue," commanded Mrs. Tabrum peremptorily, "and go see that Mary Maria keeps the fowls turning a while yet."

"Very well, my gillyflower, very well," piped senility, "but don't 'ee take on, my little blue love-in-a-mist, happen 'tis no more than a broken leg has overtook your husband."

"Polly," said Mrs. Tabrum, who saw that Phyllida was on the verge of tears, "take thy ancient master away. Hark," she finished, with an impressive forefinger.

" What are us to hark to, pretty pink? "

" Ef I doant hear a great tom-cat a-scratching in the tulips, my name be'ant Dorothy Ann Tabrum."

As at this moment the tempest outside was howling with unsurpassed fury, it is extremely doubtful whether the buxom lady spoke the truth, but her husband was alert at once and hastily snatching down a blunderbuss labelled ' Loaded on Tuesday sennight ' Simon Tabrum moved stealthily from the room.

" You must pardon my ancient old husband for his flowery manner of speech. 'Tis not disrespect he do mean, but love and charity wi' his neighbour, having as it were been sown a power of years ago and being now apt to let his withered branches fall on the heads of all manner of folk."

As this long sentence was evidently considered a full and proper explanation of the dodderer's inconvenient habit of prophecy, Phyllida smiled very charmingly and said she quite understood.

" And now let us gossip of thy wedding," said Mrs. Tabrum in a cosy tone of voice, " or would 'ee rather go to thy chamber, pretty miss? "

" Oh! indeed I will stay here, thank you. Mr. Amor might come at any moment."

" Polly! Polly Patch! "

" 'Ess, mistress."

" What for are 'ee standing there, lolloping thy great cap, dollop. Be off, great clockface, be off, pundle, to Mary Maria, and tell her to keep the fowls a-turning and a-turning."

Polly Patch curtseyed solemnly and retreated slowly, murmuring to herself, " and not to put my thumbs in the soup."

" Do you think he will be a very long time? " asked Phyllida, turning suddenly to the landlady and looking indescribably wistful.

" What I can't make out, my lamb, is how he came to leave 'ee on such a night. That's what I can't make out at all. Now at my bride-ale, for all I was wedding a man old enough to be my ancestor, why it was bride-ale, I do warrant. My aged husband being a publican and a sinner, there was a mort of merry-making, I tell 'ee, and 'twas only when Tabrum slipped on the floor and cracked the back of his faded head as we finished, and me forced to use the holland smock as I won at Ascensiontide smock-racing. Oh! his head was so raw as an egg, and running faster than ever I run for the smock."

"How dreadful," murmured Phyllida, not quite sure whether the narrative should offend her maiden sensibility or not.

"But he was out wi' the hens next morning," the talkative lady continued, "out wi' the hens and scratching away in the garden as hard as any of 'em. But, I tell 'ee, I did souse his head wi' vinegar when I got 'un indoors. The house smelt like a jar of pickle for a week o' Sundays after. But there! Tabrum he gets ascited. Don't matter whether 'tis his own or another's wedding, he's all the while jumping around like a Shrovetide pancake. And talk—well, 'tis babble, babble, and all of men and maids as was under yews twenty green years ago. I tell 'ee, we all laffed when he began telling 'ow he kissed my grandmother coming out of Evening Prayer one frosty night. 'The moon was on her back,' he says, 'ay, and ecod! so was she!' Pretty times, pretty times!"

What farther free confessions would have rippled from Mrs. Tabrum's cherry-ripe lips, it would ill become a modest writer or reader to speculate. They were cut short by the lurching entrance of Charlie and Dicky Maggs, the two postillions.

It would have been hard to find a more ill-favoured pair of ruffians in a day's posting. Both of them had dismounted very regularly at every house of call on the road and arrived at the *Basket of Roses* with a considerable cargo of bad spirits. The prospect of a long wait, while the horses were changed and their fares supped, encouraged them to farther excesses, and a lucky summons to the drawer to reach down a special cordial gave them an opportunity to finish off the greater part of a bottle of Plymouth Gin.

Fortified by this, annoyed to find that Vernon had not arrived, and half afraid they would lose their wages, they had come in to extract from Miss Courteen as much money as they could, being willing and anxious to drink away every minute of the wait.

"Ve're vet, Miss," said Charles.

"And it vouldn't be amiss if ve could 'ave a little piece of gold as 'ud varm us wiv its shining," said Dicky.

"Mr. Amor will settle your charges," said Phyllida.

"And be off, you ruffians," exclaimed Mrs. Tabrum, enraged by this impudent invasion of the Travellers' Room.

"Shut your mouth, mother Appleface," hiccoughed Charlie.

"And fork out somefink on account, Miss," oozed from his brother.

The latter began to move with uncertain steps after Phyllida, who shrank towards the shelter of the inglenook.

"Jacob! Jacob! Simon Tabrum! Polly Patch! Mary Maria!" screamed the landlady, snatching at the only article of offence in reach, which happened to be a pair of bellows. With these she puffed away furiously, to the enormous delight of the drunken postillions, who continued to advance and indeed probably found the air of the bellows very grateful to their heated brains.

It is unlikely that anything more serious than a volley of oaths would have occurred, if a tall elderly gentleman in a chestnut-brown frogged riding-coat had not come in at that moment; but as he did come in, no doubt the room was the sweeter for the interruption.

"Oh, your honour," said Mrs. Tabrum, "will 'ee please turn out these drunken rogues, seeing as all the house is away at their business and no one near by."

The elderly gentleman clenched his riding-stick a trifle more firmly and directed his steel-grey eyes—equally potent weapons—towards the abashed brothers. They did not wait to be addressed, but hurried as quickly as the fumes of liquor allowed them, to the more congenial atmosphere of the taproom. It is comforting to reflect, while they twisted their way out, that Charlie and Dickie Maggs were hanged at Tyburn for a peculiarly atrocious robbery and brutal assault upon a blind rat-tamer, who, with many clinging rats and mice and a scarlet-frilled dog, was a familiar figure in the villages round London. It is not perhaps so comforting to reflect upon the poor old man lying insensible in a puddle, with his tame rats and mice wandering aimlessly in and out of his innumerable pockets and his scarlet-frilled dog with three broken ribs moaning in the middle of a quickset bush. Egad! I vow the Tyburn horse never responded so readily to Jack Ketch's whip and never a pair of rogues went so ashen grey at the tide of a mob's execrations in all the livid chronicles of quick and evil ends.

The elderly gentleman in the chestnut Surtout turned from the exit of Charlie and Dickie Maggs to survey the subject of their insolence. It would have puzzled an onlooker to say precisely what effect was produced on the elderly gentleman's countenance by this deliberate inspection of Miss Phyllida Courteen, now melting in tears of apprehension and only barely restrained from hystericks by Mrs. Tabrum's plump hands in extensive motion.

When the iron-grey clouds of a chill December afternoon dissolve for a moment in the scud of a high gale and shed a ray of pallid sunlight on a spent blossom, we are almost glad to see the thin azure thus displayed as quickly veiled, and welcome the sullen twilight that succeeds. The elderly gentleman's countenance took on for a brief moment a strange light, but the frosted smile betrayed so much grim sorrow behind that it was quite a relief to see his face resume a normal frigidity as he muttered a regret and inquired into the chances of a good night's lodging.

CHAPTER XXX

SIR GEORGE REPINGTON

"IT is now eight o'clock," said the elderly gentleman, "if this young lady has no objection, I will eat a light supper in this apartment; and if you, ma'am, have no objection, I will retire to my bedchamber immediately after the meal. I do not require a heavy supper," he added as Mrs. Tabrum's jolly face began to pucker with the impatience of a good housewife to enumerate the plentiful dainties of a well-stocked larder.

The latter perceiving that Phyllida was recovered of her alarm, and anxious to prove to the elderly gentleman that his appetite was in the wrong by producing a flock of savoury dishes as speedily as possible, hereupon curtseyed, and was soon audible in shrill pursuit of little Polly Patch.

The Travellers' Room of the *Basket of Roses* was plunged into rosy quiet. The Dutch clock swung a languid pendulum to and fro with gentle tick; the fire whispered and crackled faintly; the lattices occasionally shook before a more unruly blast; a mouse stood up in a dark corner and squeaked; the huge oak dresser occasionally tapped; two unknown birds, screened till morning by chintz foliage, sometimes stirred on their perches; the elderly gentleman sometimes rapped his mother-o'-pearl snuff-box; Phyllida sometimes smoothed her forget-me-not flowered skirts; and away in the taproom was a tinkle and murmur of taproom sounds muffled by several intervening doors. Yet, however fair the surroundings, it is impossible for two people, unacquainted, to maintain a graceful silence for long. The elderly gentleman began to tap his snuff-box more frequently while Phyllida would smooth her skirts more persistently and from time to time cast a sidelong glance in the direction of the elderly gentleman. The latter felt the undercurrent of strong emotion so keenly that he was worried by this steady inaction into a curiosity quite alien to his character, and plunged into a conversation consisting principally of a large number of direct questions on his side and a small number of indirect replies on the part of Phyllida. At last, after a tiresome quarter of an hour in which the only solid piece of information given and offered was the fact that he was going to, she departing from the salubrious town of Curtain Wells, the elderly gentleman produced from the upper left-hand pocket of his waistcoat an oval case of worn Morocco leather. Phyllida observed that he rapped this in just the same decided way as he rapped his snuff-box and felt a certain incongruity in his manner, as he took from it the miniature of a young girl and offered the portrait for her inspection, asking whether she detected a likeness.

The girl, depicted with the meticulous art of the worker on a small scale, recalled at once the features of Mr. Charles Lovely. Phyllida hesitated for a moment before assigning the likeness to such a man.

"You observe, Madam, the resemblance to yourself?" said the elderly gentleman.

"To myself?" replied Miss Courteen taken aback.

"For what other reason should I show it to you?"

"To say truth, sir, it reminds me more of a gentleman——"

"Eh! what's that," he interrupted. "Not young Charles Lovely?"

"Indeed, sir—'twas he occurred to my mind."

"You know him?"

"I have stepped a minuet with him," replied

Phyllida, now more than ever on her guard against the steel-grey eyes of the elderly gentleman.

"This was my sister, his mother."

If you had asked the stranger what prompted him to confide so suddenly in Miss Courteen, I doubt he would have been unable to tell you. If his clerks could have seen Sir George Repington, head of the great banking house of Repington, at this moment they would have been indescribably shocked to hear him announce this piece of personal information. The clerks in busy Throgmorton Street firmly believed that the great Sir George Repington lived a desolate and severe life surrounded by calculating machines of enormous complication; they would have gasped to imagine his bleak financial solitudes disturbed by a young woman in an inn-parlour. The chief cashier, indeed, might have emitted one of his dry hacking little laughs; but then the chief cashier had grown old in the service of the Repingtons and, having known Sir George as a young man, enjoyed a privileged cynicism. Moreover, the chief cashier when he was junior clerk had carried half a score sealed notes to Thistlegrove Cottage—a diminutive paradise five or six miles along the Hounslow Road. There, amid the chirping of many linnets, young Master Repington would swear eternal fidelity while the sun-dyed sleepy air coloured his dear one's lips as deep as rubies and enchanted with gold her soft brown hair. No doubt the present scene of this small history would have awakened a delightful memory from the dusty recesses of the chief cashier's brain, for all that the end of Thistlegrove Cottage was a businesslike affair on a level with many other successful monetary transactions of the great house of Repington and Son.

Phyllida was somewhat embarrassed by the sudden announcement of his relationship to that dreadful Mr. Lovely, who had lampooned the whole of the fashionable world. She wondered if the elderly gentleman was aware of his nephew's late indiscretion, whether she ought to break the news of his odium, and finally with a maid's inconsequence fell to wishing she had never eloped since the step had involved her in so awkward an adventure.

Sir George, noticing her embarrassment, introduced himself.

"My name is Repington, ma'am—Sir George Repington." As he said this he received the miniature from Phyllida, and having, as it were, fondled the oval for a second, replaced it in the upper left-hand pocket of his waistcoat.

The introduction put Phyllida deeper than ever into a quandary. She felt the genteel movement to be a low curtsey coupled with the graceful revelation of her name, but this was just the act she could not bring herself to perform. What a vast number of polite difficulties attached themselves to an elopement, and how she wished with all her heart she had never been so foolish as to brave them unaccompanied.

"The resemblance is certainly very remarkable," said Sir George Repington.

Phyllida clutched this conversational straw.

"I doubt, sir, 'twould ill become me to allow the compliment."

The stilted reply did not seem to offend the elderly gentleman, for he bowed very gallantly and tapped the lid of his snuff-box with an air.

"And my nephew, ma'am, what does Curtain Wells think of my nephew?"

Luckily for Phyllida who was racking her brains to devize a polite method of informing Sir George Repington that his nephew had offended the whole world, that is to say the whole world known to the residents and visitors of Curtain Wells, Mrs. Tabrum came back to say that a pair of fowls were on their way.

"A morsel of cheese is all that I require, thank'ee," said Sir George to this information. "A morsel of cheese, well-aired sheets and———"

"A bit off the breast," murmured Mrs. Tabrum coaxingly.

"Well-aired sheets and——"

"A grilled drumstick," insinuated the landlady.

"Well-aired sheets and——"

"The liver wing."

Sir George Repington capitulated and sat down to supper with Phyllida opposite and a great bowl of daffadillies between them.

Nobody ever found out what exactly was the elderly gentleman's unspoken requirement.

Sir George was enjoying himself—a very unusual occupation for that grim and solid man of business.

Phyllida, on the contrary, was becoming more deeply embarrassed every moment. She could not help picturing to herself the awkwardness of greeting her dear Amor in the presence of such a man. Moreover, she could not understand why the latter preserved such a lack of curiosity. She, a heroine to herself, was unable to appreciate the point of view that took her and her adventure for granted. She almost resented Sir George's acceptation of her as part of the furniture of a wayside inn.

As a matter of fact, the banker was abroad to enjoy himself, and the discovery of a maid sitting solitary in the firelight of an inn parlour only struck him as whimsical in so far as she resembled his dead sister. Having, after a lapse of many grey years, put on once more the mantle of youth, he was very ready to welcome a face that consorted so perfectly with his mood.

But as supper went on, and the elderly gentleman inquired no farther into the well-being of Mr. Charles Lovely, while Mr. Amor did not arrive, and the drunken postillions remained in the tap-room, and the Dutch clock ticked on quite unperturbed by the raging of the storm without, Phyllida began to regain her equanimity, and even to converse so trippingly with the elderly gentleman that elopements and Gretna Green marriages floated away while she chattered of her dearest Morton, betrayed the latter's partiality for young Mr. Chalkley, compared her boldness with the more modest behaviour of a certain Miss Jenny West, who was the third daughter of a parson who lived four—no five miles from where they lived in Hampshire, jumped from the tale of Miss West to the tale of Miss West's brother who scandalized the country by stepping eight consecutive gavottes with his cousin from Hertfordshire; and ultimately confided to Sir George her profound contempt for Mr. Moon and her immense distrust of Major Tarry. Yet, at the very moment when she was telling Sir George of a ludicrous chase of the Major's wig one windy March morning in the preceding year the furious gale was blowing his sodden pigtail to and fro without a curse from the little soldier in whom stern death had begotten a divine and everlasting indifference to the minor amenities of polite appearance. Sir George Repington was near to the capture of his fled youth that fire-lit evening. He was back in the old South Gallery at Repington Hall sitting in the wide window seat at the West End, and opposite to him with flushed exquisite face sat his sister Joan, rippling joyfully through the fair meadows of life like a glittering brook. The musick of Phyllida's conversation revived for the elderly gentleman many a crimson dusk. He thought with a sigh of the South Gallery now, with its hollow echoes, its dust and long line of contemptuous ancestors, and of himself as, with severe tread, he ran the batteries of many immutable eyes.

Old Tabrum would quaver in from time to time to survey the comfort of his guests, regaling them with some particularly choice floral anecdote. His wife too would peep to inquire whether the roasted fowls fulfilled her expectations, and once little Polly Patch put her cap round the door and asked if his honour would like the warming-pan left in his bed or merely whisked three or four times over his already well-aired sheets.

* * *

Phyllida made a careless remark about her mother, and Sir George Repington hoped that Mrs. Courteen (Phyllida had some time ago divulged her name) would not be alarmed by the strife of the elements. Phyllida made a very careless reply to this, by reassuring Sir George about her mother, who, as she pointed out, would be not at all likely to observe the wildness of the night in her anxiety to secure her hand against the prying glances of my Lady Bunbutter.

"Is that Sir Moffyn Bunbutter's lady?" said Sir George.

"Yes, indeed, sir."

"Sure to be, sure to be," Sir George commented. "Who'd have thought of seeing poor old Sir Moffyn's lady here of all places?"

"But she's not here, sir. She is at Curtain Wells."

"But your mother?"

Phyllida saw her mistake, but, being unused to falsehoods, made no attempt to extricate herself from the situation provoked by her own carelessness. As a happy compromise, she blushed and made queer little excavations in the salt-cellar.

"You've no brother and your father is dead?" went on Sir George, fixing the abashed young woman with his sharp eyes. "Then you are alone in this inn?"

The statement, put so baldly, sounded very dreadful to Miss Courteen. Moreover, she had an uneasy idea that the elderly gentleman was beginning to feel himself compromised by her company, so she made patterns in the salt-cellar more fantastick than ever, blushed till the shells of her ears seemed veritably to crack in the furnace of outraged sensibility, and looked very guilty.

"Alone?" the elderly gentleman repeated.

Phyllida's whispered 'yes' was only just audible above the languid ticking of the Dutch clock.

The antique landlord broke the tension by putting his head round the door and demanding from Sir George whether he preferred to sleep in the Dorick Summerhouse with a view of the surrounding country, or in the Green Vista with a more comfortable bed, if not so wide a view. Antiquity was followed by his wife, who hustled him fairly into the candlelight and explained that all their bedchambers were named to suit the flowery eccentricity of her husband.

"Thus we have the Parterre," said old Simon in support of his wife's explanation, "the Pleached Alley (though that is more truly a passage). The Sun Dial (a warm attick), the Quincunx, the Bosquet, the Arbour, the Green Gallery, the Cascade (or stairway) and for my dear hollyhock and myself, the Columbary."

"God bless you, sirrah," said Sir George rather testily, "I'm no Dutch garden-maker that I should fret about such vagaries of taste. Oons! plant me where you will, I wager I shall not open till daybreak."

This quip pleased the old landlord enormously, and he retired upon a chuckle prolonged sufficiently to convey him to the farthest ends of the house, whither he was followed by his anxious wife.

Left alone once more, Phyllida and Sir George looked at each other over the remains of that genial supper.

Neither broke the silence for a while. The elderly gentleman was the first to speak.

"Don't you think it is somewhat unwise to travel alone, especially as your postillions do not seem a very trusty pair?"

"I am not really alone," said Phyllida, "I'm—I'm—expecting—a—a—companion."

Sir George Repington raised his eyebrows and seemed about to make a severe comment upon this halting explanation, but, leaning his elbow on the table and his cheek on his hand, he changed his mind and in cold deliberate accents, so cold and so deliberate that you would have sworn a weight of emotion was sunk beneath them, began a tale. Since this tale must either be told by me or by Sir George himself, inasmuch as it concerns one or two of our characters, I will let the original author give it to you in his own words, nay I will give the story the distinction of a chapter to itself.

CHAPTER XXXI

A TALE WITH AN INTERRUPTED MORAL

SIR GEORGE REPINGTON filled up his glass (he was drinking Port wine), motioned Phyllida to a seat on the right, sat himself down opposite, and, to the accompaniment of thunder and lightning and wind and rain, proceeded to entertain her with some vastly interesting details of his domestick history.

"I have already shown you the portrait of my sister Joan, and you will remember that I remarked upon the resemblance between you and her—I did not think at the time that such a coincidence would fulfil itself even more completely.

"We were left orphans soon after I reached my twenty-fifth birthday, and I will admit that I experienced a keen sensation of pride in the responsibleness of a great financial house and a very attractive young woman. Pray, remember I was still young. We lived when we were in London at a pleasant house in Soho Square, on the side nearest to the Oxford Road, but spent much of our leisure at Repington Hall, a fine old family mansion in the county of Surrey, near enough to the town to make our visits there very frequent."

Sir George sighed at the pleasant memories as he sipped his glass of Port wine.

"We spent many golden days at Repington Hall and our friends, carefully selected, as all young people's friends are, found the long June evenings on the great sloping lawn not less pleasant than we did. Egad! I can see them all now and hear over the long silences that invariably punctuate such intimate conversation the lowing of the cows in the home farm and the deer crunching the sweet long grass beneath the broad oak-trees. And in Spring what a choir of nightingales sang in the gnarled whitethorn trees by the sunk fence, and in late summer what myriads of grasshoppers chirruped in the twilight. Yes, yes, I can see them all—young Harbottle Ramsey—he's my Lord Sodor and Man now—succeeded his uncle who was executed after the rising in '45—well—well, Harbottle was always a staunch Whig, and by gad, so were all of us in those evenings at Repington. Then there was Burnet, Cinderton's eldest son—he is Cinderton now—Burnet was always monstrous careful about his cloaths and always carried a small Persian rug to sit upon. I remember we used to call it the hearthrug—Harthe-Brusshe is the family name—and now they tell me he's a positive martyr to the lumbago. Yes, yes, Ramsey and Burnet and Belladine, I wonder what's become of Belladine,—he was a famous fop—poor Belladine, poor Belladine—he never recovered from the blow. And then there was Roger Quain.

"He was my best friend, and the happiest day of my life was that on which he was betrothed to my sister Joan. I tell you no such rousing toast was given at Repington since the news of the Boyne victory was brought in to my father. She and Roger were betrothed in July and should have been wed in April."

The old man—for, with the progress of his tale, such the elderly gentleman seemed to become—took a longer sip at his glass of Port as if to brace himself for the climax of the narrative.

"They should have been wed in April. But that winter was a busy one in Throgmorton Street, and my sister Joan, having caught a chill, was ordered to remain in the country—her only companion, a foolish cousin of my mother's. I was not at home more than twice all the winter. I never knew of that blackguard's visits till March. He used to come every day—every day until I forbade him the house—a white cockade papist crammed with disloyalty—always bragging of some outlandish petty rebellion on the top of some d——d Scottish mountain or other. He filled her head with his Jacobite twaddle—a fool who, earning his livelihood by dice and cards, was willing enough to upset all law and order for the sake of the plunder which he and his fellows might very well have acquired at the expense of better and honester and more loyal men.

"He wound himself round her heart with his false French oaths and cursed lovemaking.

"I sent for Roger; he came down with Belladine—I shall always believe that Belladine loved her too—and I told Roger he must keep an eye on his treasure, or 'twould be stolen from him. The wedding was fixed; the guests were invited; and one fine morning I went down to the orchard to see how the apples were setting (there had been a shrewd Easterly wind for some days) and—and—I found him dead—Roger Quain—my dearest, oldest friend—Roger Quain dead. Gadslife! young Madam, if you had seen, as I saw, the fallen apple-blossoms reddened by his blood, I do not think you would be making a runaway match; and she, my beloved sister, eloped with his murderer—with Valentine Lovely, Esq., Jacobite, Papist, rake, spend-thrift, drunkard, gamester, and prodigal!"

Sir George Repington rose from his seat and in the passion of remembrance broke with his grip the thin stem of his wineglass, so that the spilt liquid as it trickled over the hearth stones and stained the ashes conjured up the old scene all too vividly and horribly for poor Phyllida.

"But why did Belladine let her go with that blackguard—that is what I never knew—that is what I would like to ask Belladine—what can have happened to Belladine?" the old man muttered to himself, "and why do I tell you this?" he went on, "why—because ——"

But unfortunately the moral of this story was never properly related, though 'tis easy enough to guess the import, for at that moment in came the long-awaited Mr. Francis Vernon, splashed from head to foot in mud and wearing a deep cut over his left temple. After all, Major Constantine Tarry did succeed in delaying the elopement if only for an hour or two because Mr. Vernon's mare had shied at the dead body and flung her rider over the hedge in her unwillingness to pass so damp and gloomy an obstacle. If the veteran's ghost was able to spare a moment from his enthralling conversations with Alexander the Great and other notable captains in Elysium, I make no doubt at the sight he gave vent to an attenuated cackle of pleasure.

Nothing sets a woman off to such disadvantage as the need to introduce a pair of men whom instinctively she knows to be hostile to each other. They never make the slightest attempt to help her out of the awkward position, and, indeed, add to it by such haughty behaviour, such ruffling of crests and bristling of limbs that under the circumstances the most polished gentlemen become uncouth savages or dogs eager to squabble over a debated bone.

In this instance Mr. Vernon stared Sir George Repington up and down, while the latter, who was not accustomed to such freedom of regard, took snuff very aggressively and looked as if he would like to give the intruder a moment's notice, as indeed he would. Phyllida tried to stem the tide of embarrassment by remarking in a hushed voice that Sir George had been kindly entertaining her in the absence of Mr. Amor.

"Has he?" was the latter's frigid response.

"And oh, Amor," she went on, "those odious postillions pushed their way to the room and wanted money and Sir George kindly came to the rescue and bade them begone."

" Did he? " was all that Vernon would vouchsafe in thanks to this timely assistance.

Phyllida, abashed by her lover's bad manners, seemed inclined to apologize for them with tears. And now Sir George did what most Englishmen would have done under the circumstances—he walked out of the room in a very stately way. No doubt the banker thought the strength of feeling which had led him to reveal his life's tragedy would kindle an equal emotion in the heart of Miss Courteen and that when he returned he would find the raffish intruder gone.

This was in fact the precise result of his withdrawal. When he returned, Mr. Vernon was gone. But neither was Miss Phyllida Courteen anywhere in sight.

CHAPTER XXXII

THE HORRID ADVENTURES OF BEAU RIPPLE AND MRS. COURTEEN

WE will, if you please, take for granted the persuasions used by Mr. Vernon to induce Phyllida to continue upon her headlong course. He rode beside her on this second stage of her adventure, and I shall have something to say of that drive together through the darkness of wind and rain. We will take for granted Sir George Repington's indignation, expressed with many a z——ds and many a pinch of snuff, and since there are a number of fine folk abroad on this most atrocious evening, it is only just that we should pay them the compliment of relating their horrid adventures.

You have not forgotten, I hope, the sensation created in Curtain Wells by the sight of Beau Ripple and Mrs. Courteen ensconced in the former's vivid yellow post-chaise, driven by the former's diminutive groom Pridgeon. You made one of a host of conjectures, or rather you would have done had you not been in the heart of the secret, thanks to the honest, straightforward way in which I have treated you throughout this story.

They went off with 'Tally-ho' and 'Whoo-whoop, gone away!' They rattled over the cobbles and clattered over the kidney stones and jolted prodigiously over a kerb that protruded too far into the road. They bumped over a log of wood dropped by old Mother Hubbard in her frantick endeavours to gain the protection of the pavement, they ground the face of little Miss Muffet's favourite wax doll to minutest grains of powder. They experienced a second's muffled progress as with two wheels they rolled over little Tommy Trout's Easter coat and with the others made a broad smear over little Sammy Green's satchel and cracked his new Horn Book into a thousand splinters.

As for Mr. Ripple, every time he rose to a wayside obstacle and fell with a genteel plump into Mrs. Courteen's wide lap, he had a sensation of the acutest disgust; with disgust, too, he viewed his cushions of fawn silk and ivory sattin dedabbled with the widow's copious tears—these cushions made salt with a mortal widow's grief that were never intended to be spoiled with anything less ethereal than the glittering milk of the Queen of Heaven.

Extreme dizziness overtook the Great little Man when, in accents hoarse with hysterical sorrow, the wretched woman by his side begged the loan of his handkerchief. Then, indeed, he nearly called to Pridgeon to check their mad course, turn the horses' heads stablewards, brooding for a sensuous second upon the delights of a warm meditative bath, made sweeter with Citron Essence.

Poor Mr. Ripple! As the mile-stones fled past and the chilly March twilight crept over the dusky fallows and peered above the black hedgerows, he thought with unutterable pangs of the cheerful and comfortable town of Curtain Wells. His china shepherds and shepherdesses called to him over the bleak country, and in the distance like elfin bells he heard the reproachful tinkle of his elegant lustres.

At the turnpike Mr. Ripple asked the keeper whether a post-chariot had lately come under his jurisdiction.

" Dick who? " inquired the janitor.

" Have you seen a post-chariot? " said Mr. Ripple, petulantly.

" No, I ain't. Have you seen two bullocks as 'ave lost, stolen and strayed theyselves hereabouts—the red 'un with a———"

"Drive on," said Mr. Ripple.

"That's gentry," commented the gatekeeper as, spitting on the bust of King George which reposed in the palm of his dirty hand, he retired to brood over a well-thumbed pamphlet that set forth with convincing ribaldry, the imminent danger of another Popish plot.

"Drive on," said Mr. Ripple, "we shall have a heavy shower presently."

They were bowling down a broad village street with a merry jingle of harness and rhythmical clatter of hoofs, while the cracking of little Pridgeon's whip, nearly as big as himself, made many inquisitive bodies huddle in the low doorways of the cottages to survey the gallant equipage.

"Reg'lar delooge, your honour," said Pridgeon, turning round on the box.

Mrs. Courteen was already so wet with the tears of outraged motherhood that the addition of rain could scarcely have affected her comfort. Nevertheless she shuddered so expansively that she squeezed her companion closer than ever to the side of the chaise.

"Shall we put up at the *Green Dragon?*—very comfortable Inn, the *Green Dragon.*"

"No, no, Pridgeon, drive on. If it rains, it rains."

Such a platitude from Beau Ripple can only have been provoked by the intensest despair. A ploughboy's epigram would not have seemed more out of place. The Nine Muses were certainly waked from their harmonious lethargy, and a small boy, playing *Sally in our Alley* on a Jew's harp, twanged a discordant echo of their shocked sensibility. A platitude from Beau Ripple! The very chaise collapsed in ignominy. Bump—bang—whooooo! The gay vehicle was on its side and the front off-wheel was whirling madly down the broad slope of the street, to the enormous delight of the boy with the Jew's harp and the immense consternation of a flock of geese in whose company it made a noisy entrance into the village pond.

Pridgeon turned once more on the Jimmy and, having pulled up the horses and gazed at the Tableau, remarked:

"Blow me tight if I didn't think the wheel 'd do that afore we started. Blow me right and tight!"

By this time, all the village stood in a circle and supplied an exhaustive commenting upon the sad event.

"She's putt her futt through her petticutt," whooped grandmother.

"So her 'ave and toored 'un proper."

"Blarm 'un if the old buoy's knee ain't streaked like somebody's baäd baäcon."

"So it be, buoy, so it be," came the delighted rejoinder.

"Look, see the seat of his breeches!" cried a shapely hussy.

"I never saw such a power o' mud, why, 'e's like a brown paäper plaster behind. Poor soul!"

"Horse ain't hurt?" asked a sharp-featured, bow-legged individual with professional anxiety.

Four or five hobbledehoys had assisted the Beau to his feet and volunteered to show him the way to the *Green Dragon*. As that hostelry stood exactly opposite the scene of the disaster, the offer savoured of something more than mere friendliness.

Mrs. Courteen was whirling round and round, like a kitten after her tail, trying to ascertain the precise amount of damage close to her train; a good-natured booby stuck his foot on the skirt to steady it for her inspection, and in doing so made the rent more irreparable.

"Better go to the *Green Dragon*, your honour," said Pridgeon, as spruce as when he started.

"Better go to h——, you dunderhead," said the Beau, very white with well-bred passion and the shock of the catastrophe. No fragile vase of Dresden or of azure Sèvres, no figure of opalescent Worcester, no violet-flowered teapot of Lowestoft that ever fell from a proud cabinet through the careless sweep of a chambermaid's broom, was to be so deeply commiserated as Mr. Horace Ripple. These painted monuments of care betray their inherent beauty even in the dainty particles that proclaim their wreckage, but a fop with muddied breeches—why, in the very first chapter of this story we trembled to behold the circumference of the least dignified part of the Beau's anatomy protruding from beneath a bedstead; and on that occasion, it was gay with the flowers of a silk dressing-gown.

I do not think that the Great little Man ever recovered from this outrage to his personal attire, for to the very end of his modish days, he would wear a coat cut an inch or two lower than was readily allowed by the least conservative tailor in his employment.

As for Mrs. Courteen, who followed meekly in the wake of her wounded escort, she could not refrain from wishing that the Major and the Justice were at hand to console her with jealous attentions and rival sympathies, and when the first round drop of the swift-approaching storm hit her plump on the nose and washed away in its downward course the last vestige of powder from her face, she regretted also the tributary fingers of Betty.

In the hall of the *Green Dragon* their reception was almost servile. Great Cobblebury, for all its pompous name, was too near to Curtain Wells to attract the attention of many travellers, and the *Green Dragon* depended for custom almost entirely on the thirstiness of the surrounding population. Guests, therefore, received very excellent service for their money. The host, one George Upex, had watched the advance of the chaise with sleek arms beneath a protuberant apron and thumbs that twiddled sleepily; but the smash aroused his hospitable instincts, and by the time Mr. Ripple and Mrs. Courteen had reached the doorway of the inn, he was back from the kitchen, where he had hastily ordered the immediate insertion into the capacious oven of several dishes, and was ready to usher the stranded travellers into the parlour.

"And what will your good lady take?" he inquired, with his rubicund face cocked at what he considered a very appetizing angle.

"She is not my good lady, sirrah," rapped out the Beau.

"Not at all, your honour—beg pardon," said Mr. Upex, putting up a gigantick hand to an equally gigantick mouth as if he would force the latter feature to eat the indiscreet question it had so grossly emitted.

"How long will it take to mend the damage to my chaise?" demanded Mr. Ripple.

The landlord made a rough calculation in his mind.

"About an hour to cook the—to mend the—er—chaise," he replied.

"Have you a bed?" asked the Beau.

The landlord beamed. They were going to spend the night under his roof, and mentally he saw himself on the next day obscuring the sunlight of the parlour with a very long bill.

"A bed, your honour? Yes, indeed! Oh! yes." Mr. Upex paused. "A bed?"

"Yes! a bed—a b-e-d—bed."

"For one night?"

"One night—no! now, sirrah, now." Mr. Ripple stamped his little foot, probably to shake off the mud of the humiliating accident.

"Now?" Mr. Upex looked surprized, that is to say the mouth of Mr. Upex remained fixed in a cavernous gape.

"Why not now?" exclaimed the peremptory Beau. "Ain't your beds aired, landlord? Ain't they made yet?"

"Oh, certainly, your honour."

"Then show me upstairs at once. I shall lie down until the wheel of my chaise is mended. And shew this lady another room, and send two or three chambermaids to attend to her."

Mr. Upex looked much relieved.

It was not such a shameless affair as he had been led by wanton ambiguity of phrase to believe.

"What about the duck?"

"What duck? What duck?" asked Mr. Ripple fretfully.

"The duck your honour ordered—that is, was about to order when I interrupted your honour."

"Send up three slices of the breast on a small tray to my chamber, and don't put any stuffing on the plate, the odour of sage upsets my appetite."

"Indeed?" said Mr. Upex, quite frankly interested by such a nasal idiosyncrasy.

"Yes, and send out a woman of taste and discretion to purchase a nightcap."

"I wouldn't say, your honour, as how one of the maids wouldn't oblige your—er—the good lady."

"For myself, landlord, for myself."

"I beg your honour's pardon."

Mr. Upex hurried off to execute his guest's requirement and presently returned to escort them to their rooms.

"When my man comes in," said the Beau, "send him up to me with the nightcap."

Pridgeon had rescued the wheel from the pond and, having successfully directed two bumpkins to trundle it to the blacksmith, arrived at the inn with an admiring retinue of idlers, whom he regaled with quarts of bitter beer. The woman of taste entrusted with the purchase of the nightcap (she was the scullerymaid) returned with the vestment neatly wrapped in paper, and, meeting her master on the stairs, was told to hand it to the diminutive groom, who chucked her under the chin with the parcel and took his bow-legged way upstairs to Mr. Ripple's temporary apartment.

Outside he rapped smartly on the door, which was

cautiously opened sufficiently wide to allow the urbane countenance of the Beau to peer round the corner.

" Is that you, Pridgeon? "

" Me, y'r honour, with a present from Great Cobblebury."

The Beau took the nightcap, and in its place handed muddied smallcloaths, smeared coat, and wrinkled waistcoat.

" Have these cloaths thoroughly brushed."

" Yes, y'r honour."

" And bring me three slices of breast in an hour's time."

" Yes, y'r honour."

" And don't get drunk to celebrate your carelessness."

" No, y'r honour."

" Poor clod," murmured the Beau to his polite self, as he closed the door of his chamber and double locked it against intrusion.

I think it would certainly be indiscreet to spy upon Mr. Ripple's retirement. How did he spend his time in bed? The whisper of book-leaves tempts me to suppose that he read several of the bitterest odes, very possibly a whole satire of Quintus Horatius Flaccus, that poet so fierce but withal so urbane. Meanwhile Mrs. Courteen, surrounded by three maids, respectively known as Susan, Joan, and Elizabeth, held forth upon her misfortunes to a sympathetick audience.

She stood in the middle of her chamber, a massive figure pouring forth ludicrous complaint. It was as if a stork should seek to emulate a nightingale.

Susan knelt on the floor and industriously stitched away at the ragged train; Joan knelt with innumerable pins stuck between her pearly teeth and judiciously fastened several gaps in her attire, while Elizabeth, who was being courted by Johnny, the *Green Dragon's* sibilant hostler, rubbed away at the mud with as near an imitation of the sounds produced by her lover's stringy throat as the softness of her own would allow.

L*

"I have been greatly distressed," said the widow, "grossly deceived, intolerably put about for, though Mr. Ripple has the character of a block of marble, it don't become a woman to be seen alone with a man anywhere, especially in a yellow chaise which attracts everybody's attention. I vow I heard that odious young Miss Kitcat laugh from her balcony as we flew past—yes, flew—and such bumping! I dare swear I'm bruised from head to foot, and my skin shows the smallest mark. I remember when I was a young woman, I stepped a minuet with young Mr. Heavibois of Heavibois Hall, and I declare he might have been taking the grossest liberties all through the evening, for the way my wrist was marked. Lud! it was as purple as my grandmother's silk coverlet that was given to her by a young lieutenant in the Navy, and was thought to belong to the wife of the Cham of Tartary, though I dare say he bought it in Cheapside for ten shillings, being a young gentleman on whose word nobody could rely, that is the worst of men, young women, you cannot trust 'em. And now my own daughter has run away with a London spark, and I, her own mother, must give up half a score routs and my Lady Pickadilly's drum—the most fashionable affair of the kind that will ever be known in Curtain Wells, for my Lady Pickadilly is newly come from town with her second son the Hon. John Hyde, as quiet a young gentleman as ever said Bo! to a goose, and here we are nearly into April, and if my daughter drowns herself from London Bridge, why then I shall be wearing black at the Fêtes Champêtres and a pretty figure I shall be truly! though, indeed, if one had the courage to wear a white velvet vizard, I might very well pass for an Allegory of Moonlight—and yet that would never do, for to be sure that malicious creature Mrs. Dudding, whose Conversazione last month was the completest failure ever known, would make one of her odious epigrams about poor Mr. Moon, the best natured of gentlemen and the very personification of the milk of human kindness. To be sure, his ankles are very big, but indeed I vow if one were to regard all the defects in humanity, very few of us would be able to hold up our heads. Mr. Ripple himself is the smallest man in the Wells, but nobody esteems him the less for that. To be sure, I think he was very ill-advised,—though for that matter he was never known to take anybody's advice but his own—very ill-advised, I say, not to speak more severely to my daughter. I was always so careful of her modesty that I never allowed her to sit in the Maze with an odious little nudity in stone always hovering about, till I declare they should have planted ivy to climb up his shameless legs. I'm sure nothing could be more Biblical than such vegetable apparel. Cupid they call him: Stupid I call it." Mrs. Courteen here paused to take a longer breath and Susan exclaimed:

"La! ma'am, what to do wi' your petticoat I doan't know. It comes peaping through your gown like Tom o' Coventry in the Christmas mumming."

"Pin it, child, pin it," said the widow.

"La! ma'am, we ha' used nigh forty pins already, and thee'll be like a hedgehog soon."

"No matter, child, no matter how I appear. I must do my duty as a mother, but I vow I blush when I think that near everybody takes us for man and wife. To be sure, I don't mind, and always say that if the world wishes to talk, the world will talk; and there once was a time when I was talked about from one corner of the county to the other. And now this improper affair of my daughter's will set every idle tongue wagging again. My own maid Betty, who was privy to the whole unhappy intrigue, was truly frightened when she found how far ignorance and wilfulness had taken her. 'What will they say at Courteen Grange, ma'am, and what will Mr. Rumble the carrier say, and Mrs. Rumble and the old widow who keeps the shop and poor old Jonas the gardener and all the good folk of the shire?' 'Ah,' said

I, ' what indeed? ' Ugh! child, you're running pins into my—into my legs! "

" Dear life, ma'am," said Susan the culprit, apparently not much abashed by the accusation, " 'tis difficult to find a bit of leg to run a pin into, for, O my soul and body, you're shining like a starlight night, wi' pins all over 'ee."

So the rehabilitation of Mrs. Courteen went on with diffuse anecdotes on the side of the widow, with similes from deft-fingered Susan, with much displaying of pearly teeth from Joan, and with a gentle cooing from Elizabeth, who was betrothed to the hostler of the *Green Dragon* Inn.

Outside it was raining faster than ever, and the wind was beginning to moan under the eaves and away in the remote corners of the house. A flash of lightning and a terrifick burst of thunder that followed immediately upon its heels undid half an hour's steady pinning, owing to the violent tremours with which it afflicted poor Mrs. Courteen.

It made Mr. Ripple break a Cæsura and, worse, it made him try to mend it with a false quantity. Altogether the prospect was extremely uninviting, and the succulent odour of roast duck was certainly no temptation to precipitate his departure. However, the duck came to an end, and the morsels of it which began to freeze upon his plate made him so impatient of farther delay that when Pridgeon knocked at the door and informed him the chaise was once more fit for the roads, he called for his bill and, as I believe, (such a sweet change had Horace and roast duck wrought in his mind) hummed a popular jig while he buttoned up his breeches. Soon he was tapping delicately at the door of Mrs. Courteen's chamber, saying:

" Come, ma'am, I hope you're rested. Our horses are waiting—'tis a most atrocious night—but never mind, ma'am, never mind, we shall sleep the sounder," he had almost said " for having done our duty," but not even the stress of an untoward adventure could condemn his spirit to a second platitude that stormy night, and he altered the unfinished sentence to " for not having to endure Mrs. Dudding's epigrams. Foregad, ma'am," he went on, " she churns the sour cream of her intellect and produces, after infinite toil, a very rancid wit."

Then the Great little Man pattered downstairs, condescended to felicitate Mr. Upex upon his timely meal, inquired the name of his cook, said she was a good woman and would go far, listened to Farmer Gruby's opinion that this rain would do a power o' good to the land, condoled with him upon a bovine loss which he was still lamenting, bade Pridgeon stand another quart of ale each to the good fellows who had assisted to talk about the accident, raised his monocle to a bill of sale affixed to the wall, inquired into the state of the roads before them, evoked an atmosphere of respectful adoration by presenting the landlord with a card inscribed ' Horace Ripple, The Great House,' and finally won the perpetual devotion of Mr. George Upex by writing in his neatest hand at the top right corner of the engraved card ' Recommended by.' The landlord vowed he would have the precious voucher of identity framed and hung up in the parlour underneath a painting on glass of his gracious Majesty K—— G——, and in close proximity to a likeness of Lord Breda's prize bullock Jupiter, which several drunken loyalists had been known to salute in mistake for the K——.

Mrs. Courteen sailed downstairs, followed by Susan, Joan and Elizabeth, all of whom were kept busy picking up pins, which they stuck between their teeth, to the great disappointment of Mr. Pridgeon, who would have very much liked to snatch a kiss from each Hebe in turn, and, seeing that the hostler was standing outside in the rain, I dare swear that but for the pins he would have been successful in his amorous project. Off went the chaise into the gathering gloom, spattering the onlookers with mud, and almost drowning with its clatter the hearty cheers of the inhabitants of Great Cobblebury.

And now the Beau, whose urbanity had been restored by Horace and roast duck, entertained Mrs. Courteen with delightful tales of fashionable society. The most violent jolt no longer availed to upset the balance of his sentences. The widow was deeply impressed by Mr. Ripple's charming behaviour and, though she could not appreciate his anecdotes at their value, was put into a very pleasant disposition of mind by a half-fledged fancy that the Great little Man was slowly succumbing to her ample fascination. As for little Pridgeon, his diminutive inside was so replete with cordials and old Jamaica rum that he was quite impervious to the weather and he sang a large number of country ballads in a very engaging Alto voice.

Suddenly, as they were driving over a wild stretch of commonland, dotted with huge clumps of gorse and a number of stunted and wind-bent thorn-trees, the chaise stopped with a jerk, spoiling the climax of one of the Beau's best stories, describing how he had compelled the Duchess of Hereford to apologize to a flower girl.

"What's the matter?" he cried out.

"Nothing," said Pridgeon, "but we're just underneath the gallows with a very notorious reskel swingin' over our heads—reg'lar old scarecrow he is—can't you hear the chains, y'r honour? He's bobbin' about in the wind like a cork in a puddle."

"Drive on, rogue," commanded Mr. Ripple sternly.

"It 'ud be a pity not to see 'im. Blue Jenkins vas his name—I'll hold up one of the lamps and you can take a good look at 'im. There was hundreds used to walk 'ere of a Sunday afternoon when he was just turned off, ecod, y'r honour ought to take a look at him."

"Will you drive on, sirrah!"

Suddenly Mrs. Courteen uttered a loud scream; and very uncanny it sounded in the tempest.

"What in the name of—what's the matter?" exclaimed Mr. Ripple.

"I hear horses," said Mrs. Courteen, and screamed again.

Pridgeon cocked up his ears.

"She's right," he shouted. "There's a couple of 'em coming up behind us!"

"Good G——! Highwaymen!" said Mrs. Courteen, clinging to Mr. Ripple. The latter did not lose his presence of mind.

"Drive on, you puppy! I'll see to the priming of my pistols." With these words the Courageous little Man dived between the widow's agitated legs and groped for the elegant walnut case of his exquisitely chased pistols.

"'Tain't no good," shouted Pridgeon, as he lashed the horses to a gallop. "'Tis only a mile afore we reaches Long Hill and they'll catch us walkin' there."

"I warn you, madam," said Mr. Ripple calmly, while the postchaise rattled through the storm, "I warn you that I shall certainly shoot once, if not twice."

But Mrs. Courteen had fainted away and only half a dozen pins released from their responsibleness whispered a faint and ineffective answer.

CHAPTER XXXIII

THE HIGHWAYMEN

THE rumour of Phyllida's elopement took definite shape just as the candles were being lighted for the nuts and wine. It lent quite a flavour even to the inferior Port that disgraced most of the dinner-tables at Curtain Wells. And if a flavour was lent to moderately bad wine, what a truly celestial aroma was given off by the fragrant pots of tea in the parlours. Curtain Wells was always famous for the finest blends, and I venture to think that the sad affair of Miss Courteen inspired every hostess to a perfection of art unequalled before or since. Never were the gentlemen so quick to follow the ladies from the spent dinner. Moreover, the absence of Beau Ripple permitted a recklessness of conjecture, a venom of Innuendo that would have made the rumour famous, even had it proved devoid of the slightest foundation.

Many inclined to the theory that Mr. Ripple had arranged the prologue to suit himself, and vowed they had seen fervent stares exchanged between him and Mrs. Courteen. One inventive young gentleman started a report that Mr. Vernon was the Pretender; but this was contradicted by old Lady Loch Lomond who, having been one of the ladies-in-waiting at St. Germain's and watched the young prince in his bath, was positive that Mr. Vernon did not resemble him at all. The young gentleman's ingenious suggestion lent a momentary glamour to the heroine of the affair, but with the destruction of his story by Lady Loch Lomond, publick attention was again concentrated upon Beau Ripple. An extravagant explanation of his roundabout method of courtship was found in a whispered legend that in early youth he had married one of the daughters of the Grand Turk and escaping from the turbaned alliance four months afterwards through the friendly offices of a fig merchant from Smyrna who smuggled him out of the Bosphorus and landed him at Lyme Regis in Dorsetshire, had spent the rest of his enforced celibacy in dread of vengeful scimitars.

Then somebody remembered the codicil to Squire Courteen's will, and the story of young Mr. Standish who left the neighbourhood in such a hurry. One of the abetters of this last tale mentioned that Mr. Ripple was badly in need of money, and finally everybody agreed that here at last was the true explanation of the yellow chaise. The Beau was trying to make up his losses by wedding Mrs. Courteen secretly so that the lawyers should not lay violent hands upon her inheritance. This was such a satisfactory and circumstantial account that everybody sat down to Quadrille without their play being the more distracted than usual. Meanwhile the author of the latest explanation went from house to house to burble the news in the company of his two witnesses. The three of them were received everywhere with acclamation as soon as it transpired they were the bearers of the authoritative account; and though they were all of them bores of the finest calibre, they enjoyed a considerable popularity which compensated for all the slights and snubs they had received in the past at the hands of rank and fashion. Having discovered their talents, they all three existed for ever afterwards on the sources of false information and published books of memoirs and thought themselves great men and, in fact, are to this very day consulted by social historians.

Meanwhile another rumour was flying furiously round all the shops that Mr. Lovely was on the verge of making a hurried departure from Curtain Wells. Mr. Ripple owed nothing to the tradesmen; consequently his yellow chaise caused no consternation in commercial hearts, but Mr. Charles Lovely owed large amounts. Every shopkeeper in the High Street vowed he would know the true facts of this reported flight. Under the great archway of the *Blue Boar*, they pattered—all of them dressed in snuff-coloured suits and all of them with suspiciously long envelopes protruding from their left-hand pockets. There was Mr. Crumpett the Confectioner and Mr. Frieze the Tailor and another tailor called Charges and a third called Trimmings. There was Mr. Cuffe the hosier, and Mr. Trinket of one toyshop and Mr. Leonard of another, and Mr. Wheeler the coachbuilder; there was fat Mrs. Leafy of one flower-shop and little Miss Bunch of the other flower-shop, and old Mrs. Tabby of the ribband shop, there was Mr. Filigree the Goldsmith, and Mr. Tree the boot-maker, and Mr. Buckle the saddler, the young Washball the barber's senior apprentice. In fact, the only creditors absent were Mr. Daish who was at that very moment listening to a plausible demonstration of Mr. Lovely's prospects, and the ex-limner Mr. Canticle who would have scorned to associate himself with such a snuff-coloured rabble and had, moreover, been paid something on account more lately than the rest.

"What the deuce is this seditious gathering?" exclaimed Lieutenant Blewforth to little Peter Wingfield as they swung round the corner and plunged into the voluble assemblage. Suddenly there was a noise of a window being thrown up, and a stillness fell upon the dingy throng as they beheld the debonair countenance of our hero.

"Speak up, Charles," bellowed the Lieutenant, "I support your candidature. D——e," he muttered to Wingfield, " d——e, if I knew Charles was a Parliament man."

"L-listen," said Mr. Wingfield, standing on tip-toe

and craning his little neck to hear Charles' views on the political situation.

"Gentlemen," Mr. Lovely began, with a hand gracefully buried in the opening of his embroidered waistcoat, "Gentlemen, I am sensibly flattered by this deputation."

A simultaneous grunt acclaimed this remark.

"I say, I am sensibly flattered. It is always a pleasure to—to——"

"Charles 'll never be elected, if he talks to 'em so slow," commented Mr. Blewforth with a shake of his burly head.

"I say, I am sensibly flattered."

"That's all very fine, Mr. Lovely, but what about my bill?" shouted Mr. Filigree who being better able to stand a loss was bolder than his companions.

"Ay—yes—to be sure, your money," Charles started off again. "Well, gentlemen, I say, gentlemen, money is a very wonderful thing. It is the panacea or cure of all earthly ills, like sleep in the play it knits up the ravelled sleeve of care. Money! to be sure!"

"He's trying to make 'em swallow the new taxes," said Blewforth sagely.

At that moment somebody twitched Mr. Lovely's coat from behind, and he retired from the open window; the angry snuff-coloured crowd looked at each other, conferred for a moment, then pattered quickly back by the way they had come. From the tangle of their murmured confabulations, two ominous words floated back to the Lieutenant and little Peter Wingfield— 'Sheriff's Officers!'

It was Clare's announcement of the arrival of Betty in the best parlour of the *Blue Boar* that had distracted Charles' attention from his creditors. He found her trembling from head to foot and playing with the buttons of her scarlet cloak.

"My young mistress, your honour, my pretty lamb has gone."

" Miss Courteen? "

" Little Miss Phyllida."

" With Vernon."

" No, wi' Amor."

" How long ago? "

" Nigh three hours or more. The Bow and the Widow have galloped after 'em, but what I do say is, 'tis no work to set an old couple to catch a young couple: oh! your honour, if ever in this sweet Springtime you loved my dear one, will 'ee follow her now and bring her back to me? "

The news of Phyllida's elopement so crudely announced staggered him, notwithstanding his anticipation of such an event.

Hitherto his love for the maid had been a pleasant fancy, an impulse to day-dreams but nothing more material.

That very morning as he wandered in the watermeadows, he had been so full of the outside effect of his attitude there had been no room for the personal desire. He had tried to convince himself he was sincerely anxious for Phyllida's future happiness; but the true position he should have taken up was a determination to possess her for himself whatever the cost. She was young and fair, rose-flushed and adorable, and 'twas a pity to waste so much freshness on Vernon dulled by pleasure and—not quite well-bred.

Now a sense of personal loss stung him into action. Besides, he and Tony had vowed to transform life into a gay adventure. Here already was a quest worthy of their highest hopes.

" I will certainly go," said Charles.

" Ah! you have a true heart."

" Have I, Betty, have I? "

" 'Twas on merry Valentine morn, you saw my pretty one."

" So 'twas."

" When thrushes and blackbirds do maäte."

" So they say."

" Take it for a sign, will 'ee? "

" I will."

" And say when you come to her and have sent that wagabone packing off to his Lunnon, say the linnets are piping away down in Hampshire, will 'ee? "

" I will."

" Say that us'll soon be harking for the cuckoo in the greenwood, and look see, give her this; 'tis a little white däisy I picked. Bid her look 'tes none the less beautiful because the edge of her petals are gone red wi' the cold March wind. 'Tes a däisy, the same as before—a little white däisy."

Hastily putting the frail flower in Mr. Lovely's hand, the maid ran to the door. There she stayed a moment.

" And say, will 'ee, that I'm coming to kiss her and hug her and comfort her as soon as the Wells waggon can bring me."

" That's a good maid—a loyal maid," said Charles to himself when Betty was gone, and, as he looked at the tender blossom somewhat shrivelled by captivity, a fallen tear trembled like a dew-diamond on the golden heart of the gathered flower.

And now the problem of escaping his duns vexed Mr. Lovely more acutely than before. Daish had been pacified by generous Clare with £50 on account. The horses were saddled and ready; and by the greatest good fortune when Charles looked out into the inn-yard, there was not a snuff-coloured soul in sight.

Blewforth came in with the news of Sheriff's Officers, and Clare appeared in the gallery all buttoned up for the journey: " Where shall I tell Daish to send our baggage by the Wells' stage waggon? there's a good inn called *The Basket of Roses* about twenty-five miles away, d'ye know it? "

" No," said Charles, " is it on the London Road? "

"Yes, on the London Road."

"Then 'twill suit me very well. Shall we set out at once, Tony?"

"No time to lose," shouted Blewforth.

Daish came shuffling in to say the horses were growing impatient of the cold.

Off went our romantick adventurers: up they got on their horses: down tinkled a couple of new silver crowns on the cobbles.

"Thank 'ee, yer honours!" shouted Jimmy Trickett the hostler; and the third detachment of the Love Chase set out amid the thunderous farewells of Lieutenant Blewforth of the *Lively*, as jolly a sound to put heart into a pair of handsome young gentlemen on a gallant quest as they were likely to hear throughout their wanderings.

They were gone when the snuff-coloured crowd pattered back with a Sheriff's Officer in tow, and Mr. Jeremy Daish was a person of sufficient importance to be able to despise their snuff-coloured threats. After all he had fifty pounds on account and there wasn't a brewer amongst them.

As they cantered along the same road which we have already followed three times, Charles told his friend of Betty's request and Tony was as urgent as he to do all in his power to thwart Mr. Vernon. Honest Anthony Clare was very proud of the handsome rider by his side. I do not think he would have allowed that any one was quite the equal of Mr. Charles Lovely in accomplishment or bearing. He could not avoid a feeling of self-congratulation when he saw the maids among the daffodils of narrow cottage gardens run to lean over their green gates and watch their course away down the road. What a fine fellow he was in his full trimmed grey riding-coat and brown buckskin breeches. How well the azure waistcoat became him; how eagerly his blue eyes danced to the rhythm of their horses. How far ahead down the billowy road he gazed, as if to conjure up the vision of the galloping chariot that held his hope of happiness.

And when they, too, rode into the storm, muffled in their full cloaks of black Bavarian cloth, what a romantick figure Charles made as he spurred his iron-grey steed to farther exertions.

There was musick in the south-west wind of that tempestuous twilight. It sighed through the bare hedgerows and whistled round the broad brims of their beaver hats. There was musick in the clap of horses' hoofs on the wet road. There was musick in the big horse-pistols tapping against the saddle-bows.

They were passing a great barn where a host of yokels were thrashing a stack that had lain too long, and a rare sight these were, knee-deep in the amber corn whence the rats fled ceaselessly.

" Shall we catch them, Tony? " asked Charles.

" I think we shall."

" But in time? " Charles dug his spurs in deep to cover the blush that was flaming over his cheeks.

" And will she turn back? Oh! Tony, Tony, she must, she shall, turn back."

In Great Cobblebury they stopped to give their horses a feed, and heard of the accident of the yellow chaise.

" Z——ds, these clumsy vehicles travel fast enough," muttered Charles.

When they started again, the darkness clung round them like a pall. The blown branch of a tree brushed against Lovely's elbow in a narrow part of the road and he shuddered, as though an unseen hand were warning him to pause.

" 'Tis a plaguey rough night," he shouted over the wind, clapping his hat tighter and leaning close to his grey's warm slim neck.

They were crossing Dry Tree Common where Blue Jenkins was swinging in a shameful cradle, and Clare shouted he could see the lights of a chaise in front.

"That's Ripple for a hundred," cried Charles spurring on his horse, "gadslife, what a speed they are making. Hurry, Tony, hurry."

A dazzling flash of lightning seared the sky long enough to illuminate the ghastly figure on the gallows. Clare's chestnut mare shied violently and threw her rider head foremost into a large clump of gorse. It was a matter of some difficulty to catch the frightened animal, but Charles by mere determination succeeded in doing so, for all the night was now black before the rising of the moon. By this mishap, Clare was in much the same state of prickles as the widow, without the help of deft-fingered Susan.

"What the plague made you do that?" said Charles fretfully. They had lost five valuable minutes through the behaviour of the mare. Tony laughed with great good humour.

When they reached the foot of Long Hill, they could see the lights of the chaise once again. It was finding the heavy pull very difficult. The rain was pouring down the ditches on either side with a gurgling sound, heard all the more clearly, because in the shelter of the slope the wind was quiet. Just before the summit, the carriage stopped and a bullet sang between Clare and Lovely who were now a bare twenty yards behind. Mr. Ripple believed in the advantage of an offensive campaign.

"Stop! stop!" shouted Charles, "we are not highwaymen."

The Beau recognized the voice, and in accents wherein could be detected the faintest note of relief said:

"Charles—Mr. Lovely! and why, may I inquire, are you abroad on such an unpleasant night?"

"Why, sir," called out Charles, "what have you been about? There's a dead man lying in the road."

"Good G——!" said Mr. Ripple, "a dead man?"

"Bring a lamp," called Clare.

Pridgeon descended from the box and, having tied

the horses to a withered fir-tree, snatched one of the lamps from its socket.

As he came along, Charles observed by the wavering light primroses in flower.

"Surely, surely," said the Beau, "I cannot have killed this man."

"No! No!" cried Clare who was kneeling beside the body. "He has been dead some time. Z——ds! 'Tis the little Major."

"The little Major?" echoed Ripple sharply. "So 'tis! So 'tis!"

"All alone in the storm," said Charles in a low voice.

"It may have been highwaymen," said Ripple.

"So it may, so it may," Clare agreed.

"And it may have been Vernon," said Charles, "d—n him."

"Charles," said the Beau, "I owe you an apology. I have been obstinate. This should never have been allowed to happen."

Charles grasped his hand in the darkness.

After all, Mr. Ripple was not in his kingdom and they were all levelled by the presence of Death.

"We cannot leave the body here," said Tony.

"It must travel in the chaise," said Charles.

"What about Mrs. Courteen?" questioned Mr. Ripple. "She is in a swoon."

"You are sure he is quite dead?" asked Charles and wondered at the futility of the remark.

Nobody troubled to reply.

"Perhaps it would be better to send a waggon," said Clare. "We are not many miles from Roseland-in-the Vale."

"Somebody has cut off his epaulettes," said Charles.

"Then it may have been footpads," said the Beau. "No wayfarer would rob the dead."

"It is a very dark night," said Clare simply.

"He fought at Fontenoy. Let us lift him out of the

mud," said Mr. Ripple, vaguely recalling long stories which the dead soldier had poured into his ears.

"He gave his life for her. We must certainly lift him out of the mud," said Charles.

"A dead body is dangerous to horses," said Clare, "I will take his head."

Just then the widow screamed again.

"Say nothing of this to Mrs. Courteen," said Mr. Ripple to the diminutive coachman.

"I knew something 'd 'appen," replied the latter. "I knew something 'd 'appen when I see'd as how somebody had stuck a bunch of primmerroses in Blue Jenkins's toes."

CHAPTER XXXIV

OLD ACQUAINTANCE

CHARLES said he would ride on to the *Basket of Roses* and bid the landlord prepare a supper against the arrival of the rest. Clare stayed behind to protect the Beau from the hysterical excitement of Mrs. Courteen, who would not be pacified by anything less formidable than an armed escort. She had made up her mind that highwaymen were abroad, refused to allow the chaise to drive fast lest they might gallop unaware into a thieves' ambush, and alarmed herself with so many imaginary bogies that she almost succeeded in making Mr. Ripple fire point blank at Mr. Anthony Clare's shadow looming huge in the hedgerow.

Charles reached the *Basket of Roses* not long after the departure of the lovers, and on hearing the news immediately spurred his grey horse to pursuit. For a couple of miles he plunged along a road that was almost a swamp, fired to greater exertions each minute by the sight of the ruts made by the chariot in front. Suddenly his horse began to go lame; the road grew worse; the ruts proved to be those of a country waggon. He was riding in the wrong direction, so he turned his grey round and walked her back to the inn. While he was inquiring into the possibility of securing a fresh mount, a voice from the parlour called out to know if any person was inquiring into the whereabouts of a young woman.

"She supped alone with the old gentleman," whispered Mrs. Tabrum.

Charles was not proof against a natural curiosity, and

decided to wait at the inn till the arrival of the others. He ascertained that Vernon had changed horses so it was evident that he intended to post as fast as possible Eastward. His own horse must be tended if they were to proceed that night. There was no other in the stables, and as he was sure of catching the chariot before morning, he felt there would be no harm in learning why Phyllida had supped at a wayside inn, alone with an elderly gentleman. What was Vernon about meanwhile? Why had he not accompanied her? Charles ordered supper and stepped into the Travellers' Room.

"You were asking about a certain young woman," said Sir George, fixing him with deep set eyes of cold steel.

"I was indeed, sir," answered Mr. Lovely pulling forward an armchair into the blaze and stretching his damp legs towards the genial warmth.

"My name is Repington," said the old gentleman.

"Eh! What?"

"Sir George Repington."

Charles stared at him.

"And mine, sir, is Lovely, Charles Lovely."

"My nephew—humph—'tis your existence which has attracted me so many miles West."

"I did not think you knew of my existence," said Charles half sneering.

"You never condescended to inform your uncle of your movements."

"Sir," said the nephew, a smile of bitter recollection twisting the corners of his mouth. "I did not flatter myself that any attention on my side was welcome."

"What! you remember our only interview?"

"I was eight years old, sir."

"Is that a date in youth's short calendar that breeds a specially sensitive disposition of mind?"

"You turned me out of your house."

"On the contrary, nephew, you chose to go back to your father."

"Why wasn't he admitted, too?"

"Because," replied the uncle, "on a former occasion I was unfortunately compelled to invite your father to leave my house."

"By what right?"

Sir George raised his eyebrows.

"Truly, nephew, I think you are indiscreet for a young man of such fashion."

"I have the right to know," Charles burst out. "In all that I can remember of my childhood, you stood like a shadow in the corner of the room, you were the nightmare that haunted my pillow. You used to write sometimes—oh! I can remember your letters in their fat pursy envelopes. I can smell the sealing wax, black sealing wax, now. My father would go out with an oath and my mother would sit by a window with your letter in her lap, weeping, weeping."

"Did she weep, boy?"

"Ah! that pleases you, eh?"

"No, no, I was thinking what a laugh she had once—what a laugh. I expect I was hard—I was—Charles, nephew, give me your hand—I——"

The old man faltered in his speech and, as if the room were dark, groped for our hero's hand; the latter drew back.

"No! thank 'ee, Uncle, once is enough."

The old man did not heed the insult.

"Perhaps I understand your feelings, boy, I've read your poems."

Charles was touched for a moment, but hardened himself as he thought of that wide staircase down which, clutching the balustrade with both hands, he had stumbled alone. A child does not easily forgive a slight, and Charles still regarded his uncle with the eyes of a child.

" Did she speak of me before she died? " murmured the old man with a wistful eagerness.

" She may have spoken," said Mr. Lovely, " the fever was high."

" Or laugh—before she died? Nephew! to-night a young woman came to this inn alone. She smiled like my sister, she laughed like my—like your mother and like your mother she went away with the wrong man."

" What do you mean? " cried Charles too much startled by the sudden violence of his uncle's speech to resent the criticism of his father.

" And you have ridden in pursuit? Then you are her lover—eh? She's played you false as Joan played Roger false, and you are riding after her, and you will shoot him and marry her, and bring her to Repington Hall. 'Fore Heaven, I would give all my fortune to hear that laughter ripple along the lonely corridors of Repington Hall. They used to sit in the sunny window seat; and he would lean over the sill to pluck the roses that blew beneath. I cut the tree down when he was killed, and in the orchard where Lovely murdered him I planted cypresses."

" Murdered him? " cried Charles impressed against his will by the old man's passion.

" Aye, murdered him. Roger was no swordsman, he was a gentle kindly creature who loved old books and old friends, that's why I cannot understand Belladine, why did Belladine let him fight, and what became of —Good G——! " said the old man, " he's come back." Charles looked up and, seeing only Beau Ripple standing in the doorway, concluded that his uncle was gone mad.

" A pinch of snuff, George? " said Mr. Ripple.

" Thank'ee, William," said Sir George. " This is my nephew, William—young Charles Lovely."

" We are already very good friends," said the Beau.

The exchange of courtesies effected by the Beau with that unfailing tact which characterized his least actions shed a new serenity over the situation and, though

Charles was completely puzzled by a surprizing junction of personalities, he, too, with a profound instinct for the correct attitude, bore a part in what was apparently nothing more out of the way than a conversational episode in a social evening; yet three twigs in a whirlpool do not jostle one another much more roughly than the same three twigs in a puddle.

"How's the gout, George? You threatened at one time to become an easy prey to our physical Alectro."

"Better, William, thank'ee, far better. I found that hard work kept it off; or else I grew to drink less Port. I've dined solitary for a round number of years now."

"Your uncle looks well, Charles. Egad, I believe after all gold is better than iron for a man's health whatever the apothecaries tell us. Where is Clare?— a good fellow that friend of yours, Charles. I like Mr. Clare."

Tony came in from the stables at that moment and was presented to Sir George Repington.

He had often heard Charles rail against his uncle, but, perceiving no strain in the relation between them, entered the gathering with an easy grace, and gave a very humorous account of their departure from the Wells.

"Tut, tut," exclaimed Mr. Ripple, for Ripple he must remain, since as Ripple he achieved immortality.

"Tut, tut, I cannot have these riotous assemblies. This comes of leaving Curtain Wells. By the way, where is Mrs. Courteen?"

"She has an audience, sir," said Clare, "and is, therefore, as happy as can be expected under the circumstances."

"Who is Mrs. Courteen?" This from Sir George.

"A lady in whose company I have set out upon a very restless adventure. Cupid, George, has been shooting his arrows of late, without much regard to our mortal comfort. I believe the young rogue was unduly elated by the success of his Valentines."

"Sure, you aren't abroad on a love-affair, too, William?"

"Not of my own, George, but I have an onus in the matter. Some one has stolen a porcelain shepherdess from my booth in Vanity Fair."

"That would be the young woman with whom I supped to-night in this inn. Her name was Courteen."

"What! then we all have an interest in this matter, and can discuss the proper conduct of it over the very excellent supper whose arrival I anticipate without apprehension. This is a capital house, George."

"The landlord is an oddity," said Clare, "called me tulip and onion in a breath, and begged to be allowed to brush the mud off my boots which he said was a famous manure for carnation gillyflowers. I 'faith, the old boy made me feel devilish unclean."

Mrs. Tabrum came in to say the widow would not take supper with the gentlemen. She was much fatigued, and would be glad to retire to bed if Mr. Pipple—or was it Ripple—had no objection.

"None whatsoever," replied the latter in a pensive tone of voice. He was meditating rather sadly upon the circumscription of human fame.

A mere five-and-twenty miles from Curtain Wells, and already there was a doubt as to whether he were Pipple or Ripple.

"The widow don't intend to proceed," said Charles, when Mrs. Tabrum had curtseyed her way out.

"She is a foolish woman," said the Beau.

"But you are not going to leave the daughter to her fate," asked Sir George. "As you——" he stopped.

Charles looked up; Mr. Ripple gravely took a pinch of snuff. "I think," said the former, "'that I shall be more likely to catch the chariot. What's o'clock?"

"Half-past ten," said Clare. "Your horse must rest an hour or two yet; I'll ride with you."

"That would be wiser," said Sir George eagerly. "Then nobody will say Charles took an unfair advantage of him. Although—" Again he stopped in a sentence, and again Mr. Ripple took a pinch of snuff.

It was strange how Sir George had identified himself with Phyllida's fortunes. It seemed as if he were staking his hope of a happy old age upon the result of this love chase. The meeting with Phyllida had filled up the rift which time and disappointment had created. He felt that fortune owed him reparation for his sister's loss; and could not help thinking what an appropriate instrument of the Fates had risen up in the person of his nephew. Sir George Repington had become so much accustomed in his large financial experience to the theory of just exchange that he was inclined to put too blind a confidence in the scales, and was too sure that the balance would adjust itself at some time or other. His nephew had not shown himself greatly enraptured by this late reconciliation, and Sir George had been lonely long enough. He was anxious at eventide for company. Death came suddenly like a clock that strikes in the night, and Sir George was afraid of the grey dawn stealing over the tree tops through the gaunt windows of Repington Hall. When the time came for him to face the vast uneasy realms of immortality, he would like to feel that somewhere on this small green earth, some hand would wave a sorrowful, a last farewell. He would cherish these two lovers; the maid would bring him and Charles together in friendship and charity. Everything pointed to a fortunate issue. He no longer brooded resentfully over calamities that were forgotten long ago. Belladine had come back. He and Belladine would sit on the sloping Repington lawns. June was in front of them. Already, like balm upon the old man's wounded heart, there stole the murmurous peace of the longest day. He saw the golden light, and the long shadows of the elms. He heard the caw of homing rooks and the flutter of thrushes in the great Hall shrubberies. In dignity and in rustick ease he would move with measured meditative steps like an

English squire to his last account—not account, that savoured too much of Throgmorton Street—to his last bed, his virtues recorded in a Latin eulogy and for a memorial Charles and Phyllida, perhaps a grandson George, certainly four weeping cherubs to guard the four corners of his cenotaph.

Our hero was in that state when a host of conflicting emotions fight for the mastery. So much had happened in this eventful day. Everything and everybody appeared in a new perspective. Beau Ripple, seen by the firelight of the Travellers' Room, was no longer the exquisite despot of a world in miniature, the impersonal porcelain monarch, the rarest and most valuable piece in an universe of Bric-a-brac. He was in some way connected with the tragedy of his uncle's early life. The sovereign marionette of amber and tortoise-shell, of perfumes and pomades, whom Charles had known hitherto, was only an elegant exterior. Underneath the sattin, it seemed, there lived a man—one Belladine, of whose existence Fashion was ignorant. The well-dressed Attitude called Horace Ripple would be revered long after his decease. His epigrams would be quoted. He would represent a period in the frivolous archives of Curtain Wells, but Belladine whose heart had quickened to something more vital than a pretty measure, Belladine who had known tears and laughter, Belladine the Man would be forgotten. Charles pondered with passionate commiseration the myriad heartaches of poor humanity that were once esteemed worthy of exaggeration until a new intrigue caught the publick tongue, and contemplated regretfully the inevitable and gradual insignificance of all scandal. Truly, it was more consoling to regard Beau Ripple, that inexplicable phenomenon, than try to gain the acquaintance of Mr. William Belladine who had once played an important part in his uncle's life.

The latter, too, was different. He had only existed in Charles' mind as an aversion of childhood, but

Charles no longer objected to sleep in the dark—the habit had come to him unconsciously. After all he owed Sir George Repington no grudge; it would be absurd to cherish an animosity that was based on a jejune domestick patriotism. The time had long gone by when he thought his own father the finest gentleman in the world. Yet was not this power of taking so much for granted, this passive acceptance of change and decline, a surrender of his youth? Was he, in fact, already divesting himself of all passionate reality? Charles experienced the despair of the devout man whose faith deserts him. He wrestled with his doubts and suddenly (it seemed a miracle) beheld on the ingle seat a swansdown muff. Youth returned—a harlequin with the supple wand of illusion. He stood once more in peach-coloured velvet coat, staring up to a balcony over whose railing dimpled the most enchanting face in England.

"This was your mother, boy," said Sir George almost timidly, breaking in upon his dreams.

Very tenderly, Charles took the locket from the old man, and the sight of the fresh young face brought back to his mind queer old nursery rhymes, and his mother's voice and the smell of a pot of musk and the cries of London coming in through an open window. There was a mist over Charles' eyes and a lump in Charles' throat as he shook his uncle's hand.

The latter wondered at himself for having been content to remain so long without the consolation of an acknowledged heir. For all these years, he had worked without an object. Now the great house of Repington and Son should be incorporated with some equally famous house and a delightful leisure was at last imaginable.

It warmed the old man's heart to hear Charles declare the importance of immediate pursuit, to hear him shout for his horse to be saddled, lame or sound, to see Mr. Clare look to the priming of the pistols and when, on the threshold of departure, the old man saw his nephew pick up the swansdown muff and cram it into the deep pocket of his great cloak, he could scarcely forbear a loud huzza, such vigour and determination were plainly visible on his nephew's attractive countenance.

One incident, just before he set out, served to chill our hero's fervour and discount his conviction of success. He was coming back from the stable and, as he passed the staircase that led to the bedchambers, perceived Mrs. Courteen beckoning from the corridor. He stopped to bow; and in a tone where politeness and condolence and hopefulness were pleasantly mingled, as good as promised the speedy restoration of Miss Phyllida Courteen.

"Sir," said the mother, "you are generous indeed to a fallen young woman."

Our hero frowned at this description of his love.

"And equally generous," she continued, "towards the fault."

Charles made a movement, but the widow plaintively ignored the interruption.

"They have told me of your generous resolve, but I would warn you, Mr. Lovely, that interference in these matters is generally disastrous. The child has done wrong—I do not wish to extenuate her crime—for crime it is when you consider her mother's indulgence of every whim. I know nothing of the eligibleness of the gentleman in whose company she has chosen to shock the sensibility of her mother's small and select circle of intimate friends."

Charles began to fidget.

"He may for all I know be a man of fashion, of rank, of fortune. He may, on the other hand, be a play-actor, an attorney's clerk, or a journeyman tinker. In either case it seems unlikely he will make an offer of marriage. Pray do not put such an idea into his head. Marriages forced upon reluctant suitors commonly turn out unhappy for both parties."

The widow must have been immensely in earnest, monstrously eager to secure her ambition, for never before had her speech betrayed such power of coherent expression.

"Let her go on her way," said the mother. "Let her find out for herself the results of rebellion; when the villain deserts her, she may not be quite so unwilling to stone the damsons next August. Let her learn her lesson, Mr. Lovely, and pray do not persuade her to come back. Her reputation is tarnished; and I am not at all inclined to bear the burden of her ill-behaviour, as I should do, Mr. Lovely, as I certainly should do since the world is censorious, and apt to visit the sins of the children upon the heads of the father, as the Bible says."

Charles could scarcely believe that Mrs. Courteen was in earnest.

He knew her for a worldly-minded woman, careless of everything save her own pleasures, but for such depths of callousness he was not prepared.

"Indeed, madam," he said coldly, "my only excuse for obtruding my presence upon Miss Courteen at such a time is my sincere hope that she will honour my solicitous regard with the bestowal of her hand."

"The child must be punished," insisted the mother.

"Indeed, madam, I venture to think we may safely leave that office to the small and select circle of your intimate friends."

"I cannot understand what attracts—" Mrs. Courteen began, then changed to "what makes men so generous."

Mr. Lovely regarded her contemptuously.

"So I should think."

"Cruel Mr. Lovely," moaned the widow. "Cruel to suggest that I am ungenerous. Why, I have never mentioned the pearls which were taken out of my jewel-case."

"They say that Miss Courteen's necklace vastly becomes her mother."

"Do they, indeed, sir?" said the widow with an affected sigh.

Charles made an impatient gesture.

"Do you imagine, madam, that I am going to tire a good-hearted horse for the sake of allowing you to bask in the flattery of your friends? By G——! I tell you that one of 'em is already dead—shot for the sake of that daughter whose ruin you contemplate so tranquilly."

The widow turned pale.

"At any rate," Charles continued; "at any rate, the little Major with all his strut died like a cock of the game."

"The Major dead," half screamed the widow; and even that information, so brutally delivered, provided the thought that now more than ever was it necessary to prevent Phyllida's marriage.

"Aye, dead! He'll be here in the morning when the Wells waggon arrives."

Charles turned away from the widow, thinking how impossible it was to believe that a mother could be so heartless. The desire to cherish Phyllida surged over him in a wave of tenderness; but when presently he and Clare set out from the inn-door, under the tail of the storm-cloud shedding stars in slow retreat across the sky, he felt Despair upon his heels and pondered the infamy of this beautiful world. Poor hero! he was a gamester even in his emotions and, having staked his hope in one wild throw, was fearfully watching the issue. What a maddening melody the cubes made when rattled by the hands of Fate.

Pray remember, before you dismiss the widow to your eternal disdain, that she may have loved young Mr. Standish, that rugged Squire Courteen may have been very brutal in his cups, that such a malicious Codicil might have soured a woman less dependent upon the amenity of life. Finally, pray remember that she was a woman who did not wrinkle easily, and the consequent temptations of a deceitful mirrour. Looking-glasses, like human beings, lie more often than is commonly supposed, but possess an unlucky reputation for truthfulness which seldom hampers humanity.

Left alone with Sir George, Mr. Ripple took advantage of the opportunity to explain to his old friend certain events on which the latter had long brooded in vain.

CHAPTER XXXV

THE CUTTING OF A DIAMOND

"AND what is your life, William?" asked Sir George Repington, leaning back in his chair and removing his wig.

"My life, George," replied Mr. Ripple, "is a gem carved by a cunning workman to stamp any material sufficiently plastick to record an impression. My life, George, is a conductor of musick. Of itself it produces no sweet sounds, but evokes a fair harmony from many and diverse instruments."

"You had ambitions once."

"I have gratified the most of them."

"Yet your life has not been active."

"No?"

"As for example mine has been."

"I do not know, George, that my contemplative existence has produced less than your phrenzied encounters with mathematical alliances and numerical intrigues. The manipulation of human beings is quite as active. We have neither of us done a vast deal."

"I have had a great influence upon the political situation, more than once," said Sir George proudly.

"So have I," said the Beau.

"Indeed?"

"I have tamed the wives of the most of our ministers."

"But you are not a man of intrigue?"

"Heaven forbid!" said the Beau devoutly. "No, no, George, my knowledge of Olympian intrigue taught me to be wise. I found that the gods never improved their dignity by amorous descents. To be sure, on one or two occasions, they made an effort to assert their divinity by dramatical effects unworthy of a country conjurer, but I do not believe that they ever recovered from the indiscretion of familiarity with their inferiors. No! no! George, I am not a man of intrigue."

"Then what is your life? How do you pass your time?"

Sir George Repington had lit a churchwarden pipe and accentuated the inquiry by waving the long stem. Mr. Ripple took a pinch of snuff and, settling himself deeper in his chair, began to relate his manner of existence in a clear and modulated tone that agreed well with the comfort of the room. The narrative took its own course and reminded one of the purring of a cat amid the flickering shadows cast by firelight on a gaudy rug.

"I assumed my present name—Horace Ripple—partly out of respect to the poet, partly out of respect to my father's mother. Belladine was too metallick, too lustrous an appellation for a man without any desire to agitate the peace of the world. Besides, there were other reasons why I should forget my patronymick. As Horace Ripple, I rode one fine morning into the town of Curtain Wells, procured a pleasant house in the Eastern Colonnade and waited upon Beau Melon. The latter received me very graciously and was pleased to compliment me upon the trimming of my waistcoat. (I have often contemplated the revival of that auspicious fashion.) I was lucky enough to render the great Beau a trifling service, in the matter of adjusting the discordant claims of two dairymaids who were quarrelling rather loudly over the young Earl of —— well, his name don't matter. Melon had been entrusted with the harvesting of the young nobleman's wild oats. After that I was able to lend him five hundred pounds and half a dozen epigrams, also to put him in the way of a neat translation of a song by the passionate Catullus, whereby he secured the hand of the famous, wealthy, and eccentrick Contessa Dilettante. He married, bequeathed to me his house, his notebooks, and his goodwill, so that in a paltry five years I succeeded to the sovereignty of Curtain Wells. Our season endures from October until June. During that time I am as busy as a monarch should expect to be. I have made many alterations during the years of my rule; for instance, the Assemblies once held every Wednesday are now invariably held every Monday."

"But what the d——l does it matter which day they are held!" interrupted Sir George.

"Of course, it does not matter. Nothing matters. Nevertheless, George, when I announced the change, I tell you my throne, for a moment, tottered. However, I triumphed over the malcontents, and I venture to think it would take a very bold man to suggest they should ever again be held upon Wednesday."

"But, my dear William!" said his friend, "this is nonsense. 'Tis absurd for you to sit there and congratulate yourself as though this were doing something."

"My dear George," said the Beau very blandly. "Did I not read last year in the *Intelligence* that you were agitating yourself confoundedly in order to secure some great financial advantage by altering the date of the despatch of bullion to Portugal?"

"You did, William, you did," said Sir George, setting his shoulders back at the proud thought of a great victory won.

"And what the d——l does it matter whether the ships sail in February or March?"

"You don't understand—the depression of the markets, the——"

"Precisely so," interrupted Mr. Ripple, "and you, my dear friend, do not understand the depression of Monday and Tuesday in the time before my great reform."

"But mine was an affair of international importance."

"And mine was an affair of domestick and social importance. Gadslife, do you suppose that my subjects care a jot about your schemes, if their own bodies are uncomfortable? Do you realize that many an election depends—yet why should I dispute the question. Nothing matters, but everything is of the very greatest importance."

Sir George was bewildered by the Beau's sophistry and argued no farther. After all, as he told himself, the atmosphere of Throgmorton Street had probably stultified his outlook. He himself only regarded it as a necessary, purgatorial prologue to the paradise of the life of a man of leisure. Belladine was a man of leisure, and if Aristotle's politicks were not corrupt, must know more than himself about the affairs of the whole world. So Sir George kindled a fresh pipe with a burning coal, and listened to the continuation of Mr. Ripple's placid narrative.

"I perceived," the latter went on, "that pleasure was the most inexorable fact, setting aside birth and death, in the human economy. Before my time, the diversions of Curtain Wells, though conducted on a lavish scale of expense were somewhat haphazard. They did not always fit in with the moods of the pilgrims of Æsculapius. Too much was left to private enterprize. There was not enough organization and, worst of all, there was not enough stress laid upon the ascetick duties, whose fulfilment would lend such a flavour and zest to relaxation. I instituted, therefore, a rigour of exercise and diet, I insisted upon the sacred character of the Pump Room, I glorified the taking of Chalybeate by a ritual at once subtle and magnificent. In a word, I founded a new religion and, as the auctioneers have it, made of Curtain Wells a true Temple of Hygeia. Having trained my subjects to make themselves uncomfortable in a modish way, I was soon able to urge the necessity of enjoying themselves on the same principle. To this end I arranged that every month should have its specifick pleasures, which would be welcomed as we welcome each flower that succeeds in its season. I will not fatigue you with too much detail, but I can honestly affirm that when the great Aquatick Gala or Fête Aqueuse comes to a dazzling conclusion, when the showers of bursting crimson, violet, and golden rockets dim the lustre of the Dog Star on the last night of June, the whole of the fashionable world retires to verdant solitudes with a profound admiration for me and a fixed determination to grace the grand opening Assembly on the first night of October."

"Indeed," said Sir George Repington, on whose mind a new prospect was breaking, "and how do you pass your time during the intervening months?"

"I meditate, George, I meditate in a charming rural retreat which I possess in the green heart of Devonshire. There I spend leafy days in pastoral seclusion. I have my plane tree, my jug of old Falernian. I have my spaniel, Lalage, and an impoverished female cousin who performs very engagingly upon the spinet. I sit in the austere musick-chamber with shadowy white walls, empty save for two or three tall black oaken chairs and the curiously painted instrument. I listen to the cool melodies of Couperin and admire his unimpassioned symbols of the Passions where a purple domino is the most violent, the most fervid emotion. I hear above the chirping of the crickets, the faint harmonies of Archangelo Corelli and the fugues of Domenico Scarlatti, whose name is so vivid, but whose musick like the morning is a mist of gold. I sit in a library hung with faded rose brocades and tarnished silver broideries. There I meditate upon the bloody deaths of Emperors and the grey hairs of Helen of Troy. There I move serenely from shelf to shelf and hark to the muffled thunder of volumes clapped together to exclude the odorous dust. I ponder Religion and Urn Burial and pore over the lurid histories of notable comets. At dusk of a fine day, I step out into the dewy garden to watch the colour fade from the flowers and the stars wink in the lucent green of the western sky. Presently I step indoors, light a tall wax candle set in a silver candlestick, go sedately to bed and fall asleep to the perfume of roses and jasmine and the echo of a cadence from the *Anatomy of Melancholy*."

" And that is your life? " said Sir George.

" That is my life."

" William, would it have been your life if things had been different on that April morning? I thought my life was as I would have wished to spend it; I have worshipped dull columns of figures and the dust of counting-houses, but to-night when I saw that child, when I saw that nephew of mine, I feared old age and wished I could somehow have thought less, calculated less, striven less, and loved more."

" George," said Mr. Ripple, tapping the lid of his snuff box with not so brave an air as usual, and, as he spoke, his friend apprehended in a moment's illumination that all this decorated narrative had been evoked to defer an explanation which he had felt all the while was inevitable.

" George," said Mr. Ripple, " if upon that morning in April, I could have made up my mind, I should, I believe, have—and yet I don't know," he broke off, " I doubt I was never intended to be a man of commonplace action."

" You did not interfere? "

" I loved her, too."

" You loved her? "

" I saw she cared for him alone, and, when Roger fell, though I had my pistol loaded and levelled, I had no heart to fire. But I was never brave enough to tell you I had let him escape and, having waited too long— oh! well there it is—I waited and could not bear to resume my old life. And indeed, George, I think I have been a happy man. You have conjured up the ghost of Belladine to-night and Belladine was and is and will be miserable to the end of his days, but pray dismiss him, vex not his ghost, and take snuff with Horace Ripple of the Great House, Curtain Wells. We are both too old, George, to do anything now. We must depend on young Charles."

"And if he should fail?"

"We are both old men. We should, therefore, both be able to suffer another disillusion."

"I suppose that is true," said Sir George rather sadly. "William——"

"Horace," corrected Mr. Ripple.

"William," persisted the other, "did I ever mention Thistlegrove Cottage to you?"

"Not that I can remember."

"'Tis a fine night, full of stars," said Mrs. Tabrum, entering the room with a tray full of brightly burning candles, "and what time would your honours like to be waked up in the morning?"

"I will ring my bell," said Mr. Ripple.

"I will ring my bell," said Sir George Repington.

The two old friends took each a candle, and went upstairs to bed. From the corridor casement they looked out.

"What a laugh she had," says Sir George. A gust of wind extinguished his candle, and he shuddered.

"That is the way I shall go out."

"That is the way we shall all go out," said Mr. Ripple.

"And nothing afterwards?"

"Darkness."

"And nothing else?"

"Perhaps a hand in the darkness."

CHAPTER XXXVI

THE SCARLET DAWN

THE post-chariot that held in its musty recesses Miss Phyllida Courteen and Mr. Francis Vernon rattled on its way with all the vigour imparted by four fresh horses and the exhilarating effect of Plymouth Gin upon the post-boys.

A smell of saddlecloths and damp cushions, of leather straps and the dust of oat and hay, clung to the vehicle, while over them was wafted the permeating steam of horses' flanks and the pungent odour of hot lamps.

"Phyllida, my Phyllida, at last."

"Why did you let me travel alone? I was frightened."

"My dear," said Vernon, "indeed, I do not know how to explain my neglect, but I wanted to ride out of the darkness and find you alone in the firelight like a maid in an old tale. It must have seemed cowardice to you."

"I was frightened," murmured Phyllida, growing breathless at the recollection of Mr. Charlie and Mr. Dicky Maggs lurching round the table in the Travellers' Room.

"You longed for me?" Vernon moved closer to his love and took her hand.

"Amor," said the girl shuddering, "I think I am frightened now. I think we will go back. I think I have done wrong."

"You think all these foolish thoughts, dear life. I

know that to-day will be to you a day of days for ever."

He held her now in his arms, and she with a sigh yielded herself into his keeping. Soft she was and timid, like a bird which has fallen from the nest, and in the gloom he could still see her wide blue eyes and above the jangle of the chariot he could hear her whisper.

" I love you, Amor, I love you."

" My Phyllida."

" Amor, dear, dear Amor."

" 'Tis not my name, dear one."

" 'Tis the name you told me."

" My name is Vernon."

" To me you will always be Amor. Amor means Love. I asked the Archdeacon and he told me that Amor meant Love."

Vernon was taken outside of himself. As he kissed those lips more soft than the petals of flowers, the other lips he had known seemed cracked and dry. In the darkness, he felt her eyelashes upon his cheek as they drooped to a blush, and a passion of remorse swept over him. He would wed this child at the end of the journey. He would love her for ever. That was certain. Oh, yes, there was no doubt he would love her for ever. He had plucked this flower in a wanton moment, had thought to wear her for a scented month and fling her away. O execrable intent!

" My Phyllida, my Phyllida! Why do you love me? "

" Why do you love me? " Her hand nestled in his.

" I don't know, because—because—oh, because I do love you, because you have driven me mad with your blue eyes and your hair and your lips. My Phyllida, my Phyllida! "

Vernon was no longer conscious of acting. This was no scene set with chairs at appropriate angles. The raffish Mr. Francis Vernon of London, the clever Mr. Francis Vernon who vowed every woman had her price,

Mr. Vernon the hero of half a hundred squalid intrigues was dead. Why should he not forget him, taking for his own that fortunate pseudonym which had set him as high as the angels? With a gesture of dismay, he drew from his cuff a greasy King of Hearts and spurned the dishonourable cardboard with his foot.

" Amor! "

" My dear! My lovely one! My heart! "

" Once I climbed up a high hill at home in Hampshire."

He held her more closely.

" I climbed a hill and stared for a long while right into the sun. I was giddy. Amor! Amor! I feel now as I did when I stared for a long while into the sun."

" Phyllida! Phyllida! "

" You'll never not love me, Amor? "

" Never, I swear it."

" I could not bear you not to love me. Once I knew a young woman whose lover forsook her and she used to work woollen flowers all day long with a tambour frame, because she was working woollen flowers when he told her that he loved her, and she never did anything else all the years that we knew her; and, Amor, she is working them now, and oh, I'm afraid when I think of her working those woollen flowers."

Vernon in his new frame of mind could scarcely forbear telling his love of the ills he had intended towards her. He had caught a passion for frankness and would have poured into her ears the whole of his past. He could not endure, to such elation had he been carried, that Phyllida should be ignorant of the worst of him in order that for the future she should know more truly the very best of him. But he was wise and, though Cupid had lent him his own wings, he would not play too many aerial pranks, soar too near the sun, fall and break his neck. It was indeed a form of abnegation that prevented him from showing Phyllida his own bad self. It was bitter to hear her murmur, with a white hand on his sleeve,

"I knew you were true, my true love, all the time, all the time."

Nothing tugs at the heart-strings of a man like a young maid's plighting of her troth. Nothing makes his brain reel like her first kiss freely given.

"Oh, Phyllida, Phyllida! I'm not fit for you."
"Foolish Amor."
"Are you happy, my dearest?"
"Oh, so happy."
"We shall never be parted again."
"Never!"
"I did not know that life was so wonderful."
"I thought it was," she murmured, as she nestled to his heart, "because Spring was always so sweet, and now I need never mind the Winter."
"All the years I did not know you, my Phyllida, were wasted years."
"Amor!"
"Phyllida!"
"How I shall always love you."
"Always?"
"To the end."
"Once," she said with a sigh, "I longed to grow old, and now I would like to be always young."
"Ah! Phyllida, my Phyllida, don't speak of age. I've wasted so much of my life."

He thought with anguish of the dead Summers he had known and wondered with a great dread whether they would come again. If, while he could still feel this splendid passion, they should be grey and dismal, he would never forgive himself for having revelled in the warmth and gaiety of those irrevocable seasons.

"You are not sad?" she asked, jealous of his silence.

"I wish that life were not so short."

Our villain was beginning to examine the foundations of his existence upon this earth, where hitherto he had jogged along, accepting the most outrageous calamity and good luck with placid superficial mind. Meditation upon the brevity of a life, which at any moment a tavern brawl might extinguish, would have seemed to him before this passionate conversation a lunatick method of spending time. Poor villain! he had not enjoyed much leisure for meditation. He was born in a hurry, his mother being under contract to appear as Millamant a long while before she should. He was brought up in a hurry at Alleyn's School to be murdered in a hurry by some Richard III. Moreover, in youth he had assisted at so many tinsel deaths that it was not surprizing he should regard them lightly. Even his mother's death within sound of the orange girls outside Drury Lane struck him as nothing more final than a last appearance.

Now for the first time, there broke upon him the stunning fact of inevitable decay and, being a self-indulgent man, he had for a moment nothing more dignified than petulant despair with which to meet this sudden apprehension of mortality.

"'Tis monstrous," he declared, "a fearful thought that you and I should ever grow old and die. I cannot bear to think of your brown hair growing white. Phyllida, you cannot grow old."

Love had made a woman of Phyllida and already, with gentle touch, she soothed his anguish.

"Dear Amor, I know that if we love each other truly, we shall never grow old to each other."

"Phyllida, I love you," and clasping her lissome body breathless to his, he defied the lightning of the Gods.

And now a new fear assailed him. 'We shan't be followed,' he had contemptuously informed old Mother Mawhood at Blackhart Farm. In sudden dread he leaned out of the window of the chariot, and strained his eyes to pierce the darkness. He could see nothing save the shadows of the postillions against the hedge, hear nothing save the clatter of the horses. The loneliness and gloom affected his spirits and with a shudder he sought again the musty interior of the vehicle. He caught his love to his heart.

" What did you see? " she asked.

" Nothing, but I was afraid. I could not bear to lose you now."

" You saw nothing? "

" Nothing."

" And heard nothing? "

" Nothing. Why do you ask? "

" Oh, Amor, I thought I saw the shadow of a man on horseback."

" Fancy, my sweet, fancy." Then, with a sinking fear, he remembered he had told Mother Mawhood of the pearls. He called to mind the postboys' insolence, the look that passed between Charlie and Dickie when he told them he would ride in the chariot. He sprang in alarm to open the window, but the carriage pulled up with a jerk which flung him back against Phyllida. The glass crashed to the heavy butt of a pistol and, as he stretched out for his own fire-arms, he saw the postboys resting long barrels on the sill and, by the lamp which one of them held, a masked face that with thick brutal voice demanded their money.

" Hand 'em over."

" Hand what over? " said Vernon, in a futile attempt to delay his humiliation.

" The pops first," said one of the Maggs, winking humorously in the direction of Vernon's pistols that in leathern holsters lay harmless on the dusty floor of the chariot.

Now occurred one of those astonishing coincidences that have tempted the speculation of many sages since the beginning. A field-mouse chose that very moment to cross the road. A large white owl spied the diminutive pilgrim and having tasted no food that stormy night, swooped daringly upon his prey under the heads of the standing horses. Terrified by the soft white apparition, the leaders plunged forward. In a moment the chariot was bumping and jolting at a wild pace down the road, having broken Charlie Maggs' big toe in transit. The blackguard deserved a scar for his carelessness, if for nothing else, and the limp he earned that night was some time afterwards the means of proving his complicity in the affair of the blind mouse-tamer, thereby ridding the world of a very dirty rascal. Mice were fatal to Charlie Maggs. It is satisfactory to know that the adventurous animal avoided the owl, and it is also consoling to learn that the latter never adorned a gamekeeper's pole, but died a natural death in the hollow trunk where it had spent actually all the days of its life.

It was a moment or two before Vernon understood that the danger was averted; then he bent low to reassure Phyllida, who was crouching in the darkest corner of the chariot.

"My dear," he cried, and for all the swaying motion caught her to him with a certain grace. "My dear, there is nothing to be afraid of now."

"Oh! Amor!" she sobbed, abandoning herself to the horror of remembrance, "that face—that black face."

"My sweet, you shall never see it again."

"It will follow us."

"If he should I have something here that will frighten him away fast enough."

Vernon waved a pistol which he had picked up even as he caught hold of Phyllida. But the masked face did not pursue them and, after a mile or so of noisy swaying progress, Vernon began to consider the possibility of stopping the carriage. He leaned out of the window and nearly had his eyes put out by a bramble sucker.

A survey from the other side, where the remaining lamp lent a wavering illumination, showed they were travelling at an alarming pace down a deep rocky lane. Vernon noticed that the boulders in places trespassed considerably upon the road with projecting points, and there seemed every likelihood of the chariot being presently wrecked like a rudderless boat. However, runaway horses and drunken men share a large amount of the world's luck between them, and notwithstanding the headlong speed, every boulder in turn was successfully avoided. Farther along, the surface of the road grew worse and, every other second, one of the wheels would grate against the side of a deep rut with a horrid jar. They were going downhill now and Vernon strained his eyes to discover the lie of the country. The pace was harder than ever, and it seemed impossible for four horses to survive the roughness of the road and the steepness of the descent.

Suddenly above the clatter they heard the roar of water: at the same moment the front wheel struck some permanent obstacle: the chariot dipped forward: Phyllida and Vernon were flung in a tangled heap on the floor, while the sudden cessation of movement made the noise of the water sound very portentous in the gloom. Vernon extricated himself from the vehicle on the lighted side, jumping out, splashed his way through mire and puddles to the horses' heads. The two leaders with that unexpected philosophy which in horses often succeeds the most fervid excitement were cropping the young herbage peacefully, while the wheelers were only slightly more restive through their inability to reach the same sweet pasture. Vernon snatched the solitary lamp from the socket and went to help Phyllida alight. As she stood upon the step and gave him her little hand, he divined with a sense of awe, begotten by the solitude of the surroundings, that she was truly his. He was Adam greeting Eve with the mystery of woman all about her in that primaeval Spring.

The scene of the catastrophe was peculiarly solemn. The chariot had struck a column of stone that rose suddenly out of the ground as if the finger of a Titan had been frozen into perpetuity to mark some early and gigantick travail of his mother Earth. The lamp with feeble yellow light made monstrous shadows of the huge features it sought vainly to illuminate. So far as he could judge they were nearly at the bottom of a deep ravine along which swept a torrent whose magnitude was impossible to estimate, since the roar of the waterfall gave it in the darkness a dreadful importance.

"It must be close on two o'clock," said Vernon, "let's leave this disastrous vehicle. We may find shelter somewhere over this valley."

Phyllida drew the riding hood round her and, taking her lover's arm, silently acquiesced in this proposal.

As they drew near the waterfall, the thunder of it made her shiver. They crossed the torrent by a stone bridge that seemed to have become a natural feature in the landskip.

On the far side by a common impulse they stopped and Vernon leaned down to kiss her face.

"My Phyllida," he murmured; and held the lamp so that he could see the shimmer and gleam of love in her eyes. They stood silent, enraptured, and the hot yellow lamp away down in the depths of this world-forsaken valley became the very torch of Hymen.

With slow steps they climbed the opposite hill, deserting the waters and the rocks, the ferns, the little bridge, for the grey starshine above the gloom. Yet the awe of that solemn ravine, which they had reached after such peril, enthralled them still and I think both felt as if somehow their love had been consecrated by a divine being. It was quite a relief from the strain of reverence when Vernon informed Phyllida that there was no sign of any human habitation.

"What shall we do with the carriage?" asked the latter.

"Don't fret about that."

"And the horses?"

"They must take their chance. I wish I knew the hour."

"You said it must be two o'clock."

"The sun does not rise till half-past five. Three hours and a half. I wonder why we left the chariot. It would be wiser to go back. You will be cold in this open country."

The wind was blowing shrewdly up there in the starlight, and Phyllida would not deny she was cold and tired.

"We had better go back to the chaise. 'Twas warmer in the valley."

Yet both of them felt a strange disinclination to risk the disillusion of return till, suddenly, up there in the wind and starlight, terror caught them, and the noise of water tumbling over rocks gave them a sense of security from this wide place of silence.

"'Tis a monstrous uneasy country," said Vernon, voicing in common speech the sense of woe that oppressed him.

"I feel frightened," Phyllida agreed, "let us go back to the water."

They stopped to listen as people will whose minds have been much wrought upon. There was nothing but the lisp of the wind in the bents of last year's grass and a melodious sighing in the boughs of larches. Yet never throughout that adventurous night had Phyllida's heart pattered at such a pace, never had she been so near to shrieking aloud. Without longer delay they turned back in the direction of the coombe, walking with quick steps as if to avoid an invisible pursuit. Half-way down the hill, Vernon stooped to gather a primrose.

"Here's a daisy," he said.

"A daisy," Phyllida cried. " Why, foolish Amor, 'tis a primrose," and whatever fiend or goblin followed in their wake fled in affright at the sound of her rippling laughter. I think nothing shows more conclusively that Mr. Vernon was in love with Miss Courteen than his indifference to her ridicule.

"Sweetest," he said, " I'm ignorant of the best things like flowers," and forthwith began to tell Phyllida of his life in London, so that when presently they stood again upon the bridge, he was raising his voice in order to describe his first impressions of rustick Marybone, to which he added a very nice account of the view of the Hampstead Hills.

Under the influence of this narrative, the scene lost some of its grandeur. An air of grottoes, of stone embellishments, arbours, and cunning recesses shed itself over the landskip. One heard comparisons with this or that famous haunt of sight-seeing mobs. In fact, both Vernon and Phyllida, being English, felt their late raptures were unbecoming, and having excused a lapse into sensibility by the fright they had suffered, proceeded to declare that the chasm, far from being Titanick, would make a mighty fine site for an excursion of pleasure. At least Vernon clothed the opinion in words, Phyllida was too much fatigued to do more than murmur a weary assent.

They found the chariot just as they had left it and the four horses browsing upon the grass. He handed her into the vehicle, made her comfortable with what rugs and cloaks he could collect and left her to rest with the assurance he would remain close at hand. She gave his hand a tired clasp and almost immediately fell fast asleep. Vernon tethered the horses to various stumps in the vicinity, and proceeded to doze and dream away the cold hours before dawn in the shelter of a particularly large and overhanging ledge of rock. The sound of the falling water that deafened him with its roar when first he heard it, now soothed him like a gentle lullaby.

I cannot do justice to the scene: Rembrandt with his powerful and gloomy imagination could have etched it. He would have made the two lovers present themselves to the onlooker in their right proportions to the scenery. You and I are too near to the candlelight of Curtain Wells to believe in the romantick desolation wherein they seemed of no more importance than the ferns that hung down their green tongues to the limpid pools hollowed from jagged rocks. Vernon, huddled in the shelter of the crag, with his hat pressed over his eyes, his knees arched as high as his chin, might well have been a belated herdsman who, having flung himself into this valley to avoid the upland wind, had been bewitched by the magick of running water to dream away the night. The horses in the black shadows and the ruined chariot had an air of Gothick melancholy; the yellow lamp that glimmered fitfully in the heart of the abyss served only to throw into more huge relief the neighbouring rocks, while it lighted the thresholds of gaping caverns that stretched beyond to unimaginable depths of solitude and gloom. The night wore on and over the hill the lovers had found so depressing to their spirits, like a sword in the twilight, lay the first grey streak of dawn. Phyllida and her lover slept while the features of the landskip began to win again their own outlines, while the rocks that were wrapped in the warm velvet of night appeared with a cold sheen. The grey streak widened to a broad lake whose margin was flecked with the faint hues of lavender and mauve. Birds began to twitter and chirp in the trees and bushes that overhung the rocks below, while the winds of dawn fluted in the small withy bed beside the bridge.

Very wan in the morning twilight, Mr. Charles Lovely and Mr. Anthony Clare clattered down the deep lane that led to the valley. Their horses' flanks glistened with the sweat of hard travel and the riders rose hardly to the jerking downhill motion.

Just as the rose-tipped fingers of Aurora plucked the lavender from the skies, Charles and Tony caught sight of the chariot and just as they pulled their horses to a standstill, Mr. Vernon woke up. It is characteristick of the latter's new-found consideration that his first action was to warn them with a gesture of Phyllida's presence fast asleep inside. Charles tapped his holsters in reply and pointed up the opposite slope. Vernon rose to follow his pursuers with a backward glance in the direction of the chariot.

When they were over the bridge and out of Phyllida's hearing Charles reined in his walking horse and inquired if Vernon was willing to give him satisfaction.

"For what?" said the latter with a sneer.

"For insulting my Muse," said Charles, determined if possible not to make Phyllida the subject of the quarrel.

"Your muse?" echoed Vernon, with the faintest intonation of surprize, "but I promised you satisfaction for that a month hence."

Vernon was equally determined that Phyllida should be the direct occasion of the duel, if duel there must be.

The rosy heavens became a sheet of vivid scarlet intersected with the golden bars of the fast rising sun. Up he came in a blaze and dazzle of glory, lustrous and invigorating; still the colour was not quite effaced, and on the three men that scarlet dawn made an invincible impression of disaster and woe. A red sky is a warning to shepherds and sailors, no doubt it was ominous to lovers.

The summit of the hill was reached and involuntarily the three paused in their wrangling to marvel at the extensive landskip suffused with the amber haze of earliest morn. The homesteads in sight seemed untenanted: there was not a single column of curling smoke to mark the presence of humanity.

Where they were standing, the road was bordered on

either side by a wide stretch of level sward. On the left was a spinney of larches showing as yet no crimson plumes of Spring, round which numbers of rabbits gambolled in air that sparkled like golden wine. It seemed indeed more like July than April, and only the bare trees told the true tale of the season's youthfulness. Up here on the top of the world the three men drank in the beauty of the universe and, having as it were performed their orisons, turned to arrange the details of a bloody encounter.

"I promised I would meet you where you would in a month's time!" repeated Vernon obstinately.

"But I prefer to meet you now," replied Charles.

"I have no one to act for me."

"Mr. Clare will act for both of us."

"That is an irregular proceeding."

"I don't care."

"And Miss Courteen?" Vernon was resolved to drag Charles to the real point of issue. "What is to become of Miss Courteen?"

"In either event, Mr. Clare will be able to escort her back to Curtain Wells."

"D——n you," said Vernon, roused by his enemy's assumption of guardianship. "And what if she wishes to stay with me?"

"Mr. Lovely has her mother's authority to conduct her home," interposed Clare.

"What you two prim busybodies don't appear to understand is that Miss Courteen prefers to remain with me."

"Miss Courteen is not her own mistress. She is not of age," said Clare.

"And pray how do you propose to make her accompany you?"

"Why, in this way," interrupted Charles, shaking off his friend's arm, "in this way, Mr. Vernon. If you decline to meet me with pistols, by G—— I'll thrash you senseless with my crop."

Vernon's hands twitched for a moment, but he had learned a new restraint, gained a new dignity from the wondrous ride and with scarcely a perceptible quiver in his voice begged to point out to his friend Mr. Lovely that if he shot him, he should not scruple to shoot Mr. Clare were the latter to stand in his way.

"But what if you're shot, sir?" cried Charles, betraying in his eagerness the true reason for his desire to force an instant encounter, "as by G—— you deserve to be for murdering the poor little Major."

Vernon was perplexed.

"The Major? Is he dead? I had nothing to do with his death." The simplicity of the denial almost convinced his listeners that he was speaking the truth.

"Come, Sirrah, will you meet me?" said Charles, lifting his crop.

"Listen, you pair of puppies," said Vernon between his teeth. "I could have put a bullet into either of you at any time during the last five minutes, and by heavens, I don't know why I kept my finger from the trigger. Yes, I do," he shouted. "I've got a chance of happiness and I'm not going to throw it away by having your blood on my head. You're an interfering pair of fools, but I cheated one of you at cards and I played a low game over the book, and by G——, I believe my father was a gentleman. I'll meet you, Mr. Lovely, now."

With these words he flung down on the grass at Charles' feet the two pistols which the skirts of his riding-coat had concealed.

"I'll step fifteen paces," said Mr. Clare, hiding his emotion with a piece of practical utility. And, as he began to measure the ground, away down in the broken chariot Phyllida woke with a start. She was surprized by the daylight and called to her lover. Only birdsong answered her voice. In sudden dismay, presentiment hanging over her like the aftermath of an evil dream, she jumped from the chariot. Intuition, perhaps the remembrance of last night's fear, made her look towards the summit of the slope. In silhouette against the golden sky, she saw three figures. Breathless with horror she ran in their direction. Up the hill she laboured. It was still cold from the night air and foreboding was heavy upon her heart. Up the hill she struggled, leaving in her path many fluttering pieces of muslin where eager feet had torn the frail flounces. Down the road, she saw them level their weapons. "One, two, three," came in measured tones along the still air of the morning. There were two shots, the scud of frightened rabbits to their burrows, a reeling figure, a cloud across the sun, a mist over life, and she was kneeling in the dewy grass beside Amor.

"Oh God!" she screamed. "He's dead. Oh! Oh! Oh!"

That anguished cry wounded Lovely deeper than any leaden bullet, for it killed his hopes.

At the touch of his dear one, Vernon opened his dark eyes.

"Here's a bunch of primroses," he murmured, "not daisies. I picked them, Phyllida . . . for you . . . not daisies . . . primroses. . . ."

And so with thoughts of flowers, Mr. Francis Vernon died. Pray let that sentence be his epitaph.

Charles, watching the maid stare into the sun with eyes whose light seemed fled with the swift-flying soul of the dead man, wished passionately—wildly—that he were the quiet body there in the dewy grass.

"What shall we do?" he murmured brokenly to Clare.

"Leave her alone for a while."

"What a mistake it has been."

They walked away with cautious steps and spoke in whispers as if they were afraid.

"What right had I to interfere between lovers?"

"You did it for the best."

"I know, I know, but what a d——d number of silly actions are done for the best."

"To-day is the first of April," said Clare, seeking with a commonplace to relieve the tension of Charles' distracted mind.

"Is it? What an April fool fortune has made of me."

CHAPTER XXXVII

APRIL FOOLS

THE last ejaculation of Chapter XXXVI will serve as an admirable summary of the positions in which a number of our characters found themselves on April the First, in the year whose annals include this small history.

There is a peculiar happiness of choice in making the first day of that treacherous and feminine month coincide with the humiliation of a large number of worthy people. We plunge into April with a prodigious expectation of jollity: we delight in the sound of her name, liquid as the song of a thrush; we strut in the sunshine, fling off our surtouts, recline on banks where the painted adder lurks and the East wind cuts down from the high pastures, and altogether behave in a very foolish fashion. The heavens have taken a deeper blue; so among the cowslips we contemplate their azure until a black squall blows along, stings our rash necks with perilous hailstones and drives us headlong to the shelter of the pale green hedgerows. There on the drifted leaves of dead Octobers, we are scratched by the crimson thorns of briers and, slowly acquiring an extensive rheumatism, wish very sincerely we had never stirred from the hearth where the wise pages of Montaigne or La Rochefoucauld lie dog-eared through our precipitate adventure.

Yet, after all, it is better to be a fool in April than a wise man in November. Pit and boxes hear the ravings of the mad Ophelia with the sense of superiority secured by plush, but the most of them would be better men and women for having gathered that nosegay of columbines and rue.

So drop a tear for Phyllida. She was the heroine of the piece, the gentlest, tenderest maid. Sorrow has laid his grey fingers upon her heart and, though she may grow old and wise and wed a squire with well-tilled acres and spacious hall, to the end of her life a poignant experience, on which you have been the privileged intruder, will modulate her lightest laugh with a deeper harmony.

At the *Basket of Roses* there were April fools that day.

"Charles made up his mind and did no good," said Mr. Ripple. "I hesitated, and was in no better case. What is one to do?"

Sir George Repington was quite broken up by the affair. Years ago he had built a bower in April which was destroyed in a morning. In old age, Spring fooled him again.

Like the heavy footnote of a tragedy, Mr. Moon, lately arrived by the Wells' waggon, employed himself with practical suggestions. Mr. Lovely must retire over the water for a while, the sooner the better. Mrs. Courteen and Miss Phyllida must return to Hampshire. He would make posting arrangements; their baggage must be sent after them. Tarry must be buried in the parish church at home; he could not allow a neighbour to lie in a strange churchyard. For once in his life, Mr. Moon was of real use to a situation and, in the protracted discussions of expedients for hushing the matter up and conveying the principals safely into seclusion, the grief of many hearts was temporarily allayed.

"You must come back with me to Curtain Wells, George," decided Mr. Ripple, "we must not allow the world to invent any more explanations of the affair. I doubt the wildest rumours are flying round. In a month or two, Charles can return if he will; meanwhile you and I, George, will give ourselves the pleasure of paying his debts."

In the dusk of to-morrow's dawn, the vivid yellow chaise of Beau Ripple rattled over the cobbles of Curtain Wells, and drew up before the Great House. A dexterous and hurried toilet was performed with Mr. Mink's assistance and the watchers from the windows, ignorant whether the Great little Man was returned, were immensely gratified to see him emerge from his front door, goblet in hand, and wearing a new buff suit of unparagoned cut with very full trimming round the skirts.

The Exquisite Mob buzzed around the Beau's pedestal with a scarcely contained curiosity. Mr. Oboe, the Physician, was almost more subservient than usual, and not a single person inquired after his neighbour's health or expatiated upon his own. Gog and Magog exposed their ivory teeth in a permanent smile of welcome, and in the kitchen of the Great House, Mrs. Binn, the Beau's intelligent cook, prepared a breakfast of the most savoury character. His ascent to the rostrum produced an expectant silence.

"My lords, ladies and gentlemen," he began, "I owe you a profound apology. You will, of course, understand that in my capacity as Master of the Ceremonies of Curtain Wells, I am under no obligation to any one, but as Horace Ripple, I feel that my conduct in deserting you yesterday morning without any notice of my intention deserves an explanation. When I inform you that a domestick difficulty not entirely unconnected with my censorious office called for hasty adjustment, you will, I am sure, pardon me for not divulging the details of a very unfortunate affair. If I may trespass to such an extent upon your good nature, I should like to make my late adventure the subject of a short admonition. As you are aware, I am not accustomed to mingle with the practical politicks of my matutinal oration any allusion to your moral welfare: I should esteem it highly impertinent on my part, were I to usurp in such a way the prerogative of our friend the Rector. Nevertheless I am inclined to make an exception to my rule this morning, the more so as I feel it my duty to inform you of my impending resignation."

The Beau raised his monocle in order to regard the consternation of the Exquisite Mob.

"That event may not occur yet a while; at any rate I shall remain in my present position during this season. Next October, however, I hope to present you with a younger, I will not say worthier, successor. Naturally I shall spend the greater part of my time in Curtain Wells, but with the advance of years, I shall wish to be excused from many of your more nocturnal gaieties. That desire I could not gratify were I still to hold the reins of responsibleness. However, this is not an oration of farewell, so I will not longer emphasize the melancholy topick of mutability.

"The advice I would offer you this morning is, next to the duty of a regular course of Chalybeate, the most important item in human happiness. My lords, ladies and gentlemen, never meddle with other people's business when it happens to concern the heart or the soul of a human creature. Do not, because you are older or because you have read more widely or because you have travelled across Europe or because you have dined with a Minister, or because you suffer from any of the numerous delusions of superiority, do not be too sure that you are competent to interfere with somebody who has enjoyed none of these accidental advantages. Admonish the erring child, warn the impetuous young woman, chide the libertine, reproach the gamester, set an example of continence to all the world, but abstain from direct interference; and if an unpleasant doom overwhelms the object of your interest, pray do not suppose that you would have been able to avert it. My lords, ladies and gentlemen, you are one and all the genteelest of companions, but so far as my theology has taken me, you are none of you gods or goddesses, except in the hyperbole of poetick dedications.

"You have already heard the announcement of your forthcoming entertainments; let me add to their number with a very cordial invitation to the Great House, next Tuesday week. Finally, let me add that during my tenure of office, I shall hope to make these personal encounters a very frequent delight to your obliged humble servant Horace Ripple. Oh, and pray let me assure you that my absence yesterday morning was in no way due to any desire on my part to celebrate the festival of the First of April. My lords, ladies and gentlemen, your very obedient."

With these words the Great little Man descended from his pedestal, and was presently in affable conversation with a number of men and women of rank and fashion.

You will remember that when, it seems an age ago, we first saw Beau Ripple and the Exquisite Mob, we also met Mr. Vernon and Miss Phyllida Courteen. For my own part, I feel that the Pump Room on this morning lacked vitality for all its glitter and stir of elegant movement. I miss the swansdown muff and the blushing, eager face of Phyllida. I miss those little notes that dropped like feathers from the wings of Love. I miss the ingenuous artifice and sweet stratagems of Phyllida and Betty and for all it would nearly break my heart to see her misery, I would fain be walking behind them away down in some budding Hampshire lane. They are still in a postchaise, however, and the musty odour is wringing her heart with an agony of regret. In what a world of memories will she live the summer through. The cuckoo will call in the green wood and the nightingale thrill the moonshine with her passionate song, but Phyllida will stare into the sun.

In a dip of the billowy downs, the harebells wave from their fragile stems and ladies' slippers glow with red and orange flames. Far below you can see the flashing wings of kestrels and hear the lapwing's desolate cry. The beech trees rustle and in the long dry grass the wind sighs continually. There she will sit hour after hour in the summer heat, until she can forget.

And yet, little heroine of a sad tale, I wonder whether you would not have drooped in London and spent long lonely evenings while the twilight stole in from the murmurous streets of the city. I wonder whether after all you were not happier with a flock of rosy children, a portrait by Mr. Romney, and the most comfortable corner in the great Hall pew. Upon my soul, I am not competent to give an opinion.

Phyllida's mother certainly thought that everything was for the best. In her case optimism brought its reward, and she secured Courteen Grange as a dower house, where she continued for many years to be very spritely company for all the dowagers and many of the old bachelors in the neighbourhood. It is perhaps strange she did not marry Mr. Moon, but to confess the truth, the death of Major Tarry destroyed some of his charm. Without that brisk veteran to stir his ponderous courtship, the Justice became wearisome, possibly with greater opportunity of intimacy, more cautious. No doubt in the course of his legal researches, he came upon the Codicil to Squire Courteen's Will, and his election to the Chairmanship of the Bench rendered him oblivious to anything more trivial than Immortal Renown. If we can judge of his qualities by the epitaph in the South Aisle of the Church, he united in one person the austerity of Solon, the severity of Draco, the wisdom of Solomon, and the domination of Aaron. He never finished his great essay on Peace, but as his mural biographer justly remarked, 'His was now the Peace that passeth all Understanding,' so that presumably the publication of his fragment would have been a superfluous tribute. One particular distinction belongs to Mr. Moon. He was never made an April fool. And if the quiet tea-tables of Newton Candover were temporarily disturbed by the escapade of Miss Phyllida Courteen, why the parson benefited by an increase in his congregation. But even the most impudent curiosity could not long survive Mrs. Courteen's circumambient frankness.

CHAPTER XXXVIII

BEAU LOVELY

CHARLES was perfectly right when he said Fortune had made an April fool of him. He should have accepted the ill omen of Valentine morning, for it was certainly very unlucky to mock the God of Love with a false pledge of affection. He was never intended for Phyllida. As Betty rightly pointed out, they were too much alike. Pray do not suppose that he was not an utterly miserable man for a long time. He was; but, in compensation for being born a poet, he possessed the latter's faculty for enshrining a reality in a sentiment. Phyllida came in time to stand for the symbol of elusive youth. During his retreat abroad he suddenly discovered that what he suspected was true, he had grown old. His father had enjoyed a perennial inducement to commit foolish actions in the quiet disapproval of his wife. Charles, however, in receipt of a handsome allowance from his uncle found he no longer had the slightest inclination to play. Wine had never attracted him save in moments of high excitement and he was willing to let his love for Phyllida occupy for ever the sacred inmost shrine of his heart.

Clare remained with him as long as he thought Charles needed his company, but word arriving that his cousin had died, he returned to Devonshire, and in the following year you might have read in the *Gentleman's Magazine* 'Sir Anthony Clare of Clare Court, Devon, to Miss Arabella Hopley with £10,000.'

To the end of his days he always said that if he lived his youth over again, he should not have acted otherwise than he did upon the first of April 17—. But Tony Clare was obstinate in many ways, and, as I believe, never admitted the virtue of even a new manure very willingly. Before Clare left Charles had received a letter from Beau Ripple inviting him to reside once more at Curtain Wells.

"That is impossible," said Tony stiffly.

"I suppose it is."

"You forget that foolish satire."

"I take it that Ripple intends me to succeed him as King of the Wells."

"The publication of *Curtain Polls* has made that impossible."

"I don't know. It might incline them to respect me."

Charles was very lonely in Paris after Tony had gone, and when war broke out again, he decided to go back to England. Just before he started he received a second epistle from the Beau.

THE GREAT HOUSE,

June 15.

MY DEAR CHARLES,—*Our season will presently evaporate in this atrocious heat, and your Uncle and I intend to visit Repington Hall. He is now somewhat recovered of his Disappointment and very anxious to consult with you as to the advisableness of selling the Property. I agree with him in thinking that you would not enjoy the somewhat gross seclusion of a rustick Squire, so that you will oblige him by returning to England and letting him know your feelings in the Matter.*

I cannot see you can do better than take up your permanent residence in Curtain Wells. I do not wish to urge you into a contemplative Existence too prematurely, but to a man of your temperament the opportunities of observing human Character must make an imperious appeal. These I can offer you together with the pleasant pastime of ruling the fashionable World. You need not fret yourself with any early indiscretions. They will very soon acquire a romantick Interest of their own, and I confidently look forward to your success in the splendid Office I have long wished you to fulfil. You will have the benefit of my Advice which I hope you will not find too obtrusive. Come, what do you say? There is a capital house contiguous to Curtain Garden. I fear I cannot yet resign the Great House. Your Uncle is willing to buy this property for you and eagerly looks forward to your acceptance of his Offer.

In this hope he is cordially joined by

Your devoted

HORACE RIPPLE.

Charles hesitated no longer and hurried as quickly as possible to Repington Hall. The canary-coloured footmen received him with extreme deference, and he found the wide polished staircase quite easy to climb. He had been a little afraid of his uncle's sentimental reminiscence, but as it turned out his fears were groundless. Nothing was said about the past and the conversation was almost entirely of a financial character. He spent the remainder of the summer with Sir George Repington at Scarborough, returning early in the autumn to form the establishment of his new residence, Dragon Lodge.

He bought a monocle of such thickness that the human countenance seen through its glass was reduced to the merest pin-point. He procured two Chinese mutes —Heaven knows how or where—but their names were

Ho and No. His eccentricities would exhaust another volume of description. He was the famous Beau who appeared on the first of the month in a light-coloured suit that gradually deepened until, on the last day of the month, it always achieved blackness. When asked by somebody the reason of this mode he replied that he was mourning the flight of time: when asked farther why he was not perpetually funereal in his costume he replied that the first day of the month always revived his hopes of immortality. It was observed, however, that in April his dress did not alter and those who rashly inquired the reason for this exception were severely rebuked for their curiosity. His library was one of the finest in England, although it did not contain a single copy of *Curtain Polls*. The Great Dr. Johnson on one occasion complimented him upon the selection of his authors, the decorousness of his bindings, and the rigidity of his ladders.

As Mr. Ripple had prophesied, the indiscretions of his past in course of time acquired a romantick mystery of their own. He was credited in turn with a faithless wife immured in a Gothick dungeon in the North-West of the Island of Sicily, with a prodigiously passionate affair with a German princess in which he was said to have pinked four Royal Dukes, and with innumerable other entanglements quite impossible to recount. All these tales only added to his prestige, while his wealth and amiability gave him a reputation second to none of the Beaux of the past. He wrote a number of verses, but never published another volume, and was probably the original whom Sir Benjamin Backbite copied, though his reasons for not printing were quite different from those of the later fop.

He would sometimes return early from assembly, rout, or ridotto to pay a visit to Mr. Ripple. He would usually find the latter engaged in a game of picket with Sir George Repington and, after entertaining the two old gentlemen with a witty and satirical account of the evening's entertainment, he would walk slowly back to Dragon Lodge, stare meditatively at the new motto he had adopted, *Fui decorus*, step into a small ivory room that opened out of the massive library and take from a cedar-wood drawer a white swansdown muff.

EXPLICIT